Somebody Tell Aunt Tillie She's Dead

Christiana Miller

Somebody Tell Aunt Tillie She's Dead
Christiana Miller

HekaRose Publishing
Second printing publication date: March 2013
Copyright © 2010, 2011, 2013 Christiana Miller

Cover Art by: © Ariel Manigsaca | Dreamstime.com
© Klara Viskova | Dreamstime.com
© Olesja Makarova | Dreamstime.com
© Christos Georghiou | Dreamstime.com
Cover Design by: Tara Shuler

HekaRose Publishing
All Rights Are Reserved.

ISBN-13: 9781461168232
ISBN-10: 1461168236

RANDOM PRAISE

"This was so much fun to read I didn't want it to end! If you are looking for a paranormal story that has it all, this is it!"

—Wickedly Bookish

"A must-read for paranormal lovers. Christiana Miller is an author to keep an eye on!"

—Melanie's Book Addiction

"Get ready for a psychic roller coaster ride. This book is a tour de force novel of magic, spellcraft and over all chills."

—Everything Magical and Middle Eastern

"A charming, well written, fun novel well worth the read. Ms. Miller's humor is delightful! Come fly with her through the bewitching life of Mara—you won't be disappointed!"

—FMAM Mostly Mystery Reviews

"If you want a great indie paranormal adult read that will keep you turning the pages and guessing what will happen next, pick up this book and give it a read."

—My Guilty Obsession

"A spellbinding tale about the families we are born to--and the ones we choose. It captivates from the first page and holds on until the final, shocking conclusion. You won't want to miss it!"

—Barbra Annino, Author,
Opal Fire: A Stacy Justice Mystery

"A fine romp through spookyland, with enough paranormal creepiness to chill your blood. Witches, demons, magic spells, oh my! Enough intrigue and magic spells to keep you on edge, and Miller's hilarious one-liners leave you begging for more. Highly recommended for fun but scary reading on dark, stormy nights."

—Bonnie Turner, Author,
Down the Memory Hole

For my Dad who, after he died, whispered the idea for this story to me in my dreams, for my Mom, who always asks about the book, and in honor of Lord Grundleshanks, the late, great, magickal toad.

ACKNOWLEDGMENTS

Big THANK YOU's go to:

Troy, who thought immortalizing Lord Grundleshanks was a fitting tribute for a magickal toad, and who inspired me by surviving against all odds.

Mark and Griffin, for putting up with having a writer in the family. My mom, who's been asking me for years when the book's coming out.

Jill and Carrie for being my beta readers. My Backspace, Kindleboards and Facebook crews for their continued advice and assistance. My manager, Leslie Conliffe, for her patience.

A big thank you to Mike Campbell for coming up with the title—I will forever be grateful. Even if I do keep trying to change his name.

Thank you to the amazing readers who snagged editing errors and brought them to my attention: Linda Rae Blair, Tim Gordon, Kerstin Day Peterson and Mark Miller. Your sharp eyes are very much appreciated!

But most of all, I want to send a big thank you to my children. To my grown-up kids, who have taught me to live life on my own terms and to AR, my baby girl and muse, who inspires me and teaches me, everyday, how to reach for the stars.

SOMEBODY TELL

AUNT TILLIE

SHE'S DEAD

TABLE OF CONTENTS

Part One Killing Aunt Tillie

Part Two Aunt Tillie's Revenge

An Excerpt From:
Somebody Tell Aunt Tillie We're In Trouble!

PART ONE

KILLING AUNT TILLIE

CHAPTER ONE

*AT THE BEGINNING OF this whole, surreal journey, I had no idea
you could be evicted from your body as easily as you could be
booted out of your apartment. Easier, actually, since there's
none of those pesky laws in place to protect you. But it all started
out so innocently—with a streak of bad luck.*

* * *

ONE OF THE PROBLEMS with being a witch is when you ask the
universe a question, it generally gives you an answer. Or just
enough of one to ruin a perfectly good week.

But since it was my birthday...

And since I was an eternal optimist...

And mostly 'cause I was stuck at the longest red light in the
history of traffic, with nothing else to do, I dug my tarot deck out
of my purse and pulled three cards for the coming year.

Death. Three of Swords. The Tower.

Transformation. Sorrow. Change through destruction.

Happy birthday to me.

Damn it. I shouldn't have looked. You'd think I'd know
better by now. Damn tarot cards always suckered me into
peeking into my future and I just about always regretted it.
Because the hell of it was...

They were usually right.

* * *

After a quick stop at Trader Joe's, I was finally home. I
propped the grocery bag on my hip, wrestled open the wrought
iron gate and placed my hand on my mailbox. *Mara Stephens,*

Apt 1-C.

I stood for a second, hoping my unemployment check was in there and tried to read the vibes. This was a game I always played with myself—a small psychic exercise to keep my 'sight' sharp. But I didn't feel any sense of urgency or hope. Just a whopping dose of dread.

Great. So my guess was no check, but at least one major bill I'd have to pay. I unlocked the box and quickly sorted through the mail. A sale flyer from the Crooked Pantry, a birthday card from a temp agency and—yup, there it was, sure enough—a pink notice from the Dept. of Water and Power.

Good thing I had plenty of candles to fall back on. And a swimming pool. If I got desperate, I mused, I could always shower over the drain in the courtyard, using the garden hose. People washed their dogs there all the time. And my shampoo was considerably less toxic than flea dip. I wondered if Lenny, (my landlord), would let me set up one of those portable, camping shower stalls.

Tucked into the back of the mailbox was a reminder about the rent. At least that was one thing I didn't need to worry about. Lenny knew I was good for it. How much longer I'd be able to pay the rent though... that thought made me queasy.

Suddenly, a wave of panic hit my stomach and clenched it hard. Forget crawling, gooseflesh positively raced across my arms. I struggled to breathe. Whatever was wrong, it all seemed to be coming from the direction of my apartment.

I dropped my mail into the grocery bag and peeked around the corner of the mail stand. Behind the screen door, my front door was wide open.

Shit! I ducked back behind the mailboxes and fumbled through my purse for my cell phone.

I flipped open the phone and hit 9-1-1.

Busy.

I hung up and tried again.

Still busy.

Bloody hell. No wonder the crime rate was so high in Los Angeles. I didn't know what the non-emergency number was, so I decided to call my home phone and warn the intruder to clear out.

2

If I was lucky, it would just be a break-in. A simple case of anonymous robbery. I'd warn whoever was in there, that I was on my way home, and they'd hit the road with their haul.

But as I punched in the first three digits, the phone beeped, the battery icon blinked and the screen went black.

Damn it. I shoved the phone back into my purse and took another look at my apartment. The living room lights had been turned on against the gathering dusk. But why would robbers turn on the lights? Didn't that negate the whole idea of stealth?

I crept closer. That's when I saw Mrs. Lasio, the new building manager, planted like a bull in my living room.

Great. Just freaking great. Why did it have to be her? Why couldn't it have been some whacked-out crack-head carting off my TV?

* * *

Mrs. Lasio was a heavyset, older Latina woman who always wore an ostentatious gold cross that could double as a weapon. It was heavy enough to do serious damage if you whacked a mugger with it and no security person would ever dare confiscate it. She was trouble from the minute she walked into the building courtyard. She made no secret of her feelings about me. After she met me, she added a blue and black eyeball-shaped amulet to her crucifix, as protection against the evil eye. But, other than that, she'd always left me alone. *Until now.*

* * *

I slammed open the screen door.

"What are you doing in my apartment?!" I yelled, dropping the grocery bag on the carpeted floor. Then I winced when I remembered the eggs. Ye Gods, this was turning out to be a shitty birthday.

Mrs. Lasio was so mad spit flew out with every sentence. "Look at this devil shit. I warn Lenny about you," she said, making the sign of the cross. "*Iesu Maria. Brujaria.* Devil magic."

I looked around my living room. Third-hand furniture, wall-to-wall bookshelves and various dragon and gargoyle statues that I quite liked. Okay, so I was having a second childhood in my twenties and grooving on my bits of gothic statuary. Sue me.

But Mrs. Lasio was very pointedly looking at the alcove in the wall. It's where the built-in wet bar used to be, before I took a sledgehammer to the counter and remade it into an altar.

There was a chalice and athamé (cup and knife, together they represented the union of male and female), a small cauldron, incense and candles on top of the altar and a pentagram plaque on the wall (representing fire, earth, water, air and spirit). Next to the sink, where most people kept their barware, I had a tribal skull, (made of resin), sandwiched between a statue of Hekate and a statue of Baphomet, with various tarot decks spread out in front of them.

Nothing too out of the ordinary for a young witch, but how was I going to explain it to someone as superstitious as my building manager?

"What are you talking about? It's not evil, it's Wicca. You know, Mrs. Lasio, like on TV? *Charmed? Buffy? Witches of Eastwick?* Good magic, white dresses, Goddess moons, blessings of the earth? Do you watch TV?"

She picked up my statue of Baphomet and waved it at me. "Is Satan."

"It's Baphomet." But with its wings, horns, half-human/half-goat appearance, I had to grant that maybe, just maybe, it gave a bad impression. *Damn it.* I was so screwed.

I took a deep breath and tried to explain. "Baphomet sits at the threshold between order and chaos, life and death, male and female. He's representative of the duality of the manifest universe and the cosmic unknown." He just looks kind of scary. Although I didn't say that last part out loud.

Mrs. Lasio snorted, unswayed by my speechifying. "You think I am stupid? I see this in Church. You worship *el Diablo.*" And she threw the statue across the room.

I almost had a heart attack, but Baphomet just bounced harmlessly on the couch cushions before settling to a stop. "What is wrong with you? You break into my home and now you're throwing my things around? Screw this. I'm calling the cops. They can deal with you."

Mrs. Lasio scuttled to stand between me and the phone. "I smell something funny. Maybe your apartment on fire. Maybe you have drugs. I have to check before I call *policia*."

My jaw dropped open. How far was this woman going to stoop, to spy on me? "How many weeks did it take you to think that one up, Mrs. Lasio? Or did you have help?"

"I no like you, *bruja*. You are hazard to building." Her eyes narrowed as she played her trump card. "I am Manager. And you... you are evicted."

* * *

And that was how it all began. If I had known then, what I know now, I would have packed up every objectionable item the minute Mrs. Lasio moved in and I realized how narrow-minded and bigoted my new building manager was. After all, if witchcraft is in your blood, you don't need the accoutrements. They just make it easier to focus. If it's in your blood, you can craft stark naked, wearing a paper hat and waving a toilet brush.

* * *

"Evicted?!" I sat down on the couch before my knees gave out. "You can't do this. I've lived here for ten years," I whispered. Even after my dad died, I moved into a smaller apartment, but I still stayed in the building. Most people my age were saving to buy their first house but I loved my apartment.

We had rented it, sight unseen, from Chicago. The minute I saw the ad, I just knew it was the one. I could feel it in the way the blood rushed to my head and my skin tingled. And sure enough, when we pulled up in the moving van, I had immediately fallen in love with its 1970's-style architecture, triangular arches and quaint little pool with seahorse imprints. It was my bit of retro-paradise in the middle of hot, smoggy Los Angeles. How was I supposed to just give it up?

The image of the Tower card kept flashing in my mind. *Chaos and destruction.*

"My soul is going to heaven. Is not going to hell. You take your devil garbage and get out." Mrs. Lasio crossed herself again. "I have priest come bless this building."

"There's no way Lenny will let you do this to me." I said.

Lenny was our neighbor when we moved in, but then he won a chunk of money on *Who Wants To Be A Millionaire* and bought the building. Other than my dad, I'd known him longer than anyone.

"He saved, *bruja*. I take Lenny to church with me and Jesus find him. He not under your spell no more."

That must be why I was suddenly in her sights. I inwardly cursed the fact that I was on a month-to-month lease instead of a yearly contract. But Lenny was as commitment-phobic in his business contracts as he was in his relationships.

"Great. Good. Fabulous. Maybe Jesus will defend the two of you in court when I sue your ass. Ever hear of religious persecution, Mrs. Lasio? The ACLU will hang you from a flagpole."

Mrs. Lasio crossed her arms, the fingers of her left hand tapping her flabby upper arm. "You are like little dog with big words. Yap, yap, yap." She glared at me. "You no pay rent, you get out. You evicted."

"That's ridiculous! Lenny knows I always pay my rent. He's never gotten it later than the fifteenth."

"Too bad for you, rent is due on first. My nephew is lawyer." She slapped an eviction notice on the coffee table in front of me. "You get out by end of month. No funny business, or I keep security deposit. I'm watching you, *bruja*."

And with that, she left, slamming the door behind her. I thought about throwing a curse at her, but it wasn't worth the coin. Few things were. Dumb karma. Dumb threefold law. Dumb me for not paying the rent sooner.

* * *

Damn it. I should have known better. Mrs. Lasio was more religious than most priests I'd met, taking fanatical to a whole new level. Every Easter, she hosted a Passion of the Christ movie night and then paraded around the block with her friends. The men held mock crosses on their back, while the women wailed at the top of their lungs and flicked holy water at anyone who had the misfortune of being on the sidewalk. I should have realized she'd never tolerate a witch living in her building. I should have known she'd jump at the first chance to get rid of me. But I just hadn't been paying attention.

* * *

I studied the eviction notice again. It certainly looked official. Could Mrs. Lasio have done this on her own? Without Lenny knowing about it?

I read down the page. Nope. There was Lenny's signature, in his neat, careful penmanship. It was official. The weasel had kicked me out. So much for him considering me to be family. I had three weeks. How was I going to find a new place to live in three weeks?!

I tore the notice into thirds and tossed the pieces on the coffee table. Then I picked Baphomet up off the couch, before I accidentally sat on him, and looked him over. He wasn't that bad. Almost attractive—in a demonic sort of way.

"What's wrong with people nowadays?" I asked him. "The Knights Templar worshipped you for ages. They were Christians. Well, okay, so maybe they were heretical, but still."

The phone rang. I did my best to ignore it as I carefully positioned Baphomet back on the altar. "Not that I'm not a social person," I told Baphomet, "but how much humanity should anyone have to suffer in any given day?"

After a few rings, the answering machine kicked in and a sexy male voice came on the line. "I know you're there, bitch. Pick up the phone."

I rolled my eyes. Only Gus could make *bitch* sound like a pet name.

I picked up the receiver. "I hate when you do that."

He laughed. Gus was my best friend and chosen family. He was like the brother I never had. We were each other's standing date and occasional wingman. He was also one of the few self-proclaimed witches I'd met with real ability. His 'sight' was annoyingly spot-on and he could be pushy as hell. Unlike me, Gus reveled in his witchiness. The only thing stopping him from tattooing a scarlet W on his forehead, was that it would clash with his wardrobe.

Once you got past our shared sense of humor and our shared love of men, we were total opposites. I was your typical, pale, Scottish-American with a fondness for jeans and tee-shirts. Gus, on the other hand, was an eccentric Greek-American Celtophile. With a flair for the unfashionable. Seriously. His wardrobe was like Pirates of the Caribbean meets The Craft. Long, flowing shirts, blousy pants and gnarly Celtic man-jewelry. And yet, somehow, he was able to pull it off without looking like a stowaway from a Disney flick.

* * *

"So? Don't keep me in suspense. What happened?" Gus asked. "I could hear you screaming all the way in West Hollywood."

"Hold up, let me get the headset on." As soon as my hands were free, I walked into the kitchen and started putting groceries away. Yay, most of the eggs were still intact.

"Out with it. Tell Gus what's wrong."

I sighed. "My unemployment's about to run out. I can't find work. I've just been evicted. I'm spending another birthday—that everyone forgot, hello—alone. And my tarot cards hate me. Other than that, I'm fine."

"Sounds like you've had a full day."

"Fuck off." Bastard. I could practically see him trying not to laugh. "I'm so glad my misfortune amuses you."

"I didn't forget your birthday, I'm planning a surprise."

"That's what you said last year." I finished putting away the fridge food and started on the dry goods. "But you get points for consistency."

"You are in a foul mood. Why don't you tell Lasio you've lost your way and you're ready to be saved? She'll be all over that."

"Because that would be lying. And lying is wrong. Didn't your parents ever teach you that? Or were you raised by wolves?"

I expected Gus to make some kind of smart-ass remark, but all I heard was silence.

"She thinks I should move into your sardine tin with you," I added, still waiting for a reaction.

Now I could hear some odd thumps, followed by quiet breathing.

I made a face at the telephone. "I'm sorry, is my life falling apart boring you?"

"Hush. I'm trying to catch Lord Grundleshanks eating. There's a cricket marching on his damned head and he's about to... stay oblivious. Damn it, Grundleshanks."

I rolled my eyes. What was it about boys and distractions? Were single-track minds were a male genetic marker?

"Whatever. Call me when you break up with the toad." I said, hanging up the phone.

* * *

I searched through the fridge until I found what I was looking for—my secret stash of brandy-filled, bean-shaped chocolates from Trader Joes. I opened the box to find one, solitary, lonely, little bean nestled in the corner. Figures. I should have known I'd be almost out of chocolate. It was just the way my luck had been going lately.

I sighed, bit into the tiny chocolate and brandy confection, and tossed the box in the trash. Then I pulled the tarot deck out of my purse. It was a Thoth deck and normally, I liked using it because it was loud, unequivocal and unambiguous in its messages. Although, sometimes, it could be way too blunt.

I shuffled the cards within an inch of their lives and pulled three cards for the upcoming year.

The order was different, but the cards were the same.

Three of Swords. Tower. Death.

Son of a bitch.

CHAPTER TWO

LATER THAT NIGHT, I was whipping up a bowl of frosting when I heard a scratching sound at the door and the doorknob turned.

I grabbed a knife from the butcher block.

The only way in or out of my apartment was the front door. So if someone was breaking in, one of us was gonna be screwed. And it wasn't going to be me.

The door creaked open.

I clutched the knife harder.

But as the door opened all the way, I saw a goofy grin, long hair and a pirate shirt.

Gus. Looking inordinately pleased with himself. Gus once told me learned how to pick locks on the Internet. Personally, I suspected he had spent a previous life as a cat burglar, given how proficient he was at it.

"Damn it." I swore, as I put the knife away. "Haven't you ever heard of a doorbell? Or privacy? You just shaved five years off my life."

"I tried your doorbell. Didn't work," he said, putting his tools back in their case. "I don't know why you won't just give me a key."

"Because your name's not on the lease. What about knocking? What if I was in here, having sex on the living room floor?"

He snorted. "I'd wonder if the Jurassic age had returned."

"Ha. Funny. Very funny." I narrowed my eyes at him, but it didn't seem to faze him any. "Fuck off and go bug somebody else."

"Hey, be nice to me, Miss Thing. I come bearing good

news."

I looked at him suspiciously. He looked good, he smelled even better. Gus blended his own essential oils and he was wearing an amber/patchouli mix that was warm, sexy and incredible.

I gasped. "You found a new boyfriend and you're on your way to Bordello?!" Bordello was the hot, new nightclub in downtown L.A. It featured live Jazz and Blues bands and Gus and I were both dying to try it out.

"Oh, ye of little faith. Would I come over here just to rub my water wealth in the face of a woman who lives in the desert?"

I rolled my eyes. "Of course you would," I said, spreading frosting on my still-warm cake. When some people get depressed, they can't eat. When I get depressed, I bake. It's why my clothes never quite fit. Good thing I didn't get depressed too often, or I'd look like Jabba the Hut. "Well, don't just stand there. If you're on your own tonight, sit down and pull up a plate. Have a piece of my home-baked double chocolate fudge Kahlua cake."

Gus arched an eyebrow over at my trashcan. "Since when does a box mix count as baking?"

"Hey, I put in additional ingredients. It doesn't come with Kahlua in the mix, you know."

He picked up the box and checked it out. "Partially hydrogenated vegetable oil. You have any idea how bad this is for you?"

I shrugged. "More for me, then."

He shook his head and dumped the box back into the trash. "Eating yourself into a coma is such a chick thing."

"In case you haven't noticed, I am a chick." I said, annoyed.

He hooted. "With those hips, who could miss it?"

"Jackass. Just for that, I'm wishing myself a new best friend."

I carefully finished sticking the candles in the cake. Birthday cakes just don't taste the same without candles. Then I fired up the candles. Despite his misgivings about my dietary choices, Gus turned off the lights and, as I carried the platter out to the dining room table, he sang the Happy Birthday song.

I took a deep breath and made a wish for more time. Just in case my stupid tarot cards were right. Then I blew those candles out as hard as I could. To my relief, I got them all out in one go.

* * *

Some people may think it's silly, but the whole ritual of birthday wishes has always seemed to me to be a simplified form of spellcrafting. You send your wish to the Gods, by using your breath to blow the flames, (and your wish), from the manifest world to the unmanifest world, hoping your wish will be granted and returned to you in manifest form.

* * *

Gus turned the lights back on. "You want to tell me what that was about? There was a bit more *oomph* to that, than your standard birthday wish."

I shook my head. "If I tell you, it won't come true. And with the way my life's been going, I need all the help I can get."

He sighed. "You've gotta think positive, Mara."

I gave him another slit-eyed look. "That's easy for you to say. You have a job."

"My dear, divalicious witch girl, you're looking at this all wrong. Unemployment is the Gods' way of putting you on a new career path. You should be dancing on your coffee table, giddy with the possibilities, not trying to eat away your sorrows."

"Really?" I pulled the candles out of the cake and cut a super-sized slice. "Because panhandler just doesn't seem like much of a career path to me. Go figure."

"It's all about attitude, my little magic mushroom. Change your attitude, change your life. Embrace what the future brings you."

I laughed. "When did you turn into gay Oprah?"

"Bite your forked tongue, woman. I am an original. The Gods made man with everything at their disposal and then used the leftover, unnecessary bits to create woman."

I raised an eyebrow at that. "There are days when I wonder why we ever became friends," I said, shaking my head. But I couldn't quite hide my smile.

"Because I bring *'fab-u-lous'* into your monochromatic

life," Gus said, looking triumphant. "Now, hush up and prepare to be thrilled. Are you ready for your birthday present?" He smiled, pleased with himself. "You, Mara Stephens, are about to embark on a new career. Courtesy of *moi*."

I stopped with a bite of cake halfway to my mouth. This wasn't going to be good. I could just feel it.

He waved his arms, clearly visualizing some kind of billboard above the Hollywood freeway. "*Mara Stephens, Fortune-Teller to the Stars*. And it starts tomorrow."

"What?!" I screeched. "Seriously?"

I had made the mistake of reading Gus's cards once. He thought I was spookily good. So he's made it his life's mission to make me regret it ever since. Although he calls it '*getting Mara to embrace her abilities.*'

"Tell me you're joking. I am so not on speaking terms with my tarot cards at the moment."

"Mmmm. Let me see..." He looked off into the distance, then turned back to me. "Yup, pretty sure I don't care. Whatever happened, apologize to the cards and get over it." Then he leaned forward and pinched my waist. "Now, assuming it still fits over your self-indulgent rolls, get your best witchy outfit together. The fate of a ninth grade class depends on you!"

"You are out of your mind," I slapped his hands away from my love handles. "I am not going to play Witchy-Poo to the post-toddler set. Besides, I'm busy tomorrow. I have to track down my weasel of a landlord and throttle him."

"It pays two hundred fifty dollars for three hours work."

My jaw dropped. "Well, why didn't you start with that? My schedule just cleared."

"That's my girl." He winked, smug in victory. "Do your best not to scar them for life and everything will be fine. Tomorrow, you conquer the ninth grade. Next week, Dame Fate is ours for the taking."

I laughed and rolled my eyes.

Gus lit a cigarette and took a drag. He was perpetually trying to quit, but he had the self-control of an infant.

I took the cigarette away and ran it under cold water as he started hacking up a lung. "Talk to me about conquering Dame Fate after you conquer your disgusting nicotine addiction. I thought you were quitting."

"Something's got to kill me. Without my vices, I could live forever and that would really fuck up the natural order of the universe." He gave me a wicked grin, kissed me on the cheek, and wafted out in a nicotine, amber and patchouli cloud.

* * *

That night, I tossed and turned, lost in a nightmare world that felt eerily familiar.

I ran through the woods, driven by a sense of imminent doom that was so strong, it pulsated through the air. Branches tore at my ankle-length skirt. I struggled to breathe against the confines of my bodice, but I couldn't slow down.

Driven by a sense of urgency that I didn't understand, I increased my speed, until I burst out of the woods and into a clearing, next to a small, stone cottage. I forced open the heavy oak door and ran in, panicked.

Blood seeped through the walls, running down in rivulets, pooling on the dirt floor. Blood streamed over my booted feet, soaking my skirt. A rising tide of blood filled the room, the iron smell overpowering.

I turned to run out, but the door was blocked by a large, tattooed man, holding a knife.

He plunged the knife into my stomach and twisted it. The pain was unbearable, the sheer burning as the blade cut through muscle, tissue and organs.

I gasped as he slowly pulled the knife out.

On the point of the blade was the bloody, mutilated head of a newborn, its mouth open in a silent cry.

The baby's eyes snapped open...

A burning red...

A fiery window into hell...

I felt myself falling into the flaming abyss...

* * *

I bolted upright, sweating, breathing hard. It was 4:00 a.m. and I was freezing cold. I knew Los Angeles was technically a desert climate, so the night could be a lot colder than the day, but this was ridiculous. I jumped out of bed and shuffle-ran down the hall to the linen closet, shivering the whole way. If it got any colder, it was going to snow inside my apartment. I snatched a fleece blanket out of the linen closet and wrapped it around me. But as I was turning to go back to bed, I noticed a light on in the living room.

I held my breath and listened.

Male voices.

At least two of them.

And neither one sounded like Gus.

What the hell was going on? I thought about calling the cops, but my cell phone was in the living room, along with the landline. And, unlike apartments in Chicago, there was no back door for me to sneak out of. I toyed with the idea of the bedroom window, but the screens were screwed in so you couldn't open them. And the toolbox with the screwdriver was under the kitchen sink. *Crap.*

I took another deep breath and held it, straining to hear what the voices were saying, while I tried to figure out what I should do next.

"Look at me."

That sounded like John Travolta.

Was I freaking out over nothing?

Did I go to bed and leave the TV on?

On the bottom shelf of the linen cabinet, next to the kitchen towels, was my Mag-Lite. I picked it up and hefted the weight. Sturdy. Oh, yeah, that would hurt an intruder. On a good day, it might even deflect bullets.

I held it like a club and crept down the darkened hallway, my heart in my throat, and carefully opened the door between the hallway and the living room.

There was a guy sitting on my couch, smoking a cigarette and watching *Get Shorty*.

I lowered the Mag-Lite. "Gus?"

He turned toward me.

Not Gus.

Not even close.

CHAPTER THREE

"DAD?" I GAPED AT him. He looked like he was in his twenties, with a full head of blond hair, instead of the graying strands he had when he died. This wasn't the first time I had seen a ghost, but it was the first time I'd seen one so up close and manifest. Like he was really sitting there.

"Hi, pumpkin." He lowered the volume on the TV. "I've been waiting for you."

I set the Mag-Lite on the coffee table and sat down in the chair next to the couch. "You look all... *Rebel Without A Cause*-ish."

"Yeah. One of the perks of being dead. You're not limited by time." He exhaled, sending smoke up in a cloud. "I can be whatever age I want."

"And you smoke?!"

"I did when I was younger. I gave it up when you were born. What's it gonna do now, kill me?" He laughed and leaned back, relaxing against the couch. "We don't have a lot of time. You officially turn twenty-seven in," he looked at my clock, "three hours and twenty-one minutes."

"You came here to wish me a happy birthday?"

"No, I came to warn you."

Great. Fabulous. Figures. It probably had to do with the crappy tarot cards I pulled today. I pressed my fists against my temples, but his voice went on.

"I tried to get here sooner, but it's tough to time appearances from a dimension where time doesn't exists. Do you remember your mom?"

My head was starting to throb. "She took off when I was a

kid. How much am I supposed to remember?"

"She didn't take off, she left to protect you."

"Tom*a*to, tom*ah*to." I muttered.

"You remember how hard we looked for her?"

Yeah. I remembered. We had spent most of my life searching for her.

"I never told you this, but I tracked her down at your Aunt Tillie's house. I begged her to come back home, but she was afraid. She said she was cursed. And whatever was coming for her, she didn't want it to touch you, or even know you existed. Three days later, on her twenty-seventh birthday, she vanished."

I felt a chill crawl up my spine.

"You need to lay low. Stay off the Otherworld grid. You can use your sight to stay alert for danger, but other than that, stay in the shadows. I won't be able to help you, without drawing attention to you. You'll be on your own." He reached over, patted my hand, and started to fade. "I love you, pumpkin."

"Dad! Wait! Come back!"

But he was gone.

* * *

I picked up the remote control and turned off the TV, but the sudden stillness creeped me out. So I turned it back on and snuggled into my blanket.

What did he mean, she was cursed? Did that mean I was cursed, as well? I felt woefully under-informed about the entire thing. I wished he had stayed longer. Although, to be honest, I was surprised he made it back to this side of the veil at all. My dad was a normal human being. He wasn't like my mom. She was born a witch, as was everyone in her family line. And her magical talents had passed into me. But did that mean her curse had passed to me as well?

My thoughts turned to my dad. He was brave enough to marry a woman he couldn't really understand and human enough to keep her grounded and safe in his reality. Well, for as long as he could, at any rate. Until he couldn't. And then she was gone. I remembered all those times when I was a little girl, and it was just me and him. We would sit on the couch and I would snuggle into my dad's arms as he watched TV, until I fell asleep. In the middle of feeling scared and alone all the time, the only time I truly felt safe was when he was holding me.

* * *

When I woke up, I was in my bed.

What the heck?

I got up and went to the hall closet. My fleece blanket was still folded up, on the top shelf, untouched. The Mag-Lite was still in its place. It was as if last night had never happened. As if it had been nothing more than a dream.

I walked into the living room and turned on the TV.

SoapNet.

Not exactly a channel that would air *Get Shorty*.

I sighed. So it was going to be like that. One of the reasons I hated dealing with ghosts, was that they always screwed with my sense of reality. They had the ability to make dreams seem real and reality seem surreal. But it made sense that my dad wasn't able to really show up in my living room. It took a lot of energy for spirits to become manifest. It was much easier for them to interact in the dream realm.

And then I noticed the time.

Damn, damn, damn. I was going to be late.

I took the fastest shower known to womankind, then ran around my apartment like a demented wind hag, throwing everything I could possibly need into a box. Gus's big job opportunity was this afternoon and I still needed to meet with Lenny before I drove over the hill.

* * *

Fifteen minutes later, I was sipping a chai latte at Aroma, the local coffee shop/bookstore, waiting for Lenny. An hour later, I was on my second over-priced latte, paging through a book I couldn't focus on. I looked up at the clock. Then I looked at my watch, but it gave me the same time.

I was starting to feel like an unwitting character in a never-ending Beckett play.

Just as I was giving up, the elusive Godot swept into the shop. And *'swept'* was exactly the right word for it, with his white Panama hat and white alligator shoes. Perfectly groomed from stem to stern, wearing a pale yellow shirt and white linen pants. Lenny looked like a summer day in Florida. He smiled at me, but his eyes were twitchy.

He bypassed the coffee line and headed directly for the table. I groaned. Without food or coffee to anchor him to the table, he'd be jackrabbiting out of here the minute I turned my back.

"Yes, baby doll," he said, sitting down and taking off his white Panama hat. "What can Lenny do you for?"

I placed the shreds of the eviction notice on the table, hoping he'd say Lasio had forged his signature, but he just shook his head.

"Wish it weren't so."

"C'mon, Lenny. You've known me since I was a kid. You're like family. And family doesn't evict family."

"Sorry, sweet-pea, but I've got nothing to work with here. Gloria is one wigged out *mamacita* when it comes to you. If you were actual blood, I could maybe use that. But since you're not..." he shrugged.

I cursed to myself. How long had Lenny been on a first-name basis with the evil hag? "Mrs. Lasio's just really old world. It's a total over-reaction."

"Honey, we live in a Moral Majority world. Flaunt your religious beliefs and sexual preferences at your own peril. It's something we boys have known for centuries. Done is done."

"Seriously?" I couldn't believe what I was hearing. "Did time turn backwards while I was asleep? Are we going to be fighting over civil rights next? This is the new millennium, isn't it?"

"New, old, who cares? Honey child, read the newspapers. Creationism made a comeback and science is just another theory." He sighed. "You chose to live an alternative lifestyle. I told you to stay under the radar. You got careless."

"She broke into my apartment," I protested.

"Sorry, cookie. That's just the way it crumbles. You'll be fine."

I slumped down, head in my hands.

Lenny reached over and patted me on the shoulder. "Don't

stress, sugar. The Lord will provide."

"He fucking will not."

"Language, sugar! I may be old, but I have delicate ears."

I sighed. "You know what they say, Lenny? It's not the Earth the meek inherit, it's the dirt. I'm kinda done with dirt." I looked up him. "So, what she said about you is true? You're born again? You found salvation?"

Silence from his end. A jogger outside the window seemed to catch his full attention.

I nudged his leg. "Lenny? Cough it up. And be straight with me."

"Perish the thought."

"If you're going to let Mrs. Lasio ruin my life and turn me out in the streets, at least give me a crumb. What's really going on?"

His blue eyes were bright in his elfin face, his white goatee and mustache neatly trimmed. Everything about him screamed hot date. Call me crazy, but I had a feeling the effort wasn't made on my behalf.

Lenny forced a smile. "Sorry, lamb chop, but I'm dating her brother and they take their religion very seriously."

"You found Jesus in order to get laid?" I practically choked on the remains of my latte.

Lenny shot me a look and I put up my hands in surrender.

"I'm down with that, really. I'm just trying to figure out why I have to lose my home over it."

He sighed. "This family can eke out drama like a salt-water taffy pull. They're very hot-blooded, close-knit. If she's upset, she calls Manuel and gets him upset and my sex life is for shit, darlin'. And she has been freaked about the devil stuff since the day she met you."

"It's not devil stuff," I snapped. I was getting so tired of being labeled as evil.

"Of course not, sugar. But it doesn't matter. The truth never has. Life is all about dealing with people's perceptions of the truth. Unfortunately, Gloria's perception of you means you just got voted off the island."

My emotions were bouncing between disgust, despair and anger. Despair must have won, because Lenny leaned forward and patted my hand.

"I'll give you a good reference. Heck, I'll even give you your full security deposit back, plus last month's rent check. But I need you to pack up and not cause a fuss."

I crushed a napkin in my fist and tried not to cry. "I hope he's worth it."

"Oh, he is, baby doll," Lenny gave a happy sigh. "He's absolutely incredible. He used to be a gymnast and he's still got a body that defies the laws of physics. At our age, that's saying something."

Just then, a well-muscled, older Spanish hunk, in a tank top and sweats, walked in through the door.

Lenny waved his white Panama in the air. "Yoo-hoo, Manuel! I'll be right there, darling." He turned back to me. "Sorry, love. Must run."

"You don't happen to own any other apartment buildings, do you?" I asked, in a last ditch attempt.

"Not yet. But I've always got my eyes open."

A couple of air kisses, a fragile hug, and Lenny was off with his Latino dreamboat. I looked down at my empty latte mug, feeling completely disconnected. And then I noticed the time.

Gus was going to kill me.

CHAPTER FOUR

I THREW A PRAYER up to the traffic Gods that Coldwater Canyon wasn't nightmarishly backed up and jumped into Sally, the cherry-red, vintage Mustang convertible I had inherited from my dad's mid-life crisis. *Look out, ninth graders. Witchy-Poo's on her way!*

I spent a few minutes imagining how cool and sophisticated I looked in my dad's car. But, as I floored it over the Canyon, the wind did its best to force-feed me my hair, destroying the illusion. I coughed and spat hair out of my mouth. Well, no one would ever mistake me for being graceful. Or even stylish, really, unless it was a really good day. But at least the car was bitchin'.

While it was a hot summer day back in the Valley, over on this side of the hill, a cool breeze flowed in from the ocean. Now, this would be a great area to live in. Beautiful mansions, gorgeous views, tree-shaded streets, swimming pools that glittered like gemstones. Maybe in my next life.

With a sigh, I stopped daydreaming about things that were out of my reach and focused on Gus's big job. From what I had Googled, Lyra had taken his name from the Italian word for money, *lira*, when he immigrated to America and it brought him luck ever since.

He quickly married up, using his wife's business contacts to make a small fortune in promotional merchandise. Then he took a big risk and invested in a string of B-grade movies, featuring A-list has-beens, that paid off in a big way. A couple of surprise hits and a growing cult following later, he was swimming with the celebrity elite.

I turned up a side road and was suddenly at the sprawling, Greco-Roman inspired, Casa de Lyra. The wrought iron gate was open and a marble fountain, featuring naked male cherubs pissing water, held a spot of honor on the front lawn. I almost laughed out loud when I saw it. Given the cancerous quality of L.A. tap water, piss was a pretty apt metaphor.

But what struck me most, as I parked my car, was the marble driveway. What would possess anyone to put in a marble driveway? That had to be a bitch during rainy season. I could just imagine Mr. Lyra's wife sliding down the rain-slicked driveway on her designer Christian Louboutin heels, arms windmilling, as she struggled to get her balance. But maybe Mr. Lyra had so much money, he paid rubber-booted servants to carry his family members from their chauffeur-driven car to their ornate front door during monsoon weather.

* * *

I schlepped my box of occult tchotchkes to the door, where a beefy security guy carefully—and way too slowly—searched it. I glanced at my watch. Party guests were due to arrive in thirty minutes.

"Can you hurry it up?"

"You were supposed to be here an hour before the party." He said, oblivious to my distress.

"I don't need that much set-up time," I lied.

Then, just when I thought he was done, he started searching me.

I jumped. "Hey, easy there! This gets any more intimate, I'll expect a ring."

He raised an eyebrow at me and I could have sworn the corner of his mouth twitched, like he was trying not to smile. "You keep squirming, it's going to get a lot more intimate."

"Sorry. I'm ticklish. Isn't there supposed to be a female guard doing this?" I grumbled.

"This ain't the airport, sweetheart," he said. "Shoes off."

I slipped out of my Birkenstocks. "If there's a cavity search involved, I'm quadrupling my fee."

He grunted, gave me my shoes back, and handed me off to a harried maid.

* * *

The maid pulled me through the mansion at a brisk trot, past Renoirs, Monets, a Steinway baby grand, antique furniture, brightly-colored balloons, streamers and a *Happy 14th Birthday, Kimmy* banner.

Within minutes, I was unceremoniously deposited in a closet-sized, harshly lit room. Good thing I came prepared, because doing readings in that type of environment would suck. I shook off the resentment I was feeling about the security at the door, quickly touched up my make-up and slipped into a long, flowing, green gown. It was a tight squeeze, but I didn't hear any seams rip. So far, so good.

I opened up my box of Gothic kitsch and got to work.

* * *

Twenty minutes later, I turned off the lights and looked around, pleased. The play of light and shadow from the candles softened the small space and gave it some much-needed depth. I had draped Celtic print fabrics over the hideous goldenrod-colored counters, anchoring them in place with pieces of dragon statuary.

Then, I spread out my more esoteric tarot decks, using them as decoration to punctuate the space. Flickering tea lights were reflected in the mirrored walls, like hundreds of fireflies. It felt like a magical moment, stolen out of a summer's night. The room positively glowed with an air of mystery and promise.

I kissed the top my crystal skull for luck and put it on the reading table next to a bowl of quarters. Then I twirled in front of one of the mirrors. In the candlelight, I looked pretty damn witchy. With my long hair, Goth-style make-up and the bust-friendly cut of the dress, I kind of looked like a young, woodsy, Elvira.

Suddenly, I was hit with a wave of *déjà vu* so strong it made me nauseous. It was as if the world had somehow shifted and I was looking at my reflection through a crack in time.

I stared at the mirror. Frightened eyes stared back at me. I tried to remember what year it was and the answer that came into my head shocked me.

Breathe, Mara. Just breathe. It's really not the seventeenth century.

And then a smile started, so slow and wicked it made the skin on my spine crawl. My hands shot up to my face.

I wasn't smiling.

But my reflection was.

* * *

I squeezed my eyes shut and tried not to scream. I had to get a grip. I couldn't afford to let these people think I was losing my mind. When I opened my eyes again, my reflection had returned to normal. I turned on the room lights and looked at the mirror again.

It was just an ordinary mirror, showing the reflection of a too-curvy, modern-day girl wearing Ren-Faire-ware and too much make-up.

I opened a bottle of water with shaky hands and took a swig. *What the hell was going on? Was I losing my mind? Was this the curse my dad warned me about? Or was someone from the other side trying to reach me?* Maybe it was a brain tumor. I had heard that tumors on the temporal lobe could cause visual and aural hallucinations.

* * *

Yeah, in case I didn't mention it earlier, that's the other problem with being a witch. Since we deal so much with the unseen world, it was entirely too easy to step over the line into fantasy and madness. I'd seen other people go that route. Gus had lost his last lover that way. Although, really, that was kind of his fault, for initiating a non-witch into the mysteries.

Witches are born with a multitude of ancestors in our heads, so we learn to deal with the voices and visions from an early age. When the door between realms is opened for a normal human, their minds can snap, unable to deal with the sudden chaos in their heads.

However, even witches can cross the line from having a foot in both worlds, to becoming completely non-functional in the mundane reality of this world, utterly consumed with the world of the Unseen. Which is why a witch must be both born and made. A true witch must be a hedge-rider between the mundane and the supernatural. And it's a very delicate, very important balancing act. Fall off the hedge, you can tumble into utter madness -- and that's if you're lucky.

So I've always tried to keep a tight rein on my 'sight' and ride it, rather than allowing it to ride me. Although lately, I seemed to be failing at that more often than not.

Unfortunately, what I didn't realize at the time is that the more you access the Otherworld to work your will, the more access it has to you, as well. Something I wish I had known before I crossed the line between living my own life and becoming a conduit for an entity that shouldn't exist in our world.

* * *

I drank a swig of water and tried to steady my hands. Whatever was going on with me, I didn't have time to deal with it right now. I took a few deep breaths to calm down. I had a job to do. I turned off the room lights, let my eyes readjust to the softer candlelight, and threw open the door. The Reading Room was ready for business.

The girls trickled in, slowly at first, but as word of the fortune-telling witch got around, a line formed down the hall.

All the girls were obsessed with their careers. Thirteen- and fourteen-year old girls. And these were careers in progress, mind you, not dream careers in the future.

Welcome to Hollywood.

Girl after girl:

"I'm ready for something sexier. Should I take that Miramax role?"

"My agent sucks. Will I be screwed if I fire him?"

"I think my accountant is ripping me off. Can you take a look?"

"My mom is seriously cramping my style. Bitch thinks she has final say over what jobs I take. Can I sue her? Become one of those kids without parents?"

Yeesh. Too bad I nixed the tip jar. I could have paid my overdue electric bill with their spare change.

And then Kimmy, the party-girl, walked in, hiding behind a tough-girl facade. Her clothes were one size too small, her makeup was two shades too dark and her heels were three inches too tall. I looked at her and I could feel my stomach sink. She was going to be trouble.

Just like the others, there was only one thing on her mind and she wouldn't be swayed from it.

"Are you sure? You don't want to know about boyfriends?"

Kimmy popped her gum. "Yeah, like, whatever. It's my party, right? I want to see my career."

"What about school? High school? College?"

"No, dope. Fuck college. My career. Now. Don't you watch TV? Do I get nominated for an Emmy this year or what?" She shuffled the cards, barely able to get her hands around the full-sized deck.

I took them from her and indicated the bowl of quarters. She pulled a quarter from the bowl and tossed it in front of the crystal skull as I laid out the cards...

And then I put the cards back in the deck and had her try again.

And again.

But no matter how many times I had her re-pull the cards, I couldn't get away from porn stardom and drug addiction. Trying to turn that into something I could tell the poor girl was completely nerve-wracking.

"Not this year, but you're definitely going to be nominated for an acting award. And win." *And trust me, you don't want to know which one it is*, I thought to myself.

"Now we're talking. You got any advice to, ya know, maximize my career potential?"

I looked down at the cards and tried to think of how to reach her. "Follow your heart, but don't fall for the easy answers, the easy outs, the easy highs. They'll destroy you."

"That's it?"

"Don't be in such a hurry to grow up."

"Yeah, thanks, *mom*. You suck."

Okay, so it wasn't exactly what she wanted to hear, but from what the cards were showing me, she was going to have to learn to deal with disappointment. As she stood up, I got sudden flash.

"You're going to have a surprise math quiz this week. Don't cheat. You'll be caught."

"Cool. Now that I can use."

* * *

After twenty-four readings, I was thrilled to close the door behind the last future Oscar-winner and call it a day.

Damn, but my head hurt.

Readings always gave me a pounding headache, right in the middle of my forehead. My third eye. Or, as the more scientific types called it, my pineal gland. Like any muscle, over-exertion caused pain, and twenty-four non-stop readings had to count as torture in anyone's book.

Food. I needed to get something to eat. A thick slab of salty meat. Maybe some lamb chops. With some of that mint sauce that Gus gets from England. That would help ground me out. I wondered if Gus was busy, what he was doing for dinner, and if I could talk him into cooking.

* * *

As I pulled off my gown and dropped it into my cardboard box, the overhead lights flashed on, momentarily blinding me.

I heard a softly accented male voice by the door. "*Scuza, signorina.* Forgive me for interrupting."

I whirled around. Mr. Lyra was leaning against the door, grinning at me like a hungry wolf. A dangerously handsome, hungry wolf, the bulge in his pants clearly outlining his agenda.

And here I was, pretty much naked. Without even a shadow to hide behind.

Shit. This had the potential go really, drastically wrong.

CHAPTER FIVE

WELL, THERE WAS NOTHING I could do about it now.

"I'm sorry, I thought I locked the door," I said. I quickly rummaged through the box for my street clothes and pulled on a pair of jeans.

"It does not always catch. I must call a locksmith for repairs."

He was still watching me. His eyes slowly traveling over every inch of me. It was unnerving.

"It's refreshing to see a woman who is so easy about her body. So unconcerned about her weight."

I blinked. What an ass. I would never be heroin-chic, but it's not like I was Dumbo. I enjoyed food and I had curves. It's what a woman was supposed to look like. "That's me. Built for comfort, not for speed."

"But why ruin such a beautiful body with all those markings?"

I could feel the muscles in my face tightening as I looking for my bra. "Tattoos? I happen to like them."

I found my bra and, turning away from him, I quickly shoved the girls in. But my fingers seemed impossibly big and clumsy as I tried to fasten the hooks.

Mr. Lyra came up behind me and brushed my hands away. "No need to worry. I never object to a beautiful woman in my house. Especially one who wears her skin so defiantly."

As he hooked my bra together, I could feel his breath warm on my skin. His fingers lightly brushed the curve of my neck, my shoulder...

I was appalled to find my body tingling to his touch. It had been way too long a dry spell. I quickly stepped away from him and pulled on my shirt, trying to keep the box between us.

He smiled, showing off perfectly enameled teeth.

Caught in the surreal moment, I wondered how much the cosmetic dentistry had cost him and what—if anything—his hygienist had worn under her smock.

He laughed. "Such unusual eyes you have."

I bet. Whenever I got angry or embarrassed, they turned an icy cold blue. Although I had to give him props for looking above my neck.

He held up my check, his eyes dark. "You do a little extra service for me? I give you bonus."

My breath caught in my throat. "Sorry. Not part of the deal," I squeaked. I coughed and pretended to clear my throat.

As I reached to take the check from him, he gave me a cold smile and grabbed my wrist. "Perhaps it should be. I am not used to paying a woman so much for so little," he said, still smiling, but squeezing just hard enough to hurt before he let go.

I resisted the temptation to check for bruises and shoved the check in my pocket. "You're married, you have a house full of children and a door that doesn't lock. Trust me, anything else would be a bad idea."

Although I was beginning to understand Kimmy's reading a bit better.

"Besides, this fortune-telling gig isn't as easy as you might think," I said, as I walked around the room, blowing out the remaining tea lights and throwing them in the trash.

"You make up stories, entertain the women and children. Will I marry Justin Timberlake, Miss Lady Witch? Maybe not, but you will find someone just as handsome or as rich. See? I can be *strega* too." He sat at the reading table and lowered his voice. "We are not so different you and I. We both gamble on the future, tell people what they want to hear."

"Actually, most of the time, I wind up doing exactly the opposite." I tossed out the last used tea light and started boxing up my dragon statues.

He laughed. "So you are not only bad whore, you are also bad businesswoman."

I resisted the urge to clock him with a dragon. Instead, I dug through my bag to see if I had any Advils left. This exchange wasn't helping my headache any. I found a travel packet wedged into my cosmetics bag and downed the pills with the warm remains of a soda.

"Experiencing other people's pain, seeing their lives play out in front of you, it's not as much fun as you may think," I said.

"*Bah.* I know who you are, better than you do." Mr. Lyra stood up and brushed imaginary lint off his trousers. His erection gone, he seemed bored with the game. "You live in a world of make-believe and you act as if you do the world a favor. You cry about this gift, but it's *pazza*, crazy. You are here because my daughter, she is in love with Buffy and all the *stregoni* on the television. You are human party favor, no more."

As I gathered up the moody, haunting Templar cards I used for decoration, Mr. Lyra continued, his voice sharp. "You do not deal with life or death, nothing is at stake for you. Is all just a game."

"You sound like a man who needs a reading and doesn't know how to ask."

"So you charge me for another hour? No. *Grazie.*"

"On the house. Short reading, one question. If you have the nerve for it," I said.

He looked at the cards. I could tell he was tempted.

"Tell me, Mr. Lyra, are you better off walking into the future as a leap of faith, every day an unknown adventure? Or, for a smart man like you, is it better to move forward having all the information?"

As I flipped through the Templar deck, I noticed Lyra's face blanching at some of the images: horned gods holding skulls, winged angelic figures challenging humans, lusty women cavorting with skeletons.

"It's a question that's always plagued me. Is forewarned really the same as forearmed? Can this," I tapped the deck, "give you the power to turn the Hand of Fate to your favor? Or is it just another way to ruin a perfectly good week?"

"No blow job?" he asked, sounding almost hopeful.

"No blow job."

"Okay. Show me the future, *strega*. When am I going to

die?"

Of course. Why would I expect anything different? "Are you sure?"

"Is it too much question for you?"

"It's not me I'm worried about."

"That is the answer I want."

I shuffled the cards. "Take a quarter out of the bowl and offer it to the skull. Silver must change hands, so this reading belongs to you. Unless you want to know when I'm going to die."

* * *

Which really was a question I had been majorly on the fence about, ever since I pulled the tarot cards on my birthday. Although, I was so invested in the answer, I didn't think the cards would tell me, even if I wanted them to. Once you get too invested in the outcome, the cards have a tendency to shut down. That's why they say people can't read for themselves. It's utter crap. You totally can read for yourself. Up until the point where your fears take over and render your sight impotent.

* * *

Mr. Lyra snagged the last quarter out of the bowl and tossed it in front of the skull, where it joined the rest of the quarter brigade. I shuffled the cards again and had him cut the deck. He slid one card out of the middle of the deck, put it on the bottom and handed the deck back to me.

One by one, I laid the cards out.

The Emperor: a winged, horned man, surrounded by books and skulls.

Three of Swords: a woman entreating Death, while comforted by an angel.

Nine of Swords: a woman crying over an angel's felled body, broken swords littering the earth.

Ten of Swords: ten swords buried deep into an angel's body.

"Four years," I said, turning over the *Six of Swords,* which showed two women journeying across the water in a sword-filled boat. "If you don't change the path you're on, you have four really rough years, full of anger, betrayal, sorrow and pain."

"You are fucking with me, yes? None of those are the Death card."

"The Death card is for spiritual transformation and change. You wanted to know about your mortal death." I cast my sight out into the universe, to double-check my answer. It still held. I tapped the cards on the table. "You will die of your own doing. Too stubborn for your own good. You have very little time left, to change your path."

"Impossible."

I closed my eyes, hands spread wide over the cards, as I focused on Mr. Lyra's body. "Cancer. Lower down, either colon, or prostate, maybe testicular. You should see a doctor as soon as possible, while it's curable. The window's closing."

He cursed at me in Italian. "If you think this is funny..."

"I'm not laughing." I gathered up the cards and put them away. "See a doctor, Mr. Lyra. Or you'll be dead in four years."

Unbeknownst to us, Kimmy had walked in with a piece of birthday cake for her dad, just in time to hear this last piece of advice. She burst into tears—big, racking, screaming sobs—and dropped the plate, smearing thick icing into the imported Oriental carpet.

Mr. Lyra took Kimmy into his arms, "Hush, my beauty, it's okay. This witch is not like Willow. She is a liar and a phony."

The butler appeared at the door. Lyra handed Kimmy over to him. "Take her. My wife has Percocet in the bathroom, give her half-dose."

As the butler left with the girl, I turned to Mr. Lyra. "I'm sorry, I didn't know she was there."

He shot me a dirty look. "Take your things and get out. You are finished in this city. I will see to it. I make one phone call, no one will hire you again."

"Mr. Lyra, please. Even if you don't believe me. For your family's sake, please see a doctor while it can still make a difference."

But he turned on his elegant, imported leather heels and walked away.

"And for God's sake, stop sedating your daughter," I hollered at his retreating form. "You're really not doing her any favors."

33

But he ignored me. I pocketed the quarters from the skull and quickly finished packing up. I barely had the lid fastened on the box when the burly butler returned. This time, his sights were set firmly on me and he looked pissed. So I did what any self-respecting witch would do.

I grabbed my box of goodies and ran.

* * *

Outside, I quickly tossed the quarters from the readings into the fountain of pissing cherubs, as an offering to the spirits, and then jumped into my car. At least I had a paycheck. Call me paranoid, but my next stop was going to be the bank. Just in case Lyra tried to put a stop payment on it.

As I floored it out of there, checking in my rearview for pursuing bodyguards, I really hoped I was wrong about Lyra and his daughter. Nobody deserved a fate like that. At least the reading I had done for the mother had gone well.

Mrs. Lyra was an easy read, her past, present and future laid out clearly in the cards. From starting her own business with a female partner, to her current struggle to expand and an upcoming affair with a young, male secretary. Reading her cards was like reading a Jackie Collins' novel. And Mr. Lyra's death, should he choose that path, would leave her a very wealthy, very vulnerable widow.

As I drove, I tried to shake off the residue from the readings. *What a day*.

Above me, the sun dipped below the canyon and the underside of the clouds lit up in bright orange-red waves—an ocean of fire racing across the sky.

It's the Devil's palette, my dad always said. *Beautiful to look at but deadly.*

Although, thanks to the air initiatives, the deadly part was getting a little less so. But the beauty of the view did its job. I could feel my teeth unclenching and the throbbing in my head downshift a notch.

As I crested the hill, I glanced in the direction of Lyra's fortress-like mansion.

Good luck, Mr. Lyra. I thought at him. *You're going to need it. You and me both.*

CHAPTER SIX

WHEN I GOT TO GUS'S apartment, he was hard at work, dashing the hopes of the next Great American Screenwriter. He worked as a freelance reader, which meant he set his own schedule and he could work from home, but he got paid crap. Although he seemed to have a knack for finding boyfriends with enough cash to subsidize his lifestyle.

I pushed aside a stack of scripts and flopped down on the couch. Gus's apartment was tiny but interesting. A shelving unit with four animal tanks separated the living area from the temple space. In the tanks were a laid back boa constrictor, a bad tempered iguana with a vicious bite, a horned dragon badly in need of some PMS-regulating medication and Gus's most recent pride-and-joy, Lord Grundleshanks, the poisonous toad.

"How'd it go?" Gus asked, taking a plastic bag of crickets over to Grundleshanks's tank.

"It's gone. The evil Mrs. Lasio has won the war. Maybe I can pitch a tent on the beach."

"What I meant was, how'd the party go?" He opened the lid to Lord Grundleshanks's aquarium and dropped a cricket into the mud.

"Ah, my stint as a fortune-telling whore to precocious, budding porn stars."

He laughed. "Sounds like you were a big hit."

I snorted and walked over to the refrigerator to snag a bottle of organic lemonade. "If hit means being banned from ever setting foot in Beverly Hills again, then yeah, sure. It went swimmingly." I sighed and unscrewed the cap. "So much for the great new career path. I've been blackballed in Beverly Hills.

What am I supposed to do?"

"Shop in the Valley?"

I rolled my eyes. Trust Gus to make a joke out of my life falling apart. I debated telling him about the cards, my dad's ghost, the weird visions. But Gus would probably see it all as being cool, a confirmation of my inherent witchiness, and he'd book me at the next party as a Medium.

"Hey, could you stop that? You're scaring the toad."

"What?" I had no idea what he was talking about until he pointed at my head. I touched it and winced. Ouch. I'd been banging it against the fridge door without realizing it.

"I don't mean to come between you and your inner masochist, but if Grundleshanks is upset, he might not eat."

"Sure, no problem. I can always take it up again later." I walked back to the couch, feeling like an idiot.

Gus made a face at the tank. "What are you? A fierce toad warrior or a warty doormat? Don't you dare let that cricket have its way with you." He pointed at the cricket tank. "If word gets out, none of them will respect you. Not a one. What will you do when your food rises up and revolts?"

I glanced at the toad tank. Grundleshanks, who looked kind of like a lump of muddy goo with two eyeballs poking through the surface, didn't seem particularly fazed. A cricket marched and hopped over the muck, completely oblivious.

"Seriously? My life's falling apart and you're giving a pep talk to a mud lump?"

"Sacrilege, woman! Lord Grundleshanks the Deadly is a most important toad. A poisonous toad. The Emperor of Toads." Gus tapped on the glass. "I can't believe he's letting that cricket jackboot all over his head. Come on, boy. Crickets are just glorified cockroaches. Chomp, chomp."

"Maybe you should stop reading him Pinocchio at bedtime."

"You know what you need?" he asked, looking over his shoulder at me.

"A new life?"

"A big dose of Gus. I believe it's time for our birthday outing. And it starts as soon as the toad eats." He turned back to the aquarium.

"I don't know if I have that long to live." I muttered.

But Gus was determinedly staring at the mud-embedded Grundleshanks, as if willing it would make it happen. It wasn't until I started humming the Jeopardy theme and threatened to go home, that he finally conceded defeat.

* * *

As Gus got dressed for our night out—heaven forbid he wear his lounging-around outfit, when he could swap it for something snazzier—I wandered through the apartment and into Gus's temple room. A skull on a dolmen-like stone altar grinned at me. The walls were painted with vines and trees, and there were twenty-one wands hanging from wall hooks. Each wand was made from one of the sacred woods, such as birch for new beginnings or blackthorn for protection. It really was a very interesting room. I always felt at peace in there.

Eventually, I found myself back in front of the toad tank. Two eyeballs were slowly rising out of the muck, fixated on the oblivious cricket. The air between the two animals was charged, even if the cricket didn't quite seem to realize it.

Suddenly, Grundleshanks's tongue shot out at the speed of light and the cricket was gone.

Gus walked out of the bedroom but I couldn't take my eyes off the toad. "That was amazing. I had no idea he could move so fast."

Gus stopped dead. "Grundleshanks ate?! And you saw him?" He stomped over to the cage. Sure enough, the cricket was gone. Gus sputtered, beside himself. "Grundleshanks ate! Damn you, Grundleshanks. You treacherous amphibian. Traitor of the first degree. The minute my back is turned!"

"Chill, Gus. It's just a toad."

"I have been watching him for weeks. I have fed him and watered him and watched him and waited and nothing. Nothing. He's shy, he says. Doesn't want to eat in public, he says. But let a pretty girl come over..." He glared at Grundleshanks. "Show-off."

The eyeballs on top of the mud lump calmly blinked back at him.

"I'm going to need an entire bottle of single malt to get over

37

the betrayal. You understand, my disloyal amphibious friend, that you're putting me right into the drunk tank?"

I couldn't help but laugh. "I need to find you a Toads Anonymous group. You do know you have a hugely co-dependent relationship with your squat little friend, right?"

Gus sniffed. "Less talk, woman, and more movement. The pub awaits."

As we were walking out, I snuck a look back at Grundleshanks and I could swear that he winked at me. I almost said something, but I quickly squelched the impulse. Gus really wasn't very good at dealing with betrayal, real or imagined, human or animal, and I didn't want to spend the rest of the night hearing about the toad.

* * *

The Laughing Hound Pub was housed in a quaint wooden cottage, white with gold trim, with British, Scottish, Welsh and American flags hanging from the roof. The outdoor tables were usually filled and tonight was no exception. We walked in, weaved past a dart game and scored a table in the back, away from prying ears.

In Los Angeles, actors and writers tended to lurk around every corner, practicing *'human observation'*, (a.k.a. eavesdropping), so you had to stay on the ball. There was nothing creepier than realizing your private conversation was being transcribed by a desperate screenwriter. Except, maybe, seeing it replayed on some low-rent cable movie.

It didn't look like that would be a problem today, though. The pub's clientele was filled with self-involved Anglophiles, soccer fans and homesick Brits.

I sat down and ordered a shandy, much to Gus's amusement.

"A shandy? What the hell is that? Beer for wusses? Get a pair of balls. Order a real drink."

"It is a real drink."

"Bloody lemonade."

"With a pale ale kick."

"More like watered-down piss if you ask me." He looked up at the waitress. "Black and tan, with a whiskey chaser."

"And Black and Tan's a real drink?"

"No, Ouzo's a real drink. Whiskey's a real drink." Gus grinned. "Black and Tan is a thirst quencher with body."

By the time we got around to placing our order, the drinks were on the table.

"Okay, on to the next thing. Let's find you a new apartment." Gus spread out the apartment rental section of the Recycler and wielded a highlighter over it like a sword of Damocles. "What can you afford?"

"Nothing. My unemployment's running out and I don't have a job."

"What are you paying now?"

"Lenny hasn't raised my rent since I moved in."

"Which means?"

"Six hundred."

"For that cavernous place of yours? With a pool and outdoor grill? What kind of spell did you weave to get a deal that delicious?"

"Now do you understand why I don't want to leave?"

Gus leaned over, putting on a bad New Jersey accent. "You want I should put a hit on this Lasio broad? Concrete shoes, TNT, dyn-o-mite? Get rid of her and you're sitting pretty."

I laughed and shook my head. Just then, the waitress arrived with our order. Scotch Eggs for me and Shepherd's Pie for Gus.

She looked really familiar. I stared at her, trying to figure it out.

"Do you want something else?" she asked, tucking a long piece of blond hair behind her ear.

"No, I'm sorry. It's just... I swear I've seen you before."

"Yeah. I get that a lot."

Gus looked up at her. "Hey, weren't you the girl on that sitcom?" He turned to me. "Remember? It was about a teenage witch in Beverly Hills and her cat friend."

"Oh, yeah!" I looked at the waitress again. "You were great in that. You were the cat, right? I mean, after the witch turned the cat with the Cartier diamond collar into her human best friend with a Cartier necklace."

"Yeah, that would be the one. Before that, I was played by a stand-in cat."

"Wow," Gus munched on a slice of cheddar. "What are you doing here? Researching a role?"

She sighed and jingled the change in her apron pocket. "Nope. Just making a living."

She walked off, leaving me in stunned silence.

Once she was out of earshot, I reached over and smacked Gus's arm. "If she has to pick up work as a waitress, what freaking hope do I have? This economy sucks."

"You are a witch, my dear. She is but a mundane woman, a sycamore in the forest of the trees of life. You have talents no mere mortal can possess."

I rolled my eyes and cut into the Scotch egg. It was my first time trying it, so I was a bit curious. It turned out to be a hard-boiled egg in the middle of a banger (a mixture of sausage meat and flour).

Gus folded up the Recycler. "You doubt me? You are more powerful than you think."

I rolled my eyes. "Gus, you may be able to magic yourself a house out of monopoly pieces, but I can't."

"Pish tosh. You're obviously not trying hard enough."

I couldn't think of an answer to that, so I speared a piece of banger on my fork and waved it at Gus. "How come Brits have mongo thick slabs of pork for bacon but they can't figure out how to make a decent sausage?"

But Gus was completely focused on the tabletop, where he had crossed his fork over his knife and was now drawing a circle around it with a spoon. Then he closed his eyes and hummed—a tuneless, droning sound.

"Would you stop that?"

"Hush," he said, holding up his hand. "I'm crafting for you."

I took a swig of my shandy and hoped no one was watching. "You sure are. You're crafting me a headache."

"Cynicism is for sycamores. Tell Gus what you want."

"Money. A house. A boyfriend. Hot sex."

"One thing at a time. Money. Toss some coins into the circle."

I dug into my pocket and took out a quarter. I tossed it into the circle Gus had created on the table.

He chanted: *"Money go and money come. One hundred thousand times this sum. Money come and quickly though. Within a fortnight it must flow. Money come, my will be done. And with a breath, this spell is done."*

He exhaled on the coin with a loud growl, momentarily attracting the attention of the other pub-crawlers. I ducked my head to avoid meeting their gaze and eventually they turned back to the soccer match on the television.

"There you go," Gus said, cracking his knuckles. He picked up the quarter and tossed it into his water glass. "Money's on the way."

CHAPTER SEVEN

AFTER DINNER, THE WAITRESS and the bartender brought over a bowl of treacle pudding with a birthday candle stuck smack in the middle of the spongy glop. And much to my amazement, embarrassment and, (though I'd never tell Gus), delight, they started singing.

"Happy birthday, uh! Happy birthday, UH! May the candles on your cake burn like cities in your wake! Happy birthday, uh! Happy birthday, UH!"

Soon, it seemed like the entire bar had joined in. I put my hands over my bright red face and tried not to laugh at the boisterously out-of-key, drunken rendition of the never-ending Mongolian Birthday song.

"Now that you're the age you are, your demise can not be far. Happy Birthday, uh! Happy birthday, UH!!"

After ten more verses and just when my candle was down to a nub, they were finally done. I blew out the candle to a round of applause.

Gus turned to me, grinning. Inordinately pleased with himself. "Surprised?"

"Mortified."

"Same thing."

"I'm going to have to kill you if you ever do that to me again." But I couldn't get the goofy smile off my face.

"You'll get over it. And thanks to my spell, you'll be rich in no time."

"Uh-huh. That lottery ticket better come in soon, or I'll be the little old woman who has to live in a shoe."

"Oh ye of little faith. There's more than one way to

influence the web of fate." With his eyes closed, Gus waved his highlighter over the Recycler, then randomly stabbed an ad. "Here you go. Call it up."

I leaned over, quickly scanned the ad and laughed. "Are you kidding?"

"What's wrong with it?"

"I'm not living in Vernon. It's all slaughterhouses and sweatshops." I plucked out the candle remains and poured custard syrup on top of the still-warm pudding.

Gus waved his spoon at me. "They have a nice little tent city next to the expressway. And lots of free roaming dogs. You've always wanted a dog."

"You know what? You're right. All that community and Toto too. After we eat, let's run to Office Depot. Pick out my cardboard box. Maybe I can even build me a new-fangled corrugated home."

"No need. I have a tent you can borrow. Live in style." He stuck his spoon in the treacle. "How is it?"

"Crunchy."

"Really?"

"Are they supposed to leave the eggshells in?"

"That would be a no. How is it otherwise?"

"Good. You better try some of the custard though, before I wolf it all. That's amazing stuff. It should be illegal. It might actually be better than chocolate."

Gus took a spoonful and stabbed at another random ad. "What about this one?" he asked, pushing the paper towards me.

"This is about Grundleshanks, isn't it?"

"What?"

"You're trying to punish me."

"What's wrong with that one?!"

"East L.A.? I take it you're supplying me with a Kevlar wardrobe?"

Gus narrowed his eyes. "You're busting my balls, woman, and I'm all out of steel-plated jockstraps." He flipped to a different section. "I suppose Chinatown is out?"

I licked my spoon. "If you stand still too long, taggers cover you in graffiti."

"You're impossible, you know that?"

"I like where I'm at."

"Too bad they don't like you."

I made a face, Gus dipped his spoon into the treacle and we both fell into a troubled silence.

* * *

After dinner, Gus talked me into going to see a nearby *'charming studio with room to grow.'* The place was stifling hot, the water faucets spewed rust, the kitchen was full of ants and the security gate was broken.

"But there's a small garden you can grow herbs in and a swimming pool."

"Swimming pool?!" I cast my mind back to the front courtyard of building. "Wait, you mean the over-sized duck pond? That was a swimming pool? It had algae growing in it."

"How picky can you afford to be?"

I sighed. "Fine. How much?"

Gus waved the page from the Recycler. "A rock-bottom seven-hundred a month. It's like a gift from the Gods."

One more minute of Gus the Cheerleader and I was going to strangle him. "Keep it up and I'm going to knee you in the goonies."

"What?" He gave me a hurt, puppy-dog look. "What did I do?"

* * *

Before I knew it, I was in the building manager's apartment, actually filling out the paperwork for the god-awful sinkhole. At least, until I dropped my pen. As I bent over to pick it up, my pentacle fell out of my shirt, into plain view. The building manager took a look at the pendant, the tattoos that peeked out of the bottom of my tee-shirt sleeves, the Celtic man-jewelry Gus was sporting and suddenly remembered the apartment had already been rented.

Gus got so upset he launched into an almost physical rant over religious discrimination. I thought he was going to clock the guy. I had to drag him out of there with promises of a Shrek marathon and a big bag of Twizzlers.

* * *

Four hours later, Gus finally went home, quoting the *'onion boy'* dialogue between Shrek and Donkey all the way back to his SUV. I sprinkled vervain and sea salt into a hot tub and had a long, decadent, candle-lit soak. I hoped the cleansing properties of the salt and herb would send all the negative energy of the day down the drain with the dirty bath water. And it seemed to work. I went to bed feeling a bit more relaxed.

* * *

Unfortunately, a peaceful night wasn't exactly what was waiting for me when my eyes closed.

* * *

The same cottage, shrouded by night. This time, the night was full of life. I could hear the gossipy chatter of crickets, a rustling of small scavengers in the underbrush, the haunting sound of victory as an owl caught a field mouse, even an angst-ridden howl of a distant coyote.

Suddenly, I was inside the cottage, standing in front of a full-length, antique mirror. The bald, tattooed man stood behind me. He slowly unlaced my corset, watching my image in the mirror as the fabric fell to the floor.

My breasts were magnificent and full, swollen under my pale white skin. As I stared at my reflection, the aureoles darkened and my nipples grew incredibly large and thick. The man cupped my breasts with his hands, kneading at my nipples until milk flowed out of them. I leaned into him and sighed.

His image shifted and he turned into a long-haired man dressed in a flowing white shirt, breeches and boots. I struggled, but I couldn't get away. He held me hard around my waist and brought up a bloody knife. Placing the tip of the knife on my breastbone, he slowly sliced my chest open. The pain of the blade was like liquid fire.

He peeled open my skin, exposing my inner organs. My lungs expanded and contracted against my ribs. He turned me to face him and he opened my ribcage as if it was the lid of a jewelry box. He reached in past my lungs and removed my still beating heart.

He brought the writhing organ to his mouth and bit into it,

45

letting the blood run down his chin.

Then he turned into Mr. Lyra, standing there, laughing at me, still holding my heart in his hand.

* * *

I gasped and sat up, rubbing my chest. I tried going back to sleep, but there was no escaping that restless, nightmarish dreamscape. Every time I closed my eyes, I was right back in it.

So I gave up and walked over to the kitchen. These dreams were driving me crazy. The microwave clock said it was four a.m., and I was more exhausted than when I went to bed.

I started the coffee pot brewing and got a container of half-and-half out of the fridge. I may as well get a jump on the day. The thought of going back to sleep gave me the heebie-jeebies.

I swear, I should TiVo kid's TV and watch it before going to bed. That way I could dream about harmless things like Caillou or the Wonder Pets instead of malevolent, knife-wielding men. Although with my luck, I'd still dream about that damn cottage. It would just be relocated to Sesame Street and a furry red Muppet would be wielding the blade.

* * *

When I went out to water the plants a few hours later, I found a fresh copy of the eviction notice taped to my door, along with a mini-calendar with the days of the month marked off. Just in case I forgot how little time I had. Talk about a knife to the chest. Next time I saw Lenny, I was going to shake my traitorous little Dutch uncle until his little gold ear studs fell off.

CHAPTER EIGHT

AFTER A WEEK OF apartment hunting and nightmares, I was exhausted. Since my only source of income was unemployment, pentacle or no pentacle, no one was willing to take a chance on renting to me. I signed up with another temp agency but they all said the same thing—business was slow, the number of available temps was ridiculously high and they'd let me know when they had something.

* * *

Thursday night, I sat out in the courtyard, watching the stars, as I tried to let go of my worry and angst. Not that there were all that many stars visible in the Los Angeles sky. But if I relaxed my focus, I could almost see a constellation or two twinkling behind the clouds and ever-present haze of city lights.

Gus walked up as I was about to turn in, a bottle of Ouzo in hand. "I thought I'd stop by and help you take the edge off," he said, unscrewing the cap.

"A night of floating in a dreamless, drunken stupor sounds like bliss." Anything to escape the nightmares. *To sleep, perchance not to dream.*

"Any time you need a night you can't remember, keep me in mind. Gus's bar, at your service."

I went into the apartment and came back with a big bottle of Fiji water and two glasses full of ice. Gus mixed the drinks and handed me one.

I took a small sip. Cool, licorice-y and delicious. I sighed in contentment. It had been a long time since I'd had ouzo.

We drank in silence. I let my eyes wander about. The

jacaranda trees were in full bloom, their delicate purple petals lazing about over the pebbled deck. There was a nasty crack that ran across part of the deck and down the pool stairs—a remnant of the Northridge earthquake, a scar that would never heal. But the underwater pool lights lent everything a wavy blue, surreal glow and made the courtyard seem magical.

I waved a hand at my plants. Poor things. They did their best to look like a menacing urban forest around the pool. "Who's going to take care of them after I go?"

It was one of the few accomplishments I was proud of, turning my black thumb into a green one. The thought of Mrs. Lasio forgetting to water my babies was depressing.

"I'm disappointed in you. You're being a lousy witch."

"You try finding an apartment without a steady income."

"You could have had that place on the corner if you didn't go out of your way to fuck it up."

"That was an accident."

"I don't believe you."

He kind of had a point. I could have put up a shield, deflected the manager's gaze. Bottom line was, I didn't care. I hated the place.

"You could craft for Mrs. Lasio to have a change of heart. Or a change in circumstance. Something that would make her go away."

"That old battle-axe? She's as stubborn as they come. Besides, I don't like the idea of using magic on people. It's not right to take away their free will, just to impose my own."

"So have her find her dream house. Positive karma points and it would get her off your back."

Probably. But it really galled me to craft up something nice for her and then have her win the lottery or something. And I couldn't craft up anything nasty, because being nasty tended to backfire. That's how my dad found out I had inherited my mom's 'witch' gene when I was a kid. When I really wanted something, I would wish for it and more often than not, it would happen. I thought everyone could do it. I didn't know it was something special. But if I wished for something bad to happen, man, did I pay for it.

When I was seven, I was furious at Tommy McGregor,

because he'd shoved me into a mud puddle and ruined my brand-new dress. So I wished that something bad would happen to him. I even drew a picture of him with spots all over his face. Three days later, he got chicken pox. Two weeks later, so did I. Even worse than him. Followed by the German measles. Karmic payback can be a bitch.

So, in general, I've tried to steer clear of magic whenever I could. For my own safety, if nothing else. Unlike Gus, who'd spellcrafted his way through life. How he got his ass around karma, I have no idea. He must have done something really good in a previous life, because he sure seemed to get a free pass in this one.

"Fine. Then why don't you just get to know her on a mundane level. Make friends. Let her see what a wonderful person you are."

I laughed. "Little late for that. I'm never going to win her over. She's positive she already knows who I am. She's so full of preconceived notions, there's no room in her head for the truth."

A pair of curtains twitched up on the second floor. Gus looked up, curious.

"Mrs. Lasio," I explained. "Making sure we don't toss any animal sacrifices into the pool."

I sighed. Gus must have seen the despair leaking out of me, because he topped up my glass with more Ouzo, then gave me the Gus version of a pep talk:

"You, my love, have got to change your attitude. You pull in what you push out. You keep putting out this negative, *I'm a victim of life* bullshit and you are going to be living in a shoebox. In the streets of Vernon."

Gus rummaged through his man-bag, (because, as he frequently told me, *'men don't carry purses'*). After a few minutes, he pulled out a wooden pipe, hand-carved to look like a witch's head. He filled the bowl with a vanilla-smelling tobacco and tamped it down with his thumb.

I looked at him in consternation. "What are you doing? You don't smoke pipes."

"I know," Gus lit up and puffed on the pipe to get it started. "But this looks really cool. I mean, c'mon. It's a head. I'm smoking head. How cool is that? And it's a hag's head at that."

"Well, that's appropriate. As long as it's going to kill you, why not carve it into the shape of the Hag? At least it smells better than those god-awful cigarettes."

I leaned back in my chair, enjoying the vanilla scent of the tobacco. Above us, the moon was just rising, low in the sky and orangey red, like the glowing eye of a dragon. I sighed and tried to hold back tears. I was going to miss this place.

"What kind of witch are you if you refuse to bend fate to your will?" There went Gus, getting back on his soapbox. Whenever Gus got rolling on one of his witchy tirades, there was no stopping him. "You know what you need. Stop panicking and figure out how to get it."

"Did you come over to lecture me or to hang out?"

"A bit of both, actually." He re-lit the bowl and took another puff. "Call what you need to you. Your desire will create the void and the universe will rush to fill it. Spellcrafting 101. It doesn't get any easier than that."

"I just don't think people should use magic to do things they can accomplish mundanely." I said. I knew I was being stubborn, but I couldn't quite shake my Dad's warning to lay low.

"Why the hell not? Might as well have everything working for you on all fronts. And if you have the ability, not using it is just criminal. Stupid. Criminally stupid."

"But magic can be tricky. Uncontrollable, cantankerous. It's always a risk. You get what you want, but in a way where you don't want what you get."

That was the difference between normal humans and witches. If humans want something, they pray for it. Their God takes it under consideration, and if it fits the grand design, God grants their prayer.

Witches, on the other hand, plunge ahead blindly. Their preferred method of prayer is spellcrafting. Their Gods and Goddesses take the spells under consideration and, if they find the potential outcomes sufficiently amusing, they step aside and let the witch have it, in a *'be careful what you wish for'* type of way.

Like on my last birthday. I had made a wish that the universe would help me figure out what I was supposed to be doing with my life. You know, the old *'what am I supposed to be when I grow up.'* And the universe responded by promptly taking away my dead-end job, so I'd have time to find my bliss. Magic can be a tricky thing.

"God is in the details. Bind it with specificity and you're good to go." Gus said.

I sighed again and sipped my drink. I'd been sighing a lot lately." I miss the days when getting laid was my biggest problem. Maybe I should become a kept woman. No responsibilities, no bills, just lots of sex and high-priced gifties."

"If that's what you want, Little Miss Difficult, you're gonna have to stop saying no." Gus tapped his pipe into a pot of dirt, getting rid of the used tobacco.

"I just wish I could go to sleep and have everything magically fixed by the time I woke up."

"And I wish I could win the lottery. But sometimes, you have to focus on doing what's necessary rather than what you want. And what's necessary for you, is a new home." He slipped the pipe into his man-bag, then stood up.

"Where are you going?" I asked. "Don't you want to stay and be my shoulder to cry on?"

"I just stopped by to light a fire under you. I have a hottie waiting for me at Rage."

"Rage?! Bastard. I never get to go anywhere fun."

"That's because you're always broke. Go forth and be witchy, little woman. The echoes of one realm makes ripples in the other." He kissed my cheek and then he was off, trailing scents of amber, patchouli and vanilla behind him.

As I watched Gus get into his SUV, I couldn't stop thinking about what he'd said. He had a point. Why was I being so reluctant to use magic? It's not like I was making a frivolous request. Incipient homelessness combined with joblessness was a big deal. Could I really afford to be hamstrung by what might only be a dream about my dad?

* * *

As I stood up to go in, a crow flew into the courtyard and a long, black, wing feather slowly floated down. I caught the feather as the crow settled on the second-floor iron railing, loudly cawing.

I looked up at him. "I've already had one lecture tonight. I don't need one from you, too."

He cawed one more time, turned around on the railing and lifted his tail. I dodged under the overhang, barely avoiding a runny white plotz. While some cultures considered it lucky if a bird poops on your head, I considered it kind of gross and something to be avoided at all costs.

* * *

Later that night, with Gus's words ringing in my ears, I decided to put my doubts aside. After Mrs. Lasio was asleep, I closed my blinds and got out all my witchy accoutrements. I wasn't quite sure what I was going to do, but I had a feeling it would require more *oomph* than just wishing.

I lit two candles: a red one for illumination and a blue one for the ancestors. Given Mrs. Lasio's hypersensitive nose, however, I skipped the incense.

Then I placed the cauldron in the center of the room, poured in a little bit of rubbing alcohol and fired up the liquid with a long-handled lighter. The sudden flare quickly spread into a small pool of blue fire. Flames licked up the side of the black iron, casting playful shadows across my tattoos.

I waved the crow's feather over the cauldron, sweeping the air currents in a circle, as I waited for guidance from the ancestors, for words to pop into my head.

Within minutes, I started chanting: "*Lady of the Cauldron, Lady of the Grail. Be with me here, guide me through this trial. Show me strong, show me true, just what it is that I need to do.*"

I got a clear visual in my head and opened up a box of modeling clay. As I softened and shaped the clay in my hands, I circled the cauldron, continuing to chant:

"*From the currents of the air, from the feathers of the birds, from the darkness of the void, I make you.*"

I formed the clay into a rough image of a bird. I pushed the crow's feather into the clay.

"*By the power of the Goddess of the Witches. By the power of the Horned God of Old. By the power within me, until your task is accomplished, live and be free!*"

I brought the clay bird up to my lips. "*With my breath I give you life. Fly where I can not. Fly and search on my behalf. Fly and bring me back a home."*

I took a deep breath, so deep it felt like I was pulling it up from the center of the earth. It went through my entire body until I exhaled loudly into the clay bird fetch, with the intent of breathing life into it. I tossed the bird into the cauldron and blue flames flared up.

To my shock and amazement, I saw the spirit of the fetch as it left the cauldron, soared through my patio door, and out into the night.

When I looked back at the cauldron, the blue flames curled in on themselves, then were sucked back into the iron and extinguished.

Utter darkness enveloped the room.

CHAPTER NINE

I TURNED ON THE LIGHTS. *What the hell was going on?* I had never seen a fetch take life like that. I mean, as much as all those fantasy books and movies about witches would have you thinking that Otherworld realms are three-dimensional and you can interact with fairies as if they were solid beings, the reality is usually quite different.

As a witch, you can 'see' other dimensions, but it's a third-eye thing. It's almost like having an overactive imagination, but one that's eerily accurate. Fleeting impressions on your mind's eye. Not full-on, 3-D hallucinations that are as solid as my hand.

Was it because of my birthday? Did turning twenty-seven activate some kind of latent powers? Did it have something to do with entering my Saturn return, astrologically? I thought about it for a second and then shook my head. It was probably a brain tumor. That made more sense. And it would explain the impending doom portents in my tarot cards. If I had any health insurance, I'd go see a doctor.

Unless I was just losing my mind. I'd certainly seen it happen to others. Traveling too far into the Otherworld, too often, can negate your ability to return to the mundane world.

What if my dad had been right with the *Do No Magic* warning? What if it wasn't just a dream, what if it had been a full-on visitation that I chose to ignore? Well, hell, even if it had been just a dream, what if it was my subconscious warning me that I was about to go too deep and cross a line I couldn't uncross?

I sighed. I just hoped it wasn't too late to find my way back.

* * *

That night was the worst yet. When the nightmares hit, they hit hard.

I was walking through a forest, when I emerged onto the shoulder of a paved road. It was early and the sky was a swollen bruise, all purple-red, as the sun violently erupted into morning.

On the other side of the road, a forked pathway led back into the woods. If I took the right fork, I knew the path would lead me to a lake. Even though I couldn't see it, I could smell the algae-filled water and the rotting fish.

If I took the left fork, I knew beyond doubt the path would take me to the stone cottage. It lurked there, on the edges of my subconscious, like an unspoken threat, beckoning to me.

I decided to try the path to the lake for a change. As I walked to the center of the road, a Volkswagen Cabriolet appeared out of nowhere, speeding towards me. The top was down and the driver, an old woman who looked half-corked, was happily singing along with the radio. She seemed completely unaware of me as the car sped up.

My feet felt like they were rooted into the road, I was unable to move. As the car was just about to hit me, a large screech owl soared down and flew directly into the windshield.

The woman screamed and twisted her steering wheel.

But the owl shattered the windshield, its bloody body hitting her squarely in the face, like a feathered missile. The sheer force of it pushed the woman's thin facial bones through to the back of her skull. Death was swift and merciful.

The car continued on its trajectory, until it slammed up against a lightning-blasted oak tree, blood spattering everywhere.

The front end of the car crumpled and the woman's corpse fell forward. Her lifeless body hit the horn on the steering wheel, a last cry of protest, her head falling to the side.

Disturbed by the noise and motion, a flock of crows rose up from the tree. They circled the ravaged flesh that would soon be their dinner. One of the more adventurous crows leapt through the busted-out windshield and, reaching quickly and carefully with his sharp beak, dug out what was left of the woman's right eye.

For one stomach-turning second, the crow turned and faced me, the eye speared in its beak, the pupil looking right at me.

* * *

I sat up with a gasp and clicked the bedside lamp on. 4:00 a.m. I reached for the glass of water next to the bed, took a sip and held the glass to my forehead. The beads of moisture felt good against my hot flesh.

* * *

At some point, I must have fallen asleep again. Because the next thing I knew, rays of sunlight were piercing my closed eyelids through the openings in my blinds. I could hear birds arguing over stray pieces of bread and a dog across the street, yapping its little lungs out.

I got up, closed my blinds tighter, and went back to bed. I was just nodding off again when Mrs. Lasio walked past my bedroom window, loudly chastising her youngest daughter, Lupe, over the latest boyfriend fiasco. In the short distance to their car, accusations of '*putana*' and '*ashamed in front of God*' and '*that nice priest*' echoed through the courtyard.

I buried my head under my pillow to muffle the cacophony.

And it almost worked.

Until Gus burst through my bedroom door with all the force of a tidal wave.

* * *

"Wake up, sleepy-head!" he said, jumping onto the bed and bouncing up and down.

I groaned. "How did you get in? I locked the door. I put garlic over the windows. Are you even supposed to be out in daylight?"

"I'm the mighty, the invincible, the immortal Count Gusula. C'mon, wake up! We've got things to do."

I groaned again. "Weren't you just here yesterday?"

"And if you're lucky, I'll be here tomorrow." He got off the bed, opened up a green duffel bag he had brought with him and dumped his dirty clothes on me. "Come on, woman. Rise and shine. Laundry's not going to do itself, you know."

"Ugh," I opened an eyelid. "Get your stinky ass sweat socks off me."

"Get out of bed and make me. I brought quarters," he said helpfully, raining them down on the pile of laundry.

An errant quarter hit me in the head. "Ow!" I swept off the covers, sending clothes and quarters flying, and sat up. "I see," I said in a chilly voice. "Since I own a broomstick, you've obviously mistaken me for your maid."

"Jumping Cernunnos, woman, but you're cranky in the morning. And here I was being generous."

"How do you figure?"

"I brought enough quarters for both of us."

Gus gave me his best little boy smile while I contemplated flushing his quarters, and his head, down the toilet.

I clenched my teeth together into a smile. "How thoughtful. Maybe next time, you could also bring your mother. I'm sure she'd love to spend her weekend doing your laundry."

"Is this your everyday, general crabbiness? Or is it that special time of the month?"

"You don't value your life much, do you?"

"*Hormones, hormones, lovely little hormones,*" Gus sang. "*Give 'em chocolate, give 'em salt, give 'em a credit card and let them sort themselves out. But you never give 'em a gun. Hormones, hormones, lovely little...*"

I gave him the hairy eyeball, then flopped back down on the bed and put my pillow over my head.

Gus shook my arm. "It's no use sleeping your life away, Goldilocks. Time marches on and you'll still have to move."

I shifted the pillow so I could glare at him. "I'm starting to understand why you have no other friends."

"I'm so charming they can't take the competition." Gus grinned.

I snorted. "I have an idea. Why don't you take the quarters and you do all our laundry, while I sleep?"

"Step back, you evil daughter of Eve," Gus held up two fingers in the shape of a cross to ward me away. "Spinning, weaving and laundry is woman's work."

"Oh, it is so on." I thwapped him in the face with my pillow and soon we were rolling around on the bed, tussling like children, until he pinned me in a wrestling hold.

"Come on, give it up. Say it. Gus is the King of the Witches."

"In your dreams." I got an arm free and elbowed him in the stomach. He tried to pin me back down and with all the strength of my pre-caffeinated morning irritation, I punched him in the arm.

"Ow!" He swung my arms behind my back and knelt on my hands. "Gus is Master of the Universe. You can do it."

With a loud grunt and a determined effort, I reared up and flipped him off of me. He fell off the other side of the bed and landed face-first on the pile of dirty clothes. "Give up yet?" he asked, his voice muffled.

I had to laugh. *What a goof.*

Gus climbed back on the bed. "At least you're hitting like a boy now, instead of that girly-girl slappy shit. I'm having a positive influence on you."

I got out of bed and stretched through an even bigger yawn. Gus leaned against the headboard, interlocking his fingers behind his head and stared at me.

"What are you doing?" I asked, irritated.

He grinned. "Enjoying the view."

I rolled my eyes. "If you don't stop looking at boobs, the West Hollywood boy's club is going to revoke your pink panties."

"What boobs?" he asked with mock innocence. "I was looking at your tattoos. Zulu does incredible work."

I laughed. Trust Gus to take the sexuality out of naked female bodies. I pirouetted in front of the mirror. On my back, there was a huge tattoo of a human morphing into a winged dragon. On my thigh was an elaborate Tudor rose, with the vines snaking into a knotwork leg-band. There was a crowned skull with a serpent slithering out of its eye socket on my belly and an intricately shaded, Celtic knotwork armband with a triple horse motif around my upper arm. It really was nice work.

"When you die, I want your skin."

I stopped, arrested by a visual of myself as a rotting, skinless corpse. "Why?"

"Book covers, drumheads. Can't let that kind of artwork go to waste."

"You just want an excuse to pound on me all day."

"It's a bonus," he admitted with a grin.

I snorted. "You want any other parts, or can I keep the rest?"

Gus thought about it for a second. "Well, your head, of course. Can you imagine? You would make one hell of an oracular skull. And your bones. Femurs, fingers... I can make all sorts of things out of you. Bone flute, bone grail, bone walking stick. The list is endless."

"So pretty much, you're just going to dig me back up and recycle my entire body."

"Sacrilege, woman. Bones become fragile when you bury them."

"They become really fragile if you cremate them."

"Much better to put a few dozen beetles in the casket with you and let them do their work. Above ground. After I skin you, of course."

Ick. This post-mortem imagery of me was a bit much, first thing in the morning.

"You know who's carrying caskets now?" he continued. "Costco. I can even get one delivered. How great is that?"

I was starting to feel decidedly queasy. I rubbed my stomach, "Whatever happened to talking about things like politics or religion or what I want for breakfast?"

But Gus was still thinking out loud. "This kind of thing is impossible when you live in an apartment complex. Could you give me a six-month warning before you kick the bucket? So I can rent a house?"

"Yeah, sure. I'll put it at the top of my to-do list. Freak."

"Great. It's a plan. So, my domestic little Goddess, you get on the laundry and I'll go pick us up a couple of lattes."

I thought about it for a second. I really didn't have anything else to do. "Get me a pumpkin scone with that latte and I'll think about it. Any other wifely chores you have in mind though, you're on your own."

"Just me and my hand, as always."

"Really didn't need that visual."

As I was about to walk into the bathroom, Gus picked up a glass of thick, grayish water from my nightstand. "Gross. How long has this been sitting here?"

Ewww. I looked at it and cringed. Did I actually drink from that glass last night? "It didn't look like that when I went to bed."

"You must be having some interesting dreams." He held the glass out to me like it was full of nuclear waste. "Please, take your spirit scum away from me."

I grabbed the glass from him. That water was going to go in the toilet, first thing. It was just nasty.

I looked over at him. He still hadn't moved from the bed. In fact, he looked like he was debating taking a nap. "Hey, barista boy. Why are you still here? Get moving. Quad shot, half and half, extra foam. And I want it ten minutes ago."

"Four shots? Are you sure..."

As I glared at him, he hastily revised what he was going to say.

"...I shouldn't make it six? Maybe seven? After all, why stop before you go into cardiac arrest?"

My eyes narrowed and my upper lip curled over my teeth. So, Gus did what any self-respecting male witch would do—he beat a hasty retreat.

*   *   *

I could hear a muffled trumpeting sound and an off-key rendition of *"Off Gus goes to save the day!"* as he marched through the living room.

I laughed and shook my head. Who could stay mad at someone as goofy as him?

But as soon as I opened the bathroom door, everything went to hell.

I heard an ear-splitting scream rip through the room.

It took me a few seconds to realize I was the one screaming.

CHAPTER TEN

GUS CAME RUSHING BACK in from the living room. "What the hell?"

But then he saw it.

Lying in a shower of glass on the tiled floor, was the bloody, beat up body of a crow.

"One for sorrow, two for mirth, three for a wedding, four for a birth," he muttered.

One for sorrow. I couldn't stop shaking. I wondered if this was the same crow that was hanging out in the courtyard last night. The thought that it probably was, was making me hyperventilate.

"Breathe, Mara. Slow breaths. Slower. What is wrong with you? I've never seen you freak out like this. It's just a crow."

I took a deep breath and it all came out. From the nightmares to the vision of my dad and his warning to stay away from magic before some mysterious curse finds me, to the weird hallucinations and my secret late-night ritual, to the too-vivid dream that wrenched me awake and now, the crow on my bathroom floor.

And then I started smacking Gus.

"Ow! What?! What did I do?!" he asked, trying to dodge the blows.

"This is all your fault. You and your *'what kind of witch are you'* bullshit. I was right. Just because someone can do magic, doesn't mean they should. Now look what's happening!"

"Are you kidding?! I wish something like this would happen to me. Color me jealous."

I wanted to shake him. "Of what? That I'm cursed and

living on borrowed time? Or that I've got a brain tumor?"

"You are such a hypochondriac. You don't have a brain tumor."

"So you think I'm cursed. Thanks."

"You're not cursed."

"Oh, my God. What if I killed someone in my sleep?!" Every option was just getting worse.

Gus laughed. "You're not a God. You can't kill people in your sleep."

"You didn't see this dream!" Okay, so maybe I was being a little hysterical, but still.

"Are you kidding me? You can't even swat a bug without sending up a prayer for its soul. Maybe this is just a sign from above that you should open a pagan pet store. You can call it A Murder of Crows and we can specialize in selling familiars."

I sat on the toilet and buried my head in my hands. I could hear Gus sighing. I knew he thought I was being a wuss, but I couldn't help it.

"All I'm trying to say, is you're maturing into a full-blown witch. How cool is that? Most people don't get that option. They're all WYSIWYG. What you see, is what you get. You, on the other hand, have layers. Like a parfait. Next time you want to do a spell, call me. I'm dying to do magic with your new, improved, witchy self, if only for the visual effects."

I shot him a look that would fry an egg.

"Look, if you really think you're cursed, let's go see Mama Lua. Before you turn it into a self-fulfilling prophecy. If anyone can help you, she can."

A shudder ran down the length of my spine. Mama Lua was well known in the pagan community as a witch doctor who was a bit overly familiar with the dark side. She was said to be expensive, but worth it.

I shook my head. "Just because I'm having nightmares, doesn't mean I need an exorcism."

"But what if you're being gas-lighted by some spirit who wants you to *think* you're cursed? Let's get an outside opinion."

"And sometimes a cigar is just cleverly disguised bubble gum. Besides, I can't afford it."

Gus shrugged. "We'll just talk to her. A casual

conversation. It can't hurt, right?"

Well, that was a matter of opinion.

He stepped around me and scooped up the bird in a hand towel. "What are you going to do with this?"

I grimaced. I desperately wanted that bird out of my apartment. "I don't know. Dumpster?"

"Blasphemy, thy name is woman! When the Gods give you a gift, it's impolite to spit in their many-splendored eyes."

"Call me ungrateful, but I would happily trade it in for a toaster."

"If that's the way you feel," he shrugged and wrapped the bird more securely in its towel. "Can I have it?"

"What are you going to do with it?"

"The list is endless."

I shuddered. "I believe you. And considering your plans for my body, I don't even want to know. You are totally, completely gross."

"I'm resourceful. Witch, remember? It's what we do. Recycle everything. The ultimate in green living."

"Fine, take it, whatever. Just get it out of here." I looked down at the mess on the floor. Broken glass, feathers, blood. The bathroom looked and smelled liked death. "I'll make you a deal. You clean up the mess and take the bird away, and I'll do your laundry without complaining about it. But I still want my latte."

He gave me a thumbs-up and I walked out of bathroom.

*   *   *

Gus had the mess cleaned up in fifteen minutes. As much as he may not like being domestic, he had the cleaning thing down. The bathroom was spotless.

But, as we swapped places and I turned on the shower, a creepy suspicion snuck up on me.

I poked my head out of the bathroom door. "Wait, what are you going to do with it?" I asked, pointing at the towel-wrapped crow in his hands.

Gus looked back at me from the hallway. "I haven't decided yet."

"I mean, now."

"Right now? Fridge."

I could just see the decomposing black body nestled up against the cheese and lunch meat. "Not mine, right?"

"Where else? I don't think Mrs. Lasio's gonna let me use her fridge." He whistled the theme from Snow White as he walked out the door, down the hall and around the corner, to the kitchen.

I quickly wrapped a towel around myself and ran after him. I grabbed his arm. "Gus. Not a question. Not. Mine. You want it, keep it in your own fridge."

"What kind of a witch are you?"

"One with a high ick factor. I mean it, Gus. I don't want it in my fridge."

"Fine. It won't go in the fridge. Wuss."

I looked at him, suspiciously. That win was almost too easy. But I decided to let it go. Why fight a win, right?

*　*　*

As I stood under the stream of hot water, I could feel the ick and the creepiness of the morning wash down the drain with the soap residue. When I finally came out of the shower, Gus was in the bathroom, poking through the drawers.

"That was quick." I said, drying off.

"Does this really work?" He held up a vibrator made out of a pink gel-like material and turned it on. The penis squirmed and rotated, slightly bending, so it seemed to be taking a 360-degree bow.

"Yes it does and turn it off. He's the only boyfriend I have. I don't want you wearing him out," I wrapped a smaller towel around my hair and squeezed out the excess water.

"You never let me have any fun," he grumbled. "Your two-thousand calorie breakfast is on the dining room table."

"You had time to get rid of the crow and get coffee? Did you learn to teleport?" I walked into the bedroom and pulled on a tee-shirt and jeans.

"Light traffic," he shrugged, tossing the vibrator into a drawer and following me.

A bad feeling started rumbling in my gut. "So... what did you end up doing with the bird?"

Silence as Gus followed me into the dining room.

"You did take him home, right?" I asked, getting my coffee and scone from the table.

"Kind of."

I dropped the scone back in the bag and turned to him. "Gus? Where's the bird?"

"He's not in the fridge."

I stopped, arrested in mid-movement, coffee halfway to my mouth. "Well... that's good. But... what aren't you telling me, you lying little bastard?"

"You cut me to the quick, woman."

"Gus?" I put down the coffee and gave him a slant-eyed look. "Want something cold to drink?"

"No, I'm good. I had a non-fat chai latte."

I strode over to the kitchen and opened the fridge. I scanned all the shelves as I snagged a bottle of water. "Huh."

Gus opened the Starbucks bag and took out a protein box. "I'm hurt at how little you trust me."

"Uh-huh." I said, glancing at him.

He took the egg out of the box and salted it, trying to look innocent.

I closed the refrigerator door and stood up. The freezer door caught my eye, seeming just a little bit brighter, a little more highlighted than the rest of the refrigerator. "Gus! You didn't!"

"You never said—"

"—Freezer? I never said freezer? I assumed it would be obvious."

"See? That ass-u-me thing always gets you into trouble." Gus said, polishing off the egg and scarfing down the small triangles of cheese.

I gave a strangled scream and opened the freezer door. Sure enough, there it was, in a Ziploc freezer bag. Hand towel and all.

"Ziploc keeps things fresh. It never leaks. The company guarantees it. Look at the stripe. Sealed tight. Besides, it's not like you have a lot of food in there. Crow-flavored ice cubes is a small price to pay to keep me happy," he said, waving an apple slice.

I slammed the freezer door shut and chased Gus through the living room, tackling him on the couch.

"Ouch! Gus abuse!" he protested, blocking me with a raised

forearm as I smacked him with a couch pillow. "You're being unreasonable."

"Don't even get me started, you big baby. You've turned my kitchen into a bird morgue." I said, smacking him again. "I can't believe you."

"Hey, you need me, so be nice."

"What for?"

"Mama Lua's for one. And tomorrow is Pagan Pride. We rented a vendor table so you could make some cash-ola, remember? Who else is gonna help you?"

I gave him a blank look. "Oh, shit. I totally forgot."

"Beat me to a pulp and you're on your own."

I thought about it for a second. "Fine. But the bird goes."

"Of course it will, dear heart. Eventually. Everything does. Besides, it's already in the freezer. It's not like it can leak out any more bird cooties than it already has. So, finish your coffee and let's go see Mama Lua."

I groaned.

"It's not that bad," Gus said, patting my leg. "Think of it as an otherworldly diagnostic. Your life is for shit anyway. Let's go see if some other entity is giving you a helping hand on the road to Hell, or if it's all just your imagination."

I sighed. It was going to be a long day.

CHAPTER ELEVEN

THE CROOKED PANTRY ADVERTISED itself as a place for groceries only a witch could love. It was the only occult store in a ten-mile radius. Mama Lua was behind the counter, blending oils. She was a large Jamaican woman who'd lived in New Orleans for the last ten years. Until the day her Orishas told her to leave. She quickly packed everything she owned and moved to Los Angeles. A week later, Hurricane Katrina hit the Louisiana shore.

The Orishas loved Mama Lua and Mama Lua loved them back, if all the offerings of chocolate, money and orange slices were any indication.

I pulled Gus back outside the front door. "I can't do this." I said, gripping his elbow hard.

He tried to pry my fingers off his arm. "Could you just act normal for a few minutes? You're making this much more epic than it needs to be. Besides, we need supplies for tomorrow. So why don't we start there and just ease into the whole curse thing?"

We walked back into the store. Mama Lua gave us a slant-eyed glance, but didn't say anything.

"Hey, Mama Lua." Gus said, leaving her Alegba a quarter for luck. "Got anything new in?"

Alegba was a large stone, painted half red with one black eye and half black with one white eye. And he seemed to enjoy his gifties. He was sitting on a tray with coins, candy, orange slices and a cigar. What the hell. I tossed a quarter on there, too.

"Oh, honey child. Mama's always got something new." Mama Lua picked up the cigar, lit it and blew smoke over

Alegba, muttering something that sounded like a prayer in Yoruban. Then she carefully put the cigar out and placed it back on the tray. "What you're looking for is in the back. Next to the herb rack."

Gus dragged me past the bookshelves, clothing racks, the jewelry counter, a veritable garden of statuary and over to a small shelving unit in the back of the store. It was filled to overflowing with small containers of oils, resins and miscellaneous supplies: Graveyard Dust, Blue Balls, Florida Water, Dove's Blood Ink, Bone Dust and Dragon's Blood, amidst a host of others. And it was right next to a massive, rotating herb rack.

While Gus poked through the herbs, incenses and oils, I went to the front of the store to hunt down small candles and stones to create spell-crafting packets for the fair. I also scored some parchment paper and a pen that looked like a witch stirring a cauldron.

I took an armload over to the cash register, then I went back and snagged a package of Blue Balls and a few bottles of Florida Water to cleanse my apartment.

Mama Lua rang up the total to a shocking sum, but after eyeballing me, she subtracted ten percent from it. "For you, a special discount. Mama Lua looks out for all her little children."

I gave her a relieved smile. The numbers had been making my stomach twist. But even with the discount, I didn't know how I was going to afford it. I only had twenty dollars in cash and my checking account was down to a hundred and fifty dollars. This was going to wipe me out.

Gus noticed my discomfort and slipped Mama a wad of cash along with his purchases of herbs and oils. "It's on me today, Mama," he said.

"It's too much," I said to him, under my breath.

"Don't worry about it. You can pay me back whenever you get a job," he whispered back.

*   *   *

Mama Lua packed up our witchy supplies. When she handed the bags to me, our hands touched and a little jolt of electricity passed between us. Mama Lua gasped and I jumped.

She pointed at me. "Stay," she said, steely-eyed.

I wanted to run out of there, but my feet felt like they had been nailed to the floor.

She walked over to the door, locked it and turned the sign to *Closed*.

Then, she turned and looked at me, opening her sight.

I felt a shiver run the length of my body.

"You," she said, crooking her finger. "There is evil around you. Dark shadows. Come with Mama Lua."

I looked at Gus, apprehensive.

He gripped my elbow. "It's what we came for," he muttered.

"I know." I hissed. But it didn't make the thought of following Mama Lua into the bowels of the store any easier.

* * *

In the back of the Crooked Pantry was a yard with eight shade trees, all sorts of flowering plants and herbs, and crates of chickens, surrounding an outdoor temple area. The whole thing was bordered by a ten-foot-tall privacy fence, covered in ivy.

The reason for the privacy was because the back of the store butted up against a residential neighborhood. Besides using the outdoor temple to perform her own multitude of secret Yoruban rituals, Mama Lua also rented it out to other groups for their rituals. So it was in her best interest to block out prying eyes.

Not that it made a difference to the disgruntled neighbors. They had tried to shut Mama Lua down a number of times. Rumor had it the neighbors finally called a cease and desist to their war on Mama Lua, when they woke up to find chicken feet on each of their doorsteps.

Personally, I thought they got off lucky. I wouldn't mess with anyone who practices Voudoun, Candomble or Santeria. They can be pretty dang scary when they're crossed. Mama Lua scared me, at least. I shuddered to think of what might have happened to the neighbors, if they had continued to harass her.

* * *

Mama placed me in the center of the temple area and told me to stand. Then she took three chicken eggs out of the hen coop and put them on her altar. She walked around the temple, bowing and lighting candles in each of the directions. When she returned to the altar, she lit a cigar and blew smoke in each direction, before picking up a fan made of rooster feathers.

She turned to me, blowing smoke at and over me, circulating it with the feathers as she circled around me. My eyes watered and I tried not to cough.

Mama Lua put the rooster fan and the cigar back on the altar and picked up a bowl and one of the eggs. She set the bowl at my feet and ran the egg over my body, chanting in Yoruban.

When she was done, she cracked the egg in the bowl.

The yolk came out solid black.

"Oh, my Gods." That was me.

"Holy shit." That was Gus.

"Bad juju. Very bad." That was Mama Lua.

"So I am cursed?"

But Mama ignored me. She dumped the toxic egg remains into a pot of barren earth she kept next to the altar.

Then she bowed to her altar three times, chanting in Yoruban and lit another candle. She picked up the fan and the cigar and blew more smoke at me, fanning it down the length of my body.

Then she picked up a bottle of gin and circled me three times. Each time she was in front of me, she would spray me with a mouthful of gin and chant in Yoruban, alternately pleading with the heavens and spraying me with gin.

I tried not to flinch. Some of the gin got in my eyes, stinging them. I could feel my eyes tearing up, but there was no way I was going to interrupt her to go wash them out. I looked over at Gus, to see if he was laughing, but he just had an intense, interested look on his face.

Then Mama Lua got another egg and ran it over me again. This time when she cracked it, it was gray.

Mama made a face, displeased. "I will try one more time. If the egg is still dark, you must return. We will prepare a black hen."

She took a vial of oil, put a little on her finger and anointed me with it, marking my forehead, throat and hands with magical sigils. Then she picked up an Oshun doll she had made from feathers and rocks and used it to do a blessing on me, making sigils in the air, while chanting in Yoruban.

I sent up every prayer I could think of, that the egg would come out normal. I had heard that if you have to return for one of her full-bore cures, it involved a lot of blood and gore. A wild dance in the moonlight, culminating in the slitting of a sacrificial hen's throat and a frenzy of blood. Just the thought of it made my stomach turn.

After another go-round with smoke and gin, Mama Lua picked up the last egg and ran it over me again. As she cracked it, I could feel myself shaking. This time, though, when the yolk fell into the bowl, it was a bright, cheery yellow. The air rushed out of me and I realized I had been holding my breath.

She nodded, happy. Mama Lua bowed to her altar again, chanted something else in Yoruban and blew out the candles.

When we went back into the store, I gave her Alegba the last twenty-dollar bill I had left. You can't have Orishas do that kind of work for you without leaving them something.

* * *

Gus was bouncing up and down like a kid, all the way back to my place. "That was cool! Did you see that? That was so cool!"

"Really, not so much, if you're the one turning the egg black. It's kind of creepy."

"Who knew you had that much toxic spiritual residue on you?"

"And you've been with me all day. Aren't you afraid some of it may have rubbed off?"

"Not me. I'm like magic Teflon."

"Uh-huh."

As we walked into the apartment, I glanced at the clock and was shocked to see how late it was. "What should I make for dinner?"

Gus opened my refrigerator and rooted through the crispers. "Ever hear of fruits or vegetables?"

"There's fruit-flavored gummy bears in the cupboard."

"You're hopeless."

"You just noticed? Produce is expensive."

"Tell me you at least take vitamins," he said, giving up on the fridge. "I have no idea what you can make with the ingredients you have in there. Are you sure you even know how to cook?"

"Hey, I know how to do a lot of things. Just because I don't do them often, doesn't mean I don't know how."

"Thank goodness for that. Or your sex life would be completely doomed."

I frowned. Fucker. Too bad he was right.

* * *

I cooked up a Mara Surprise, (which was pretty much everything in the fridge, mixed with eggs and some seasonings), studiously avoiding the contents of the freezer, while Gus took a shower. Dinner turned out to be edible, which was more than I expected.

Afterwards, Gus flipped on the TV. There was a Cary Grant marathon on AMC. While he watched *Bringing Up Baby*, I dumped a packet of blue balls in a bucket of Florida water and cleansed the apartment—physically, psychically, magically— until it felt as clean as I did when that third egg cracked yellow.

Around eleven, Gus stood up and walked down the hall to my bedroom, dropping clothes in his wake.

"Hey! What are you doing? Aren't you supposed to be getting ready for a hot date with your latest conquest?" I asked, picking up the clothes as fast as he could toss them.

"Yeah, that. It's over. He woke up this morning covered in hives and he thought I had cursed him. How ironic is that? So I'm all yours, *chica*." He crawled into bed.

"So that's why you came over so early this morning?!"

He shrugged. "He was hollering and jumping around so much, I couldn't get back to sleep."

"And was he right? Did you do something to him?"

Gus feigned shock. "I'm so maligned."

"Gus... ?"

He sniffed. "Oh, fine. Maybe I did mix a little pennyroyal in the massage lotion. He deserved it. I caught him in a hot clinch with that curvy tranny singer over at the Queen Mary, when he thought I was in the john."

I couldn't quite contain a snort of laughter as I tossed his discarded clothes in the hamper. Knowing Gus's easily hurt feelings and sensitive jealousy meter, the guy was lucky he only got hives.

Gus stretched and flopped down on my pillow. "And now, I'm exhausted."

"Hey! That's my side, bubba!"

"Life is about sharing, Miss Thing." Gus yawned. "There's no point in me going home. We've got an early day tomorrow. You should try and get some sleep." He rolled over and opened an eye at me. "I expect a fresh pot of coffee in the morning. Two eggs, bacon, maybe a tin of sardines. I'm a growing witch and I need my protein." And within seconds, he was sound asleep.

Bastard.

But later that night, with Gus's measured breathing and soft snores filling the air, I felt at peace for the first time in ages. When I slid into bed, he put his arm over my body and pulled me into him, spooning me in his sleep. I slowed my breathing down until it matched his.

As I drifted off to sleep, I idly wondered if this was what married life was like. With the addition of sex, of course. If Gus didn't feel so much like my brother, he'd be perfect for me. It was a good thing he was gay, or I might be tempted to overlook the whole sibling aspect. With that tan skin, those chocolate-brown eyes and long, wavy hair, he was entirely too sexy for his own good. But nothing seemed to fuck up a friendship—even in the pagan world—quicker than sex.

The last thought I had, as I snuggled into him, was that this feeling of safety was worth giving up some bed space for. And this time, when my eyes closed—I don't know whether it was due to Mama Lua, the house cleansing or Gus—the dreams stayed at bay.

If I had known then, that it was going to be my last night of peace, I would have slept in later.

CHAPTER TWELVE

SATURDAY MORNING, THE VALLEY was already insanely hot and the only direction the temperature was heading was up. But even the heat couldn't get my spirits down. Not today.

I loved going to pagan fairs. I loved the vending tables of supplies that you couldn't find anywhere else—unusual knick-knacks, one-of-a-kind handmade items, bizarre pieces of esoterica no one else would want. Pagans were generally a very handicraft-oriented lot, valuing personal effort over factory perfection. Unlike most people, they considered the flaws in an item to be a bonus, something that made it unique.

Most of all, I loved the loud, boisterous, fun of it all. The music, the spectacle, the sense of camaraderie. The only thing I disliked, in fact, was the lack of adequate shade from the scorching California sun and my current status of needing to conserve money. So, in deference to my own weaknesses, I decided to leave my checkbook at home to avoid temptation.

* * *

It was way too hot to get decked out in full, gothic-style witchware. So I hummed pagan songs while I dressed in a light, Celtic-print skirt, a spaghetti-strap tank top (with built-in boob shelf) and a sun hat. Then I slathered Coppertone SPF 15 on all my exposed parts, slipped my feet into a pair of Birkenstocks and I was ready to go.

Gus, on the other hand, was still in the bathroom, primping. I pounded on the door. "You have three minutes and I'm out of here."

"Hold your hell hounds, woman. You can't rush

perfection."

"You are such a girl. What are you doing in there? Brazilian wax?"

The door opened and Gus came out and pirouetted for me. He wore a Celtic sarong around his waist, a tank top and a straw sunhat. "Ta-da!"

I looked at him and laughed. "Great, we're the Bobbsey Twins."

"Nonsense, dear. It just proves we're cut of the same cloth."

"Are you saying that between the two of us, we're sharing custody of only one brain?"

"You always look at the down side, don't you?" He said, so loftily that I just had to laugh.

Yup. I loved fair day and there was no one better to share it with than Gus.

*　*　*

We arrived an hour before the fair opened and set up our table with a *'Spells Sold, Fortunes Told. $25.00'* sign.

Gus schlepped the enormous duffel bag of supplies from the SUV and I arranged everything on the table. As the other vendors finished setting up and customers filtered in, I was surprised at how many people, despite the insane heat, had shown up in full regalia. Old-fashioned, long-skirted gowns, tightly bound bodices with overflowing cleavage, full-length capes, leather sandals, walking staffs. Many wore homemade leather belts that held their athamés, drinking horns and leather purses. I even saw a few people (both genders) wearing tiaras and fairy wings.

The great thing about paganism, was that it was very accepting of all walks of life. Everyone was embraced with equal gusto. From rocket engineers to Goth kids to recovering addicts to transsexuals. If you enjoyed people watching, it was a veritable feast for the eyes. So I sat back and enjoyed the parade of people.

A bearded woman walked by, lecturing a skinny guy with a pocket protector. A woman in her seventies held hands with a guy in his thirties. A leather-clad guy strolled by with three amorous Goth girls on leashes. A young woman stopped to check out my booth, arm-in-arm with two really hot guys. One of the guys wore a baby carrier with an adorable three-month-old girl peeking out of the top. After they left, I leaned over to Gus.

"I can't even get one guy and she's got two? How not fair is that? I wonder if she'd share?"

"Dream on," he snorted, checking out the guys' asses as they walked away. "Sharing is for when you're looking to trade up or for when your relationship's getting stale. I don't think she's got either problem."

An older woman with over-permed, over-dyed hair and funky, horn-rimmed glasses walked up and planted herself in front of the table. "I want a spell to make this guy I know fall in love with me," she said, snapping her gum.

I looked up at her, considering. "Bad idea. Usually, if you force someone to fall in love with you, you get stuck with them long after you want them to get lost."

"You really suck as a business woman, you know that?" She used the bottom of her shirt to wipe sweat off her forehead, unintentionally flashing us her bra in the process.

I cleared my throat. "So I've heard. How about a spell to bring your true love into your life?"

The woman blew a bubble and popped it. "Will it work on this guy I know? He's really hot."

"If he's your true love, it will totally work."

"Okay. Done. And make it sizzling. I want someone who can rub my legs together and start a forest fire, if you get what I'm sayin'."

Gus chugged on a water bottle to keep from laughing and promptly choked, instead. I smacked him on the back, as hard as I could, while she dug a fifty out of her wallet and laid it on the table.

"Put double the magic in it."

I nodded. While Gus snagged the cash and squirreled it away, I put together a bag with a small red candle, a mini-stick of dragon's blood incense and wild rose incense, and a rose quartz crystal.

"When you go home, light the red candle for passion. Fire up the incense, it's a mix of dragon's blood for power and rose for love. Hold the crystal to your heart." I took out a piece of parchment paper and picked up my cauldron-stirring witch pen. "Then say this spell I'm writing for you three times."

"That's it?"

"Yup. After you say it, burn the paper, and leave the candle and incense lit until they burn out. Then do your best to forget about it and the universe will work its will."

"You're sure this'll work?"

Gus stopped working on the house of tarot cards that he was building, to back me up. "Ma'am, do you know who you're talking to? She's the best damn witch in Los Angeles. Of course it's going to work."

"If you say so. I ain't too used to this witchy stuff. It's my friend's bag. She's so gaga about it, I figured I may as well try it out."

I concentrated for a minute and then quickly wrote a chant on the parchment paper.

Love and sex are whirling,
Lust be in thy turning.
Bring my true love to me.
The one who holds my passion's key.
As the flame consumes the candle bright
I call to love with all my might
Come to me, within these days of three
As I desire it, so mote it be.

I handed the bag and the parchment to the woman. "There you go. Three days and he'll be yours."

"Cool." The woman cracked her gum a final time and left with her treasure.

Gus gave me a thumbs-up sign. "See, I told you. You're a natural. Now quit your whining and hand me the sun block. I'm starting to pink up."

I reached into my bag and handed him the Coppertone.

"Not that one. The REAL sunblock."

"Oh, excuse me. I forgot you need SPF 4800." I took back my SPF 15 and handed him a tube of Neutrogena SPF 90. "You're so weird."

"Not weird. Smart. I could get caught out in the Sahara desert for a week with a tube of this and not break a tan."

* * *

By the end of the day, we had made five hundred dollars towards the moving fund and, much to Gus's amusement, I was sporting a bright red sunburn. Gus, on the other hand, was cool, comfortable and not the slightest bit crispy. Which was pretty freaking amazing, considering that the temperature was in the triple digits and the sun had been relentless.

But, best of all, I had managed not to spend any of the money. Which was a first for me. I have a weak spot for handmade crafts. So it was a surprisingly good day. Until I came back from the port-a-potty.

* * *

Gus was sitting behind my table with a big, Cheshire cat grin on his face and the type of self-satisfied air that could only mean one thing—trouble.

"What the hell's up with you?" I eyeballed him, wondering if I should make a run for the car.

"Oh, ye of little faith. You're going to thank me later."

That didn't bode well. "Unless you're giving me a winning Lotto ticket, I don't think so. I don't think you've ever done anything that made me want to *thank* you later. Strangle you, yes. Thank? Not so much."

"You wound me, woman. Not to mention, you have a short memory. But I'll overlook that. With your aging female hormones, memory lapses are to be expected."

"Keep it up, I'm gonna dump your body and forget where I left it. All right. Cough it up, grinning boy. What are you up to?"

Gus clapped his hands. Whatever it was, he was obviously excited about it. "This is our big chance. The coven that was supposed to do the closing ritual pulled out. Their HPS was dressed up like an Anne Rice character, in full gothic regalia, and she passed out from the heat. They're desperate for someone to pull a group ritual out of their ass."

"Too bad we don't have a coven."

"I'm your coven. And you're witch queen for the day. So I volunteered us."

I looked at him in horror. I could already feel my stomach twisting. "What's the statute for justifiable homicide in California?"

"Pish posh."

"Pish posh, nothing. Goddamnit, Gus. I leave for twenty minutes and you and your inner diva drag me into hell. Do you remember that little talk we had about me not doing any more magic? Do you remember the gray water and the black egg?"

"It's not magic, it's public ritual. Besides, Mama Lua lifted the curse, so you've got nothing to worry about. You'll be fine. I even snagged a donation of yummy, carb-laden treats, so we have libation."

"Great. Maybe if you wave a chocolate chip cookie over me, the fairies will take pity and drop a ritual into my head. I swear, I can't leave you alone for a minute."

"There's no need to be snarky, Miss Thing. You don't like me taking initiative? Maybe you shouldn't take so long in the port-a-john."

I counted to ten before I said something I couldn't take back. Then I kicked off my sandals and stretched my toes in the grass. "Look at me," I said, pointing at my feet. "I can't High Priestess a ritual. I'm wearing a sarong and Birkenstocks, for fuck's sake. Get one of the tiara-wearers to do it. They live for this kind of shit."

"A real witch can craft with a paper hat and a blade of grass if she has to."

"I'm not laughing."

"I'm not joking." He was getting that obstinate look on his face that I've come to know and loathe. "Think fast, because we're on in thirty minutes."

I seriously thought about strangling Gus, but that would waste precious time. We needed some kind of game plan, a.s.a.p. Before I got torn apart by a group of pissed-off, over-heated pagans who wanted a closing ritual.

CHAPTER THIRTEEN

TIME PASSED QUICKLY. TOO quickly. Before I knew it, there was a massive group of tired, happy and broke pagans gathered in the clearing for our closing ritual.

"Ready or not, here we go," I muttered.

I still didn't want to do it, but Gus had his heart set on being the center of attention. I tried to talk him out of it, but it was useless. He had been dreaming of this moment ever since he got booted out of the last coven he was in. To be the biggest deal in the center of a large pagan gathering and thumb his nose at the people who had betrayed him, (at least, that was Gus's version of events). And he had been doing so much for me this week, I just didn't have the heart to stomp on his inner diva and destroy his fantasy. Especially after he spotted some of his ex-coven members roaming around.

So I stood up, put on my best public face, and went out to take on the crowd.

* * *

Thankfully, everyone was more than ready to call it a day. Gus and I hurriedly set up the space, using a borrowed cauldron, with the top covered by a round slab of wood, as our makeshift altar. On top of the altar, we placed a loaf of bread, a huge pitcher of apple cider and a large wooden spoon that I had snagged from concessions.

The crowd joined hands, one after the other, chanting *"Hand in hand, the circle is cast,"* as they surrounded us.

Then Gus and I alternated calling quarters from the center

of the circle. Unlike Wiccans, who used Golden Dawn quarters, we both used the Northern quarter system.

"In the East, I call on the divine fire of illumination and creativity." Gus said, facing East.

I turned to the South. "In the South, I call on the lustful joy of the fertile earth."

Gus turned to the West. "In the West, I call through the water, to the land of the ancestors, for their wisdom and guidance."

I faced North. "In the North, I call upon the winds of creation to bring clarity."

I took over the circle and explained the working. "This is the time of year where we reap the rewards for our work. It's the time of the harvest, when crops are transformed through the sickle blade. Wheat becomes flour, flour becomes bread, bread sustains us."

Gus picked up a loaf of bread and placed it on the altar. "We're going to transform this bread into that which sustains us spiritually."

The crowd cheered.

Gus continued, "What we need you to do, is create an energy cone. You're going to gather in around us and walk deosil—that's clockwise for you newbies—while doing a *Mah* chant. We're going to gradually increase the volume, pitch and pace while my beautiful high priestess here crafts what we need into the bread. Then, when she's ready, she'll yell *'Now!'* That's when you're going to throw all your energy to her and she'll redirect it into the bread. If you get lost, follow me. I'll guide you."

I placed my hands above the bread and started crafting different attributes into it, as Gus whipped the crowd into a steadily growing rhythm with the *Mah* chant.

"Joy. Laughter. Tolerance." I said. *"Wisdom. Patience. Inspiration."* Behind me, the chant grew in intensity and strength, until it became a solid wall of sound. By now I was yelling to be heard over the crowd. *"Truth. Knowledge. Love."*

The bread was so ready it was vibrating. The *Mah* chant was on the verge of climaxing.

As it reached its ultimate crescendo, I shouted *"Now!"*

Everyone screamed and released the energy to me and I threw it into the bread.

A brief moment of silence and the circle erupted with laughter and joy.

Then Gus picked up the pitcher of apple cider and knelt in front of me. Everyone quieted down as he started talking. "I hold the womb of the Lady, from whence all things come and to whom all things return."

I picked up the large wooden spoon. "I hold the instrument of the Lord, that which stirs the Lady's womb and brings life into fruition. The spark without which there is nothing."

I pointed the business end of the spoon to the sky and then slowly turned it over and brought it down until, with a final thrust, it penetrated the liquid in the pitcher and brought more cheers. Then I shook some drops of cider onto the bread.

Gus and I both poured ourselves some cider from the pitcher and then handed the pitcher off to the circle to be passed around along with paper Dixie cups. As Gus removed the board from the cauldron, I held the crafted and anointed bread up over my head.

"One piece for the sickle, for Death always takes his due," I said, tearing an end off the bread. "So, fuck off, Death and leave us the hell alone."

The crowd cheered, repeating my sentiments. I threw the piece as hard as I could, and it disappeared into the trees.

"And one for the ancestors, in honor of who we came from and to honor those who will come after us." I tore off the other end piece and placed it in the cauldron.

I held the rest of the bread up in the air and showed it to the crowd. "And the rest for life! May we all receive help when we most need it and least expect it."

As the crowd cheered, Gus and I each tore off a piece that we fed to each other and then we passed the bread around to the waiting throng. The bread was quickly devoured and the pitcher drained and refilled, then drained again.

Everyone seemed sated and happy with the ritual as they fanned out to enjoy the remaining food, which was now free, at the concessions table.

As Gus and I walked past a small group, we heard them

talking about how uplifting the ritual was. The best one in years, apparently.

Gus turned to me with a smug look on his face. "I told you, you could do it."

I shook my head. "I just hope I don't regret it."

* * *

When we got home, Mrs. Lasio had tacked up another eviction notice on my front door, along with an updated calendar. I pulled them down.

"What a bitch," Gus said.

"She doesn't want me to get too comfortable, I guess. "I looked at the calendar and felt my stomach clench. "I'm running out of time," I said, trying to keep the desperation out of my voice.

Gus took the calendar from me and tossed it in the pool.

Later that night, he tried to cheer me up by inviting me to go with him to Club Frack, a new bar in Silver Lake, which was rumored to be a reincarnation of Club Fuck. Gus was so excited about it, he was practically buzzing. But he was a lot more into the alternative sex scene than I was.

As far as I was concerned, why bother lighting the fire if there's no one at home to put it out? It would just be an exercise in frustration.

After Gus took his frozen crow from the freezer and left, I scrubbed the freezer clean and signed up for a free trial for an online apartment rental service. Unfortunately, they didn't have anything in my price range.

So I slathered my sunburn with aloe and went to bed.

* * *

That night, the dreams started again.

I ran through the woods. Branches slapped and cut my face, but I couldn't stop. I could sense the cottage behind me, as if it was chasing me.

I tripped on a branch and went sprawling face-first into a clearing. Suddenly, the cottage loomed in front of me. I had come full circle, without knowing it.

A crow soared by overhead, cawing. The earth shook and rose up under me; a thick, musty wave, carrying me to my fate, as the cottage door opened.

"No!" I screamed.

I clawed at the dirt, trying to find a root to hold on to, but the earth was as pliable and as buoyant as black water. I slammed into the cottage and wedged my body against the doorjamb, fighting against the tidal wave of black ooze.

The moonlight glinted off of a crystal casket inside the stone cottage.

A voice, a whisper, traveling through the dream like a breeze. "You can fight me all you want, witch, but you are mine. I have searched throughout time for you."

As the black tide drew me closer, the lid of the casket slowly creaked open. I looked inside and screamed. The woman inside was me.

* * *

I bolted awake, breathing hard. 4:00 a.m. Damn it. I wondered if I could get my twenty dollars back from Alegba. Then I wondered what Mama Lua would do, if I told her that her Orishas were falling down on the job. Probably tell me it was my fault for going out and using magic. Gus and his inner diva. What the hell had I been thinking?

CHAPTER FOURTEEN

SUNDAY MORNING, I WAS so into my stake-out of Lasio's apartment, (spying on her apartment through an opening in my patio blinds), I didn't even notice Gus walking into my living room, carrying a box of Krispy Kremes and two lattes until he waved one under my nose.

"Smell. Coffee. Good."

I took the latte and waved him away.

"Mmmmm." He bit into a donut and wafted it past my face. "Still warm. Sugar and caffeine. Everything one needs to soothe the savage beast."

I rolled my eyes and went back to ignoring him. Sooner or later, Lasio would have to come out.

Finally, he shut my patio blind, cutting off my sight line. "*Hola, señorita. Como esta?*"

"Don't do that," I hissed, quickly re-positioning the blinds. "You better hope she's not watching. I will wring your neck if you screw this up."

"Obsessed much? Did I mention Krispy Kremes and over-caffeinated lattes? Your favorites? I can't believe you're turning down the nectar of the Gods, just to spy on your building manager."

I grabbed a donut and crammed it into my mouth, just to shut him up. Then I washed it down with a big gulp of latte.

Big, big mistake.

My eyes bugged out, my tongue burned and I ran to the kitchen and spat the whole mess out into the sink.

"Goddamn, that was hot." I turned on the cold water and stuck my tongue under the stream. As Gus turned to say something, I snapped, "Don't look at me. Watch out the patio. Tell me if you see her."

He obediently took over my position at the patio blind. "If I knew you were going to chug it, I'd have gotten you an iced latte, goof. What's your problem?"

I popped an ice cube out of the freezer and ran it over my tongue. "I couldn't sleep. So I decided to have a yard sale. I've posted notices all over the internet."

"Like she won't notice it on the internet?"

"She doesn't have a computer."

"Really? I've heard of people like that, but I thought they were an urban legend."

"She thinks they're the work of the devil. She won't let her kid have one either. They fight about it all the time."

"Great. When do we commence the money-making?"

"As soon as Mrs. Holier-Than-Thou gets her butt out of here. She's got church today. Keep your eyes on her apartment and tell me when you see her go. But don't let her see you, because she'll think we're up to something and she won't leave."

Gus dutifully continued watching the courtyard through the blinds. "I know I haven't been to church in awhile, but I don't remember *'thou shalt not sell thy crap'* as being one of the amendments."

"Commandments." I corrected, filling a glass with ice and pouring the rest of my latte into it. "If she gets a look at what I'm selling, she'll flip. She'll call every priest in a twenty-mile radius to do an intervention. And then she'll probably try to have me arrested."

"Really? Well, that sounds promising. Anything I might be interested in?"

"Maybe." I grabbed another Krispy Kreme and popped it into my mouth, savoring it slowly this time. "Man, these are good. You are an evil, evil man."

"What? I got six for each of us. I thought that was pretty nice of me."

"I'll make sure my thighs write you a thank-you note."

Gus licked warm frosting off his fingers, dismissing my concerns. "They're glazed air. Air has no calories."

An upstairs door opened and slammed shut.

"Finally!" I rushed over to the blinds, shoved Gus aside and peeked out. "If we didn't have the fair, we could have done this yesterday."

"It was Saturday. She went to church on Saturday?" Gus asked, looking over my shoulder.

"All weekend, every weekend. On Saturdays, her women's group cleans the church, runs errands for the priest, that kind of thing. So everything's ready for Sunday. Then Sunday, they have service all morning and a reception in the afternoon."

Mrs. Lasio was in her finest dress and sensible shoes and gilded up to the eyeballs with gold jewelry. She clutched a tan handbag and slowly climbed down the stairs, followed by a mutinous-looking Lupe.

"And you know all this, how?" Gus asked.

"Lupe decided she wasn't going to go anymore. Mrs. Lasio had a cow and they totally had it out with each other on the patio. I think Mamma Lasio's been trying to hook her up with the priest. Or the priest's brother. It was a little confusing."

"How *Thorn Birds* of her." He paused. "I thought priests were supposed to be celibate?"

"So did I. But according to Lupe, the guy is a raging queer. I thought Mamma Lasio was going to wash her mouth out with laundry detergent and pool water. This place has been like a soap opera ever since they moved in and *I'm* the one getting evicted."

"Go figure," he said, dryly. "So, assuming it's the priest, is he cute?"

"What do you care? He's a priest."

"Priests have needs."

"And you think you could fill them?" I snorted and rolled my eyes. "I thought you were allergic to organized religion."

"Hey! I'm a spiritual person. Spirituality is spirituality, regardless of the name of your God. Or Gods. Whatever."

I snorted. I heard the wrought-iron gate close behind Mrs. Lasio and Lupe. As soon as they were out of sight, I handed Gus a sheaf of flyers. "Quick. Plaster the neighborhood. And no dawdling. I'll start setting up in the courtyard."

Gus glanced at the flyer. "A Cauldron and Broom Sale. Catchy. You come up with this yourself?"

"I told you, I couldn't sleep. Chop-chop. Time's a wasting."

I said, pushing him out the door.

* * *

An hour later, Gus had the neighborhood papered and I had finished dragging everything I could live without, out into the courtyard. All the normal stuff, like furniture, books, CD's, DVDs, as well as all the witchy accoutrements I could part with. Most of them had been gifts (a lot of them from Gus), but I figured he wouldn't be too heartbroken. Besides the occult tchotchkes, there were wands, staffs, scrying mirrors, extra tarot card decks, animal bones from the Bone Room and a boar's skull I had gotten on E-Bay, and which Gus promptly claimed as his own. I was going to keep the box of witchy stuff my mom had left behind, but other than that, I needed to majorly downsize, in case I wound up living in my car.

As word got around, people started trickling in. Soon, the courtyard was crowded with an interesting mix of tattooed, long-haired, body-pierced Goths and aging Hollywood wannabes looking for a supernatural boost over the competition.

Gus nudged me. "What's the deal with Aunt Bee over there?"

I looked up. "Ellen Reese. She's a hoot. She owns the gift shop over by Ventura and Colfax. When she wants something, she hangs her St. Anthony upside down. If that doesn't work, she sacrifices a chicken in the light of the moon and serves it up at her church luncheon. You can bet she keeps that quiet."

"Wow. And people say witches are bad."

"Catholic Strega. Don't mess with her. She has some big-time juju."

"How do you know all this stuff?"

"I met her at last year's Pagan Pride, after she had drunk a bottle of mead. She told me all about her special chicken salad."

"Hey, have you thought about my suggestion? I emailed the owner and the job's still open."

I sighed. Gus had emailed me late last night, all excited about a job posting he'd found at Club Frack. "I am not getting a job as a stripper."

"There's good money in it. Especially while you're still limber enough to kick your heels over your head."

I ignored him and went back to selling off my life. No price too low.

* * *

By afternoon, everything had been sold, (for far less money than I had expected, but I sucked at negotiating), and I was making extra cash reading cards for people.

Suddenly, Mrs. Lasio and Lupe walked through the wrought-iron gate—much sooner than expected. I felt my heart lurch in my chest. Mrs. Lasio took one look at the courtyard and started screaming bloody murder.

While most of the people there would think nothing of facing off with demons, the wrath of Mrs. Lasio was more than they could take. That courtyard cleared out faster than a town square in a Godzilla movie.

I stormed into my apartment and slammed the door in Mrs. Lasio's face.

* * *

"Mara, honey, I'm very upset right now." The irate voice of my treacherous landlord resonated over the phone.

"You're not the only one." I said, stirring macaroni into a pot of boiling water.

"What were you thinking?!"

"I don't know, Lenny. Money, maybe? I'm being shoved out of my home at the end of the month." I looked at the calendar. Oh, my gosh, this month was passing incredibly quickly. "So, sue me, but a yard sale just seemed logical."

"And that's exactly the problem, sugar. People suing me. I'm not insured for yard sales. For cripe's sake, I'm barely insured for guests."

"How was I supposed to know that?"

"Use your head, sweet pea. I never thought anyone would have a yard sale in the building. Criminy, girl, there's not even a yard to have a sale on. There's just a few measly inches of pebbled deck surrounding a huge water hazard. And then you pull the fortune teller crap on top of it? Do you go out of your way to be difficult?!"

"That's a cruddy thing to say."

"I don't know what else to make of it. I told you I'd take care of you and you turn around and kick me right in the Polygrips. Now Manuel isn't speaking to me. He says you're breaking God's laws by trying to see the future."

"But he's fine with the whole *'spilling his seed on barren ground'* thing?"

A long silence from Lenny. *Crap.* The filter that was normally in place between my brain and my mouth seemed to be completely on the fritz.

Finally, he cleared his throat. "Now, no more of that witchy stuff or I'll be very upset."

"Meaning you'll call and yell?" Oh, geez. It was like my mouth didn't even belong to me anymore. I needed this call to end before I said anything else.

"Meaning I'll change the locks and keep your deposit. Pull your act together and be the young lady I know you can be."

He hung up just as the macaroni water bubbled over, splattering and hissing on the flame. I quickly turned off the gas. As I poured the macaroni through the strainer, steam rose up and covered the window over the sink.

An image of the old woman from my nightmares appeared in the condensation, looking at me, sad beyond measure.

I was so startled, I almost dropped the strainer.

"It's too late..." a small voice whispered through my head.

"Too late for what?" I asked.

But there was no answer.

CHAPTER FIFTEEN

I SPENT THE NEXT week packing up everything I wanted to keep. Everything else could go to Goodwill. Not that I had any idea where I was going yet, but I may as well be ready.

Friday morning, there was a thud at the front door, like someone kicking it. When I opened it, I could barely see Gus behind the stack he was carrying. "You've got a wee bit of mail dearie," he said, dropping it on the couch. "Man, your mail lady is tough."

"That sweet little Chinese lady?"

"Sweet, my ass. And you're on her shit list for letting the mail pile up."

"It's probably all junk. Or bills. Toss it."

"No way. When I told her you weren't actually out of town, you were just ignoring your mailbox, I got a twenty-minute lecture on the evils of postal abuse. Mail delivery isn't a right, it's a privilege. So you're going to open this crap like a responsible adult."

"Bite me."

He shot me a warning glance.

I sighed. "Sometimes, you can positively be a stick in the mud. What do you think about pizza for lunch?"

"Sure. Extra cheese, extra sausage, extra 'shrooms. I'll treat. After you open your mail."

I speed-dialed the pizza place, idly sorting through the mail while I was on hold. "Junk, bill, ad, bill, magazine I've never subscribed to. Hey, what's this?"

In the middle of all the junk mail was an envelope that looked like a real letter. Curious, I tore it open. As I pulled out the letter, a check fell to the floor.

Gus bent down, retrieved the check and gave a long, low whistle. "Toss it, huh? Oh ye of little faith."

I looked over his shoulder. The check was made out to Mara Stephens, in the amount of five thousand dollars.

"Do you have some kind of secret life I don't know about?" Gus asked.

I hung up on the hold music and scanned the letter. "I don't believe this." I read it a second time, slower. "Remember Mr. Lyra?"

"You went back and gave him that blow job!?"

"Don't be an ass." I handed the letter over to Gus.

He read it out loud. "Dear Ms. Stephens, please accept my apologies. You were right. I went to the doctor and he removed five polyps removed from my colon. Consider this a token of my appreciation for the early warning. Perhaps you would consent to do another reading for me later?" Gus folded up the letter and looked at me. "Not bad. So, how much does that give us in the Mara moving fund?"

"More than I ever thought I'd have. Maybe I'll spring for pizza."

Gus tucked my arm into the crook of his elbow and pulled me towards the door. "Seeing as how you're rich and all, screw the pizza. Take me out for a real meal, woman," he swooned and batted his eyes. "Before I faint from hunger."

So, after a quick stop at the bank, I took Gus to the little Hungarian restaurant down the street. We had a delicious lunch of cherry soup and borscht for not much more than what pizza would have cost.

* * *

When we got back that afternoon, I blasted classic rock out into the courtyard, in defiance of Mrs. Lasio's 'No Loud Music' rule. May as well go out with a bang.

I put on a swimsuit and canon-balled into the deep end of the pool while Gus sat on the pool stairs, in a muscle beach tank top and white sarong, his legs barely dangling in the water. I swear that boy was more fond of skirts than any woman I had ever met.

As I swam back up to the surface, Gus looked at me from over his sunglasses. "Feel like doing more laundry? I have a couple loads in the trunk of my car."

"How can you possibly go through so many clothes? How many times do you change in a day?"

"A man's gotta look good. And just for you, I pulled in some extra from the neighbors. Are you basking in the love yet?"

"Feel free to hate me a little. Maybe you should get a wife," I said, floating on my back.

He shuddered. "Gods forbid. Women were put on this earth just to test men."

"Watch it, buddy. I may be an honorary member of the boy's club, but I'm still a chick."

"You don't count. You're a gay guy trapped in a chick's body. Although you do have your little PMS moments."

I flipped around and splash-kicked hard, completely soaking him.

"Hey! Not fair when there's no towels out here."

"Oh, crud. I knew I forgot something." I climbed out of the pool and walked over to my apartment to get a couple of beach towels.

"Hey, Mara, guess what I am?"

I turned to look. He was standing next to the pool on one leg, the other one bent behind him and his arms outstretched.

"Guess who I am. Go on, guess."

"A stork?"

"The Hanged Man, Lord of the Crossroads. Cool, huh? Hey, we should copyright that. Tarot Card Charades. I can see it now. It'll be big, baby. Get in on the ground floor."

I laughed and headed into the apartment, while Gus plotted out his next card move.

* * *

I grabbed a couple of beach towels out of the linen closet and was heading back to the screen door, when I noticed the wrought iron gate opening and a young Fed Ex guy walking in, looking around for an apartment number. I had a feeling he was looking for me, but before I could open the door, Gus waylaid him.

My 80's mix CD finished and in the sudden silence, I heard their voices echoing through the courtyard. I stood and watched through the screen door, wondering what was going to happen next.

Gus, in his best upper class British accent: "I say, old chap. Are you looking for 1-C? She can't hear you. Stone deaf, poor thing. But, no worries, I can sign for it. I'm her live-in caretaker."

The Fed Ex guy was staring at Gus, like he was some kind of exhibit at Cirque Berzerk. Then he looked down at the package he was carrying, flummoxed.

"Poor old girl. She'd be lost without me, really," Gus continued. "Constantly forgetting where she puts her glasses, her teeth, if she's had an enema or not. If it wasn't for me, the old bat would be living in a pool of watery shite. So, come, come, my good man and let me relieve you of your duty. Chop, chop."

Unsure and a bit grossed out, he cautiously gave in and handed the package to Gus. Gus signed and tossed the package on the picnic table while the Fed Ex guy beat a hasty retreat.

* * *

I emerged from the apartment, walked over to Gus and shoved him in the pool. He landed with a satisfying splash.

"Hey! What was that for?!" he sputtered, when he surfaced.

"Sorry, stone deaf, remember?" I eyeballed the Fed-Ex package on the picnic table. "Did you have fun with the delivery guy?"

"I enjoy my small amusements."

"No doubt. He seemed kinda cute."

"Not my type. Scares too easily." He paused and thought about it for a second. "Yeah, good thing you're moving. I'm pretty sure Fed Ex isn't going to make any more deliveries here."

I picked up the package. "It's from a law firm in Wisconsin."

"Maybe Lyra's wife is suing you for the five grand back."

"The way my month is going? Not out of the realm of possibility."

I ripped it open. A folder with legal documents and

Polaroids tumbled out.

I took one look at the pictures and grabbed onto the edge of the table, struggling to breathe. I was beyond light-headed—it felt like my entire body had gone numb.

"What? What's wrong?" Gus asked, climbing out of the pool. He picked up a picture and looked at it. "Nice." He put the picture down and stared at me.

The blood had drained from my face, leaving me pale, and I shook uncontrollably. I sat down on the bench and put my head between my knees. "I think I'm going to throw up."

"My psychic reactor must be tapped out, because I'm still not getting it. But if you throw up in the pool, you're on your own with that bitch of a manager."

I picked up a picture and shoved it at him. "It's the cottage from my nightmares. I can't believe it really exists."

Gus sat down and flipped through the legal papers. "Who's Tillie McDougal?"

"My Aunt on my mom's side. Technically, she's my Great-Aunt. I don't really remember her, just what I've heard from my dad. Aunt Tillie and Uncle Owen were the last ones to see my mom, before she vanished."

"Looks like you're her sole heir. She left a living trust and the order of succession was your Uncle Owen, your mom and then you."

I sat up and looked at him. "So they're all dead?"

"Looks like."

I felt the world swirl around my head and go black.

CHAPTER SIXTEEN

WHEN I CAME TO, I was laying down on the picnic table with Gus's pool-water soaked tank top draped over my forehead. Gus was looking over the papers from the Fed Ex packet. He glanced over at me. "You back?"

"I think so."

"Don't pass out on me like that again. I don't like it. And you're a bitch to lift. Talk about dead weight."

"Sorry," I croaked.

"Did you hit your head? Do you see two of me standing here? Should I take you to a hospital?"

"No, I'm good."

"Good. Remember to keep breathing. I've been looking through this stuff and, while it sucks for your Great-Aunt Tillie, this is your lucky day."

"How do you figure?" I slowly sat up and placed my feet on the picnic table bench.

"Listen to this." He stood up and started pacing, as he flipped through the papers. "As last remaining heir, you inherit everything. Except for the assets that were liquidated to pay hospital costs, property taxes, etcetera. But everything else is yours. Your aunt had set it up through a living trust, so there's no probate. And there's no mortgage. She owned the house outright. Looks like it's been in your family for a long time. And now, it's yours. Devil's Point, Wisconsin. How perfect is that?"

Suddenly, Mrs. Lasio came tearing through the front gate. "You, *brujo*, put your clothes on. This is a polite courtyard."

Gus looked up at her, a bit flummoxed. "We're sitting by the pool. I have a sarong on. What the hell is your problem?"

"In the pool you wear swimsuit. Out the pool, you wear clothes. This is not a whorehouse."

"I am wearing clothes. A sarong counts as clothing."

I took the wet tank top off my forehead, looked at Gus and started to laugh.

Mrs. Lasio was still bellowing. "I don't want to see that. No one wants to see that."

"It's okay, we'll go inside." I said, climbing down from the picnic table.

Mrs. Lasio climbed the stairs and slammed into her apartment.

Gus turned to me, flummoxed. "What the hell was that about?"

I laughed. "Your sarong is very thin, very white and it's wet. And you're standing in the sun. So you, Mr. Commando, are a 1950's peep show."

As we gathered up all the papers, Gus grinned at me. "At least you're not hyperventilating anymore. So my humiliation is having an up side."

"That's because I've decided it's impossible."

"What is?"

"This whole thing. It's all impossible." We walked into the apartment. I closed the door and turned on the air conditioning. "It's just another dream. I must have fallen asleep while I was packing boxes."

Gus reached over and punched me in the arm. Hard.

"*Ow!* Fucker! That hurt. What the hell was that for?!"

"Every time you look at that bruise, you'll know you're not dreaming."

I glared at him. "You do that again and you'll wish you were dreaming."

Gus put up his hands in surrender and dropped the papers on my dining room table.

"Are you spending the night?" I asked, changing the subject.

"Love to, but I've got a date. Speaking of, did I leave my black trousers here?"

"You did. They're hanging in the closet. And I have a bottle of that shampoo you like, if you want to hit the shower first."

Gus looked down at himself. "Think I should?" He sniffed at his armpits. "Oh, yeah. That's ripe. Why didn't you tell me I was a walking Stilton cheese?"

"Why do you think I've stayed on the opposite side of the courtyard?" I took a bottle of Jack Daniels from a cabinet poured a shot.

He laughed, kissed me on the cheek and trotted off to the shower.

* * *

A few minutes later, I walked into the bathroom, sipping my Jack & Coke. "Am I allowed to turn down an inheritance? I'm thinking living in my car is a better bet."

"That seems silly." Gus said, over the sound of the water.

"Not really. That cottage has been haunting my dreams. Anything that wants me there so bad, should probably not get what it wants." I sat on the toilet and put my drink on the countertop. "Maybe I can cash it in. Is there some kind of real estate service that'll take a house off my hands?"

"In this economy? You won't get anywhere near what it's worth." Gus shampooed his hair and yelled over the water as he rinsed. "Let's think about this logically. You saw the place when you were a child, maybe heard stories about it from your mom's family. Flash forward to now. You get evicted, and you start dreaming about a cottage that your family owns, that your conscious mind forgot. It's simple, straightforward, psychology. Maybe your sixth sense picked up that Aunt Tillie was getting old, ready to kick the bucket—"

"—Thank you, Dr. Phil. And maybe tonight I'll dream the winning lottery ticket numbers."

Gus opened the shower door and frowned at me. "You're a witch, dear heart. Why is it so impossible for a witch to dream what's going to happen in the future?" He ducked back into the shower to rinse off the shampoo. "And if you flush, I'll kill you."

"I'm not peeing, goof. I'm just sitting. Thinking. Notice that the lid's down. I normally don't pee on the lid."

"I don't trust you. You're a woman."

Just for that, I flushed.

Gus screamed as he got blasted with cold water. "Bitch!

Just wait 'til I get out of here."

"There's a problem with your logic, McFreud. This cottage that I've inherited? I've never been there. I've never seen it. But it was the last place my dad ever saw my mom alive. So it kinda freaks me out. I don't want anything to do with it."

Gus opened the shower door and poked his head back out. "Why didn't you ever tell me about your mom?"

"I didn't want to dwell on it. I'd already spent enough of my life chasing after a ghost. Ironic, huh? Now it seems like ghosts are chasing after me."

"Nothing is ever as simple as it seems."

"No kidding," I snorted in agreement.

Why'd you stop looking for her?" he asked, stepping out of the shower.

I thought of my dad and could see his bright blue eyes, aquiline nose and tanned skin as if he were standing in front of me. "My dad died of a broken heart. That seemed a good enough reason to quit."

"Sounds like real love. Or real commitment." Gus started toweling off. "Or someone who should have been committed because of love."

Devil's Point, Wisconsin. Even the name sounded like a warning. I slugged down the rest of my drink and thumped down the glass, suddenly resolved. I knew what I had to do. I stood up.

"Where are you going?"

"To give the Devil back his due," I said, over my shoulder, as I walked out.

* * *

Gus half-ran, half-hopped out of the bathroom, pulling his pants on as he hurried after me.

I grabbed the Fed-Ex package and shoved everything back in.

"Mara! Wait!"

"I'm getting rid of this," I said, tossing the package in a small, metal trashcan. I got a box of matches out of a drawer and I lit one, ready to send this gift from the grave back where it belonged.

Gus blew out the match and grabbed the box from me. "Are

you nuts? This is important stuff, Mara. You can't just burn it. This cottage could hold the key to what happened to your mom. Don't you want to see if Tillie had any pictures of her? Any memories she may have written down?"

I turned away from him so he couldn't see my eyes starting to tear up. I couldn't understand why the thought that my mom might actually be dead, felt so painful. It was easier to think of her as being out there, somewhere, living a life that had nothing to do with me.

"Besides, I'm sure they have duplicates. Burning it isn't going to make it go away." He took the package out of the garbage and handed it back to me. "Stop being a girl and man up. This solves a lot of your problems. Aunt Tillie couldn't have picked a more fortuitous time to kick the bucket. Don't run away from your gift horse just because you're having bad dreams."

"I bet the people of Troy heard the same speech and look where it got them."

"You're about to be homeless. Can you really afford to be indulging your paranoia, looking for some kind of psychic ambush?"

I sighed.

He looked at his watch. "If date night bombs," he continued, quickly buttoning his wild-colored shirt. "I'll be back for some comfort food and one-on-one freak-out time. Just try to hold it together until then, okay?" He kissed me on the cheek. "And don't hog all the Jack."

"And if it's a great date?"

"I'll call you after breakfast and you can go off on me then. I'll promise to listen to all your paranoid delusions without laughing."

"As a best friend, you kinda suck."

"Tough love, baby. Tough love. Okay, are we good?"

I nodded, reluctantly. "Go on and get out. I don't want you here anyway."

He stuck a pair of heavy silver earrings through his oversized ear piercings, put on his Celtic man jewelry, and strode off in a cloud of amber and patchouli.

* * *

Later that night, it was just me, the Fed Ex package and a rapidly dwindling bottle of Jack Daniels. I had run out of cola, and then I ran out of ice, so now I was drinking it straight out of the bottle.

I took another swig and paced the living room, trying to ignore the package. That didn't quite work, so I gave it the hairy eyeball and walked gingerly around it, expecting it to leap off the table at any second.

Between the packing and the yard sale, the apartment felt denuded and strange. I turned on the TV, but I couldn't concentrate longer than thirty seconds. I tried putting in *Murphy's Romance*, one of my favorite old-time movies with Sally Field and James Garner, (okay, so I'm a sap for happy endings), but that didn't help either.

It was odd how fate worked. I spent the last few weeks preparing to move, even though I didn't have a place to move to. I'd sold off as much as I could and I'd packed up the rest. I'd made all the preparations, without any destination. And now the destination just magically dropped in my lap. It was like the universe intervened and brought me a new home. But at what cost?

It did what you asked it to. Magic follows the path of least resistance.

"Who said that?!" I looked around, but I was the only one standing in my apartment. I eyeballed the bottle of Jack Daniels. Could Jack make you hear things?

I had to think logically. Maybe Gus was right. What if the cottage had been haunting my dreams because my subconscious was somehow aware that it was going to be my new home? I took a few deep breaths, trying to shut down my fear and calm my emotions.

Or maybe your fetch did its job too well and killed an old woman so you could have a place to live.

"Shut up!" I said, reaching for the bottle of Jack Daniels and taking another swig.

I looked around, daring the voice to say something else, but it was quiet.

I picked up the package and slowly went through the documents. Deed of Trust, pictures of the property. The pictures looked enough like the cottage in my dreams to make my spine tingle. But it was also different. It was bigger, fancier, nicer. Maybe it was just a dream after all. Maybe I was getting all worked up over nothing.

There was an envelope with a copy of Tillie's Last Will and Testament along with her Living Trust. There was also a folder with a Death Certificate. When I opened the folder, a newspaper clipping and an autopsy report fell out. I picked them up and the bottom fell out of my world.

CHAPTER SEVENTEEN

"Mara, Mara, wake up!"

The voice seemed to be coming from a mile away. I tried to grab onto the sound and crawl towards it.

"Mara! You get back here right now. Two more minutes, I'm throwing you into the pool. And let me tell you, that water's damned cold at night."

I tried to make my lips to say *'No'* but my will and my body seemed to be disconnected.

Cold. Icy. Wet. Salty. I reached up. My face was wet and salty. I opened my eyes. Gus hovered over me, an empty water pitcher in one hand, a container of sea salt in the other.

"Rude," I croaked.

"Rude, my ass." Gus said, placing a big chunk of sea salt in my mouth. "Do you have any idea how much you scared me?"

I tried to spit out the salt, but he forced my mouth closed.

"Stop fighting me. You need to ground out whatever this is."

I made a face at the way the salt burned, but I swallowed it. He handed me a bottle of water and I gulped it down, trying to wash the taste of salt away.

"Aren't you on a date?"

"I was. I was having a great time, too. Until you called."

I looked up at him in confusion. Then I looked down at myself. I was on the floor, propped up next to the couch. The portable phone was about a foot away. The contents of the package were scattered on the floor.

"Do you remember calling me?"

I shook my head. "What did I say?"

"You screamed."

"What did I scream?"

"I don't know. I couldn't understand you. The machine picked up, I heard you screaming and the line went dead. So I rushed over here. What happened?"

"Oh." As the salt worked to ground me, memories started to return, bit by bit. "I'm sorry. I don't know what got into me."

Gus picked up the empty bottle of Jack Daniels. "I do. Now what's this all about, Mara? I was in the middle of an after-dinner blowjob, so it better be good. I've never deflated so fast in my life."

The package. I kicked at it and papers went flying. "That," I pointed at the package. "That's what happened."

"Yes, we went through that before."

"You missed something," I croaked. I crawled over to the pile, scrabbled through the papers and handed him the newspaper clipping and the autopsy report.

"Gruesome." He said, flipping through it. "Especially the pictures. What idiot put these in here? Damn, when I die, no autopsies please. Even if it is foul play. Just toss me on a burning pyre. After you cut off my head, of course."

I snatched the envelope back from him. "Don't you get it?" I held up the newspaper clipping. There it was, in black and white. A small, Volkswagen Cabriolet crunched into a tree. Perched on the hood of the car was a large, black crow. Behind it was an autopsy photo, in full color, showing a ravaged corpse with a missing eye.

Looking at the clipping again, I started hyperventilating. "I dreamt Aunt Tillie's death. The whole thing. In excruciating detail. Remember? The glass with gray water? The dead crow in the bathroom? I killed her!"

"That's ridiculous. Dreaming it doesn't mean you caused it."

"She swerved to avoid me. This is all my fault."

"Breathe. Slow down. Deep breaths. Not to point out the obvious, but you weren't really there." Gus put his hands on my shoulders. "Come on, work with me here, I don't have a paper bag and I'm running out of salt." He slowed his own breathing and projected calming energy into me.

104

"You don't understand. I killed Aunt Tillie." I gasped.

"You can't even swat a spider. You always make me relocate them outside. How on earth could you have killed a person?"

I got up and paced the length of the room, holding the clip. "I killed the last of my mother's family and I've never even met her. How rude is that?"

"Miss Manners would have a field day. You should always meet your victims first."

"I'm not joking!"

"Mara, you need to calm down. Seeing something happen and making it happen are two different things."

"Semantics. Does it happen because you see it? Or do you see it because it's going to happen? It's the same thing. They feed into each other. Oh my god, I'm a killer. A stone-cold killer."

"Relax and breathe. This isn't *you*. This is the Jack talking."

"I was standing in the middle of the road. I was the reason she swerved into the tree. I have to turn myself in."

"Trust me, you'll be laughed out of every police station in the country. You weren't actually there, Mara. Read the article. It says an *owl* hit her windshield. Not an astral-projecting witch."

I gave a strangled sob and collapsed on the couch. "I was too lazy to do things the real way. I had to use magic to get what I wanted. Magic takes the path of least resistance. I wanted a new home. Now I've got it. Yay, me, right? I dreamt her death into being and all for what? Just because I needed a place to stay?"

He put his hand on my arm, but I shook him off.

"I'm going to take you to the hospital. You obviously have a concussion."

I started rocking back and forth. Gus grabbed me, stopping the rocking motion.

"You are not responsible for this. Seriously. Do you think you're such a great witch that you command the Queen of Fate for everyone else?"

"No." I sniffled, tears running down my cheeks.

"All right then. Stop taking the blame for what happens to other people. The only person under your control is you. Got it?"

I nodded.

"Now, for whatever reason, this cottage was fated to come to you. You've been seeing it because you were meant to get it. Even you being evicted played into it."

"But what about Aunt Tillie?"

"What about her? It was her time to die. You were given a gift of sight. You got a chance to see her before she kicked it. You got to spend a stolen minute with her. You did not kill her."

I nodded. I wanted to believe him. I really did.

"You're really freaked about this cottage, aren't you?"

I nodded again. "It's been keeping me up nights and now it's turning my life upside down."

"You know, there's only one thing to do," he said, looking deep into my eyes.

I stared at him, hoping he had the answer.

"You have to decide. Are you going to let your fears rule you? Or are you going to be the master of your own destiny?"

I groaned. That was not what I was hoping to hear.

He smiled at me to soften the blow. "Start packing, little grasshopper. Your new home awaits. You are going to honor the memories of Tillie and your mom, and every female in that MacDougal line, by claiming that cottage and making it your own."

I tried to smile, but my stomach had morphed into a large Celtic knot, lubricated by fear.

"Besides, if the cottage is so desperate to get you there that it killed someone to make it happen, don't you want to find out why?" Gus asked.

"No!" I yelled. But as much as I wanted to deny it and run screaming from the apartment, I couldn't quite silence the voice inside of me that agreed with him. The one that wanted to go face down the bogeyman and bring it to its knees.

* * *

In the sober light of day, the idea of moving to the cottage was as enticing as it was horrifying. Probably because Gus had been working overtime to sway me to his way of thinking. Despite my residual guilt and depression about Tillie, (and a nagging fear that Gus was wrong about his version of what happened), I was actually a little excited about the idea of starting a whole new life in Devil's Point, Wisconsin. It was just a stone's throw from the Canadian border—if you could throw really, really well, over water. And it was across the harbor from Devil's Island, with its infamous lighthouse.

The excitement was tinged with a cold layer of fear, but it was excitement nonetheless. A small, obviously suicidal part of me was not only curious, but a little eager to see the real-life cottage face-to-face and get to the bottom of what was going on.

That was the part of me that I could never quite hide from Gus. Although it made me wonder which morbid DNA marker I carried, that turned facing my deepest fears into a rush.

* * *

When Gus came up with the ever-practical suggestion of trading my precious Mustang Sally for Zed, his new Ford Escape Hybrid, I jumped at it. Normally, I'd never trade Sally for anything, but somehow, I didn't think northern Wisconsin had a terribly long summer season. And snow and rock salt weren't all that great for a convertible.

Besides, since I was going to be driving up there, the SUV just seemed more practical. So, I took Sally out for a last spin up Pacific Coast Highway and handed the keys to Gus with no regrets.

* * *

The following Friday, under the ever watchful and suspicious eyes of Mrs. Lasio, I packed up the last of my things and loaded them into the SUV. It was sad to think that my entire life could fit so easily into Zed—with enough room to still be able to see out the back window.

I had taken cuttings of my harder to get plants, like the Salvia Divinorum and the Belladonna, and let Gus keep the rest.

When he roared off in Sally, loaded down with greenery and the last remnants of my life in Los Angeles, I thought he was just transporting everything back to his apartment. But that was hours ago and he still hadn't returned.

I tried to finish loading Zed as slow as I could, but it was almost six o'clock and I had to get on the road. I was a horrible night driver. So, I wanted to get started while the sun was still out, to give my eyes time to adjust to the changing light.

I stood in the middle of the road, hoping to see Gus driving back. Except for a couple of squirrels playing tag, the street was dead quiet. I debated going back into the apartment and waiting for him, but Mrs. Lasio's nephew was already in there, changing the locks.

So I got into the SUV and willed Gus to appear as hard as I could.

Nothing.

I couldn't believe he wasn't going to make it back to say goodbye. Especially since I was moving so far away.

I thought about waiting for him in the courtyard, but Mrs. Lasio was standing guard at the gate. I looked back at the courtyard and shook my head. Damn, it looked bare without my mini-forest. With a sigh of regret, I turned the key in the ignition.

As I was pulling away, I saw Gus speeding down the road.

He parked and ran over to me, holding an aquarium. "You weren't going to leave without saying goodbye, were you?"

I put the SUV in park and hopped out, grinning. "Not happily. What's Grundleshanks doing here? He wants to say goodbye too?"

"Nope. He's coming with you."

"What?!" I stared at Gus, stunned. "But you love Grundleshanks. Besides, I don't know what to do with a toad."

Gus opened up the passenger door and put Grundleshanks on the seat, buckling his tank into place with the seat belt. "Take it up with him. The little traitor. He's the one who insisted. I tried to talk him out of it, but he'd made up his little toady mind. Just keep him fed, watered, give him new mud. Which he hates, by the way, so give him new mud a lot. And hose him down frequently. If he complains, ignore him." Gus shot Grundleshanks an evil look. "See how long you'll like living with her, you amphibian Judas."

"I can't take him, really, Gus."

"You have to."

"Why do I have to?"

"Ask little Lord Traitor yourself. He wouldn't give me any

peace until I agreed to let him go with you. And be careful taking the lid off his tank, because he can leap out and attack awfully fast, when he's in the mood. And wear gloves when you handle him. The poison he secretes through his skin can be deadly. Or a really great hallucinogen, depending on how much you get."

"I think you've been playing with the toad too much. It's starting to affect you. C'mon, Gus. Look at that face. He definitely wants to stay with you."

"I wish." Gus went back to Sally and returned with a slightly used box of latex gloves, a water mister and a plastic baggie full of crickets. "Just to get you started."

I gave it one last try. "Gus, this is really sweet, but you love Grundleshanks. To you, he's a roommate. To me, he'd just be a toad."

"That's what I told him. But it's out of my hands. Hopefully, you'll give him the care he deserves, just because he's my toad. Ex-toad."

"I don't understand."

"Neither do I. I opened his cage to change out his mud, he launched himself at me, hung onto my face and told me he had to go with you. And he refused to let go until I gave in. He got me so stoned, I couldn't move for two hours."

I looked down at the eye-blinking mud lump in the tank. "Well, if you're sure... I don't know what to say."

"He says he's on some kind of mission. Tell you what. If you don't want him, just send him back when his job is done." Gus sighed. "Just my luck to have befriended a toad on a quest." He glared at Grundleshanks. "And don't think I'm going to be pining away for you, either. There's plenty more toads where you came from."

Grundleshanks blinked at him.

Gus took a shopping bag out of Sally's trunk. "And since you insist on not taking care of yourself, I've put together a vitamin and supplement regimen that will keep you healthy."

"Gus—"

"—Hush, no fighting me on it. There's a list of what you need to take when, in the bag. I expect you to follow it to a T." Then he dug into his man-bag and pulled out a gift-wrapped box. "And this is a present for when you get there, but it's got a shelf-life and it's heat-sensitive, so don't go leaving it in Zed."

"Gus, this is really too much."

"Zip it. Not another word. Just don't expect anything else, 'cause this is the extent of what you're getting from me. Okay?" He double-checked that Grundleshanks was settled in and the seat belt would hold.

One last hug and I was off. Although I could barely see the road through my tears.

*   *   *

As I slowly drove down the street, Gus sprinted until he was running alongside Zed. He pounded on the driver side door. I stopped and rolled down the window.

"Hey, I have an idea, why don't you come back to Los Angeles with Grundleshanks when this whole quest thing is over? Not that I'm gonna miss you or anything. I mean, I never liked you that much to begin with."

I laughed through my tears. "Like I want to see your freakish Greek face. Why do you think I'm leaving?"

"Unrequited love. You're so hot for me, you have to run three thousand miles to get away from my charisma."

"It's not your charisma, it's your B.O. You do know that soap's not just for decorative purposes, right?"

Gus propped his arm on Zed and leaned in my open window. "Hey, why do you think Greeks invented olive oil?"

"Why?"

"To separate the men from the boys. And then we exported it to Scotland to separate the men from the sheep."

We both laughed. It was something we had in common—turning to bad jokes when things got too emotional.

"When you get there, have a drink for me. Scotch. Neat. Real Scotch. None of that bourbon or Tennessee whiskey crap."

"You got it." A few yards away, I could see the T-intersection leading to the main road. I looked at the cars whizzing by. "Well, this is it."

"It's not forever. Besides, you'll make new friends, forget about me."

"Never." I kissed him. "I love you, bro."

"Not as much as I love you."

I hugged him, hard, our foreheads and noses touching.

"I'm going to miss you so much," I whispered.

"Me too," he said. He put his arms around me and squeezed me tight. "Now, stop it or you're going to make me cry." Then he kissed my forehead, cheeks and lips, as a blessing. "May the Old Ones guide you on your way."

With a last, teary-eyed wave, (on both our parts), he stepped away and I turned onto Vineland.

*　*　*

Before I headed onto the expressway, I quickly stopped at a local 7-11 for a box of Kleenex, and stocked up on caffeine-loaded, energy-boosting drinks and extra B-12 supplements. B-12s were incredible for staying awake without the heart palpitations of caffeine overload.

I was going to think positive about this entire, insane, driving-a-bazillion-miles-by-myself trip and maybe, just maybe, I'd get there in one piece. Before I pulled out of the parking lot, I did a last check on Grundleshanks. He seemed happy enough. Even though the last thing I wanted in my life was a toad, having him in the car made me feel better, like Gus was taking the trip with me.

I misted Grundleshanks down with water and dropped a couple of crickets into his tank. "Are you sure you want to do this?"

Grundleshanks looked up at me and calmly blinked.

"Okay, I'll take that as a yes."

As we pulled out into the street, I glanced over at him again, wondering if toads ever got carsick. And if they did, how could you tell?

Grundleshanks gave me an especially baleful look in return and I swiveled my eyes back to the road.

Psyched up for the long drive, with the radio blasting classic rock, we settled into a routine of the vitamins and supplements Gus had put together for me, extra B-12s, caffeine overdrive, antacids, the occasional cricket for Grundleshanks and maximum speed.

PART TWO

AUNT TILLIE'S

REVENGE

CHAPTER EIGHTEEN

AFTER FIVE DAYS OF DRIVING, I felt like I was one of the living
dead, operating simply because my body was moving out of
habit. However, I had made it from the mind-numbing heat of
the Southwestern desert, through the incessant storms and
weirdly sideways-growing trees of the Texas Panhandle and into
the cool, crisp autumn of Northern Wisconsin. And I had done it
all on my own. Which is a big deal for someone who normally
can't handle a two-hour commute without pulling over for a nap.

I still made way more stops than most people would. But
the vitamin and supplement regimen Gus had concocted for me
seemed to be helping. I also embraced overnight hotel stays,
endless cups of coffee and frequent gas station restroom breaks.
Better safe than a statistic, right?

But all that caffeine was taking its toll. I rubbed my stomach
and popped another Tums. I had no idea how truckers and
Greyhound bus drivers were able to drive straight through. I was
exhausted. The fact that the trip was almost over was the only
thing keeping me from total collapse. Even Grundleshanks
looked like he could use some time on a stationary shelf instead
of a moving SUV.

* * *

Wisconsin was either freaking huge, or the freeway had
done some weird sidewinder thing, or I was lost. I slowed down
and eyeballed my map. Devil's Point looked like it was half an
inch away from Trinity Harbor. But I passed Trinity Harbor
about four hours ago. How could half an inch be taking this
long? I should have invested in a portable GPS. Although I

wondered if a GPS would even work, in the middle of nowhere.

I kept driving, looking around for some kind of a signpost, but there was nothing but trees.

Unending trees.

Followed by more trees.

Damn it. I should have just gotten the dang GPS. Especially after Lyra's check came in. Even if it only sporadically worked, it would still have been better than my map-reading skills.

When my cell phone rang, I jumped so hard I almost drove off the road.

Gus.

Gotta love his timing. I flipped the cell on, in speaker mode. "I think I found the woods where Hansel and Gretel died."

"They didn't die, they cooked the witch."

"You stick with your fairy tales, I'll stick with mine."

Gus laughed. "It can't be that bad. You're getting cell reception."

"Yay, me." The road turned to the left and dipped through a hollow. Up ahead, I could see hawks circling. "Whatever happened to commerce, industry and civilization completely assimilating the wild spaces?"

"Not everywhere is L.A., Toto. In every life a little wilderness must fall."

"Which is normally defined by a stretch of road without any Starbucks. Not this unending nature crap."

"Urban witches." Gus snorted.

"All I'm sayin', is I like my jungles with a little bit of neon."

"You're the only person in the entire country who misses concrete. Repeat after me. Trees are a good thing. Woods, trees, plants, lack of air pollution."

I rolled my eyes. "Yes, I know. Trees help us breathe and shelter us from the sun. Yay, trees. Yay, mind-melding with dryads."

"That's better."

"But they don't offer zero percent interest with no payments for a year."

"Don't make me slap you."

I looked around. The forests were full of shadows. "I would

hate to get lost out here. Way too many places for a hockey-masked, chainsaw-wielding, serial killer to hide."

He sighed. "You obviously didn't get out of Hollywood soon enough. Now, knock it off before you corrupt my toad. Or I'll fly out there and take him back, for his own protection."

"Like that's a threat? If it gets you on a plane, I'll serenade Grundleshanks daily with *Odes to Strip Malls*." I glanced down at my gas gauge. A quarter of a tank. Thank the Gods I was driving a hybrid, or I'd be sweating finding a gas station. "Hey, Zed has been a lifesaver. I'm actually getting four hundred and twenty miles between fill-ups."

"You're welcome. Sally sends her regards."

"You better be taking care of my baby."

"If *'taking care of'* means selling on eBay, she's in great hands."

"Gus! Tell me you're kidding!" Just then, an eagle, large and majestic, glided over the treetops. "Holy crap, they have eagles out here. Man, that was cool."

"Go ahead, rub it in. Not bad enough I lose my best friend, but now I'm missing out on eagles."

"Awww, that's sweet. Am I your best friend?"

"I was talking about the toad."

"Bastard. I'll send you a photo."

"Screw the photo. I already have photos of Grundleshanks. Send me an eagle feather."

"I thought that was illegal."

"If you stumble across an eagle feather on the side of the road, you're not gonna pick it up?"

"Okay, well... You have a point. I'll see what I can do."

"Hey, you taking those vitamins and supplements I gave you?"

I sighed. "Yes, *dad*." And I had been. Religiously. Even though it was kind of a pain to keep track of what I was supposed to take when and I didn't know what half of them were supposed to be for. St. John's Wort, magnesium, vervain, melatonin, evening primrose, 5-HTP, CoQ10, cat's claw, DHEA, oregano oil, olive leaf, alpha-lipoic acid, carnitine, B3, B6, B12, blah, blah, blah. One of these days I was going to look them all up on the Internet, but until then, as long as they kept working, I would keep taking them.

*   *   *

An hour later, I drove up to a crossroads and spotted a sign indicating there was a store nearby. But the sign was hanging at a crazy angle and barely attached, so the direction of nearby was a bit foggy. Great. Well, any direction was better than just stalling out in the middle of nowhere, right?

Eeny, meeny, miney, mo.

I picked up my phone and speed-dialed Gus. "Hey, do me a favor and pick a direction. I'm trying to find human life forms."

"You're the one driving the car."

"Trust me, you have as much a chance of making the right decision as I do."

"You've gone soft. All right, let me grab a pendulum." There was a pause, then he was back. I could just see him in my mind's eye, swinging a pendulum over a map. "F*e fi fo fum, I smell the blood of an...* turn east."

"Great. Thanks." As we continued chatting, I turned right at the stop sign and drove down the road a bit. Sure enough, there it was. Big J's Trading Post. There was even an honest-to-goodness hitching post in front.

"Yee-haw. You're the best. Talk to you later. And don't sell Sally! Or I will haunt your dreams and drive you crazy."

After we hung up, I parked Zed. A trading post. I shook my head. I didn't think trading posts still existed, outside of Indian reservations in the Southwest. And I'd never been in one before. I slowly got out of the car. Ouch. I'd been driving so long, my legs were stiff and my feet felt like I stuffed my shoes with pebbles.

As I limped my way through the parking lot, it was like I was walking into a piece of living history. I ran my hand across the worn hitching post and opened my mind's eye:

I could see a row of horses tied up while their owners went inside to barter; smell the warm, musky scent of their hides and the well-worn leather of the saddles.

In front of the trading post, three oak steps, worn smooth down the center, led to the front door. As I matched my gym shoes to the grooves, I could feel a buzz from the energy that centuries of boot-clad feet had left behind.

I took a deep breath and opened the door, not quite sure of what I'd find on the other side, but ready to embrace the adventure.

CHAPTER NINETEEN

I HALF-EXPECTED SOME *Little House on the Prairie* scene, with a pinched-face Harriet Oleson behind the counter, hoarding sugar and taking chickens in trade for flour.

Instead, I found blaring rock music and a tall, lanky kid who looked like he was stumbling through his early twenties. Long, stringy, brown hair that could use an up-close and personal with a bottle of shampoo, a face pitted by a thousand lost battles against acne and a pervasive aroma of cigarette smoke and stale sweat.

When I approached the counter, he turned down the radio. His name was J.J., he said, introducing himself with a crooked-toothed, nicotine-stained grin. "Jarvis the Fourth. I'm Little J. My dad, Jarvis the Third, he's Big J."

I found myself liking J.J., despite his appearance and slightly ripe odor. If the rest of the people in Devil's Point were this friendly, I might actually enjoy living here. Even though I already missed Gus like crazy.

"This place seems a lot older than two generations."

"Well, yeah, dude. It's been in my family forever. We got us plenty of J's to go around. Before it was my dad's place, it was Grandpa John's. Before that, well, it goes all the way back to Great-Great-Great-Great-Grandpa Jarvis the First. We're like, the J-men."

I smiled and looked around at the store supplies. Camping equipment, sporting goods, vintage clothes, camouflage gear, hunting rifles, children's toys, freeze-dried rations. There was even a small food section. I was surprised to see a row of cast iron cauldrons, until it dawned on me that people also used them as camping cook-pots.

"Is there anything you don't carry?" I asked, glancing at the boxes of ammunition stacked behind the counter. Charlton Heston would have loved this place. I could just picture him waiving his rifle at reporters.

"Lots of stuff. Mostly we do a lot of trade-ins, second-hand stuff. One man's junk is our bucket of gold. It's all about recycling, North Woods style." He made a dismissive gesture and I noticed that his nails were bitten down to the quick and his fingers were stained the same color as his teeth.

"Well, I'm just glad I found you. I was starting to think I was in the Twilight Zone," I smiled, mentally nudging him to tell me more while I put on a flirty facade. Not that I was actually interested in him. But J.J. seemed harmless enough and I was definitely keen on getting the scoop on my new hometown. When it came to asking for information, a little bit of flirty could go a long way.

He smiled back, warming up. "Nah, we're real enough. In a pain-in-the-ass, out-the-way, bad-teeth kind of way. At least, that's what the city folk say when they get lost up here."

"Well that seems rude."

"City folk wouldn't be city folk if they weren't rude. It's either that or they're all gushing about our quaintness. Like we're some kind of weird, old-fashioned, zoo exhibit."

I laughed. "You like living up here?"

He shrugged. "It's okay."

"That doesn't sound like a ringing endorsement."

"Dude, whadda you want from me? If you're down with boring, it's a totally righteous place to live." He leaned on the counter and flashed another gap-toothed smile at me. "We got a penny candy store, a diner that serves homemade meals, a librarian who remembers what you like and sets books aside for you. The schools are safe, the teachers are strict and the principal gets his house TP'ed every Halloween."

"Please tell me that's not the height of fun around here."

"We're not that backwoods. We got an arcade where the games are a quarter and a movie theater that shows double features for a dollar. It's Homage to 1939 this week. Wizard of Oz and Some Like It Hot." He leaned forward and lowered his voice. "We also got some righteous skunk weed growing in the woods, if you know where to look," he said, winking.

I laughed again. "I'm sure the cops love that."

"Every now and then, they'll pull up a plant and the paper will run a story on their big drug bust. Usually they just leave it alone. It's not like it belongs to anybody specific. Besides," his eyes twinkled, "The sheriff's uncle has glaucoma and he likes a toke now and then. So bustin' us would be kinda hypocritical."

"Sounds like a pretty laid back place to live."

"Mostly. But we got us our crazies up here too."

A customer walked in and while J.J. finished ringing him up, I picked up a copy of the local newspaper. It was pretty thin. Mainly social stuff, syndicated columnists, cartoons and opinion pieces. Although it looked like two farmers were getting all heated up about the ownership of a prize-winning cow.

"You guys have any festivals or craft fairs or anything like that?"

"Depends on the time of year. It's all seasonal. We're havin' our Harvest Fest next month. We also have a happenin' antiques row, if you're into that kinda thing. You here on a visit?"

"Nope. I'm moving in. 345 Oldway Lane." I said, putting the paper back on the stack. "You have any idea how to get there from here?"

"Aw, dude, the witch house? Everyone knows that place." He lit up a cigarette and I shifted to get out of the path of the smoke. "You don't look like no witch to me. Way too young and cool-looking."

"Thanks," I coughed and quickly tried to change the subject. "Why's it called the witch house?"

" 'Cause that's what it is, dude. Lotsa stories about that place. It seemed to like old Tillie though. She lived there forever. Until it decided to kill her."

"That's ridiculous." I said, but my voice wavered. I took a breath and tried to sound sure of myself. "Houses don't kill people, people kill people."

"Whatever. Wait until you actually move in. Then tell me it's not a crazy killer cottage."

Another noxious cloud of nicotine wafted towards me and I

coughed again. "You know, those things'll do you in faster than any cottage."

"That's what they say now. Ten years from now, they're gonna say a cigarette a day will keep the doctor away. Just like butter. They said butter and bacon and eggs was evil, but now they found out that fat is our friend."

But when I coughed again, he put the cigarette out. "Thanks," I smiled at him and took a deep breath of toxin-free air.

"So how'd you get hosed with it?"

"What, the cottage?" Well, there was no way I could tell him the truth. Somehow, I didn't think saying I did a ritual to get a house, the cottage heard me and decided to off Aunt Tillie would endear me to anyone. Even though that wasn't Gus's take on it. His version was that Aunt Tillie was nearing the end of her thread, so the cottage reached out to see who the next owner was going to be and I was just psychic enough to feel it. Hopefully, he was right. Because I liked his version much better.

"Tillie was my Aunt. Technically, Great-Aunt."

"That explains it. Next of kin and all." J.J. looked me up and down. "You'd be better off just forgettin' about it. Check into the B&B, have a little vacation away from the city, buy an antique, then turn around and go back home. Life's too short."

"I can't forget about a house. That's kind of impractical, don't you think? I mean, even if it's a nightmare, I can sell it." At least, that was my plan. Go, face my fears by spending a few nights in the cottage, fix it up and put it on the market. Then use the money to go back to Los Angeles.

"Not in this town, you can't." He laughed. "Trust me. It ain't worth it. No one'll buy it and you can't burn it down neither."

So not what I wanted to hear. "Why not?" I asked, wondering if the cottage was unsellable because it was a featured player in other peoples' nightmares. Or if it had a history of owners dying tragically. Maybe it was infested with termites. What if it was a white elephant built on a toxic waste dump?

"The cottage won't let ya. My Great-Great-Great-Grand-daddy tried to light it on fire one night and it turned him into a tree. Swear to God."

Well, that was an answer I wasn't expecting. I gave J.J. a sideways look.

"Seriously," he said, pointing to a faded picture above the register, of a nattily dressed, middle-aged man wearing a bow tie and an eye-patch.

"Wow, he's quite a looker." I said, fascinated. "Bet he had an interesting life."

"He was stylin', he was. Old 'One-Eyed' Jack Wilbur. He was on the cutting edge. Until he became a tree."

"Get out," I laughed. J.J. had to be pulling my leg. Either that, or he'd done one acid trip too many. "There's no such thing as a man-tree."

"Yeah? Well, when you find roots growing out of your heels, I'll send someone to water you."

"Forget water, send a documentary crew. If I turn into a tree, I want it on camera." If my fears about the cottage sounded as ridiculous as J.J.'s, no wonder Gus thought I was being an idiot. "So, how do I get to this vengeful, yet ecologically-proactive, witch house?"

"Hold on," he took out a piece of paper and drew a map for me. "You sure you want to do this, dude?"

I smiled. "I think I can handle a bad-tempered house," I reassured him. And for the first time, I actually believed it.

He shook his head, clicking his tongue against his teeth.

"Besides, I kinda like trees. In moderation." I said, thinking of Gus. "They're not as good as a Coffee Bean, but they're better than a strip mall."

He shrugged. "Your funeral," he said and handed me the makeshift map. I raised an eyebrow at him and he put his hands up in surrender. "Hey, it's all good. You've got it now and Tillie can finally rest in peace. Everything's totally righteous."

Before I left, I wound up buying some emergency equipment—first aid kit, flashlight, a map of the area, that kind of thing. I eyeballed the guns and ammo a few times. I mean, what if some rabid wild animal broke into the cottage? Eventually, I brushed the thought aside. I'd probably just wind up shooting myself anyway.

I spent a few more minutes chatting with J.J., but when another customer came in, I took advantage of the opportunity and left. If I hurried, I could take a quick tour of my new hometown and still be at my infamous cottage before sundown.

CHAPTER TWENTY

IT DIDN'T TAKE ME long to drive through Devil's Point. There was a small shopping district that included a mom and pop grocery store, an antique store, an old-fashioned diner, the movie theater J.J. had mentioned and a bookstore. There was also a mechanic's shop that was right out of the fifties, with a gas pump out front and vintage automobiles for sale, a hardware store, a thrift store and a bait-and-tackle shop. It really was an adorable, old-fashioned slice of Americana, preserved in time.

As I kept driving, I found the school, library, post office, church and town hall along with a medical center, funeral home and the town cemetery. And set back in a little picturesque clearing, was a grand old house with a sign proclaiming *Auntie Mae's B & B*.

According to J.J., if you were looking for any more action than that (or any action at all after sun-down, it seemed), the three-hour drive to Trinity Harbor was where you'd find it. Although, he'd said, winking at me, if you drove the way nature demanded and ignored the pesky road signs, you could make it in two.

"But that's like, insanely far away. What if it's an emergency?"

"We got the LifeQuest chopper. And Roy, over at Oldfield, runs a year-round chopper service for people who just want to party. Fifteen dollars a head. Comes in handy in the winters." He glanced out the store window at the parking area. "Good thing you've got an SUV. If you're planning on stayin', you might want to invest in a horse and a sleigh. Or ice skates and skis. The winters are a bitch. The roads here are nothin' but ice and snow."

* * *

After my tour of Devil's Point, I headed over to Oldfield. Besides the airfield, they had a gas station with a mini-mart. I pulled into it, gassed up, and settled my nerves with a chocolate bar and a soda. But when I offered Grundleshanks the carb-laden, chocolaty bit of heaven, he turned his toady face away, in a silent lecture on the protein benefits of crickets.

The threat of impending sunset finally made me stop procrastinating. As I got behind the wheel, I unbuttoned the top of my jeans. Ah, well. The toad might have a point. If my jeans got any tighter, I wouldn't be able to breathe. I sighed and tossed the rest of the candy bar out of the car window, into the station's trash bin.

It was time to check out this mysterious cottage, even if it meant risking life and limb to become a tree. Besides, I should probably see it while there was still some daylight left, before my imagination could imbue the cottage with any additional devilish powers.

I couldn't help grinning though, every time I thought about the cottage. Seriously. How cool was that? A witchy cottage turning a wannabe arsonist into a tree? A cottage that ecologically proactive couldn't be evil.

In fact, the more I thought about it, the more I thought it was a great idea. Turning felons into trees would certainly make for prettier scenery than cement block prison buildings and razor-sharp, barbed wire-topped enclosures. And the prison over-population problem would be a thing of the past. I'd bet there were prisoners who would even prefer being trees, to being caged humans.

Cheered by the thought and feeling a little bit better about my possibly sentient cottage, I turned down Route 41 and headed to my new home.

As I got closer though, I was hit by such a strong sense of *déjà vu*, I had to pull off onto the shoulder of the road.

I got out of the SUV to look around. The every day noise of the woods—singing birds, buzzing insects, small noises in the underbrush—did their best to reassure me, but something was making my blood run cold. I walked up beyond the bend and found a massive, lighting-blasted oak tree next to the road.

Suddenly, realization hit.

This was the same road I had seen in my dream, the same road Aunt Tillie had crashed on. Goose pimples raced across my flesh and I shuddered. I wasn't going to need the map anymore. The path from this road to the cottage was seared into my mind.

*   *   *

I walked around the oak tree. It was centuries old and sturdy as a tanker, which is probably why it withstood the impact. The only damage seemed to be a large bite taken out of the bark on the southwest side.

I looked closer. There were bits of tree bark that were still dark with blood splatter.

A whisper went through my mind, nothing more than a sudden breeze, a wordless sigh.

Without really knowing why, I picked off a large piece of the bloodstained bark and put it in my pocket. I had no idea what I was about to walk into, but I had a feeling that having something with Aunt Tillie's blood on it might give me the leverage I needed to keep her cottage under control.

*   *   *

The sun was just starting to set behind the trees as I headed towards my new home. Despite the beauty and richness of the colors—the deep shades of pink, red and purple—I suddenly felt incredibly homesick for smog and a jagged line of mountains against the horizon. So I called Gus.

He picked up after three rings. "This better be good. I'm on a date."

"How the hell do you find dates so fast? It takes me months."

"My secret club. It's a whole, incestuous, underground network that we don't let you fag hags in on. A place for us who shine like a veritable sun to share our boy toys. And our Viagra."

"You, share? When did that happen? You barely share with me, whom you have a deep and abiding love for. How can you possibly share with strangers?"

"Unfortunately, missy, you're missing the requisite body part that would make me interested in sharing. It's all about recycling. Good for the earth, good for..."

"Okay, I got it. Spare me the visual."

He laughed. The sound cheered me up. Gus had an infectious laugh. "And your second-hand boy toy is okay with us talking about him like he's a used book?"

"He's not here. He's seeing a man about a horse."

"He got you to go to the equestrian center? He must be hot." Okay, in all fairness, I was distracted, so I was a bit slow on the uptake. But as soon as the words were out of my mouth, I gave myself a mental head slap.

Gus snorted. "Oh my Gods! Get with it, girl. You're gone from the city for a few days and you've already become a hick. What happened to your kitsch-o-meter? He's pointing Percy at the porcelain. Bleeding the lizard? Shaking hands with the Vicar?"

"Okay, okay. I get it. He's in the bathroom, so we only have a few minutes. That's fine, I'm almost at the cottage anyway." I filled him in as quickly as I could.

Gus hooted with laughter. "A man tree?! Oh, you so have to send me pictures."

"I know. How cool is that?" I pulled up in front of the cottage and my jaw dropped. "Holy crap!"

"What? Don't keep me in suspense!"

"It's here. Ol' One-Eyed Jack is a rowan tree." Maybe there was something to the old legend, after all.

"Are you kidding me?"

"No!" I couldn't believe it. Standing right in front of me, big as life, was an old rowan tree with a knothole where an eye would be, a smooth patch on the other side, a gnarled growth for a nose and a hollow for the mouth.

"If I add a bow tie, it will totally freak the kids out at Halloween." I took a picture on my cell phone and sent it to Gus. I could hear him chortling on the other end. "See what I mean?"

"You better not piss off that cottage. I am not flying all the way up there just to water you."

"Screw that," I said. "You're gonna fly out here, just 'cause you'll be jealous." Behind the rowan tree was a cottage that looked like it belonged in the pages of a fairy tale. "I can't believe every one avoids this place. It's incredible."

And it was. The cottage was adorable. Fading antique pink with cream-colored trim, riots of late-blooming roses and Old Jack the Rowan tree in the front yard. There was even a front porch with an old-fashioned swing. And no neighbors to get all up in your grill. Just plant life and trees.

And, best of all, I didn't have to pay any rent or any mortgage. It was mine, for the cost of upkeep. And given what I was able to save before I left L.A., and what was left of the money that Tillie had left in her estate, I actually had an eight-month cushion, for the first time in my life. And enough left over to start a retirement account. It was almost like I was turning into a responsible adult.

I briefly wondered if I had died and no one had told me. It just felt so weird to suddenly get everything you want. *Thank you, Aunt Tillie. And thank you to your lawyers for finding me.* Although, really, I guess thanking someone for dying was a bit morbid.

I know it sounds odd, but I was starting to enjoy this adventure. I was embarking on a whole new life, one that had a house and a savings account. I finally had the time and money to afford to figure out what I wanted to do with my life. I could even afford health insurance—well, at least until the money ran out. These were all luxuries I never had before.

* * *

Looking back, I should have heeded the warning signs and run in the opposite direction. But I had no idea what was about to happen. Even my dad's cryptic warning had managed to vanish from my head. For the first time, it seemed like the hard times were behind me, and everything that was ahead of me was bright, shiny and happy.

CHAPTER TWENTY-ONE

As I GOT OUT of the car, still talking to Gus, a movement in the upstairs window caught my eye. "What the..."

"What's going on?" his voice vibrated in my earpiece.

"I thought I saw someone in the attic window."

"Someone? Or something?"

"I don't know. I'm probably imagining it." I said, doubtfully. "It's just... I could have sworn there was a woman standing in the window."

"Lucky you. You have a cottage *and* a ghost."

I sighed, exasperated. "Most people don't actually get off on finding Casper in their homes."

"You're so antisocial. There are people all over the world who've had to kill to get a ghost and you're complaining about one you're getting for free?"

"Go figure."

He laughed. "It was probably just a cat."

I hesitated. "Do you really think so? Maybe you're right. Maybe it was a cat." Or maybe I was just imagining things. "Old ladies have cats, right? It's not like I'm moving into the Hellmouth, right?"

"Guess you'll have to go into the cottage and find out."

"Right." I paused at the stairs to the front porch.

"Well? What are you waiting for? Go introduce yourself and see what comes at you."

Like I was going to rush right in, for his entertainment.

"What if it is a ghost? What if it's my Aunt Tillie? What if she doesn't know she's dead? Ewww. That would be creepy. How am I supposed to tell her she's dead?"

He hooted with laughter. "Could you web-cam that heart-to-heart for me? Or keep me on speakerphone. I'd love to hear how you break the news."

"I'm being serious."

And with that, my phone died. Damn. I should have plugged it into the charger while I was driving.

I looked up at the window again. The breeze slightly ruffled the curtain, but there was no face. I probably imagined it. Aunt Tillie must have left the window open when she had gone out and since she never came back, there hadn't been anyone to close it.

Yeah, that's what it was.

At least, that's what I hoped it was.

I stopped, struck by a sudden thought. What if it was some backwoods killer waiting for me in the attic?

Sigh. That's the other problem with being a witch—a wildly overactive imagination.

* * *

I went back to the car, plugged the phone into the charger and picked up Grundleshanks's tank. "Man up, Grundleshanks. Time to go claim our cottage."

However, as we neared the front porch, I was hit with an unmistakable urge to turn back. I shook it off and kept walking forward.

But the closer we got, the colder it seemed to be getting.

By the time we got to the front door, I could see my breath every time I exhaled. "Cold. That's not a good sign. Cold's never a good sign."

Temperature drops tended to accompany ghostly visitations. So much for Gus's cat theory. I put Grundleshanks's tank on a patio chair and rubbed my stomach to get the knots out. Then I glanced at the toad. I could have sworn Grundleshanks was shaking his head at me. But whether he was telling me to stop being an idiot, or whether he was telling me to turn back while we still could, I had no idea.

I reached out with my 'sight' and felt the energy around the cottage. The protective wards around the place were so strong, they were almost palpable, like a vise around the cottage. No wonder the cottage had a reputation of protecting itself with magic. It probably did.

"Don't take this personally, Grundleshanks, but right now, I'm wishing Gus was here with me instead of you."

Grundleshanks blinked, giving me a slit-eyed toad look.

"But you definitely run a close second."

He settled back down in his mud, mollified.

Gus would be having orgasms over the thought of living in a haunted cottage. Me, not so much. But it was such a beautiful home—at least, from the outside. But then, when I put my hand on the doorknob, goose bumps raced down my arms. I let go of the doorknob, took a deep breath and... chickened out.

* * *

I detoured down off the porch and took a quick recon around the property. Might as well see it all while there was still light, right?

There was a large back yard, full of herbs and flowers. I took a deep breath, savoring the smells of basil and wild mint and night-blooming jasmine along with the heady musk of roses. There was a flowering apple tree, a cherry tree and a weeping willow. Everything was a bit overgrown, but it wasn't too bad. The grass was long and wet, the yard was littered with fallen apples and my shoes were getting soaked, but it was obvious that Tillie had kept the place up well while she was alive.

Further down the way, there was a boathouse and a wooden pier that stretched out into a lake. At the end of the pier was a wooden platform with a heavy, wooden Adirondack chair and a wooden block for a table.

The lake was so peaceful. And beautiful. And teeming with life. There was a family of ducks waddling out of the water and back to their nest. A pair of loons glided effortlessly across the lake's surface. Then an eagle swooped down, majestic in the dying light, and grabbed a fish its powerful talons.

Unfortunately, I was running out of daylight. It was *do or die* time. So I took a deep breath and turned back to the cottage. As the sky got darker, I kicked myself in the mental keister for my procrastination. At this rate, I was going to be unloading Zed by flashlight. Assuming I could dig up enough courage to actually go inside.

I took a deep breath, fished the cottage keys out of my pocket, then climbed the stairs again, to the front porch.

"I come in peace," I announced to the cottage, feeling slightly foolish.

This time, the temperature stayed steady. No sudden dips. Whatever had been here earlier had, apparently, vacated the premises.

But when I inserted the key into the lock, the door swung open on its own.

As if the cottage had been waiting for me to arrive.

* * *

"Hello?" I said, cautiously. "Is anyone in here?"

Silence.

I slowly walked in, clutching Grundleshanks's tank.

The inside smelled musty. The furniture had accumulated a light coating of dust and cobwebs since Tillie's passing but, all in all, it really wasn't bad. I sent a quick prayer up to the Gods and tried a light switch. The ceiling bulbs flipped on, flooding the room with cheer. Thank goodness the electric company had activated my account. As I walked through the cottage, I turned on every light I could find.

The kitchen was an old-fashioned, good-sized room. There was a table and chairs tucked into a charming alcove with oversize windows. It was so different from the laughably small mini-kitchenette I had gotten used to in Los Angeles. The living room was gorgeous, with a fireplace, a large bay window and a built-in window seat. Down the hall was a library, with floor-to-ceiling bookshelves built into the walls, a standing harp and a small piano. There was even a full bathroom on the first floor.

My heart soared. A good house cleaning, a few weeks of weeding and this place was going to be phenomenal. Gus was right. He was probably right about everything. I couldn't believe I was so wrapped up in the world of my nightmares that I was ready to pass the cottage up, sight unseen.

That was the other problem with being a witch. Sometimes things that look like impending death, just mean impending change. The death of the old and the start of something new.

Nothing to be worried about at all.

* * *

I installed the toad in the living room, on an end table. "Well, Grundleshanks, it looks like we're home."

He blinked in agreement.

"I suppose I should unpack, huh?" I looked at him, waiting for an excuse on why I should put it off, but all I got was silence.

"Feel like lending me a hand?"

Not even a blink.

"Next time Gus wants to give me a familiar, I'm gonna push for a Sherpa. Everyone should have a Sherpa."

Grundleshanks sank down into his mud so that not even his eyes were visible.

"Oh, come on. Don't sulk. I'm sure you'd make a great Sherpa, if you were about five feet taller and could walk upright." I tapped on his tank, but he ignored me.

Well, he obviously wasn't in the mood to be social. So I left him alone and climbed the stairs to see what was on the second floor.

* * *

The master bedroom had an attached bathroom with a huge Jacuzzi tub. Tillie certainly knew how to live. Although, I doubted the cottage was originally built in this condition. So it must have been okay with being remodeled and updated, having floors added on to it, just not destroyed.

Across the hall was a guest bedroom, if I ever had the desire to be social. Or if I could talk Gus into a visit. And down the hall was a sweet, little room that would make a great temple space. It looked like Tillie used it as her sewing room. At the end of the hall, there was a stairway leading up to an odd-shaped door. That must be the attic. I tried the door but it was locked and none of the keys I had fit the lock. I would have to track down the key to it later.

This was so worth leaving California for, with its overpriced real estate and bottomed-out job market. Best of all, I'd been through the entire place and there was no sign of a ghost.

As I went back downstairs, I opened the windows to air out

the smell of neglect. I could already feel my spirits soar and my lungs breathing easier. I sent up a quick prayer of thanks to Aunt Tillie for leaving me the place. I felt like I was queen of the world.

Until I walked into the kitchen and noticed a small, dingy, wooden door. Probably to the cellar. This one, at least, had an old, iron skeleton key in the lock. But when I put my hand on the key, a cold wave of darkness washed through me.

The entrance to a hungry tomb...

I slowly backed away, wiping my hand on my jeans.

CHAPTER TWENTY-TWO

WHILE I'VE ALWAYS HATED underground rooms, I needed to get a grip. I couldn't start wigging out. I had a lot to do and there was no one I could call to come over and hang out with me to keep me sane.

"You can wait 'til morning, too." I told the door. I'd wait and check the cellar out tomorrow, when everything was cheery and warm and sunny. Or maybe I'd wait until I could get a bottle of holy water from the local church.

I shook my head and walked out of the kitchen. There were times I really hated living on my own. At least, back in Los Angeles, I could have called Gus to come over. Out here, it was just me and my toad. With a sigh, I trekked out to Zed and began transferring all my crap into the cottage.

* * *

As I hauled the last of my boxes into the foyer, I was grateful I had sold off my furniture. Not only would they have been an unnecessary encumbrance, but my thrift store rejects would have clashed with the charming decor and antique furniture Tillie had so lovingly put together.

I had thought Gus was silly, labeling my boxes. It's not like I had that many. But right now, I was grateful. It made unpacking so much easier. I separated out a box of occult books and schlepped them to the library/music room. Some of the bookshelves just held knick-knacks and photos, which seemed astounding to me. How can you have so much gorgeous bookshelf space and not fill every inch with books? A little rearranging and there'd be room for all of my most treasured tomes.

I hummed as I browsed through the books on the shelves. Mostly classics. The Brothers Grimm and Mother Goose and Shakespeare and all the authors I was supposed to have read in high school. There were also a large number of mythology and folklore books.

The more I explored, the more I started vibrating with happiness. Not many people are as addicted to books as I am, and to stumble across such a treasure trove... I mentally thanked Tillie again. She was obviously a woman of taste. And I loved that there was a standing harp and a small Steinway piano in the library. I ran a finger over the harp strings and the notes twinkled through the air. Everything was just magnificent.

* * *

One of the things that amazed me most, when I arrived at Devil's Point, was that I suddenly felt more capable than I ever had before. Without Gus or my Dad or Lenny to fall back on, it was all falling on my shoulders. So I could either freak out and run, or man up and face life head-on. And while there are times when facing life head-on can be vastly over-rated, what other option is there?

By the time I finished unpacking, I was exhausted and the accumulated road grime and sweat was driving me crazy. After a quick shower to wash the worst of it off, I filled the Jacuzzi tub and sat, letting the jets of warm water work their magic on my tired body. I felt guilty about the waste of water, taking a bath after a shower, but my body sure appreciated it.

When I started nodding off, I figured it was time to get out. I dried off and ransacked Tillie's bathroom cabinets, looking for something to ease aching muscles. It didn't take me long to score an economy-sized tube of Ben Gay. As I rubbed it on my back and shoulders, I reveled in the familiar pepperminty scent and warm, tingly feeling slowly spreading across my skin. I loved that smell. It reminded me of when I was a little girl and my dad was still alive. He would take me horseback riding whenever we had extra money and the next day, we would both be slathering on Ben Gay. I never was a very athletic child.

My stomach loudly reminded me that, now that I was all

clean and relaxed, it was in need of sustenance. The emergency road rations were great and all, but it could do with some real food. That's when I remembered I had forgotten buy groceries. I'd have to get on that, first thing in the morning. In the meantime, I pulled on a pair of baggy sweats and a long-sleeved tee-shirt, and went off to the kitchen, in search of any nosh Aunt Tillie had left behind.

There wasn't much in the way of food—Aunt Tillie must have eaten like a bird—but there was a veritable cornucopia of teas in the kitchen cupboard, so I put a kettle on to boil. Moroccan Mint sounded promising. I also came across a slightly stale package of Stella Doro's. Not exactly health food, but better than nothing. Best of all though, I found a mudroom off the kitchen that had a washer and dryer. And they didn't need to have any quarters inserted, to work.

*   *   *

I sat at the table in the alcove, sipping a mug of steaming hot tea and listening to the sounds of the evening. Waves lapping against the shore, wind rustling through the leaves, the haunting wail of a loon. Even the soft hooting of an owl. Just outside the window screens, thousands of crickets fiddled their insistent song, adding to the symphony. It was so lovely and peaceful.

As the night progressed and the temperature dropped, I was loathe to close the windows and shut out my private night music. So I walked to the front room to retrieve an afghan throw I had seen neatly folded on the couch.

*   *   *

It was incredibly cold in the living room. Even colder than in the kitchen. I was going to have to close windows or risk turning into a human popsicle.

As I walked through the room, I thought I saw a movement out of the corner of my eye. I froze and tried to look as non-threatening as possible.

There was a shadowy figure sitting on the rocking chair.

Great. My first night and I had spirit contact. Gus would be on the next plane out.

I reached out with my mind and felt the energy.

Whatever it was, it didn't feel malevolent.

At least, I didn't think it did.

So I took the initiative. "Hello? Can I help you?"

It didn't say anything.

I eyed the afghan longingly. "It's getting cold outside."

Still the figure didn't say anything.

It just sat there, the chair creaking, as it rocked back and forth.

CHAPTER TWENTY-THREE

"AUNT TILLIE?" I ASKED. Well, it was a reasonable guess, given that she was the most recent deceased occupant. "I know you're here. I can see you."

A cloud passed over the moon and the transparent figure slowly solidified into an old woman with granny glasses. "For heaven's sake, child. Get a wrap around you before you freeze to death."

It *was* Aunt Tillie. I moved slowly, smoothly, not wanting to frighten her and quietly wrapped the throw around my shoulders. But when I sat down on the couch, a big poof of dust made me sneeze.

I looked up, expecting the sudden noise to have frightened her away, but she was still there, giving me the hairy eyeball. As much as ghosts can, at least. Not what I was expecting, at all. I couldn't help staring at Aunt Tillie's face. It seemed so alive. Last time I had seen it, it had been twisted into a mask of horror and shock. And she still had both eyes, unlike her corpse.

"I see not much housecleaning has been going on since my passing," she sniffed, offended by the state of her cottage.

"I just got here." I protested. "This place is gorgeous, by the way. You took great care of it."

She seemed slightly mollified at that. "Of course, dear. It's my home."

"Was. It *was* your home."

She gave me a narrow-eyed look that should have shut me up, if I had any sense.

But I was so tired, my mouth just kept babbling on without

me. "I mean, I'm okay with sharing, but it's my home now. You died and left it to me."

If looks could singe, my hair would have burst into flames. But what the heck. Best to make the living situation clear up front, right? Rather than get into a fight about who had the right to live where.

"Things are not always what they seem," she said, her voice ice-cold.

I swallowed hard. I hated cryptic messages. Although they seem to be ubiquitous in the witchy world. *You have what you hold. Eyes to see, ears to hear. If you're meant to know, you will.* That kind of stuff always drove me crazy. At least Aunt Tillie didn't seem to be confused about her current state of non-being. Which made me wonder why she was still hanging around.

"Aren't you supposed to have crossed over?" I asked. "Not that I don't appreciate you being here, but don't you have some kind of time limit?"

"I've been waiting for you." She explained, as if that answered everything.

"Okay. Well, I'm here now." I said, not sure of what I should say next. I mean, would she be insulted if I wished her happy trails and held open the door? How do you encourage a spirit to move on?

"You were never meant to be here. You need to leave. It's the only way to save yourself," she said, interrupting my train of thought.

"Then why did you leave me the house in your will?"

"I didn't. I don't know how your name appeared on my will, but it wasn't by my hand. And if that doesn't convince you to leave, I don't know what will."

"I can't." I protested. "I don't have anyplace else left to go."

Tillie glared at me, annoyed. "Oh, for heaven's sake, girl. You're supposed to be able to look into the future. Can't you see what's waiting for you if you stay? What kind of half-assed witch are you? Your mother, bless her soul, gave you up to ensure this place would never find you."

"So I keep hearing. And yet, here I am."

"All the more reason you need to leave."

I shook my head. I was so tired of having this debate—

albeit it had mostly been with myself. But after all the soul searching and second-guessing I had been doing, it kind of irked me to have to rehash it all with my dead aunt.

"If my mother really wanted to help me, maybe she should have stuck around and raised me, trained me. So I'd know what the hell I was doing, instead of having to play my whole life by ear. Besides, what if I was meant to be here, all along? What if it's my fate?"

"Of course it's your fate, you idiot girl. That's why you have to fight against it. The entire point of being a witch, is so you have a fighting chance to overcome your fate." She glared at me and continued. "For being such a lousy witch, you're much too stubborn for your own good."

"And you should appreciate that." I snapped back at her. "If I wasn't, do you think I'd be sitting here, talking to a ghost? Most people freak out about things like this."

"I suppose you're right." Tillie rocked back and forth, considering what I had said. "Heaven help you, if you're the one the Devil's been waiting for." She seemed to have some kind of dialogue going on in her head, because then she went on: "Hmph. I can see the mark on you, clear as day. Just like your mother, with twice the pig-headedness." She leaned towards me. "You have the gifts but you're too undisciplined to use them properly. Which makes you useless. Worse than useless. Dangerous. To yourself and everyone around you."

"Hey! You can't go making assumptions. You don't know anything about me."

"I don't need to. Just look at what you set in motion. If it wasn't for you jumping up and down, waving flags and alerting the Otherworld of your existence, do you think I'd be dead?"

"That's not fair," I said in a small voice, swallowing hard.

"You just had to shine a light on where you were. Once they found you, I was an obstacle to be gotten rid of. If you don't want the Devil to take you as his due, you need to leave. Before it's too late."

"But I can't just go. That's impractical." I said. But my heart wasn't in it. What if she was right and I had just been making a series of huge mistakes? But what options did I have, really? "Besides, if this Devil of yours already knows who I am and where I am, won't he find me, no matter where I go?"

She started to fade. "Don't force me to do what your mother didn't have the stomach for."

I scowled at her now-translucent form. Before I could say anything, the moon came out of its cloud cover and Aunt Tillie vanished.

"Aunt Tillie, wait! Get back here! Did you just threaten me?" I looked around the room, but she was well and truly gone. "Damn ghosts. Do you get classes in how to be cryptic along with your after-death dose of ectoplasm?!"

But there was no answer. The room was almost sepulchral in its silence. I snuggled into the afghan and thought about what Aunt Tillie had said. Was I being stupid, ignoring a warning from the other side? Was leaving really even an option? Or was it already too late? I had a feeling, whatever was about to happen, I was already committed to the ride.

I closed my eyes and tried to push my sight out into the future, to see what I was letting myself in for, if I stayed. But it was like someone had stuck baffles around my head. All I could hear was my own breathing, all I could see was darkness.

I was so used to relying on my 'sight' whenever I needed it, I felt lost with it on the fritz. I had no idea how normal humans lived their lives without a sixth sense and I didn't want to find out. It must be an awfully lonely life, being confined to the here and now, with only yourself to talk to. So I kept my eyes closed and said a quick prayer up to the Gods that my sight would be restored by morning.

* * *

At some point, I must have fallen asleep. When the wind grabbed onto an empty trashcan and sent it clattering against a tree, the noise shocked me awake. I opened my eyes and looked around, disoriented. I thought I was in the living room, wrapped in an afghan, but I wasn't. I was sitting in the kitchen, freezing, my arms wrapped around my body, my tea ice cold.

What the hell? Had the entire conversation with Aunt Tillie had been in dreamtime? It had felt so real. I was sure it had been a spirit visit. I mean, all the details were there, including the drastic temperature drop. Although, as I looked around, I noticed that all the windows were open and it was pretty effin' cold outside.

I had probably fallen asleep and Aunt Tillie used my dream to send me a message. It was easier for spirits to do that, than it was to generate physical manifestations. And it explained why Aunt Tillie was able to generate such a solid, three-dimensional physical presence so soon after her death.

I quickly ran around, shivering, and closed all the windows. I wonder what she meant by the Devil was waiting to take me as his due?

"If you want to give me a decent warning, scare me off proper, a few more details would help," I announced to the cottage in general. "I'm not a novice at this, ya know. You can't just rattle my chain with vague threats and get results."

But the cottage was quiet. I sighed and looked up at the clock. I should call Gus. Ghost or dream, he would still be psyched to hear about Aunt Tillie. I looked in my purse for my cell phone, but then I remembered it was back in the SUV, charging. And it was pretty damn dark outside. Hell with it. He was on a date anyway. I'd call him tomorrow.

After I locked the house up tight for the night, I figured out an escape route in case I needed a quick getaway. Not that I was paranoid or anything, but it was good to keep your options open. Especially when you're spending the night in a haunted cottage. I also checked the landline, in case I needed to call an ambulance or the cops, but it hadn't been hooked up yet. *Crap.*

I have to say, as much as I loved the house and the property, this whole *'living alone in the woods'* thing didn't quite live up to the PR. On TV, you see women all the time, moving to the middle of nowhere, starting their lives over, finding a hunky neighbor to be their new love interest. All I had was a freeloading toad, a pissed-off ghost, and a possibly homicidal cottage.

A chilling thought butted up against my consciousness, unbidden: *I could die here tonight and no one would know.*

Then I wondered if wild animals would break in to snack on my body. Gus would be pissed. Especially with all the gross post-mortem scenarios he'd been plotting out. I sighed. I really needed to find someone to be in my life, whose focus was based entirely on me staying alive. For as long and as happily as possible.

CHAPTER TWENTY-FOUR

AS THE WIND PICKED up, I double-checked that the window shutters were all fastened. Maybe I should get the cell phone out of the car. What if there was an emergency in the middle of the night? What if a freak tornado leveled the place?

And then something thumped against the side of the house. Loudly.

And thumped again.

Probably a broken tree branch. At least, that's what I told myself.

If I was wrong, I didn't want to know about it. Besides, if a twister hit, I knew where the door to the creepy basement was. I'd just have to man up and use it.

There was another thud and the house shook.

Yeesh. Did I really want to go out there? What if there were bears? That would suck, if I went out to get the cell phone and got eaten by a bear. Screw it. I'd get the phone in the morning. Right now was hiding under the covers time. But, just in case, I decided to sleep with my keys under my pillow. That way, I could sprint out to the SUV and take off in a hurry, if I had to.

I ran upstairs to the bedroom, fighting off a yawn. It had been a long day. But before I went to bed, I climbed onto the window seat, opened the shutter and looked out. The night sky was incredibly clear. Hundreds of stars were visible: bright points of light on a giant, celestial web. It was astonishing. I'd never seen anything like it in Los Angeles. Between the lights and the smog, we get about ten stars total. Unless you counted Harrison Ford or Richard Gere. And they didn't even live in L.A.

I could totally imagine sitting here on quiet evenings,

watching the sunset over the lake, the sky transitioning from multi-colored hues into this dark, bejeweled splendor. The only thing that would make it better would be if I could move the place—property and everything—back to Los Angeles. But, until then, I decided I damn well wasn't giving it up without a fight.

As I watched, a storm cloud moved in and blocked out the stars. There was a low rumble and lightning lit up the underside of the cloud. After a few flashes, a lightning bolt struck somewhere over the lake, shaking the cottage.

I slammed the shutter closed and fastened it. I thought about warding the space, but I was just too tired to do it properly.

So I offered up a quick prayer to the Goddess. *"By your grace, keep me safe in this place. So mote it be."*

I tossed my pillows on the bed and curled up on top of the bed comforter for a few minutes, my travel blanket draped over me. I wanted to lie there and think for a minute. But the last thought I had, before falling asleep, was that this was a dead women's bed. It gave me the shivers. But somewhere between being creeped out and actually getting up and moving into the guest room, I lost consciousness for the night.

* * *

The next morning, a terrible itching woke me up. My skin had swollen to the bursting point and there were lumps all over my body. I jumped off the bed and looked in the dresser mirror.

I looked like some alien freak. My skin was red and inflamed, and I was head to foot covered in bumps. Between the itching and the pain, it was driving me mad.

I quickly dressed, jumped in the SUV and made a beeline to the local doctor's office. By the time I got there, I was so swollen, I could barely move. I wondered how much my tissues could possibly swell before bursting through my skin.

"I feel like Violet on Charlie and the Chocolate Factory, when she turns into a giant blueberry. Do you have a juicing room you can take me to, before I explode?"

The Doc, a kindly old man who looked like he was blind without his glasses, tut-tutted over my condition. "Nope. No Oompa-Loompas, either." He shook his head and scratched the side of his nose. "Looks like you have a nasty allergy."

"To what?! Devil's Point? Or my Aunt's cottage?"

"Spiders. An egg sac must have hatched in your bed. You're covered in spider bites."

"Just one egg?" I asked, looking at my now-alien skin.

"The smaller the spider, the more of 'em in the sac." He said, prepping a syringe.

Spiders. Great. As a witch, spiders are supposed to be my friends. But as a human being, I hated it when arachnids invaded my space. Outside was fine. Inside was off-limits. Although, being turned into a human spidey-snack was making me rethink my entire spider policy.

I silently cursed as the liquid fire from the doctor's syringe penetrated my flesh. But, after about twenty minutes, the swelling had gone down and the bumps were just red discolorations. Thank goodness for modern medicine.

After the doctor's office, I had lunch at the local diner and checked into Auntie Mae's B&B, so I could get a decent night's sleep and prepare myself to tackle the cottage the next day. Grundleshanks would be fine on his own. I had set him up with a breakfast feast of crickets before I left the cottage and he had plenty of mud and water.

* * *

Auntie Mae was a transplanted Irish woman who fussed over all of her guests and cooked wonderful, filling meals. She was generally wonderful. The next morning, I had come down too late for breakfast, but Auntie Mae was kind enough to go back into the kitchen and make me a piping hot meal of eggs, bacon, hash browns and pancakes. We had a pleasant chat as I ate, but when she found out I was the new owner of Tillie's cottage, she went cold.

Auntie Mae stopped talking as her plump fingers worked a dust rag anxiously and she cleaned an already spotless cabinet in the dining room. Finally, she blurted out: "I don't like to say bad about anything or anyone. But Devil House is what me mum used to call it. Evil place. Evil. Didn't hold no truck with nobody. Tillie, God rest her, was a good, God-fearing woman.

She spent most of her life in church, trying to set things right. And what thanks did she get? People say it was an accident, but I say that cottage killed her, it did."

I swallowed hard and sipped my coffee.

Auntie Mae waved the dust rag at me. "You get out, Missy, while you still can. I don't want to see no harm come to someone so young and pretty."

After promising her that I would be extra careful around the cottage, I checked out of the B&B and went shopping. Hardware store, grocery store, drug store. By the time I was done, I felt armed, rested and ready to tackle whatever other buggy surprises the cottage was hiding. But when I got home, the surprise that was actually waiting for me, knocked me on my ass.

CHAPTER TWENTY-FIVE

THE LIVING ROOM LOOKED like a battle zone. Chairs had been knocked over, the couch was on its back, lamps were on the floor.

Scrawled across the wall were the words *'Leave, Now!'* In black marker. Indelible black marker. Ugly, indelible black marker on my nice, beautiful wall. The only thing left in peace was the end table with Grundleshanks's tank.

I was so upset, I was shaking. Part of it was fear, but part of it was just anger. Was it Aunt Tillie? Or did some teenage pranksters sneak in while I was out? With the reputation this cottage had for retaliation, I found it hard to believe that it was local kids.

What if it was Aunt Tillie? What if she had figured out how to get in touch with her inner poltergeist? It was bad enough I'd let Mrs. Lasio drive me out of a home I loved, was I going to let a tantrum-throwing ghost drive me out of another one?

Damn ghosts. They think they can demand you to jump to their every whim. Just because they're dead. Like that should infer some special privilege.

I shook my fist at the sky. "There is no way I'm giving up this place to a bad-tempered, cryptic, know-it-all ghost. You're dead. I'm alive. I think it's time you move on to your new home and leave this one to me!"

Across the room, a fat, black Magic Marker rolled across the end table and bounced on the floor.

*   *   *

I stomped into the kitchen and paced around, inwardly

cussing at the lack of Jack Daniels. If there was ever a time I could have used a shot of Jack, it was now. Then I walked back into the living room and opened my spine and my third eye so I could 'see' around the entire room, maybe catch an energy signature, or see if any entities were still hanging out on the ethereal plane. It sounds weird, I know, but the whole 'opening the spine' thing isn't literal. It's a visualization, a method of tuning in to the edges of reality, or to alternate realities, where you can see the frequencies of the spirit world. You don't literally slice yourself open.

My skin got all prickly, reacting to the energy. Definitely strong, the room was practically vibrating, but whoever had been here was gone.

It *had* to be Aunt Tillie. But why would Aunt Tillie desecrate her house, when she was so capable of just nagging me to death in my dreams? Unless she wanted something concrete and scary to back up her threat, to show that she had learned to manipulate dimensional objects. And if that was the case, Aunt Tillie was the freakin' Einstein of ghosts.

The thing about ghosts, at least, in my limited experience with them, is that they don't automatically know everything and drop all their prejudices and peccadilloes once they die. Death is a process, like life. The way newborns have to learn how to manipulate their bodies and their physical environment, the newly dead also have to learn what they can and can't do. That's why it's infinitely easier for them to appear in dreams, than it is for them to vandalize your wall.

I cast my sight out through the house again. Along with Tillie's energy signature, there was something else...

Something darker and more malevolent...

But I couldn't quite place where it was coming from.

It was the same feeling I had in the kitchen, in front of the cellar door.

I wondered if that was the mysterious Devil that Tillie kept referring to? Was it an entity that lived in the cellar? Was it the cellar itself?

Damn it. I hated messing around with the spirit world. The problem in fighting with ghosts, is that they're not constrained by the laws of physics. And that automatically puts you at a disadvantage.

I pounded on my defaced wall. "No! Do you hear me? No!!! I'm not going anywhere."

I rubbed at the magic marker. It was dry.

"Couldn't you have used something that washed off?" I hollered. "Now I have to repaint the wall and it's not going to look as nice as it used to. And that's on you, Aunt Tillie."

I walked around the room, righting the furniture. "Next time you throw a fit, you'd better stick around to move the furniture back. Or I swear, I'm gonna trap your ectoplasmic ass in a brass vessel. Then you'll really have something to pitch a fit about!" I yelled, slamming a chair back into place.

In response, I heard a window shutter slam back and forth in the wind.

Okay, in all likelihood, I was probably talking to a ghost who was no longer listening. *Damn, damn, damn.* Gus would think this haunting was a hoot. And from the safety of two thousand miles away, it probably was. But it was kind of giving me the creeps.

Yes, I know, I'm a witch. I should be used to interacting with the unseen world. But late at night, when something goes bump, it doesn't matter if you're a witch or not. You'll still be hiding under the covers. Well, unless you're Gus. And then you'd probably throw a welcome party and set out a spirit plate. But I couldn't imagine anyone in this godforsaken town having the balls to party down with a ghost.

Although, that wasn't a bad idea. It might even get Aunt Tillie to lighten up a bit. Maybe after I cleaned up the mess in the living room and repainted the wall, I'd be calm enough to think about throwing some kind of party in her honor. But right now, I was too angry to make Aunt Tillie the ritualistic Dumb Supper that's usually served to the dead. Maybe later. When I no longer wanted to throttle her.

* * *

After I finished pitching my own fit, I got down to work, cleaning and vacuuming the entire house. Tomorrow, I'd have to go buy paint for the walls, but for today, I did as much as I could before I tackled my treacherous bedroom. I stripped the sheets off the bed and dropped them in the washer, then vacuumed every inch of the room and bed, flipping the mattress, so I could get both sides. By the time I was done, there wasn't a single cobweb or dust bunny or spider egg left.

After I was through, I called Gus and left him a message to ship me a case of Florida water and blue balls. As long as I was in a cleaning mode, I may as well cleanse the energy of the cottage as well as its interior.

There were fresh sheets in the linen cabinet, so I made the bed and, within seconds, I fell into a deep, dreamless sleep, exhausted. A sleep that didn't last anywhere near long enough.

* * *

Judging by the light in the room, it must have been close to dawn when I felt something touch my leg. I threw back the covers, terrified it was spiders, but the bed was full of snakes. Slithering, hissing, snakes.

I screamed and jumped to my feet. This country witch stuff was for the birds. Spiders, snakes, what was next?

I zigzagged to the closet, trying to keep from stepping on the snakes on floor. But when I opened the door to grab my shoes, I saw a huge mound of slithering, hissing snakes.

I slammed the closet door shut and clambered up on the window seat. There were snakes everywhere, slithering across the floor, across the bed. I opened the window and the shutters, to see if there was a way I could climb down the outside of the house.

The sun was just rising over the lake and the colors were breathtaking.

Wait a minute... sunrise?

Over the western portion of the lake?

Since when does the sun rise in the west?

This was a dream. This *had* to be a dream.

I jumped down from the window seat and the snakes were no longer on the floor. Written on the bed coverlet, in blood, were the words *'GET OUT!'*

"Fuck you, Aunt Tillie." I said. "I'm onto your game."

I got in bed, pulled the sheets up over my head and closed my eyes, trying to go back to where I had been before this creepy dream started.

* * *

When I opened my eyes again, the room was dark. The sheets were clean. No blood, no snakes, no spiders.

In the corner of the room, the figure of a woman glowed with an otherworldly light. She turned and walked towards me.

I looked at her face. It was so familiar and so strange, all at the same time.

I could feel tears streaming down my cheeks. "Mom?"

She sat on the edge of the bed and gently brushed away my tears. "Hush, baby. It's okay. I'm here now."

"I missed you." I was crying like an infant, but I didn't care. She got in bed with me and held me in her arms.

"I've always been with you, dear heart. Now listen to me. I don't have much time. Do not trust anyone or anything you see in this place. Everyone has their own agendas. Tillie will kill you before she'll let you help Lisette. Lisette will kill you if you don't help her. The danger for you is great. If you don't leave, you will have to face them all on your own."

"Who's Lisette?"

"Your great-great-great-great-grandmother."

"Is she the Devil that Tillie keeps mentioning?"

"One of them."

I leaned against her and she stroked my hair.

"Mom, do you think I should leave?"

"Yes." She was quiet for a second, listening to something only she could hear. "But it's too late. Lisette knows who you are now. She's watching you, plotting her move. You will have to face her sooner or later. Whether it's here or somewhere else." She kissed my cheek. "Trust no one. The danger is great, no matter what you do."

And then she vanished.

CHAPTER TWENTY-SIX

I GASPED AND SAT up. This time, I really was awake. No snakes, no sunrise in the West, (just to make sure, I looked out the window), and no mom.

Obviously, I had underestimated this place. And Aunt Tillie. I had no idea a ghost could invade your dreams and so thoroughly, totally screw with your reality. It made me wonder if the dreams I had about the cottage to begin with, weren't actually mine—or what I had fancifully assumed as the cottage looking for me—but had been planted in my subconscious by someone with an agenda.

I could ward the bedroom, to keep spirits out of it, but anything I did to ward the room against spirits would also interfere with my mom contacting me again.

So I paced and mulled it over. I couldn't actually guarantee that my mom would ever contact me again. But I was damn sure Aunt Tillie would screw with me again. And how long would it take before Lisette jumped into the mix? Mom or no mom, I needed to carve out a safe space for me to sleep, where I'd be protected from unseen entities and their agendas.

So I went downstairs, dug through my supplies, grabbed what I needed and headed back upstairs.

* * *

In the bedroom, I lit up a censor and dropped the tiniest bit of asafoetida on the glowing charcoal. I tried to hold my breath, as I made sure the smoke got in every crevice of the room.

"The good stay in and the bad stay out. By air and fire, I banish you from this space."

Man, the smell was nasty. Although nasty was an understatement. It smelled like sulfuric crap. No wonder it was called Devil's Dung. Even though I was trying to hold my breath, the smell was still making me nauseous.

I had to open the window before I gagged. The second I was done with the incense, I quickly doused the charcoal with water, dumped the nasty mess into the toilet and flushed it.

Then I mixed four glasses of water with salt and placed a horseshoe nail in each glass. I put one glass in the east, one in the south, one in the west and one in the north.

"By earth and water, I ward this space and cleanse and claim it as mine. Allow in only those I invite."

I picked up the sword I had made years ago, in a medieval weaponry class, and using a lancet on my finger, squeezed out a drop of blood and ran it down the blade. Then I swung the blade in a large, slow circle, around the room.

"By blood and iron this room is bound. So mote it be."

I felt the cottage shake and I heard a low boom as if I had crossed the sound barrier. Just in case, I checked to see if my heels were growing roots, but so far, I had no foliage on me anywhere.

"Guess my work here is done." I rested the sword next to the bed and finished washing the incense censor out in the attached bathroom.

I knew doing a warding that heavy was like using a canon to kill a rattlesnake, but I didn't want any more nights like I'd been having. I needed at least one safe place for me in this cottage.

I put fresh charcoals on the censor, lit them, and loaded the glowing charcoals with sweet-smelling frankincense. I was hoping the sweet, heavy frank would chase the aggressively noxious remnants of asafoetida out of the room. But after a few minutes, I had to leave. Even with the window open, the dueling smells were about to make me hurl.

I quickly raced around, opening all the upstairs windows in the cottage, before heading out to shop for paint. It was time to clean up after my spectral vandal. And, if I was lucky, all the smells would have aired out by the time I got back.

After I picked up a couple gallons of cream-colored latex

paint and supplies, I headed over to the Trading Post, to see if they had anything I might need. J.J. was working the counter again. Since I was the only one in the store, he followed me around, helping me out.

"So, how you liking that witch house?"

I hesitated. "It's... gorgeous. "

"But haunted, right? Was I right? I was right, wasn't I?"

I rolled my eyes. "Yeah, you were right."

"I knew it!" He pumped a victory fist into the air, pleased to get confirmation of his family legend. "See? I told you. Didn't I tell you?" He leaned forward to whisper to me. "There was even a book written about that house, like a ton of years ago. My Ma told me about it when I was a kid. Not many houses are so creepy, people wanna pay to read about them."

"Really? There's a book about my cottage? That's so cool. Is it still in print?"

"Hell if I know. Did you see the J-tree?"

"Seen him, watered him. He seems pretty happy. For a tree." I picked up a bottle of citronella and dumped it into the basket.

"I heard about that cottage my whole life. I always wanted to go check it out."

"Why didn't you?"

"No way. I don't want to be turned into no tree, taking root right next to my kin. I expect you'll be moseying on then."

"Oh, hell no. That cottage is mine. Any and all ghosts will have to take a back seat." I wasn't sure where this streak of bravado had come from, but I was feeling distinctly like Ripley in *Alien*. Or Sarah Connor in *Terminator*. *I am woman, hear me roar.*

"Ain't you ever seen any horror flicks?" J.J. asked. "People say crap like that, right before they get chopped up in little pieces."

I laughed. "Don't worry, J.J. No one's going to mulch me." At least, I hoped not.

Female roaring aside, I was starving. I'd been so busy dealing with the cottage, I hadn't stopped to eat. So I grabbed some beef jerky and pretzels to snack on in the car and a large chocolate milk. I was trying to stay away from high fructose corn syrup and trans fats, but they were ubiquitous. Even the milk had high fructose corn syrup. Oh, well. One bottle wasn't going to kill me.

I took my basket back from J.J. and handed him one of the big, black, cooking cauldrons, just in case I needed to put together something with more spellcrafting *oomph*. All I had brought with me from Los Angeles was my mom's small one. J.J. groaned under the weight as he put the cauldron on the counter.

"What kills snakes?" I asked, setting my basket on the counter next to the cauldron. Just in case my dream was actually a portent of things to come, I wanted to be prepared.

"Ferrets. They're nasty little things though. Mean tempered."

Couldn't be any worse than a room full of snakes. Snakes creeped me out almost as much as spiders. "Know where I can get one?"

"Pet shop."

"They're legal to keep as pets? They're not legal in California."

"Well that's just weird." He gave me a look, as if all Californians were mental.

"Don't give me that look. I don't know why they're not legal. I'm not responsible for California's weird pet laws."

"Maybe it's a smell thing. They can be kinda stinky."

I laughed. "Somehow, I don't think B.O. is illegal in California. If it was, a whole lotta people would be in trouble." Like half the pagan community. I'm all for back to nature, as long as it includes soap and deodorant. And clipping toenails. And regular visits to a dentist.

"In Hollyweird? I thought y'all were supposed to smell like money and gold." He took items out of the basket and started ringing me up.

I snorted. "Maybe in Beverly Hills."

Just then, a cute thirty-something guy walked in. Not my usual type—short hair, respectable looking, wire-rim glasses. Normally, (according to Gus, at least), the guys I go for look like drug dealers and thugs. But there was something about this guy. The thickness of his neck. The way his sweater caressed the muscles in his chest. The fit of his jeans.

My breath caught in my throat and my heart beat so loud it drowned out the sound of J.J.'s voice. I caught myself staring at the stranger, my mouth hanging open.

As he turned toward me, I quickly looked away. But as soon as he was out of earshot, I grabbed J.J.'s arm. "Who was that?"

"Who?"

"The guy who just walked in. Cripes, J.J., it's not like this store is full of people."

"Dudette! Like, I don't check out guys. I don't swing that way if you know what I'm sayin'. If you're looking for a date, the J-ster is at your service. Where would you like to go?"

"Sorry, I don't date smokers."

"Well that's not fair. I thought you California types were big on non-discrimination. It's that weird smell thing you people have, isn't it? Admit it. Y'all are smell snobs."

"J.J., focus!" I felt like shaking him. "Do you want me to keep watering Ol' Jack? Because he's looking like he could make a nice piece of furniture."

That got to him. He sighed. "Paul Raines. He's the new teacher over at the high school. Humanities or something."

"Really? So he just moved here too?"

"Oh, yeah. About three years ago."

"I thought you said he was the new teacher."

"He is. He's only been here three years. Have you seen how ancient the other teachers are? They've been here like, forever. Hatched out of eggs when dinosaurs roamed the earth."

"Somehow, I doubt that." I paid for my stuff. "Why do you think he moved here? It's not like this place is such a big tourist attraction."

"Hey, we're not that backwater."

I shot J.J. a look and he sighed. "Okay, yeah, you have a point. His family's from here. Guess he got lonely in the big city."

"Which city? Chicago? New York?"

J.J. looked at me like I had grown a third head. "No, dude. Trinity Harbor."

"Of course." I should have realized the term 'big city' was dependent on perspective. I snuck a look down an aisle and just glimpsed Paul's tush as he turned the corner. I thought about hanging around until he cashed out, but that was just too high school for words. A place this small—I was pretty sure I'd run into him again. Besides, thanks to J.J., I knew where he worked. And I still had another stop I needed to make, one that might help me deal with my cottage's little eccentricities.

CHAPTER TWENTY-SEVEN

THE LIBRARIAN, MRS. ANDERSON, was a sturdy, older woman with a kind face and sensible shoes. I explained to her that I had just moved into my Aunt Tillie's cottage, and I'd heard it had been featured in a book on the area.

"We did have a lovely little book about the old houses in town. It was written by one of the locals. Daniel Roake. He was the librarian here when I was a girl." She flipped through the card catalog—an honest-to-goodness, index-card system, not a computerized one. "Here it is. Historic Cottages of Bayfield County: Myths, Legends and Facts."

She wrote down the Dewey Decimal number on a post-it and handed it to me.

I searched the shelf but couldn't find it. So I searched every shelf in the area, in case it was misfiled. *Nada.*

I returned back to the librarian, empty-handed. She searched the return cart, the back room, and the shelf of books that needed to be repaired, but couldn't find it either.

She finally gave up. "We must not have replaced it after the fire. What a shame."

"Fire?" I looked around. I couldn't see any sign of water damage.

"Round about fifty years ago. A group of kids were smoking by the feed store, and one of the hay bales caught fire. The feed store, library, newspaper office and school all burnt down before it was brought under control. Tragic."

"Oh." I paused. "That seems like an awful lot of damage from a single hay bale."

"Oh, dear." She chuckled. "You are a city girl, aren't you?"

What did that have to do with anything? "I guess so," I said, blowing out a sigh of frustration.

She took pity on me and explained. "That one hay bale ignited the hundred and fifty bales next to it, and the wooden shed, and the wooden store, and it just kept spreading."

"Oh, my gosh." I said, taken aback. I could see the fire in my imagination, way too clearly. "That's horrible."

"Yes, it was, dear."

"Wow. Well, okay. Maybe I can get a copy online."

She laughed. "I seriously doubt it. The book was never widely published. Daniel—Mr. Roake—just made a handful of copies. It was a passion project for him, I'm afraid. He bound each copy by hand, with goatskin leather, and included a hand-painted frontispiece. They were truly a work of art. Back before computers were ever conceived of."

I slouched down over the counter, head in my hands.

"You could try talking to Daniel," she said, as she started checking returned books back in. "But there's no guarantee he's going to be lucid."

I perked up. "He's still alive?"

"Just turned one hundred and twelve last Saturday. Oldest man in America."

Holy crap. "I can't imagine living that long." Would it be a blessing or a curse? At that age, do you wake up every morning, looking forward to another day? Or upset that you have another day to fill?

She laughed at a memory. "Daniel certainly is a firecracker. *Good Morning, America* came out for his birthday party last month. They called him a super-centenarian. He thought they were commies and ran them off with his cane."

"He sounds like a handful." But I had to smile at the image of a camera crew running from an irascible old man. "What about newspaper articles? If the cottage was that famous, maybe the local paper would have something on it?"

"You can check the microfiche records at the paper for the newer archives, but the older archive fell victim to the fire."

I sighed. "Well, Mr. Roake it is. Where can I find him?"

"Shady Valley Nursing Home. It's down the street from the high school." She paused in her work. "If he's lucid, see if he's got a copy he'd be willing to donate to us. A book like that should be kept safe for future generations."

I refrained from mentioning how much they had already sucked at keeping it safe. The library, and most of the town, was still made of wood and stone. But for all I knew, maybe they had doused everything in massive quantities of fire retardant since the fire.

*   *   *

Daniel Roake turned out to be a grizzled old man with a lascivious sense of humor and an obsession with getting around. He had a cane, a walker and a wheelchair in his room, along with Betty Page pin-ups on his walls.

When I told him I had moved into the witch house, he chortled so much, I thought I was going to have to call 9-1-1, just in case he choked on his tongue or something.

But when he heard I was interested in his book, he perked right up. He opened his bedside table and reverently pulled out a small, leather-bound book.

"So, you have Lady Lisette's cottage. My, she turned this place upside down in her day. My granddaddy showed me a sketch of her once. She was quite a looker, she was." He eyeballed me up and down, and nodded approvingly. "Looked a lot like you."

A nurse came in to give him a bath, and despite Mr. Roake's invitation to stay, I thought it would be easier on my psyche if I didn't. I had heard stories about what happens to men as they age and I really did not want to risk seeing if those stories were accurate.

As the nurse started arranging the bathing supplies, I picked up my purse and cleared my throat, to remind her I was still there.

"You can wait in the common room." The nurse said, nodding at me. "We'll be done soon."

Daniel handed me the book. "Go ahead, take a look. I'm right proud of it, I am. Did all the artwork myself. But don't you break the spine or crease the pages, missy, or you and I are going to have words."

"I promise," I said. Then I closed the door, so they'd have privacy and went out to the common room.

* * *

A few oldsters were roaming around, watching TV, or playing cards or checkers. While some of them gave me curious glances, for the most part, I was ignored. Which was fine with me.

I settled down on a chair and gently opened the book. The leather on the cover was soft and luxurious. And the frontispiece was a beautiful painting of Devil's Point, the way it must have been, back when it was a settlement.

I slowly turned to the section on my cottage. There was a sketch of what the cottage must have looked like when Mr. Roake was a small boy. A lot smaller than it was now, and closer in shape to the cottage I had dreamt about in Los Angeles. I eagerly started reading.

* * *

The Myth: The cottage was nestled in a small clearing, deep in the Great North Woods. It was a witch's cottage, the whispers went, built by the Devil, enchanted and protected by the blackest arts. And day after day, it quivered in anticipation, waiting for the unspeakable something—or someone—to enter its realm.

Despite what should have been the ravages of neglect, time and harsh weather, the cottage thrived, a living being made of wood and stone and clay. And every so often, one of the more foolhardy villagers would screw on their courage with a jug of moonshine and move into the old place, claiming squatter's rights.

Over and over, they told themselves that the old wives tales were nothing more than just that—tales. After all, someone human must have lived in the cottage once upon a time. Someone human must have built it.

But late at night, when the wind blew wicked around the eaves and the Dark Gods of the underworld roamed the earth, the courage born of moonshine ran thin. Most of the squatters clutched their old bibles and crucifixes and ran as fast and as far as they could.

The lucky ones escaped with their lives. There were a few, the intrepid few, who were determined to remain. They fell into silence as madness descended upon them. Eventually, they vanished into the bowels of the cottage, their grimacing remains waiting, like an eerie welcome wagon, for the next claimstaker.

One year, some of the more righteous villagers called upon the might of God to defend them and attempted to burn the cottage down. But even God would have no truck with the Devil's house. Tragedy touched all who dared set out that day.

The villagers eventually came to an uneasy truce with the cottage, taking great pains to avoid it. However, throughout the years, a singular thought ran the width and breadth of the village like a soft breeze: Some day, the cottage would beckon to the one it had been built for. And on that day, the Devil would live amongst them once more.

Eventually, the cottage and all its history passed into legend. A story used to frighten wayward children. The stuff of All Hallows Eve dares and bad dreams. Until the day *she* arrived. The one the cottage had been waiting for. Lady Lisette McDougal.

The Legend: The dreaded evil that descended on the town took everyone by surprise. The villagers, from the youngest to the oldest, had been positive that the cottage was waiting for an old hag with a warty nose. A wizened old woman whose exterior merited the horrific stories told to children on cold winter nights. And they fully expected her to be accompanied by a club-footed, malformed, twisted husk of a man who collected souls like Scrooge collected pennies.

But when Lady Lisette McDougal arrived from Scotland, doe-eyed and roundly pregnant, her loveliness and grace tossed their expectations to the winds. She was ageless and beautiful; her pale white skin a contrast to her long, raven tresses. A concubine of kings, a scarlet woman of Europe, exiled to their midst. And Lucien, the tattooed, muscular, bald savage at her side, her ever-present bodyguard and companion, left them gasping.

The villagers didn't quite know if they should embrace Lady Lisette or hang her. To many of the Puritans, she was a

165

hellion, a strumpet to be reviled. Some even whispered that her companion was a demon in human form. To others, she was a wise woman and healer to be respected, who could bless or curse in the same breath.

But one thing they all agreed on was that she was touched with the charm of the exotic. She was charismatic and terrifying and the cottage quivered and thrived at her touch. Until the day she vanished, in a storm of biblical proportions, with her consort. Leaving behind an enigmatic little girl.

The Facts: The land the cottage was built on, was purchased in the late 1600's from the Ojibwe tribe, when Devil's Point was an Indian Trading Post. The original cottage was built shortly thereafter. While the cottage has expanded and been modernized over the centuries, it has withstood every challenge to its existence. When the rest of the village burnt down in the big fire of 1802, the fire surrounded the cottage, but was brought under control by the fire brigade before it could so much as scorch the timber.

CHAPTER TWENTY-EIGHT

I CLOSED THE BOOK. *Wow.* That was the history of my little cottage? I would have loved to read more about the cottage and Lisette and Lucien, but that was the extent of what he had written.

Mr. Roake's nurse came out of his room and nodded at me. "You can go back in now."

I waited a few minutes, just in case Mr. Roake needed more time to become presentable, before going back into his room, where I gushed about how beautifully written his book was. I don't actually gush easily, but the book was a true treasure, inside and out. I'd never seen another like it in my life and I was profoundly thankful to have been allowed to handle this one. As I returned the beautifully bound book to him, I asked if he really believed what he had written.

"Truth is relative. Facts are unimportant. What matters is mythic truth. Did Christ really exist? Irrelevant. The facts don't matter. The mythic truth that the figure of Christ embodies is what matters. Same thing with your cottage, young lady. It's the mythic truth you need to discover and embrace."

"I don't understand. Does that mean you don't think the Devil built the cottage? Or that the Devil doesn't exist, only the principles he represents matter?"

"What do you think?"

"I think you're making my head hurt. I know the cottage exists, because I live there. It's not a mythic place, it's stone and mortar."

"And yet, it's still a mythic place. How's that for a paradox?" He laughed. "It makes a good story. That's what's important."

"Okay, but if you had to figure out the literal truth about my cottage's origins, what would you say?"

He stopped and thought for a moment. "With the way it was built, and the markings on the foundation, my guess is a Freemason built it. A powerful one at that. I've always suspected the legend about it not being able to be harmed is rooted more in truth, than in an old man's bologna. When I was a child, anyone with sense gave that cottage a wide berth."

Freemasons. That was an interesting tidbit. When the Knights Templar were forcibly disbanded, there was a great deal of speculation that some of them fled to Scotland, eventually reemerging as Freemasons, and spreading throughout the known world.

The thought that renegade Knights Templar may have built the cottage I was living in, made my head spin. From what I had seen with the Freemasons back in California, it was easy to believe that they had a powerful magical legacy, and they were more than capable of creating the wards I had felt at the cottage.

I thanked Daniel for all his help and kissed his papery cheek goodbye. As I was about to leave though, I remembered the librarian.

"Mrs. Anderson at the library was wondering if you had an extra copy of your book that you could donate to them. The one they had was destroyed in the last fire."

He sniffed. "She can wait until I'm dead, like the rest of the vultures." But he looked pleased as he scribbled a note to himself on a memo pad. I peeked over his shoulder and read 'Leave book to library in Will.'

Well, mission accomplished. Time for me to go back to the cottage and resume my dance with the Devil. Assuming there really was one, and it wasn't just Aunt Tillie in drag.

* * *

As I was leaving Mr. Roake's room, I ran into Paul Raines. Literally. I was so busy thinking about the cottage, I plowed right into him.

"Oof!" I went down like a sack of bricks.

"Ow," he grunted. "Are you okay?"

"Sorry, I didn't see you in front of me. I'm so sorry." I said, scrambling to my feet.

He straightened up and rubbed his chest. "Man, you have a hard head."

"People have told me that my whole life. This is the first time I've used it as a weapon, though." I pressed my hand against my forehead. "Although, if your chest was any harder, I'd have a concussion. Work out much?"

"Sorry about that. Compulsive weight-lifter." He smiled at me.

Red flags went up in my head. The man had dimples, muscles, was way too hot, and he was a gym-addict. I groaned. Great. Just what I needed. Another gay man in my life. Gus was right. I had turned into a fag hag.

"You okay?" he asked again, solicitously.

I realized I was groaning out loud. "I, uh, I was just wondering where a gym was around here," I said, trying to cover.

He laughed. "Trinity Harbor."

"Figures. Apparently, everything's in Trinity Harbor. You gotta be a real gym rat to drive all the way out there."

"Isn't that what audio books are for?" he said, his eyes twinkling at me. "It's one way to get a lot of reading done."

Just then, a nurse walked through the hallway, pushing a cart of used bedpans. She gave Paul a big smile. "Paul! Daniel will be so pleased to see you. Go right in."

As she sashayed away—well, as much as a woman pushing bedpans could sashay—I turned to Paul. "Isn't he kind of old for a sugar daddy?"

"Ick. What do you take me for?" He shot me a look. "He's my great-great-grandfather. Besides, if I'm looking for a sugar anything—it's usually sporting a pair of boobs. And I'm not talking man-boobs." He said, flashing down to my chest.

I crossed my arms and turned beet red. "Sorry. It's just that when you said that you were a weight lifter, I just thought, I mean, with the gym addiction and it being so far and all."

"Only gay guys are interested in staying in shape?"

"Well, yes. I mean, no. It's just... I'm from Los Angeles. Most men out there are gay. So I'm used to gyms being a place for sexy, sweaty guys to hook up with other sexy, sweaty guys."

"Welcome to the Heartland. Our stats are a little different here. Besides, I work out by lifting weights in my garage. You're the one who wanted to know where the gym was." He walked into Daniel Roake's room and closed the door behind him.

I groaned. Great. Just great. Leave it up to me to alienate the only cute, single, straight guy I've met in years.

He poked his head back out of the room. "Wait a minute, did I miss something or did you call me sexy?"

I turned beet red. I could feel my mouth opening and closing like a goldfish that had jumped out of its tank and was flopping around on a carpet. As I turned and ran out of there, my face burning, I swear I could hear Paul's laughter all the way down the hall, out the front door, and into the parking lot.

* * *

The warding I had done on the bedroom turned out to have been a solid bit of crafting. I had a completely dreamless night. The next day, I woke up so refreshed and energetic, I felt like I had just had a two-week vacation. It's amazing what a full night's sleep can do for you.

And it was a good day to have all that extra energy. After a protein-heavy breakfast of eggs and bacon, I tackled my poor, defaced living room. I moved the furniture, put drop cloths everywhere, used paint thinner to get rid of as much of the black marker as I could, then primed and repainted the walls a gorgeous cream color.

By the time I was done, I was exhausted and hungry. So I heated up three frozen corn dogs in the oven. It took forever, but Aunt Tillie didn't have a microwave and I had sold mine. Once they were cooked, I took my plate into the living room and collapsed on the couch, satisfied with the work I had done.

"Hey, you up there." I said, waving one of my corn dogs for emphasis. "No more screwing up my walls. Or else. I don't care if you're a ghost or not—I will find a way to make you sorry. Ghosts aren't immune to everything, y'know."

I should call Gus and talk to him. When he was dabbling with ceremonial magic, he'd learned how to trap demons and unwanted spirits in brass vessels. Normally, I stayed away from stuff like that. It seemed to be on the borderline between dangerous and rude. But it was good to have options.

I stretched out on the couch and closed my eyes. Ugh. I probably shouldn't have had that third corn dog. I was starting to feel nauseous. I should have steamed some broccoli instead.

Oh, let's be honest. My diet, in general, had sucked since I left Los Angeles. It's no wonder my stomach was rebelling. Good thing Gus had made me stock up on vitamins and supplements before I left. If I was going to eat nothing but crap, maybe I should increase the number of vitamins I was taking.

* * *

I was carrying an armload of paint supplies, (rollers, brushes, roller trays, drop cloths), to the shed in the back, when I saw an old woman and a black dog dodging behind a tree. "Hey, hold up!" I dumped the stuff in the shed and took off after her. I don't know what made me follow her, but I couldn't give up. Every glimpse of her between the tree trunks enticed me onward. But it was like chasing a ghost.

I was finally catching up to her at a clearing, when I stumbled on something and fell, smacking my head hard against a tree root. "*Ow!!!* What the fuck?!"

I held my hand to my head, hoping the pressure would stop the pain. No such luck. I looked at my hand and it was covered in blood.

Don't freak, I told myself. *It's just a head wound. Head wounds bleed a lot. It's just a superficial gash. It doesn't mean that part of your brain is bulging out of your cracked-open skull.*

As I sat there, trying not to cry, I looked down to see what had tripped me. There, sticking up out of the dirt, was a small, blue-haired troll doll. I pulled him the rest of the way out of the dirt, brushed bits of dried leaves off him and put him in my jacket pocket.

While my fingers were in my pocket, I also found the corner of a handkerchief. The rest of it must have worked its way through a hole in the lining. Maybe my luck was turning for the better. I slowly teased the piece of cloth through the hole, until I was able to get the entire handkerchief out of my pocket, and I pressed it against my head to stop the bleeding.

When I looked up, the toothless old woman was sitting on her haunches, watching me, with the black dog at her side.

"Who are you?!" I demanded.

But she just rocked back and forth, silent as the grave.

I stood up and staggered, a bit woozy. I suppose I was lucky that my head wasn't gushing out blood like a geyser.

The late afternoon sun ducked behind a storm cloud. The wind picked up and the sky darkened. I glanced up. *Damn it.* I really didn't want to be out here during a thunderstorm.

Then I noticed the old woman and her dog were moving deeper into the woods. I picked up a fallen branch and, dragging it through the dirt to mark my path, I followed her.

CHAPTER TWENTY-NINE

I WALKED FOR WHAT seemed like ages. I walked long enough for my head to stop bleeding. My feet were sore and dead-tired and I was totally lost, in the middle of nowhere, chasing after a toothless old lady and her dog. Some kind of witch I turned out to be. Where the hell was a cab or a pay phone when you needed one?

A few steps later, and I had come full circle. I was back in the clearing where I had found my branch. I could see where the drag mark I was making had started. Great. Gus would bust a gut when I told him about this.

As I turned towards the direction I thought led back to the house, a weird, homeless-looking guy jumped down out of a tree and blocked my path, nearly scaring me to death. He had one crazy glass eye that was solid white and one normal eye. His clothes were old, ragged and starched with mud.

I tightened my grip on my tree branch and calculated my odds of whacking him with it, if he turned out to be some weird serial killer.

He limped over to me. "You got money?"

"You almost gave me a heart attack."

"That ain't no never mind to me. I'm the troll. And this is my road. You want to walk the troll road, you gots to pay the troll."

"What road? It's the middle of the fucking woods."

He pointed at the bulge in my jacket pocket. "What's that?"

I pulled out the troll doll.

"A troll for Troll!" he said, delighted. He carefully put the troll in his mud-encrusted pocket and ambled away.

I looked around for the woman with the dog, but she was nowhere to be seen.

Then I looked around for the Troll, but he seemed to be gone as well.

Great, I was lost in the woods with what I was beginning to suspect were either escapees from a lunatic asylum or figments of my imagination. I hoped to the Gods that it wasn't a sign that I was going to die out here. And it made me wonder just how hard I had hit my head against that tree. Maybe I had a concussion. Could concussions cause hallucinations?

I turned in the direction I thought the house was and started walking as the sun slowly vanished. The trees blocked so much of the sky, there wasn't even a sunset to see. There was just a gradual increase in the level of darkness until it was pitch black. Thankfully, I found a penlight in my jacket pocket, so I wasn't walking completely blind.

In L.A., it was never really fully dark. Between the houses that were always lit, and the businesses that were lit up even when they were closed, the traffic lights, car headlights, street lights, there was no getting away from an electrically-generated haze of light. Normally, it was one of my biggest complaints— between the pollution and the light, it was impossible to see the night sky, And after all the years I had spent in the Midwest with my dad, I really missed seeing the constellations.

But here, in the heart of the Wisconsin forest, I'd give anything for a twenty-four hour convenience store to appear around the bend. Or the moon. Or even a clearing without trees. Anything that would lessen the darkness.

I kept walking, using the stick as a staff, to keep me from tripping on exposed roots. The rustling of animals in the shrubs was creeping me out. Every time I heard leaves shift, my heart jumped. I didn't know if what I was hearing was small, peaceful animals minding their own business, or large, predatory animals stalking me. Or some crazed, rabid, rodent-like creature about to attack.

The beam from my little penlight was so small, it was almost useless.

I sighed. What if they weren't weird hallucinations? What if

I was really trapped out here with two crazy people? Maybe even two cannibalistically-inclined crazy people? Ugh. I should have taken my cell phone.

In the distance, I saw a light flicker, followed by another and another. Little fireflies of hope. I walked towards them as quickly as I could and soon found myself in another clearing.

A wolf loped up, hunting food, its luxurious coat glowing in the moonlight. I froze, not wanting to attract its attention. It paused and looked me over, clearly wondering if I had anything tasty for him. It bared its teeth and I averted my eyes. The last thing I needed was to challenge a hungry wolf. Then I thought, what am I doing? They're supposed to be more scared of us than we are of them. So I tried to make myself as big and noisy as possible, and ran straight at him.

He looked at me, letting me know he wasn't impressed, before he turned and vanished into the depths of the forest. Once he was out of sight, I continued to walk as fast as I could towards the little lights. When I stopped to get my bearings, I felt a bony hand on my ankle. I screamed, but it was the old woman with the dog. The dog's eyes glowed red in the beam from the penlight.

"I'm sorry," I gasped. My heart was racing so fast, I thought it was going to pop right out of my chest. "I didn't see you sitting here."

"There's a great deal you don't see," she said. *"And a great deal you wish you didn't see."*

"How long have you been watching me?"

"I have been with you since the beginning of time and I am that which is attained at the end of desire," the old woman cackled, showing a scattering of yellowed teeth.

Great. A homeless Wiccan. Perhaps someone's looking out for me after all. Or maybe my mom sent her as some kind of guide. "Can you help me? I'm kinda lost."

"Can you help me?" the old woman mimicked. *"Great big pillock of a girl. Can't help yourself, how can you help anyone else? Lost, lost, all is lost. When the battle has begun and the day is barely won, can your voice be brave and true? No, all is lost, cries you. Woe is me, woe is me. Time comes for all of us dearie, now it's come for you."*

The temperature dropped and I started shivering. If I didn't get eaten by wolves first, I might just freeze to death before I found my way out of here.

"What are you doing here? You don't belong here!" The Troll was back.

"I was just talking to..." I looked down but the woman was gone. "Did you see an old lady? She was sitting right here, with a dog."

He threw a rock at me, hitting me in the shoulder.

"*Ow!*" I could feel blood trickling down my arm.

"Go on, get out!"

In the distance, I saw the lights again, dancing between trees. Then I got pegged in the thigh with a rock. "*Ow,* knock it off. I'm leaving!"

Anything to get away from the crazy man with the all-too-good aim.

I rubbed my thigh and took off, following the lights. Did Wisconsin have will-o-the-wisps? Or was it a mega-swarm of fireflies?

When the lights stopped moving. I stepped out from the trees and found myself standing next to a small cemetery. There was a group of fairy lights gathered in the far corner, in front of a large tombstone with an overhanging stone angel. The lights banded together to form a figure—a female figure. She stood up and beckoned to me. I took a step back.

"Nothing against you," I told her image. "But I'm kinda done with ghosts right now."

But she came at me, relentless. Like she had all the patience and time in the world and I was a recalcitrant child. I brandished my staff like a club. "Seriously. I'm at the end of my rope with the spirit world around here. One more ghost attack and it's brass vessels for everybody."

She flew at me, her mouth open, pleading. *"Help me!"*

She pushed right through my body and then turned into a hundred bats, which flew away in different directions.

I fell backwards, my arm hitting the sharp edge of a rock, ripping open the flesh. I could feel blood running down my arm to my hand. Then I heard a scream, deep, primal, full of rage, shattering the night. It took me a few minutes to realize I was the one screaming.

The old woman and her dog walked towards me again. From the other side, the weird old man appeared from the trees. The air crackled with electricity as lightning shot from cloud to cloud and a black horse, covered in black feathers, appeared in front of me, its eyes glowing, its nostrils flared and red.

I held out my gashed-up arm and let the blood drip in a circle around me. *"By my blood and by my bone, protect me Lady, send me home."*

A loud thunderclap. The darkness swirled around me, in a vortex. Then the heavens opened up and rain poured down.

CHAPTER THIRTY

I WOKE UP ON the living room floor, cleaning supplies dropped haphazardly around me. *Had it all been another dream?* It was so vivid. Argh. Everything was so surreal. I had felt alive and awake in the dream, but now it felt like my head was full of cotton. I was getting really tired of the way this cottage kept screwing with my grasp of reality.

I shook my head and felt a sudden stab of pain. I pressed my hands to my scalp. When I brought my hands back down, they were covered in blood. I winced and stood up. I checked my reflection in a mirror on the living room wall. Besides a bloody head, I had a gash on my arm and another one on my shoulder. I looked down. There was a cut on my thigh and there was blood on the edge of the paint can next to me. They weren't the deep, *'go directly to the hospital and get stitches before you bleed out'* cuts, they were more annoying than serious, but still...

Had I fallen off the couch and cut myself on the paint can? But I was so deep into the dream, it just became part of what was happening?

That seemed kind of impossible. Who sleeps through multiple contusions and cuts?

Could it have been the paint fumes in the room? Maybe the fumes overwhelmed the oxygen in my brain?

I picked up the paint can, wondering if I had gotten hold of some lead-based paint. I wiped blood off the label and squinted at it. Latex. I put the can down and looked around at the room I had just cleaned and painted.

GET OUT NOW was written on the wall.

In blood.

Fresh, dripping blood.

Probably my blood.

Did I do that while I was unconscious? I looked at my hands, but it was impossible to tell if they had been bloody before I pressed my hands against my bleeding head.

Could it be that Aunt Tillie saw an opportunity to freak me out again and took advantage of it?

Or had someone broken in, noticed me sleeping and figured it would be a good prank? That seemed to be the least likeliest scenario.

It had to be Aunt Tillie.

Or maybe that Devil she warned me about.

I shook my finger at the ceiling. "Look out, Aunt Tillie—and anyone else who might be hanging out here—your days of tormenting me are numbered!"

Come tomorrow, I was going to ward the whole freaking house, like I had done with the bedroom. I'd just have to figure out a way to do it that wouldn't trigger the cottage's inherent security wards. Being turned into shrubbery wasn't exactly on my agenda.

* * *

I was in the bathroom, on a Bactine, Neosporin and Band-Aid spree, when my cell phone started ringing. And kept on ringing. Finally, on the thirteenth of Ode to Joy, I was done playing Florence Nightingale, so I came out and snatched up the phone rendition. Odds were it was someone selling something. Like a new service upgrade.

"No," I snapped. "I don't want to change my plan."

"Well, excuse the hell out of me."

"Gus?! Oh my Gods!" I couldn't believe how ridiculously excited I was to hear his voice. "Did you just call and hang up like ten times in a row?"

"I don't like voicemail. Did you know that in nature, up to eight percent of male sheep are gay?"

"It's about time you got around to calling me, you perv. And lay off the sheep, or the ASPCA is gonna lock you up."

"I'm just sayin'. How's it going in the middle of nowhere?"

"You'd love it. Talk about a haunted cottage. I have so

many freaking ghosts hanging out here, I'm thinking about charging them rent."

I quickly caught him up on everything that had happened, reveling in the note of envy in his voice.

Then I rubbed my eyes and yawned. "Either that, or I'm totally losing my mind and haunting myself. I'm having the craziest time sleeping out here. I have dreams that are so real, I think I'm living them. And reality is so weird, I think I'm dreaming it."

"Sabbatic dreaming. Cool."

"No. It's not cool. It's like I'm going crazy. I don't know what's real anymore. And now I'm hurting myself in my sleep. I woke up on the floor, with all these weird, bloody gashes on me, and blood all over the wall. You're not going to believe this wall. I'll send you a photo. I don't know if Aunt Tillie did it, or if I did it while I was hallucinating. Maybe I'm trying to scare myself away from the cottage. I just wish I could get a handle on what's real and what's not. It's totally crazy."

There was silence on the phone.

"Gus? You there?"

"Don't hate me."

A chill ran through me. "Why? What did you do?"

He cleared his throat. "You know those supplements I gave you? The ones for sleeping?"

"Yeah. The stuff you said would help my sleep be more restful and help me lose weight? I've been taking them. But no matter how much I take, it doesn't seem to be working."

"Uh, yeah. How much 5-HTP are you taking? I may have given you the wrong dosage."

I went into the kitchen and sorted through all the vitamin and supplement bottles. I picked up the 5-HTP. "Two pills, three times a day. Each pill is one hundred milligrams."

"Yeah. That could be why you're having out-of-control dreams."

I stared at my cell phone in disbelief. Serves me right. I should always double-check things when it comes to Gus. "And what, exactly, does 5-HTP do?"

He cleared his throat. "It increases the serotonin levels in your brain. You would have had some wicked sabbatic dreams if you were taking half that. But you're taking twice as much as I do. Sorry, I thought I gave you the fifty-milligram bottle. Anyway, your subconscious is wide open. Especially with some of the other stuff I gave you. That's probably why you've been such an easy target for your ghosts."

"You *sandbagged* me?!"

"I thought if we were both dreaming on the same wavelength, we could meet on the sabbatic plane. And how cool would that be? To be able to interact in dreamscape? I mean, I could have sworn you were there with me earlier. Did you see the black horse I sent you?"

"Made of feathers, with red eyes? Yes, I saw it. You moron. I'm gonna kill you, next time I see you. Do you know what kind of hell you've been putting me through?" I paced back and forth, wondering how pissed I should be.

"Sorry. Really. I mean... I just thought it would be fun."

"You so owe me."

"I know."

"No, you don't understand. There is no end to how much you owe me on this one." We discussed all the ways he was going to make things up to me, starting with a supply run to Mama Lua's.

* * *

If it hadn't been for Aunt Tillie's earlier poltergeisty attack on my living room walls, while I was at the B&B, I would have written off the entire haunting as being Gus-induced hallucinations—or, as he liked to call it, sabbatic dreaming. I was relieved things weren't as bad as I had thought.

Now, all I had to do, was get Aunt Tillie under control. And that was going to happen next. After all, I told myself, the living trump the dead. *Ha!* Little did I know.

CHAPTER THIRTY-ONE

THE NEXT MORNING, I woke up gasping for air. Something was wrong. I could feel it. The cottage was practically vibrating. I looked out the bedroom window, but the lake was calm and the skies were sunny and blue.

I hurriedly showered and got dressed. I couldn't shake the feeling that the cottage had battened down the hatches in preparation for something. And when I went downstairs, the feeling got stronger.

I walked through the cottage, but I couldn't pick up anything specific. Although I was starting to rethink my plan to add my own personal wards to the place. The wards that were in place were so strong, they made my head feel like it was in a vise. And the energy that permeated the cottage was vibrating so hard and so fast, I really didn't want to risk messing with it.

I went to the kitchen, took three Advils and then headed into the living room.

Grundleshanks gave me a baleful look.

"Oops! Sorry, bud. I forgot to feed you last night."

I gave him fresh water and tossed a few crickets into his tank.

He blinked, forgiving me as he slurped up the first one.

I glanced out of the bay window, at the rowan tree. It had been thriving since I had arrived. That got me thinking about J.J. and his family. And how, every day I spent in the cottage, it felt more and more plausible that the cottage actually could—and would—defend itself against all attackers.

"If I get turned into a tree," I asked Grundleshanks, "what kind of tree do you think I'd be?"

Grundleshanks snagged another cricket and blinked at me.

I saw an image of white thorns in my head.

"Really? A hawthorn? Yeah, I think so too."

Oh, geez. Not only was I talking to the toad, I was also supplying his side of the conversation. I wondered how long I could live by myself in the middle of nowhere before I completely lost my mind.

"It's better than having me supply my side." A voice whispered inside my head.

I stopped in my tracks and stared at the toad tank, shocked. "Did you just... talk to me?" I asked, incredulously.

I whirled around to see if there was someone—anyone— else in the cottage. Then I turned back to look at the toad and repeated. "Did you just talk to me?"

He blinked at me and I swear he grinned. Then he sunk into his mud.

I put my face next to the glass, so I was looking at him human-eyeball to toad-eyeball. "Let's pretend you didn't. And don't do it again. Because I'm in no hurry to be put into a loony bin."

I swear he shrugged and croaked *'whatever'* at me, just as the doorbell rang.

Keeping one eye on the toad, I answered the door and found an AT&T guy on my doorstep. "I'm here to hook up your phone and set you up for DSL and cable."

"Oh, thank goodness!" I was so happy, I almost hugged him. "You don't know how much I've missed civilization."

He smiled. "I can imagine. Even by our standards, this is pretty out of the way."

As he got to work I sent the cottage as strong a thought as I could: *He's here to help us. Do not screw with him.* I felt a little silly because I wasn't quite sure if the cottage actually was sentient, but just in case... my nerves stayed on edge until he was finally done and on his way.

* * *

"Yippee! We're back in the twenty-first century!" I unpacked my PowerBook and did a happy dance as I walked past Grundleshanks.

He just blinked at me, this time, without saying anything. He was probably debating the merits of having an owner who said things like *'Yippee'* and forgot his crickets, but he had the good sense to keep it to himself.

I was so happy, I had to call Gus and share it with him. The phone rang and almost immediately went into voicemail.

"Gus, guess what? I have a phone. A landline. And cable. And internet." I said, almost laughing as I checked my emails. "Look out, baby, 'cause I am back! Hey, is there something you forgot to mention about Grundleshanks? Like, for instance, that he can *talk*? Or is that another supplement side effect that you forgot to tell me about? Call me. I want to know if he's one talented toad, or if I'm totally losing my grip on reality."

After I hung up, I googled 5-HTP overdose and found out that if you combine 5-HTP with St. John's Wort, you can wind up with serotonin syndrome, which leads to full-on hallucinations and difficulty walking. That would explain the other night. St. John's Wort sounded familiar. I looked through my supplement bottles. Sure enough, one of the sleep concoctions Gus had given me had Melatonin, Valerian, Kava Kava Root and St. John's Wort. Add an overdose of 5-HTP and it was one potent cocktail.

I decided I was going to pound the crap out of Gus next time I saw him. No wonder my grasp of reality had gone so completely out the window. Gus was just lucky he was across the country.

* * *

By early afternoon, my stomach was growling, so I put the computer away and went to the kitchen to make something to eat and call Gus. Like before, it went into voicemail.

"Gus, you idiot. You'd better call me back and tell me how long it's going to take to get your supplements out of my system. This place is weird enough on its own, I didn't need your help to creep it out even more."

Ehhh, that sounded kind of bitchy, even for me. But as I was about to apologize, the phone went dead.

I looked around. I was standing in front of the cellar door. In fact, I had just stepped in front of the cellar door when the phone went dead. I stepped away from the door and I had a dial tone again. I took a step back towards the door and the phone went dead again.

I stepped away from the door and walked around the kitchen. It was fine everywhere else.

Everywhere except right in front of the cellar door.

"Well, that's interesting," I muttered.

I hadn't been in the cellar yet.

I put my hand on the doorknob and it was ice cold.

But just as I was about to turn the knob, I felt a hard push from outside the cottage.

* * *

I ran to the front room to check it out. If nothing else, it gave me a good excuse to avoid going into that cellar. I looked over at Grundleshanks, but whatever was going on, Grundleshanks didn't seem too bothered by it.

I climbed up on the window seat in front of the big bay window, to see if I could spot anything. The road in front of the cottage was empty, but I could hear the far-off sound of car engines through the glass.

Soon, an SUV and a pickup truck came into sight, hurtling towards each other. They were both driving erratically. One with speed, (slowing down and speeding up), while the other was swerving all over the road.

"Oh, geez. This isn't going to be pretty."

Grundleshanks blinked, still calm. I ran and grabbed the portable phone from the kitchen. But reporting that an accident is *about* to happen doesn't get you the same response as reporting one that's in progress. Especially when both vehicles are still too far away to read the license plates.

The dispatcher said they'd send a car to check it out, but she didn't sound like it was at the top of the priority list. If there was an actual collision, she told me, I should call her right back.

I looked out the window again. The SUV's were getting closer and they both seemed oblivious that there was anyone else on the road with them. Were they drunk? Or were they so used to the non-existent traffic and the apathetic police force, they just assumed they could drive like stoned pre-teens and no one would pull them over?

I thought about running out and trying to flag them down, but I really didn't want to get caught between two impaired drivers. My flesh was soft and my bones were no match for speeding metal. I called 911 again.

As I was on the phone with the reluctant dispatcher, I heard the squealing of brakes and the high-pitched scream of tires desperately pushed beyond their limits.

Then the sickening grind of metal on metal as they slammed into each other. The impact was so loud, the dispatcher agreed to send out a patrol car and ambulance, immediately.

I ran outside. The SUV had spun off in the opposite direction and come to a stop in a maple tree. The pickup truck was still spinning, like a malevolent top. It was coming closer, fast, heading right for where I was standing, by the cottage.

I hurriedly backed up, unable to look away, and prayed like hell that it wouldn't mow me down. But the truck was moving faster than I could and I was right in its trajectory.

If I hadn't been looking, I would have totally missed what happened next.

When the out-of-control pickup hit the cottage wards, instead of continuing on, there was a boom and the air glowed brighter for just a second.

The pickup truck bounced off the wards, flipping over and spinning in the opposite direction. It skidded on its top until it came to rest on the shoulder of the road.

Wow. The cottage had, literally, just saved my life. Although I was pretty sure it was just a by-product of it saving itself.

Suddenly, the cottage turning a would-be arsonist into a tree didn't seem like such a farfetched idea after all.

CHAPTER THIRTY-TWO

THERE WAS A LARGE, pasty-faced, soft-fleshed boy in the pickup that had flipped. He was hanging upside down, anchored by the seat belt. The top of the cab had been scrunched down, dangerously close to the top of his head.

I opened the door, expecting the worst, but he was conscious and breathing, and his injuries seemed superficial.

"Are you okay?"

"How'd I get here?" He blinked at me, a foggy expression on his face.

"Did you hit your head?"

He bent his neck and felt his scalp and forehead, looking for bruises. "I don't think so."

I wasn't sure if I should try to unbelt him or let him hang and wait for the paramedics. I didn't want to risk him falling on his head or neck, even though it wasn't that big of a drop.

"Oh, man. I can't believe this happened again."

"Again?" That wasn't good. How often had he flipped his car? "What's the last thing you remember?"

"I had lunch with a friend and we drank a pitcher of beer. So I went home and took a nap. I dreamt about driving to a pig farm. And then, I woke up here."

"Are you kidding me? You were sleep-driving? What kind of idiot move is that?" Although I wondered if sleep-driving was the next step after sleep-hallucinations.

"Don't judge me," he snapped. "Did anyone get hurt?"

"I don't know. I haven't seen the other driver yet. Is this like a regular thing? Have you seen a doctor?"

He blushed. "I don't like doctors. I usually just hide my car keys before I go to sleep."

"But your mind still knows where they are."

"How is my life any of your business?" he asked, oddly defiant.

"Oh, for Pete's sake. You could kill somebody. Even out here, in the middle of cow country." Irritated, I closed the driver's side door, left him hanging, and jogged over to the SUV.

Sleep-driving. I shook my head. I hated irresponsible people. Gus aside. He might be irresponsible, but I was pretty sure he'd never intentionally put someone's life in danger. Their *sanity*, maybe. Their *life*, no. At least, not so far.

The SUV had crunched into the maple tree across the way. The front end was crumpled and a very sexy and slightly shaken Paul Raines was leaning against the back bumper, his cell phone in hand.

"I already called. The police are on their way."

"Oh, ah... thanks." He said, his face reddening. He flipped the cell phone closed and winced.

"You okay?" I asked.

"Yeah, just shaken up a little."

"You're lucky you weren't in a convertible. Hitting a tree is what killed Tillie."

"I know. I'm sorry."

"Don't apologize to me, you're the one who's going to be hurting tomorrow."

Sirens grew louder. Two police cars pulled up, followed by an ambulance.

Paul quickly shoved his cell phone in my pocket. "Hold this for me, okay? Our little secret." He gave me a charming smile and then limped over to talk to the police.

* * *

After I filled the cops in on what I knew, I went back into the cottage. I pulled Paul's cell phone out of my pocket and looked at it, tempted to scroll through its history. There had to be a reason he didn't want the cops to find it. But then I looked up and caught Grundleshanks staring at me. I sighed and placed the phone on the table.

"Okay, fine." I told the toad. "Snooping is wrong. I get it. But there are times..."

I glanced out the window. There was a tow-truck hooking Paul's car up to a winch. The other guy had already left with the flatbed that had towed his pickup. As the cops pulled away, I spotted Paul walking toward the cottage. Good thing I had decided against snooping through Paul's phone. I put the phone out of my mind and turned my attention to cooking.

* * *

I had sausages in the oven and I was cracking eggs into a mixing bowl when Paul knocked and walked in the unlocked door. "Just came to get my phone."

"Have a seat. Wanna join me for breakfast?"

He looked at his watch. "It's two o'clock. How late do you sleep?"

No wonder I was starving. "I've had a busy morning. And then most of my day was taken up with these two idiots crashing into my property."

"Okay, okay," he raised his hands in surrender. "I'm sorry. Smells great in here. Can I help?"

"Sure. You could set the table."

He looked through the cupboards until he found the plates, then started setting the table as I turned back to my eggs. My goal was to make tomato-cheese-basil omelets, but, as usual, they came out looking like colorful scrambled eggs. I never did have a knack for flipping omelets. But soon, everything was done and the small table was festooned with plates of eggs, honey-smoked sausages, buttered toast, coffee and orange juice.

"Wow. Remind me to come over more often." Paul whistled.

"As long as you keep all four wheels on the road. Or walk. My cottage doesn't take well to speeding cars slamming into it."

"I don't blame it. It's a gem of a home. It definitely wouldn't have looked good with my SUV creating a new entrance way."

For someone who hadn't been hungry for breakfast, he was practically inhaling his eggs.

He must have heard my thoughts, because he looked up at

me and grinned, his smile lighting up the kitchen. "Normally, I don't eat like this. You're a great cook."

I drank my orange juice and smiled. Either he hadn't eaten in a week or I had finally learned to cook as well as a fifth grader.

He sipped his coffee. "Even the coffee is good. You ever think about opening a cafe?"

I laughed so hard I practically choked on my orange juice. "Not even once. My culinary accomplishments are insanely limited." I said. "So, what happened out there?"

"We both got lectured and threatened with jail time. Sam had to turn over his car keys and agree not to drive for the next month."

"I didn't know cops could do that."

"They can out here. They're dispensers of homey wisdom and justice. Keeps the court docket at Trinity Harbor free."

"Why were you threatened with jail time? And what was the deal with the phone? Are you some kind of rogue CIA agent?"

He laughed. Then he looked at the phone, embarrassed. "Yeah. Thanks for stashing that. I would have definitely been chillin' in the pokey if they had caught me with it."

"I didn't know owning a cell phone was a capital offense."

He sighed. "It is when you get caught text messaging. Especially if this your third offense."

"Are you kidding me? Text messaging! While you're driving? Are you an idiot?"

"Okay, let me explain. I'm not used to texting. I haven't upgraded my phone in like, three years. So the first time someone sent me a text, I thought my cell phone was ringing. I kept trying to answer it. By the time I figured out what was going on, I had run into a parked car."

I looked at him, shocked.

He held up a hand. "Being a responsible kind of guy, I paid to fix the car."

"And the second time?"

"I wasn't going to text back, I just wanted to see who was texting me. I was just looking. But Howie pulled up next to me while I was checking it out and gave me a ticket."

"And today?"

"I was actually texting. It was an emergency."

I stood up and took the plates to the sink.

"Hey, I wasn't done!" He protested.

"You are now. Text messaging. While you're driving. That's almost as stupid and irresponsible as sleep-driving. If you two had killed each other, you both would have deserved it."

"It's inexcusable, I know." He joined me, drying the dishes as I washed them. "But really, I'm not that guy who texts while he drives. It's just that my publisher was having some problems and then my publicist called, going nuts about some interview she wants me to do. I have a book about to hit the market and things are in the middle of chaos right now. And besides, it was ringing. Every time I get a text, it rings. I can't just let a phone ring and not answer it. It's not in me."

I dried my hands and grabbed both our phones off the table.

"What are you doing?"

"You'll see." I uploaded a ring tone to his phone, then I downloaded it and set it as his text message tone. I added his cell number into my phone, then handed him his phone.

As he took it, I quickly sent his phone a text.

His phone buzzed and started the new ringtone, a voice saying '*Do not pick up the phone. Do not pick up the phone.*'

"There's your new text message ringtone. Think you can leave that be?"

He laughed. "Okay. I can live with that," and he slid the phone into his pocket.

"And next time you feel the need to text someone back, do me a favor and pull the hell over. Me, the cows, the trees and my home, we would all appreciate it."

"Yes, ma'am." He smiled and looked so sincere, I felt my anger dissipate.

"So, you're a writer?"

"Yeah. I guess it runs in the family. Teaching pays the bills, but writing's my passion. You still mad?"

"You're just lucky you're cute."

"So, you think I'm cute? There's a lot of places we could go with cute. How about hot? Do you think I'm hot? A couple of days ago, you thought I was sexy. And possibly sweaty."

"A couple of days ago, I thought you were gay."

His hands strayed over to my side of the sink.

I slapped at his flirty fingers. "Don't push your luck."

After Paul left, I tried calling Gus again from my cell phone, just in case he was screening for numbers he recognized. But as I walked in front of the cellar door, I lost the signal. I stepped away from the door. Full bars. A step towards the door and it was completely back to zero bars. Just like before, with the landline. I took a deep breath, put my hand on the doorknob and unlocked the door.

CHAPTER THIRTY-THREE

AS I SLOWLY OPENED the cellar door, a cold breeze came up out of the darkness. Goosebumps raced across my arms and scalp. I grabbed my big mag-lite to use for protection, and flipped the light switch. A single light bulb flared on, turning the utter blackness at the bottom of the cellar steps into a light gray.

I carefully walked down the stone steps, one hand on the wall, the other clutching my flashlight. I couldn't see much, but I could hear the scratching and rustling of small animals.

Once I got to the bottom of the stairs, I could make out random white strings hanging down from the ceiling. When I pulled on one of the strings, another light bulb flared on.

I heard something fall and my heart leaped into my throat.

Then I felt something small and furry run over my foot.

I screamed and jumped sideways.

Okay, here's the thing. As much as I'm not afraid of things that turn normal people into jelly, like ghosts and supernatural bumps in the night, I'm at a loss when it comes to rodents who want to live in my home. I don't want them there. I don't want to see them. I don't want to see their droppings. But I don't want to see their dead little bodies either. So I'm hopeless at setting out traps. What I'd like to do is just go away and come back to a magically critter-free home. But so far, I haven't been able to figure out how to pull that off.

And what makes it worse is that the creepy critters seem to love me. They'll run right up to me and stand on my feet. Or if I'm laying down, they'll curl up next to my pillow. It's why I don't go camping any more.

I jumped around, swinging the flashlight and making lots of

noise to scare off any lurking critters. Then I yanked on all the overhanging strings, until the cellar was lit up like a police interrogation room. But at the edges of where the light could reach, it was still cobwebby, full of boxes and dark shadows, and haunted by feelings of rage and dread.

Halfway through the room, I noticed another door. I opened it. An empty storage room. I could use it as a place to store essential oils, herbs and incense. Maybe even do some blending. That is, if I could find the courage to come down to the cellar on a regular basis. But I just couldn't see spending any more time down here than I had to. My goosebumps had goosebumps.

As I walked through the cellar, I noticed that it didn't quite mesh, size-wise, with the house. It seemed to be quite a bit smaller. There was a wall blocking off the area where the mudroom and part of the kitchen was on the upper floor. I pushed against the wall, wondering if it concealed some kind of secret room. *Or if some human sacrifice had been deliberately bricked up in there,* my subconscious prompted.

"Get out of my home!" The ghostly voice echoed in the confines of the cellar and the hair on my neck stood on end.

I shuddered. It had to be Aunt Tillie. "Forget about it. This place is mine. I'm not going anywhere." I said, drawing my line in the sand.

"Get out! Or face the consequences." The voice whispered, curling around me like a mist.

A wrapped Santa Claus flew across the room, aiming right for me.

I ducked and it smashed against the wall.

"Leave here, now!"

Box after box flipped open and the contents hurled themselves at me. Pictures, plates, glasses, books, ornaments, holiday decorations, all turned into ammunition and shrapnel. I weaved and ducked as fast as I could, using my mag-lite as a baseball bat, but it was all coming too fast.

I screamed in pain as a chair nailed my leg. I tried to hobble for the stairway, using my arms to cover my face. A crystal glass hit my forearm and blood trickled down to my elbow.

"Knock it off! That hurts!"

A plate hit my shin. A sharp stab of pain traveled up my leg as one of the blades of a gardening shear embedded itself in my flesh.

"Goddamnit, Aunt Tillie. Knock it off or I swear by all the Gods, I'll call up Lisette right now and help her do whatever she wants."

Silence.

The onslaught stopped.

I yanked the shears out of my thigh and hobbled up the stairs, but nothing more hit me.

When I reached the top, I slammed the door shut, locked it and wedged a chair under the doorknob.

In the silence, I heard the light bulbs on the other side of the door explode, one by one.

* * *

An hour later, I was still shaking over the attack in the cellar, as the doctor stitched up my leg. *Fucking pushy, opinionated, tantrum-throwing, pain-in-the-ass ghosts,* I thought to myself, trying not to watch the needle and thread. This was ridiculous. Aunt Tillie could have killed me. In fact, she probably would have.

"It's none of my business, but if someone did this to you, I can have the police here in a red hot minute. One thing we do well is protect our women and children. Zero tolerance."

"I don't know if you can protect me from my own stupidity, Doc. But I promise, it's the last time I try to nudge a box of unknown stuff off a high shelf."

"If you're sure," he said, doubtfully.

As he finished up, my thoughts returned to my problem. Gus had gone through a demon-trapping phase, before he realized the downfalls of it. So he had given me lots of good tips when I ran my ghostbusting plan past him on the phone the other day. He was sending me a care package from the Crooked Pantry and Mama Lua, but I needed something now.

So, as soon as I was all stitched up, I headed over to the Trading Post, to see if J.J. had anything I could use.

* * *

When I walked in, a head-banging rendition of *Rock You*

Like A Hurricane was pulsating through the store and J.J. was deep in an air guitar solo. I thumped the counter. "Hey, J.J."

Nothing.

I don't think he even heard me over the music.

"J.J.!" I leaned over and turned off the radio.

"Hey, harsh!"

"Sorry. I'm looking for a brass vessel. You have any?"

"A whooza whatsie?"

"Brass vessel. It's like a container, or a jar. Like the magic lamp they used to put genies in? It's made of brass."

"Oh. Well why didn't ya say so?" He locked up the register and roamed the aisles with me, looking at the shelves. "Whaddya need it for?"

I thought about spinning a story, but before I could stop it, the word "Ghostbusting" popped out of my mouth.

"Off the hook! Can I watch? I can be like, *Boy Wonder* to your *Batgirl*? Or, you know, Harold Ramis to your Bill Murray?"

"No."

"Buzzkill." Then he poked his head back out of one of the aisles, "Hey, why brass? Why not aluminum or steel or, I don't know, tinfoil?"

"Because that's the way its been done for hundreds of years. King Solomon used to trap demons and wayward spirits with brass vessels. And if it was good enough for him..."

"Who's King Solomon?"

I sighed. That would be a long story. "Never mind. He lived way before you were born."

"Wait. King Solomon... is he the dude in the Bible who threatened to cut the kid in half?"

I stopped to think about it. "Yeah. I think that could be the same guy. I mean, how many King Solomons could there possibly be?"

"So, back to brass tacks, or, in this case, brass vessel," he said, laughing at his own joke. "It's just tradition?"

"It has something to do with the alchemical properties of brass. Please don't ask me to explain it, it makes my head hurt just thinking about it." That was frequently the problem with ceremonial magic. Way too intellectual.

He popped into one of the aisles, hooted in triumph, and came walking back to the register.

"You found one?"

"Voila." He handed me a long-neck bronze vase with the initials RY engraved on it.

"Does it have a lid?"

"Dude, it's a bud vase."

"I know. That's kinda my point." I sighed. Well, beggars can't be choosers. Sometimes you just have to make do. "Fine, I'll take it. But if you see something with a lid come in, can you snag it for me? Once you get spirits in, you kinda need to keep them from getting out."

He rang up the vase. "Can't you just use something else to plug it? Like a rubber ball? Or a small, round mirror? I got some of those in."

My spirits started to lift. "J.J., that is brilliant. A mirror is perfect. Do you have one that's small enough to fit?"

"Yeah, over in the arts and crafts aisle." He walked over there and snagged a bag of assorted small mirrors. "But dude, if you can really trap ghosts, we should hook up a webcam and charge a fee. Think of all the money you can make. I can be like, your agent."

"I'll keep it in mind." I said, paying him. "But I'm really hoping this is a one time thing."

I actually hated the thought of trapping Aunt Tillie against her will. But with a ghost as violent and unpredictable as that one that in the house, I had to be prepared to do just about anything.

CHAPTER THIRTY-FOUR

BY THE TIME I got home, it was late. And the thought of tackling the cellar, at night, made me queasy. Actually, just the thought of staying in the cottage tonight made me cringe. I thought about calling Paul and trying to finagle a date. Preferably an overnight date. On his couch. But how crazy would that sound?

"Hello, Paul. I know we barely know each other, but can I crash on your couch, so my Aunt Tillie's ghost doesn't kill me while I'm sleeping?"

Yeah. I could just see that leading to a second date. *Not.*

I briefly debated sleeping in my SUV, but the night was supposed to plummet right past damn cold and into stupid cold. So, I took a deep breath and walked into the cottage.

It was quiet.

Not quiet as in *'something was holding its breath'* quiet. Quiet as in, peaceful. Nobody home but us mortals. Even Grundleshanks was looking at me like I was being unnecessarily paranoid. But I grabbed his tank and moved him into the bedroom for the night, anyway, to keep me company.

* * *

With Gus's potent little cocktail finally starting to clear out of my system, I had vivid dreams, but nothing that would register on a hallucinatory scale. So by the time morning hit, I was actually feeling more myself than I had in a while. Even if the weather didn't mirror my mood.

The day started out overcast and turned stormy. Despite my newfound energy, I was still feeling a strong aversion to the cellar, so I decided to check out the attic. I've never had an attic anywhere I've lived, but I've always wanted one. I hoped it was an actual room and not some lame crawl space.

On the key ring with the iron cellar key, there was also a sturdy, silver skeleton key. I wasn't sure if it was the attic key, but I had a good feeling about it. I trotted back up the stairs to the attic, key ring in my pocket, big flashlight in one hand, a bucket of cleaning supplies in the other. I wasn't a big fan of repeatedly climbing stairs, so if the key worked, I didn't want to have to come back down to get my cleaning stuff.

I was at the top step, when I suddenly felt a push and my body went flying backwards.

I dropped everything and grabbed for the handrail, but it fell apart in my hands and I hit the stairs hard, on my back, my body twisting.

I tucked in my arms and head, resisting the impulse to catch myself with an outstretched hand. With my full weight behind it, my wrist would snap like a twig.

As I rolled, my head twisted backward. I could feel my neck at the breaking point, my head millimeters from being smashed open.

I couldn't breathe.

There was nothing I could do.

It was all happening too fast.

Was this what it was like to die?

Suddenly, I could smell my mom's perfume, and I felt invisible hands wrap around my head and neck.

My body jerked to a stop and the hands slowly lowered my head, and then slipped away.

I scrambled towards the wall, leaning against it. I looked at the broken handrail that spiked up into the air. I hadn't fallen because the rail broke. The rail broke when I fell on it.

Correction: *When a bad-tempered entity pushed me to what would have been my death.*

The hands had stopped my forward momentum. They had cushioned my head and neck.

My mom had saved me.

She had saved me.

And then, in an instant, she was gone.

I slowly stood up. Other than bumps, bruises and a twisted

ankle, I seemed to be okay. No thanks to my homicidal aunt. I limped into the living room. It was time to take care of Aunt Tillie. Permanently.

* * *

Whoever invented the saying, *'pick your battles carefully'*, was totally on the money when it came to the spirit world. Unfortunately, Aunt Tillie wasn't giving me any options.

I gathered everything I needed and carefully placed my tribal skull on the floor in front of Tillie's rocking chair. Then I mixed dried mugwort, dragon's blood resin and a couple of drops of yew essential oil into a bowl. You had to be so careful with essential oils, because some of them, even in small quantities, could be toxic.

I lined the bottom of an abalone shell with kitty litter, topped it with three lit coins of charcoal and sprinkled the incense I had just made on it.

After I cleansed and charged the space with salt water and incense, I put the piece of bloody bark from the tree Tillie crashed into, onto her rocking chair.

I added a few symbols of power that Gus had described to me and drew a holding circle around the chair with a blackthorn staff. If Gus was right, (and he swore up and down his sigils would work, even if a sycamore used them), this would keep her contained.

I drew a protective circle around the room (and me) and hoped for the best. I'd never done this before, so there was no telling what would happen. Outside, the wind grabbed onto an empty trashcan and sent it clattering against a tree.

"Ready or not, Tillie, here I come." I muttered.

I pointed the business end of the blackthorn at the rocking chair and began the ritual.

"To the ancestors I now call, open the gates of Heaven and Hell. By the ringing of this bell, set and seal this spell." I chanted, ringing a small bell.

"By blood and bone, by thorn and stone, Tillie McDougal, I command you, to return home."

I slammed the end of the blackthorn on the ground, three times.

When I looked up, I saw Tillie sitting on the rocking chair.

She glared at me. "I told you to leave."

"You tried to kill me. You stabbed me with garden shears. You threw me down the fucking stairs."

She shrugged, unrepentant. "All that's here for you is madness and death. You want to save yourself? Leave."

"I want a cease fire." I said, putting the bud vase on the floor between us. "You call off this attack now, or you can spend eternity in a brass vessel."

She gasped. "You wouldn't dare." But then she looked down and saw that my brass vessel was a brass bud vase. "Oh, that's threatening. I'm trying to help you, you idiot child."

"You're trying to break my neck." I said.

"There are fates worse than death. And if I have to kill you to keep you out of harm's way, so be it."

"Or you can trust me to take care of myself. I'm not exactly powerless, you know."

She sniffed. "You're a vile, ungrateful child. You will leave, either by your own will or by mine. I'll be damned if I let the Devil have you."

And with that, she lunged at me.

So much for protective circles and trapping her with sigils.

She coalesced into a fog around my head and suddenly, I was struggling to breathe.

She was literally suffocating me.

I clawed at my face, but my hands went right through her.

I stumbled over to the rocking chair, gasping for air and picked up bloody piece of bark.

"*By blood and bone, by mound and womb, Tillie McDougal, I bind you to this artificial tomb.*" I gasped out the words as I fought my way over to the vase, every step a battle.

Too late.

It was too late.

My vision was going black.

The darkness spread until the room was a small pinprick of light in a field of black.

I fell to my knees.

As my upper body collapsed, my fingers brushed something cold and hard.

The vase.

With the last bit of energy I had, I dropped the bloody piece of bark into the vase.

Then I felt with my fingers until I found the small, round mirror. As I was about to lose consciousness, I dropped the mirror into the vase.

It must have stopped up the opening.

Because, suddenly I could breathe.

I opened my eyes and gasped, filling my lungs.

Over and over.

Breathe in, breathe out.

The vase rocked back and forth, but it held fast.

In my mind, I could hear a scream of frustration.

Aunt Tillie.

But I couldn't hear it echoing in the house.

And I could breathe.

The vase was icy cold to the touch, but it was holding.

I had done it. I had successfully imprisoned the spirit of my Aunt Tillie.

So, why did I feel so queasy?

* * *

I sighed, ground out the energy and rubbed out the sigils with my feet. I dropped the circles and thought about calling Gus, but I wasn't ready to re-live the afternoon yet. So I set the vase up on the mantle and returned to what I had originally set out to do. Come hell or irate ghosts, I was going to see what was up in the attic.

CHAPTER THIRTY-FIVE

I OPENED THE ATTIC door, ready for anything, and was amazed to find a really cool-looking room. All weird angles and tiny hide-away nooks.

I sneezed and bumped into an antique telephone table. A mini-cloud of dust rose up. Good thing I had brought a box of disposable masks up with the cleaning supplies. I fastened one on and looked around.

Although it was unfinished, the attic looked like it had once been someone's bedroom, before it got repurposed for storage. It was roomy, with unusual, octagon-shaped windows in all four directions, that sported stained-glass edging. Depending on where you stood, you could see the lake, the woods, the main road, even the valley. You'd also be able to see both sunrise and sunset. This had to be an awesome room for a kid. Heck, it would be an awesome room for me. A little remodeling, I could turn it into a master suite with walk-in closet, full bathroom, even a small workroom.

Or a temple room, for that matter. Gus would disown me if my home didn't have a temple room. And a room where you could see both sunrise and sunset... that had temple space written all over it.

I sighed and got to work, cleaning. Well, as best as I could with a sore ankle, aching head and various bumps and bruises. I lifted a mattress and a family of mice scattered. I screamed and limped to the other side of the room, trying not to think too hard about where the mice might be scattering to.

What I needed was cats. Lots of cats. No wonder witches had cats. Forget the whole *being familiars* thing. It was to keep the rodents away.

By the time I stopped screaming, the mice were gone. I gingerly kick-pushed the mattress over to the discard pile, wondering if I could pay J.J. to come over and take the discards to the town dump. Then I went back to the bed and pushed off the box springs, steeling myself against another rodent explosion.

Which never happened. Thank goodness.

Instead, I found a wrapped painting between the bed frame and the box springs. I slid it out and took off the wrapping.

It was *me*.

It was a portrait of me. Minus tattoos. Wearing a corseted, floor-length gown and a necklace with a five-petaled rose pendant.

I flashed back to the reading room at Lyra's mansion and the image in the mirror. The way it felt like time had been fractured. Like I had been transported to the sixteenth century and was looking at myself through the wrong end of a telescope.

And then, weeks later, Mr. Roake telling me how much I looked like Lisette.

Lisette.

It wasn't me. *This* must be the infamous Lisette.

I searched the painting, looking for any clue as to when it was painted but I couldn't find anything.

I traced Lisette's cheek. The paint felt warm under my fingertips, as if it was flesh instead of canvas.

I looked at the path my finger had traced. A light pink hue brightened the pale skin, as if she was blushing. Or as if life was starting to return to her.

Wait, had she been blushing a minute ago?

* * *

I took the portrait downstairs and hung it over the mantle. It felt so right, hanging there, the focal point of the room.

I stepped back to admire it.

"Put that back where it came from, right now, young lady."

I jumped, but the voice was Aunt Tillie's. "Aren't you supposed to be in your vase?"

"There's no lid, you know." She shimmered beside me, a

barely-visible ghost, but she didn't take solid form. Even her voice was quieter. More of a whisper in my head.

"Semantics," I snapped. "A mirror's better than a lid. Just ask vampires. You're still contained, right? You can't go off on your own or anything?"

"That's right. Congratulations. I am now powerless and bound to my vase. Where it goes, I go. And I can't do anything about it."

"How bound? How far out can you wander?"

She shrugged. "Thirteen foot radius."

"Is that how it works?" I thought about it. "I can live with that. And you don't have enough power to go nuts anymore? They way you did before?"

She snorted. "This is the thanks I get for trying to save your sorry hide."

"You tried to kill me. The whole brass vessel thing is your own damn fault."

"You're a fine one to talk."

Well, she had me there. I never intended or wanted to hurt anyone, but it happened anyway. That's why magic sucks sometimes.

"I can't apologize enough for that, Aunt Tillie. But it still doesn't give you the right to launch a full frontal assault." I turned back to the painting. "So that's Lisette?"

"Christ on a crutch, I told you not to mention her name. Although I don't know which is worse—constantly calling her attention to you, or hanging her eyes on your wall."

"Don't you think you're overreacting?" I straightened the painting a smidge. "Look at her. We could be twins."

"More's the pity."

I wasn't quite sure about the care and feeding of a trapped spirit, so I thought I'd ask Tillie if she needed anything. "So, are you good?"

"By good, do you mean trapped? Unable to affect you? Unable to alter the physical world around me? Imprisoned and bored? Astounded by your naiveté? Wishing I had pushed you a little harder? Or aimed the garden shears higher? Then yes, I'm good."

"Every time I get sucked into caring about you, Aunt Tillie, you find a way to set me straight. Thanks."

* * *

That night, I dreamt of Lisette. She was in a cemetery, humming to herself, weeding. She stopped and sniffed the air, as if she could smell a shift in the winds.

She looked around, searching.

Then she locked eyes with me.

"Help me," she whispered.

* * *

I sat up with a gasp. The dream had been so vivid. It left me with a burning desire to find out more about my ancestral twin.

I wondered how aware Aunt Tillie was of my actions and thoughts while I had her bound to her bud vase. Could she sense me all the time? Or just when I was physically near her?

And, most importantly, how she was going to react if she caught me researching Lisette? She may not be able to throw me down staircases anymore, but Aunt Tillie still seemed to be holding onto her Olympic gold medal in nagging.

* * *

It was too late to go back to bed and too early to wake up. So I went down to the kitchen, made a pot of extra-strong coffee and hopped on the internet to research Lisette McDougal. Just to be on the safe side, I worked in the kitchen, away from Aunt Tillie's vase and her radius of movement. But all I pulled up were ads for professional finding services.

Once morning officially hit, I drove over to the local newspaper office. An impossibly young intern led me to their archives. It was like a mini-library with multiple computer terminals and three microfiche machines, minus books. I mean, there were a few books visible on the counter, but they were mostly directories and atlases. On the other side of the counter, an older woman in brown polyester pants and a fall-motif sweater, presided over a large scanner, a fax and a photocopy machine.

She was having a slow day, so she showed me how to work their archaic DOS-based computer archives and their microfiche machine. But after hours of trying every search string I could think of and scanning through years of Halloween issues—after all, what better day for an article to appear on the town's infamous witch house?—I still hadn't found anything useful.

After I left the newspaper building, I went over to the main library building on Vermont and Cherry Ave. I knew it was probably a long shot, and sure enough, I didn't find anything in their archives either. Although that didn't surprise me. But it sure made me wish I could turn back time to when the town's written history went back to the accounts of the first settlers in the area.

* * *

On my way home, I dropped in on Daniel Roake at the nursing home, but he couldn't recall anything more than what he had already told me. Although I had to laugh when he told the head nurse that I was his new girlfriend.

"You know what they say," I told her. "One hundred and twelve is the new sixty."

"Va-va-va-voom." Daniel said.

She scurried away, looking scandalized and he, very gentlemanly-like, kissed the back of my hand. "If I was ten years younger," he said.

"I'd probably be too old for you," I laughed.

He winked. "Stop by anytime, sugar. We're having a boxing competition this weekend. I'm the resident champ."

"Seriously?" I couldn't even imagine it. "You old people are tough."

"You better believe it." He laughed. "It's that Wii," he explained. "I thought all you young hep cats were hip to the Wii."

Wii boxing. That made more sense. Too little sleep must have been making my brain fuzzy.

"And my great-grandson should be back by then," he said, teasing me. Sly old fox.

"Back?" I tried to sound nonchalant. "Where did he go?"

"New York. He's a hotshot writer now. Runs in the family, you know."

I laughed and promised to visit him again soon. When I left, he was watching re-runs of *The Golden Girls* on the communal

TV.

* * *

Later that night, I called Gus.

"What's up, girlfriend?"

I explained the situation to him and all he did was laugh at me. "You're the witch. You want to know about someone who's dead, ask her directly."

"And I'm supposed to do that how, exactly?"

"Don't make me spell it out for you. S-e-a-n-c-e? Sabbatic dreaming? Astral projection? Mean anything? The ways to contact the dead are only limited by your imagination."

"That's the problem. I'm too close. I don't know if I'll be able to separate fantasy from reality. Besides, I've been up since four today. I'm exhausted."

"That's the best time to try to contact the other side. Did you ever open that present I gave you?"

"What present?" I cast my mind back to the last time I had seen him. He had given me Grundleshanks and then... Wait, there *had* been a small box...

"Find it. Open it. Use it. Then you can sing my praises." And with that, he hung up.

So I went looking through my things until I found it. Inside the box was a small jar of homemade flying ointment. I checked out the ingredients label. Belladonna, mugwort, wolfsbane, datura, magic mushroom tincture and toad secretions. There was also a warning to apply the ointment sparingly.

I was really skeptical about taking this any further. I love Gus to pieces but he was insane when it came to mixing up alchemical goo. I was perpetually amazed he hadn't poisoned himself. And now he wanted *me* to try his latest concoction?

I pulled a quarter out of my jeans pocket. "Heads, I try it. Tails, I go to bed."

Heads. *Damn.*

I put up a protective circle, sat on the floor and applied the flying ointment to the inside of my wrist. Sparingly. Very, very sparingly. Knowing Gus, this was going to be potent stuff and I didn't have a designated driver.

* * *

When I came to, the sun was dawning. Well, that had been a waste of time. All I had seen was vivid colors—red, silver and green—flying at me from all directions. A vortex in space opening up. Voices talking so fast, they were impossible to make out. Everything was fast. Fast, fast, fast. And then Lisette, standing in a room, in front of a stone altar, her hand on a skull.

It was the same room I'd seen in my dreams, back in Los Angeles. But what did it mean? What did that have to do with me? And why was Tillie so dead set (no pun intended) against Lisette and I connecting?

I stood up, wincing. My legs were cramped, every muscle hurt, and my feet, hands and butt were numb. I hopped around, shaking my hands and feet as the pins-and-needles pain hit. It felt like they were on fire. Ugh. I hated this part.

* * *

As soon as I could move without pain, I went out for a walk to let the early morning air clear my head. The sky was just beginning to lighten. Normally, it would be showcasing the rising sun's artistry. But today, the sky was awash in a uniformly flat color, tinged with the promise of rain. A low-lying fog hovered over the dew-soaked ground. In the trees, a lone bird trilled its morning aria, only to cut off its song mid-note.

As I walked around, I noticed a well-worn path, leading deep into the woods. And, because I never seem to be able to leave anything alone, I followed it.

It led me to the old-fashioned family cemetery I had been dreaming about. So it actually did exist. The place was just starting to fall to neglect. Some of the fence planks had rotted through and random plant life was beginning to encroach on everything. Aunt Tillie must have tended to the cemetery, until she became one of its residents. Willows, yews, poplars, oaks, apple and cherry trees stood guard over the tombstones, like ghostly sentries shrouded in mist.

I pulled my jacket tighter around me and walked among the old-fashioned tombstones, reading the inscriptions. It seemed to be my entire family, on my mom's side. Gus was going to be green with envy. An old family homestead, replete with ghosts and a private, family cemetery, was his idea of a dream come true.

In the center of the cemetery, a broken granite angel watched over a riotous overflow of roses. At first, I thought it was just a sculpture, but it was actually an elaborate tombstone. It was the oldest grave here, and it was where I had seen Lisette in my dream.

Here lies a promising witch. Too promising for her own good. 1650-1677.

It had to be Lisette's grave. Damn, she was young when she died. Only twenty-seven.

The age I am now.

A shiver crawled up my spine.

A raven cawed and landed on one of the tall, standing tombstones.

In the silence that followed, I heard someone say, *"You overestimate your talent, witch. And your importance. It will be your undoing."*

I whirled around, trying to find the voice, but I was alone.

Had I actually heard that with my ears? Or had it been my imagination?

Was it meant for me?

Or was it an echo from the past? Something someone once told Lisette?

I caught a movement out of the corner of my eye. I whirled back to Lisette's tomb, but there was no one there.

I rubbed my eyes and looked again, opening up my mind's eye and activating whatever second sight I possessed. Next to each grave, the fog swirled and started forming human shapes. Was this real? Or was Gus's ointment screwing with my head?

I blinked, but the shapes were still there. I slowly backed away, as one of the shapes beckoned me to come closer.

Instead, as soon as I got to the gate, I turned and ran.

CHAPTER THIRTY-SIX

AFTER I GOT HOME, I took a long, hot shower and scrubbed my wrist about six times, to make sure I got all of Gus's flying ointment off my skin. I was too wired to sleep so, once the sun was up and the morning fog had lifted, I decided to tackle the godawful mess in the cellar. Especially now that Aunt Tillie was contained.

With sunlight streaming in through the small cellar windows, it didn't seem as scary of a place. I should have felt the energy in the room, but I was pretty convinced that with Aunt Tillie trapped, I wasn't going to have to worry about a flying shovel whacking me in the head when my back was turned. Which ratcheted my fear level way down.

It took hours to sweep up all the glass and broken decorations, replace the lights, clean the blood stains from the floor and pick up the equipment and various odds-and-ends that were strewn everywhere. Aunt Tillie's little poltergeist-y tantrum had certainly been effective. Even the large, metal shelving unit in the back of the cellar had been knocked over.

I tried to prop the shelving unit back up, but it fell backwards and hit the wall, making a hollow thud. Hollow? I picked up a hammer and tapped the wall. It did sound hollow. I tapped on the East wall. That sounded solid. So I returned to the North wall and tapped it again. Definitely hollow.

I rooted through Tillie's tools until I found a sledgehammer. As I was about to smash through the wall, I remembered the rowan tree out front and hesitated. Obviously, wanton destruction would have to be my last choice.

There had to be a way to get behind that wall. I pounded

and knocked and prodded, but I couldn't find an opening. I hefted the sledgehammer again. Did I dare risk it? But just as I drew my arms back for a swing, I saw something silver flash between the wall slats. I dropped the sledgehammer and took a closer look. It was a type of lock. I was going to need something long, thin and narrow.

* * *

I ran upstairs, grabbed a letter opener from Aunt Tillie's desk, and went back into the cellar to try to jimmy the lock. The letter opener went partway in and stopped. I jiggled it back and forth, but it didn't release the lock. I took a barrette out of my hair and inserted that into the lock. I closed my eyes and tried to feel where the pins were, but it was hopeless. Lock picking was in Gus's wheelhouse, not mine.

Somewhere, there was a key that fit that lock. But where?

I ran back upstairs and searched Aunt Tillie's desk, pulling out all the random keys she had stashed in there. I tried them all, even the safe deposit box key, but nothing worked. Where else would she keep a key? Especially one that she wanted to hide, but not lose? The more I thought about it, the more I thought I knew the answer.

After I did the grocery shopping, I hit the bank. It was an old wooden building and, like the rest of the town, looked like it had been built in the nineteenth century. When I walked in, it seemed everyone knew everyone else. Which was no surprise, since it was the only bank in town.

The teller, Michelle, was super-sweet and chatty. "So, you're living at the witch house?"

"That's what I hear."

"Poor Tillie. That's a crime what happened to her. A real crime. She was real old though. Should never have been driving. Especially without her glasses. But she hated wearing them, so she forgot them whenever she could. Old people. I swear they need someone to parent them."

I wondered what 'real old' meant to a barely-legal teller. "You seem to know more about my Aunt Tillie than I do."

"Well, that's the downside of a small town. We all live in

each other's pockets. And everyone loved Tillie, on account of her bein' so sweet and all."

I snorted and quickly covered it with a cough. Seemed like my lethal, posthumous Aunt Tillie was very different from the Tillie everyone else remembered. Death must have made her personality take a turn for the worse. "Did Aunt Tillie have an account here?"

"All her accounts were transferred to her trust after her death."

"Yeah, I've got the trust info," I said. "I was just wondering if she had a safe-deposit box."

"Hold on, let me check." She left and came back a few minutes later. "You're right. She rented a safe-deposit box right before she died."

My ears perked up and a soft wind whispered in my head. There was something in that box I needed to see. I could feel it. "Can I see it?"

"You would need to bring in a copy of the Death Certificate and the Will."

"Seriously? I have to prove that she's dead and I'm her beneficiary? I'll bet this whole town could recite the details of her Last Will and Testament by memory."

She smiled. "You have a point. I guess we could waive the rules. Just don't tell Mr. Harding."

"Mr. Harding?"

"He's my new boss. He's a stickler for rules. Even when they're stupid." She looked around, presumably for Mr. Harding. "Follow me," she said, ushering me down a set of stairs and into the vault. "Do you have her key?"

I pulled the key out of my pocket and held it up.

Within minutes, I was ensconced in a small, private room, sorting through Aunt Tillie's safe deposit box. Birth certificate, property deed, some pictures of Aunt Tillie, there were even a few of my mom, holding me when I was a baby.

I flipped through the pictures. Wow, my mom had been young when I was born. I studied her face, looking at the similarities between us. I had her eyes. And her jaw. And her hair. That must have been hell on my dad. A visual reminder of the woman he lost, every time he looked at me. Although, what surprised me most was that I looked more like Lisette than I looked like my own mom.

Under the pictures was an unusual-looking pendant. It was a pentacle, with most of the pentagram inside an ouroboris serpent, (a snake eating its tail), except for one of the pentagram arms which jutted outside of the serpent. The point turned into a long stem, topped by an infinity symbol. I couldn't imagine anyone wearing it. It looked more like a key than a pendant for a necklace.

A key. This *had* to be it. I pocketed the pentacle key and the pictures of my mom, and returned the box to the teller.

* * *

When I returned home, Tillie shimmered and formed in front of me. She was bigger than usual and her anger was palpable. "You have to stop."

"Really, I don't have to do anything." I held up the pentacle key. "I want to see what's behind that wall."

Tillie's flesh dripped off so that all I saw in front of me was a rotting, worm-eaten corpse.

"I appreciate what you're trying to do, Aunt Tillie, but I can take care of myself. You're not going to scare me off with sideshow theatrics. So get back in your vase."

I really liked the new set-up, with Aunt Tillie being around, but not being able to physically hurt me anymore. I should have done that power-over ritual when I first arrived, instead of waiting until she almost killed me to toss her in a brass bud vase.

I walked through her and towards the kitchen. It was kind of weird seeing my body go through Aunt Tillie's, but I wasn't about to let her see me get squeamish.

She stood there, looking martyred and annoyed. "Then meet your fate, you arrogant girl."

She returned to her vase in a cloud of ectoplasm and I headed for the cellar.

* * *

Even though it would be dark soon, and going in the cellar at night was not something I really wanted to do, I was obsessed with finding out what was behind the wall. So I turned on all the cellar lights, located the hidden lock on the wall, and then slipped the key in.

The lock clicked and released, and a hidden door swung open. Behind the door were stairs that led down into a black pit. I couldn't see what was down there, but I could feel a cold, malevolent breeze racing up from its depths.

Gooseflesh rippled across my skin and my pineal gland kicked into overdrive.

I took a camping lantern from the tool table, turned it on and slowly crept down the stairs, one hand on the light, the other hand on the wall.

At the bottom of the stairs, I found a small stone room, cold as a cave, with a stone altar in the center of it. It was the room I had been dreaming about for months. This must have been Lisette's temple space.

I walked in and cast feelers around the room.

I could sense vibrations of violence and tragedy. Something epic must have happened, to have imprinted itself on the space for so long.

I placed the lantern on the altar. It didn't give off a lot of light, but it was better than nothing.

I tried to open up my sight to the past, but I didn't get anything. I needed to find a way to go back in time. Gus's flying potion hadn't really worked for me before. But what were my options?

An image of Grundleshanks flashed across my mind's eye. *Sometimes, you have to kiss a lot of toads...*

I ran upstairs, got Grundleshanks's tank, brought it down into the hidden room, and placed it on the altar. Then I drew a circle of protection around us with my trusty blackthorn staff and called on the Gods in all directions to keep us safe.

I reached in the tank and picked up Grundleshanks. For a long minute, I felt paralyzed by doubt. Did I really want to do this? I could already feel the effects of the toxins from his skin, traveling up my arm.

I took a deep breath and, before I could change my mind, brought Grundleshanks's cold little toad body up to my lips and kissed him, ingesting the poison he carried, before I dropped him back in his mud.

Soon, my whole body was vibrating. The vibrations grew stronger, until I couldn't tell if I was feeling vibrations or having a seizure.

I collapsed in the circle, my body twitching on the ground.

CHAPTER THIRTY-SEVEN

I COULD FEEL MY spirit rise, up, up, up, until it was free of my flesh. I journeyed through the blackness until I had left the confines of the cottage, my spirit traveling through the celestial heavens.

A vortex opened up and pulled me in, hurtling me backwards through time, until I landed back outside the cottage.

It looked newly built. It was much smaller than it was in my time, and the woods were much grander. I settled down on a tree stump and asked the universe to tell me about Lisette.

Lisette appeared in front of me and I felt a pull between us. Suddenly, it felt like I was both inside of her, experiencing her life, at the same time I was outside of her, watching her.

* * *

Lisette had quickly and joyfully settled in to her new life, with visions of *'happily ever after'* floating in her head. She loved the cottage and her newfound status in this new American colony, that both feared and adored her. She was so busy looking forward, she forgot to look back. If she had, she would have seen that Fate was hunting her around every corner, waiting for her in every shadow. Even Death himself crossed the ocean, seeking her out by her scent. For Death does not relinquish his loved ones so easily. And the hangman's noose still ached for her lovely, white neck.

One beautiful summer day in the North Woods, Lisette left the baby with Lucien and went out to collect fresh herbs for her wortcunning. As she walked, a layer of morning dew soaked the hem of her skirt.

Lisette paused and let the scent of the forest flow through her. She loved the dark, rich smell of the soil, the sharp green of the leafing plants, even the dank smell of rot. She loved everything about the forest, from its perfectly contained cycle of life and death, to the soft light that peeked through the tree branches.

Humming, she turned down a path that was scarcely more than an impression on the foliage, the work of small, hooved animals over time. She always seemed to find her best herbs in the most out of the way places.

As she walked, she tied up her skirts so they wouldn't drag in the grass or catch on twigs, exposing the small dagger she kept sheathed on her thigh. If the villagers could see her now! Walking about with bare legs. That would be guaranteed to stir gossip for months.

But with every scratch on her exposed legs, she cursed the unwritten rule that trousers were for men. She vowed to begin wearing them from this point forward. It was guaranteed to shock the villagers, which was almost reason enough and it might just start a trend. Women everywhere would thank her for their liberation from their treacherous, cumbersome wardrobes.

Every now and then, Lisette stopped and cut various herbs for her basket. A bit of sage, some mugwort to open the sight, a few sprigs of hemlock. She handled the hemlock carefully, touching it as little as possible, cautiously placing it inside a handkerchief to separate it from the other plants. The deadly herb's resemblance to its edible cousin yarrow was the downfall of many 'not-as-cunning-as-they-thought' folk. She could already feel the vibrations of her body increase from the small amount of toxin she had absorbed through her skin.

Half a mile later, she unknotted her skirts so her legs were covered, and rejoined the main path. As she left the sheltering woods for the well-trodden road to the Village, the sun blazed high overhead and the heat made her long to run wild and naked and free, without any concern for modesty. A body should be allowed to have its skin warmed by the sun and cooled by the shadows. Although, she thought, as she tripped on a rock, it would also help to have hard hooves to run on, rather than these soft-skinned, easily bruised feet.

Finally the General Store was in sight. She paused to knot her long, black hair up into a bun. She should have worn her bonnet, but she had been so happy to get out of the house for a bit, and away from the demanding screams of that wretched, pint-sized tyrant, that she let her haste get the better of her.

As she kept walking, a wave of unease hit her. She stopped and sniffed the air, trying to orient where this feeling of distress was coming from.

Suddenly, she felt a small hand on her arm.

She looked down into the frightened, dirty face of ten-year-old Bobby Wheeler. His cheeks reddened and his breath stammered out in short gasps.

"You have to come with me, Lady," he wheezed, "It's me mum. She's not feeling well."

"What's wrong with her, Bobby?"

His eyes shifted away, fixing on the dusty tips of his booted feet. "Her tummy aches and she's afraid maybe the baby's coming."

Could that be the cause of the distress? Lisette let Bobby pull her away, but the unease grew stronger, demanding her attention.

As she cast about for what this disturbance in the web might be, she felt a pain so intense, her blood chilled in her veins and her legs nearly gave way under her. A tidal wave of fear and anger washed over her, taking her breath away.

Every fiber of her being was pulling her back towards the woods, back towards her cottage.

She looked down at Bobby. His image was blurry, as if he wasn't really there. She blinked and tried to focus. The rate of his breathing, the direction of his glance, the sweat on his brow, the redness of his cheeks, all these were signs.

"Your eyes are full of falsehoods, little boy. Why are you trying to waylay me? Tell me true."

He swallowed and stammered his innocence, but she could smell the guilt on him the way a snake smells fear on its supper.

She drew herself up to her full height. "I've cured you, your mother, your sister, of ailments that would have killed you. I've treated you as if you were my own family. And you repay me with deception? Tell me true," she said, her eyes glittering dangerously. "Or do you think your youth will stay my hand?"

Terrified, his legs shaking, Bobby still managed to stand his ground before her. "I don't know what you..." he trailed off. "Me mum's not feeling well. I didn't mean to..."

The pupils in Lisette's eyes elongated into slits, her body gently swayed and her voice changed, the sound carrying a subtle, hissing undercurrent. "Stay your lies, they do not please me."

She took Bobby's hand in hers, stroking the back of his palm as though beckoning the words from him. *"Speak your secrets to me, little one. Whisper to me what you dare not say out loud. Upon your soul, upon Heaven and Hell, unstop your mouth and let loose your words."*

Bobby burst into tears. "He told me to delay you on your journey, Lady. I do not know why."

"Who is this *'he'* you speak of?"

Bobby sniffled and whispered the name so low, she had to put her ear next to his mouth to hear him. "He said his name was Matthew. Matthew Gilardi."

Lisette took an involuntary step back, the name ringing in her head, the fear so strong and thick in her throat, she almost choked on it. It couldn't be. Not *him.*

"This Matthew Gilardi, did he wear boots befitting a pirate? Did he sport thick, long, silver hair and a soft, inviting beard? A face almost too perfect to belong to a man? Not a blemish or mark upon him?"

Bobby looked at her, lost. Lisette placed her hands on his head and pushed an image into his mind. "Is this who you saw, Bobby?"

"Yes," he whispered, confused. "How did you—?"

But she turned on her heel and ran back into the woods, dropping her basket of herbs in her haste. She prayed that she'd make it back to the cottage in time.

She ran and ran as if her heart would burst. She paid no attention to the branches clawing at her face or the burrs and thorned plants catching on her legs and skirts. She leapt over roots and rocks. She stumbled on a patch of small, wet pebbles, barely catching herself against an old roughened oak. She didn't register the bloody scrapes on her palms. All she could think about was reaching the cottage.

As she breached the clearing, she could hear the baby screaming.

"Lucien!" She ran into the cottage and was overwhelmed by noise.

The screaming, furious, snotting tears of an infant...

Muffled scuffling sounds...

The ringing of metal against metal...

The dying wail of a man meeting a violent end...

"Lucien!!"

It all seemed to come from the bowels of the cottage, from the hidden temple room. She tried to spring the mechanism, but the shelving that concealed the door wouldn't budge more than an inch.

She threw herself against the shelves with her full weight, forcing them to swing open, their great bulk finally sweeping aside the debris that had barred their way.

The room—her temple and work area, where she could work her craft and worship her Gods in peace—looked like a cyclone had spun through it. Broken glass, scattered herbs and candles were strewn over the floor.

Next to the altar, a tear-streaked, red-faced, screaming child was safely imprisoned behind the bars of her crib.

As Lisette looked around, dazed, she caught a movement out of the corner of her eyes. There, on the floor, behind the stone altar.

She took her dagger out of its sheath, prepared to do battle with the Devil himself, when the figure struggled up to his knees.

It was Lucien, blood gushing out of his midsection.

"Lucien!" Lisette rushed over to him, just as his strength failed and he fell backwards.

She sunk to the ground with him, gently cradling his head on her lap. His breathing was slow and shallow. Blood seemed to be everywhere, bubbling out of his nose and mouth, out of the terrifying gash in his abdomen, coloring him in a palette of gore.

"No! Don't you leave me!" Lisette sobbed, her soul racked with grief and fear. "Don't leave me, Lucien! I can heal you. I know I can!"

But it was too late. He was beyond human intervention.

"No!!!" Lisette screamed. A scream that echoed through the woods and into the village. A scream that alerted the soul of the cottage to the danger at hand. A deep, primal scream from the depths of Hell itself.

Lisette turned her face up to the heavens and did the only thing she knew how to do—she reached out and summoned the Gods and Goddesses she held dear and channeled their power through her body and soul.

"I call upon the power of the Ancestors. I call upon the power of the Horned One and his dread Queen. I call upon the power of Hell itself. Rise up. Rise up and turn the blood in my veins to fire. Rise up and give me my birthright. By my blood and by my bone, I command you! Rise up and give me your power!"

The room crackled with electricity. Lisette's hair flowed on an unseen wind. Her eyes darkened, filled with magic and passion, the whites turning black.

* * *

Outside the cottage, day became night. Storm clouds gathered overhead, their interiors highlighted by flashes of lightning. In the village, people saw the commotion over the witch's cottage and ran for shelter, praying to their own Gods for protection.

* * *

Deep in the cottage, the temple room glowed with an unnatural light. A swirling vortex opened up at Lucien's feet as his spirit tried to separate from his lifeless body.

With a gesture, Lisette slammed shut the otherworldly portal.

"Death will be denied, the gate to Heaven or Hell barred. This man's soul is mine. I claim him. I own him. He is blooded to me."

She smeared his blood on her face, on her breasts, between her thighs. Taking a piece of broken glass off the floor, she cut her palm and squeezed her blood into his mouth. "Come to me, my love. For you will live again."

She positioned her mouth slightly above his and began to breathe in and out, heavier and heavier, sucking his soul into her lungs. "You. Will. Live!"

With a final breath, she pulled his soul into her. Clutching her throat, she staggered over to the human skull atop the stone altar. It grinned at her, the white bone enfleshed with wax drippings from the candle affixed to its crown.

Blood running down her face, Lisette held onto the skull with one hand and waved the other over the candle. "*Light of the Old Ones. Light of Lucifer. Light of the Black Sun. Open the gateway of the ancestors. My will be done.*"

A flame came to life and danced on the end of the candle's wick.

She wiped her bloody face and hands across the skull's face. *"Feed and live again."*

She leaned forward and breathed into the skull, exhaling from the depths of her being.

A vortex opened up on the face of the skull. Lisette screamed as Lucien's soul was slowly sucked out of her and pulled into the blood-smeared skull.

The vortex closed and the skull shimmered with an image of Lucien's face, the tribal tattoos across his chin, cheek and forehead in sharp contrast to the white bone, his dark eyes full of panic and confusion.

She knelt and tenderly kissed him, trying not to feel how cold the bone was under her lips. "All we need is to find a body for you, my love, and we will be joined again."

Clapping sounded from the shadows. Lisette whirled around. Matthew Gilardi stepped out of the shadows, his fancy, flowing white shirt and breeches soaked in Lucien's blood.

"Lovely, my dear. Quite impressive. I wondered how far along you had come in your powers." He drew a sword out of the leather scabbard that hung off his belt.

Lisette stood up, furious. "Why did you have to kill him? He wasn't one of us. He made no difference to you."

"Just a witch's play toy? Pity." Matthew nudged Lucien's

corpse with his sword, cutting through the fabric of his clothing, exposing the tender flesh underneath. "What a sad life for such a magnificent specimen."

"Damn your soul to Hell, Matthew Gilardi. You and your entire line. May the Queen of Fate destroy you..."

As Lisette weaved her curse around him, he raised his arm, swung the sword and decapitated her in mid-sentence. Her head rolled towards him and he picked it up by the hair. A look of rage and surprise was frozen on her face.

"Consider this justice. Long overdue. I should have killed you when you were a child," he said, calmly wiping the blade of his sword on her long, black tresses.

As he put the sword away, the baby began to wail, her lungs expanding to amazing capacities. Matthew walked over and gingerly took her out of the crib with one hand, while holding onto Lisette's head with the other. "And just what am I going to do with you?"

The baby reached out for Matthew's bloody trophy, grabbing hold of Lisette's face, the familiar feel quieting her down as Matthew considered his options.

* * *

I slowly returned to my timeline. As I regained consciousness, I sensed darkness... Utter darkness all around me. The bulb in my camping lantern must have burnt out.

Then I felt small feet with sharp nails climbing across my bare ankles. *Mice.* It had to be mice.

I woke with a start, gasping, cold and disoriented. As I moved my feet, the mice scattered. Was it my imagination, or was the altar glowing green? The room started to spin. I shivered uncontrollably. My skin was clammy and covered in sweat. As I got to my knees, my stomach lurched and I retched all over the stone floor.

I closed my eyes and tried to stop the whirling in my head. When I re-opened them, the room was dark, but no longer moving. I looked down at my Indiglo watch: three o'clock. But was it three in the morning? Or three in the afternoon? How long had I been down here for? My stomach flopped and I retched again.

CHAPTER THIRTY-EIGHT

WHEN I GOT BACK upstairs, it was dark outside. I settled Grundleshanks back on his table and escaped to the kitchen, before Aunt Tillie noticed I was up and about, and started reprimanding me from her vase.

I rinsed my mouth out with a mixture of hydrogen peroxide and water, trying to spit out as much of the toad residue as I could. Then I poured a big glass of milk and opened a box of Saltine crackers. I needed to cushion my stomach. As soon I could hold down the milk, I was going to get some desperately needed sleep. Once daylight hit, I had unfinished business in that temple room.

* * *

I slept until noon the next day. After a quick shower, I picked up some more camping lamps from the Trading Post, and then I hurried back down to the temple room and cleaned up the mess from the night before. At least the smell from all my retching had dissipated—somewhat. To mask the remaining residue, I sprayed a mixture of orange essential oil, vinegar and water on the area that I had been sick on.

Afterwards, I searched the room and I found the nook that Gilardi must have hidden in, waiting for Lisette. What I didn't find was any supplies, or the skull, or anything other than the stone altar.

The altar that had been glowing green.

I checked out the altar. The top was a stone slab, placed upon a wide, stone column. I pushed against the top and I felt it shift, just a tiny amount. I pushed harder and one half of the slab separated from the other half. The inside of the stone column was hollow.

I shone a light into the column. There was something hidden in there, under a thick layer of spider webs. But the thought of reaching through a handful of spider goo made me cringe. Even the thought of a feather duster full of cobwebs was *ewww*-inspiring.

So, I ran upstairs, got out the Dustbuster and brought it back down to the hidden room to suck all the dust, webs, spiders and whatever else was in there, out of the altar column.

Once it was (relatively) clean, I looked into the column again. At the bottom, I could see a curved white bone. *The skull.* It had to be.

I reached in, as far as I could, until my fingers fastened around the bone. As I pulled up on the skull, a zap of electricity sparked against my skin. *What the hell?* I yanked my hand away and felt my skin tear open.

"*Ow!* Son of a bitch."

The skull clattered back down the column. *Damn it.* I hoped it hadn't broken. My hand was stinging like crazy, but I carefully flexed my fingers and reached back down for the skull.

This time, I was able to get a good grasp on the skull and I slowly brought it up. No zaps or gashes this time. But as I lifted the skull out of the column, I could see why my hand was stinging. It was bleeding all over everything, especially the skull.

And the skull was practically humming with happiness.

I placed the skull on the altar slab, took off my tee-shirt and wrapped it around my injured hand. When I looked up, the front of the skull was shimmering. On top of the bone, I could see a face—tribal, tattooed, angry.

I swallowed. "Lucien?"

And then it was gone.

I shone the flashlight on the skull, but it was just a blood-covered skull. My imagination was really running away with me. Before I went upstairs to take care of my hand, I couldn't resist looking inside the column again. In the light, I could see the silver glint of a knife blade, with fresh blood on it. Lisette's athamé. The one she cut her herbs with. That must have been what I cut myself on.

I debated trying to get it, but with my luck, I'd sever a finger. So I gave up and ran upstairs.

*   *   *

It was freezing cold in the house. As I bandaged my hand, I heard Tillie's voice scream in my head. *"Fool! You never give blood to the dead!"*

I couldn't argue with her. She was right. I had known it the moment I felt how happy the blood had made the skull. I just hadn't wanted to think about it.

"It was an accident."

"It doesn't matter." She appeared beside me. "Do you have any idea what you've done?"

"It was an accident," I repeated.

"You have a lot of accidents and unfortunate consequences. This is exactly why your mother never wanted you using magic."

"Maybe if she had stuck around and trained me, instead of taking off, I wouldn't be learning the rules the hard way."

"Maybe if you stopped meddling in things that are none of your business, you wouldn't be such a menace."

"I'm not a menace." I said, frowning.

"Then stop feeding that skull," she said and vanished.

*   *   *

I went back down into the temple room and tried to wipe the blood off the skull, as well as the altar. But the damage was done. I could feel that it had awakened something within the room, but I had no idea what. All the same, it was kind of creeping me out. This time, when I left, I locked the door, to keep whatever it was, in.

I was really starting to worry. I called Gus, but all I got was voicemail. I called Mama Lua, to ask her about blooding a skull—or, more precisely, how to *un*blood one—but the store was closed. I tried to talk to Aunt Tillie, but she was ignoring me.

I researched it for hours on the internet, but it was the one thing no one seemed to have any interest in doing. Or, if they did, they weren't posting about it. I even asked Grundleshanks, but all he did was blink at me.

Finally, I gave up. I fed Grundleshanks a cricket and went to bed.

* * *

A warm wind blew in through the windows, making the curtains dance. But this wasn't my room. Everything was white. Like a bridal chamber. White roses, white robes, a white coverlet. There was even a white canopy over the bed.

I writhed around on the bed, feeling on edge. My skin was so hyper-sensitive, the feel of the silk sheets was almost too much to bear. I ran my hands down my body, pressing the sheets against me and moaning in pleasure when a shadow came into the room.

Moonlight hit the shadow and it morphed into a large, naked man with skin the color of Kahlúa. He was covered—from his feet to the top of his bald crown—in tribal tattoos.

Lucien.

He never said a word as he slid into bed with me, stroking my body like it belonged to him. His touch was smooth, gentle but firm. His lips were full. And I gasped in pleasure at what his tongue could do. As he lingered between my legs, I thought I'd lose my mind with ecstasy.

And when he was done, he kept going. Licking the sides of my belly, outlining my breasts, before taking my aching nipples in his mouth. Teasing, nibbling and stroking me until I was near the breaking point. He worked his way up to my neck and throat, licking, nuzzling and gently biting.

Finally, he brought his mouth to mine and he plunged his body into me, again and again, until I felt like I was riding a rollercoaster. Our bodies fit so perfectly together. It was like we had been made for each other.

We were suspended in time and space, twisting and turning, weightless. I rocked against him until the world exploded inside me.

* * *

I woke up with a gasp, only to find a pillow between my legs. Was all that a dream? Did I really just hump a pillow? I sighed and laid back down. If Lucien was really like that—no wonder Lisette had gone to crazy lengths to save him.

A cold breeze wrapped around me and inside my head, I heard, "All that and more..."

I tried to go back to sleep, to get back into that dream, but no matter how hard I tried, it eluded me.

But when I stopped trying, he came to me again and it was even better than before.

CHAPTER THIRTY-NINE

WHEN I WOKE UP the next morning, it finally dawned on me how freaky the previous night had been. I could understand dreaming about Lucien, but that erotically?

And it had felt so real. That dream had left me so incredibly horny, it was physically painful. And nothing I did seemed to ease that pain.

But what if it wasn't a dream? What if Lucien's spirit had paid me a nocturnal visit? How would he have been able to get past my wards?

* * *

After a cold shower and a brisk walk through the woods, I called Gus again. This time he answered.

"Finally. Where the hell have you been?!"

"Busy."

That was all he would say. Bastard.

So I filled him in on the days and nights of yours truly. "Do you believe that ghosts can come back from the dead and have sex with a living person?"

"No."

"Why not?"

"Because if it could happen, I would have already done it. You know how many hot gay men have crossed over? Hubba, hubba."

"I don't think you can force yourself on an ethereal partner. I'm talking about if they're interested in you. Not the other way around. It happens in Hollywood movies, all the time."

"And we all know how realistic they are."

"You're just jealous."

"You know what I think? You're just horny. You had a vision of some sexy dude that lived a million years ago and you've created a whole fantasy out of it. Because you need to get laid. Bad. Want me to call Mr. Lyra for you?"

"Shut up. What the fuck is your problem today?" Although at this point, I probably wouldn't turn anyone down. Even Lyra. Or his wife. I was so antsy, it was driving me crazy.

"I'm not the one with imaginary lovers."

"Bite me." I was tempted to hang up on him, but I had a question and I knew I'd rather ask Gus than Aunt Tillie. And the way things were going, there was no guarantee Gus would answer his phone again. "Just suppose, for a minute, it was really Lucien. How would he have gotten past my wards?"

Gus sighed. Impatient.

"Spare me the commentary. Do you know or not? It's a simple question," I snapped.

"Fine. Let's, for the moment, say you're right. You said he lives in the skull, right?"

"Yeah." Given everything I had seen, I was pretty sure he did.

"Well, you blooded the skull. So if he came to you, he would have smelled like you, like your blood. So your wards wouldn't have done squat to stop him. Can I go now?"

"Sure, little Miss Sunshine. Call me back when you find a better personality." I hung up in an even fouler mood. *Eh,* he was probably right. I just needed to get laid. Bad. Boy, did I need to get laid. I was usually fine with total abstinence—I've had a lot of practice—but not right now.

I wondered if Paul was back in town? I had been hoping that he would fall for my charm and wit, but I hadn't seen him since the accident. Not even a phone call.

* * *

When I went to sleep that night, Lucien was back. And it was the best time yet. Everything about his body just felt so right. From the curve of his muscles to the heft of his penis. But I woke up the next morning, feeling slightly foolish. I mean, here I was, either being seduced by a ghost or having a torrid affair with my freakin' pillow.

I really needed to get a man in my life. It had been way too long if even the memory of sex could make me orgasm. Suddenly, I thought of the love spell I had written for that woman at Pagan Day. A slight modification and I was pretty sure it would work for me.

I spent a little bit of time reworking the spell, then I lit a small candle and fired up some dragon's blood incense. Holding onto a serpentine stone in one hand and a rose quartz crystal heart in the other, I chanted:

"Love and sex are whirling.
Lust be in thy turning.
Bring my true love to me.
The one who holds my passion's key.
As the flame consumes the candle bright
I call to love with all my might
Come to me, within these hours three
As I desire it, so mote it be."

I passed the stone and crystal through the smoke and flame three times. Then I put them in front of the candle and burned the piece of parchment with the spell.

When the flame crept all the way down the page to my fingers, I dropped it in an ashtray, to finish the burn. Then I tried to forget about it as I waited for the candle to burn out. Spells were best left not picked at.

* * *

Three sex-obsessed hours later, there was a knock on my door. I opened it to find Paul Raines.

"Hi." He cleared his throat. "Mind if I come in?"

Paul. I almost started laughing. The one who holds my passion's key. As far true love went, I could do worse. Now if I could only get him on board.

"Hello, stranger. Right on time. I've been hoping you'd show up again." I opened the door all the way.

"Well, listen to you," he smiled, his eyes twinkling. "Miss me?"

"Don't let it go to your head. How was New York?"

"Hectic." He said, walking in.

Man, he looked good. Even in clothes, his body was well-defined and luscious. His jeans were tight and his shirt was the perfect shade of blue to bring out his eyes. Although, all I could think of was stripping his clothes off him. I wondered if I'd get the chance.

"Why are you looking at me like that?"

"Like what?"

"Like I'm a lobster in a restaurant tank."

Hmmm. How to answer that? If I said "I was just wondering if it was okay for me to jump on you now, or do we need to do dinner and a movie first?" would that make him run for the hills? Or for the bedroom?

Yeah, honesty was probably a bad idea. So I covered. Well, I tried. What I meant to say was, "Don't flatter yourself, Shakespeare. I was just wondering if you want anything to drink."

But what actually came out was, "Just wondering how you'd look naked."

I clapped my hands over my mouth and hurriedly spun away, so he wouldn't see the mortified look on my face. *Damn it.* The older I got, the less control I had over what came out of my mouth. I could feel my face flushing from my chin to the roots of my hair.

"Want a drink?" I squeaked, keeping my back to him and edging towards the kitchen.

"I can email you a photo if you promise not to put it on your Facebook page," he laughed. "Are you blushing?"

"No! I'm just... wondering if you want tea or coffee?"

"Really? 'Cause the back of your neck is beet red," he teased, still amused.

I escaped into the kitchen, where I doused my burning cheeks with cold water and put on a kettle for tea.

*   *   *

A few hours later, we had drunk the tea, made (and eaten) a pizza, and were having a lively conversation over drinks. As I poured another round of Jack & Mexican Coke (made with cane sugar instead of high fructose corn syrup), I surreptitiously gave

Paul a once-over. Way too sexy for the middle of nowhere. He wasn't as ferociously sexy as Lucien, but at least he was a living, breathing man. So he automatically had the advantage.

He was solid and just at that age when his muscles were starting to get a little soft. Rugged, but comfortable looking. With full lips and piercing blue eyes beneath his glasses. And intelligent to boot. He'd have to be, right? Since he was a teacher and a writer?

"So, what's your book about?" I asked.

"Haunted houses of the Midwest. There's some interest in turning it into a reality series, so they want me to get footage for a sizzle reel. Whatever that is. My grandfather tells me I'm an idiot for not taking a closer look at your cottage."

"Daniel knows more than I do about the history of this house—he wrote the book on it."

"As he's never let me forget. And then I stopped in at the Trading Post and J.J. Told me you're living in a *'ghost house with 'tude'.* So I was hoping I could spent a few days here. Bring in camera equipment, infrared, that sort of thing."

"Are you crazy? You can't stay here. You're way too hot."

Shit! I clapped my hands over my mouth again. I hadn't meant to say that out loud! Damn alcohol. Jeez!

"I mean, this place is way too small." The state of Wisconsin was too small. Okay, now my face was absolutely burning. And I knew he could see it, because he was laughing at me.

"Y'know, last time I tried to flirt with you, I got my hand slapped. And the time before that, you accused me of being gay."

"Well..." I couldn't really argue with him. But what was I supposed to say? I'm being visited by an evil spirit who makes me horny? That if I don't have sex with a live man soon, I'm going to go stark raving mad? "A woman's allowed to change her mind. And you're pretty damn cute in that shirt."

"Don't get my hopes up if you don't mean it."

"Oh, I mean it." More than you know.

He blushed. Ah-hah! Finally. I made *him* blush. Score one for me.

"I think you're kinda hot, yourself."

I perked up. "Really?" That was promising. "Here's to

mutual hotness."

We clinked glasses, his eyes lingering on mine. "But there's more to a relationship than just heat," he continued. "Heat, I can get anywhere. But I'm at the age now where I want the whole enchilada. So don't play this game if you can't handle the consequences."

A tingle ran up and down my body, as I contemplated Paul becoming a part of my life, not just my bed.

CHAPTER FORTY

HALF A BOTTLE OF Jack Daniels later, we were getting pretty friendly. We both liked the same things, (funny movies of all genres, classic black & whites and anything with Harrison Ford or Cary Grant), hated the same things, (hack-and-slash films), and were turned on by the same things (honesty, intelligence, integrity, humor). Over the course of the evening, I found myself moving closer and closer to him. Before I knew it, one of my hands was on his thigh, while the other hand stroked his arm, working its way up to his broad shoulders...

I yanked my hands back and sat on them. "Sorry. Sometimes they have a mind of their own."

"That's okay. I never mind an attractive woman manhandling me."

"But if a chick's doing it, wouldn't it be womanhandling?"

"Don't tell me you're one of those w-o-m-y-n feminists?"

I laughed. "No. I think I'm more of a gay man trapped in a woman's body," I said, as my hand found its way back to his thigh.

When he didn't stop me, I tossed all sense of decency to the winds and straddled his lap, kissing him. I kept expecting him to pull away, but instead, he undid my shirt, unhooking my bra with an expert twist of the wrist.

Soon, the floor was littered with clothes, as we explored each other's bodies. Now this was much better than any dream could be. It made me wonder why I had been in a self-imposed celibacy for so long. But that was back in L.A., and the men there were totally different from the man who was currently doing such lusciously wicked things to my body.

I briefly thought about moving venues, but Tillie had been quiet for so long, I was pretty sure she wasn't watching. Hopefully, she had fallen asleep. If ghosts even slept. Besides, the last thing I wanted to do was interrupt the flow.

Afterward, we lay in each other's arms, decompressing. But I was still insatiable. I couldn't keep my hands off him. And the more I stroked his body, the more aroused he became. Before I knew it, we were in the throes of ecstasy once again.

*   *   *

"I have something for you." Paul lay on the couch, glistening with sweat.

"Again? What are you? Superman?" I leaned over and kissed him.

"Give me a few hours to catch my breath, woman." He kissed me back. "No, I mean, from Daniel. A present. I dropped one off at the library before I came here. The other one's for you. It's in my satchel."

I pulled my clothes on and opened up his satchel. It was Daniel's book, the soft leather binding supple to the touch.

"He said you'd know what to do with it."

"Do I ever." I put it on display, on the mantle, next to the portrait of Lisette.

By the time I finished adjusting the placement, Paul was dressed and in the kitchen, making a pot of coffee.

"You're domestic, too?" I teased, walking into the kitchen. "How did I get so lucky?"

"Just moved to the right town."

"I guess I did." I said, smiling to myself as I set two mugs on the table.

*   *   *

Later, after the coffee had percolated...

"So, about this ghost thing," he said, sipping his coffee.

I dragged my mind back to the conversation we had been having, before we became so pleasantly distracted.

"I want to see if I can catch your ghost in action," he continued. "Temperature dips, whispers. You'd be amazed what an infrared digital camera and recorder can pick up."

I laughed. "You're not going to need all those fancy gizmos. As far as ghosts go, mine completely lack any subtlety." Kind of like me.

"I have to be honest. I've never seen any sign of a ghost here. I mean, it was before I got all the cool equipment, but still. When I was a boy, my mother used to have tea with Tillie every now and again, and I never picked up on any type of spirit emanations."

"Did she take you on a tour of *all* the rooms?" I asked.

"Yeah. What with my grandfather's book and all, she was determined to prove to my mother that her cottage was ghost free."

Somehow I seriously doubted she had shown him the entire house. "So you know about the secret room in the cellar?"

"What secret room?"

I grabbed a flashlight. "Grab your camera and get ready for the big time. This is going to rock your sizzle reel."

* * *

Paul got his gear from the car and we were soon descending into the dark cellar.

"I replaced the cellar lights. I can turn them on so we can see."

"Don't. It'll blow out the night-vision screen."

So, I didn't. As we got further down the stairs...

"Definite temperature drop." He said into his camera mic.

"Just watch where you're going. I don't want you to be so into taping what's going on, you fall down the stairs."

The camera swung over and Paul focused on me.

"Knock it off!" I said, putting a hand over my face. "Focus on the ghosts. Not me!"

He laughed. "Do you know how many people think they have ghosts? It's usually something that can be explained away by science."

"Sure it is." I muttered.

"Hey! Look at that." He pointed to the infrared monitor screen on his camera. "Isn't it amazing what you can see, using a digital? My still camera picks up things like this all the time, but I haven't quite figured out what causes it yet."

I looked at the monitor. There were red, green and white spirit balls zipping through the screen. More than I'd ever seen before.

"I hate to burst your non-believing bubble, Paul, but those are spirit balls. Proof ghosts exist. Just what you were looking for."

"Or an interesting and amusing trick of the light."

"What light? It's dark down here."

"You know what I mean."

"Not really." I opened the door to the secret room. "But if you think that's cool, get ready to have your world blown apart."

* * *

In the middle of utter blackness, the skull gleamed white, practically glowing on the altar. I turned the camping lantern on low, so I could see where I was going, and Paul focused his camera on the altar as we walked closer. "Wow."

"The first time I touched the skull, I swear I saw a face shimmer across the bone."

"Oh, yeah?" He reached out to pick up the skull.

I grabbed his arm. "Wait! Don't do that."

"Why not?"

"It's not safe."

"Really? In case you haven't noticed, I'm a grown man. I don't think I need a girl to protect me from a skull."

I dropped my hand. "Fine. But don't blame me if you start having erotic dreams about a long-dead, bald, tattooed man."

"Are you kidding me? After what we just did, you're back at the gay thing?"

"No! Nope, not me. Not at all. I'm just—"

"—What? Telling me about your personal fantasies? Are you saying I should shave my head?" He laughed and placed his hand on the skull.

Suddenly his body convulsed as if he was having an epileptic seizure, his camera dropping to the floor.

"Paul!"

He fell to the ground, eyes rolled back in his head.

"Paul! Are you all right?! Paul?!" I felt for a pulse.

He stood up and threw me off of him. Preternaturally

strong. My body sailed across the room, hit the wall and slid to the floor.

* * *

When I could breathe again, I slowly rolled onto my side, aching and bruised all over. Paul lay on his side, next to me, his hand stroking my face.

"Paul?" I looked at him and my blood turned ice-cold. His eyes seemed to be rotating in different directions. "Are you all right? Should I call a doctor?"

"That will not be necessary," said Paul's voice—but not his voice. It was like his voice box had become its own echo chamber and his voice resonated on multiple levels.

"You're not Paul." I whispered.

"No, my love. And I have you to thank. I have been waiting for so long. I hope I didn't hurt you."

"Lucien?" I asked, hazarding a guess.

"Yes, my love. I appreciate your sacrifice. I could not have chosen a better body myself."

"What? I didn't... I'm not... he's not your body. You can't keep him. And I'm not your love."

He roared with laughter and every hair on my body stood on end. "I feel so strong. Do you know how many centuries I've waited to get my strength back? I don't know what to do with myself. I want to squeeze you until I break you in half. It would be as easy as picking a flower."

"Wait! No," I squeaked. "Whatever happened to 'my love'? I think I liked that better."

He laughed, amused. His body was so much bigger than mine. I didn't remember his body being that wide. When I looked at his body again, I realized it wasn't. His body wasn't actually touching the ground.

He may have been laying down, but his body was hovering a good two inches above the floor.

CHAPTER FORTY-ONE

"OH MY GOD, ARE you levitating?" I climbed on top of him, tried to use my own body to pin his down.

As I looked at him, I could see Lucien's tattoos settle over Paul's skin.

"Stop that right now and give me Paul back." I hissed.

Instead, he stood up, shaking me off as easily as if I was a fly. Standing, his feet were still about half an inch above the floor.

"We will be together again, soon," he whispered in that bizarre, echo-y voice, as he half-walked, half-glided out of the room.

I ran up the stairs after him. "Lucien, wait! You can't abduct my boyfriend like that. That body belongs to me."

But when I got to the kitchen, the back door was wide open and Lucien was gone.

Did he go into the woods? Or down the road? It was pitch black out and impossible to see.

"Lucien! Where are you?" I hollered into the night.

But all I heard was the sound of crickets. Paul's car was still in the driveway. But his body was AWOL. And there were no footprints to follow.

Damn it. What had I done!?

* * *

The next morning, there was a knock on the back door. I opened it to find a mud-covered Paul, dirt and twigs in his hair, his nails torn and dirty. At least he wasn't levitating any more.

"Thank God. I was about to call the police. Did you spend

the night in the woods? Weren't you freezing?"

He smiled, sheepish. "A hot shower would be really good right now."

I gave him a long look. "And how many people will be inhabiting my shower? One or two?"

"Depends. Are you showering with me?"

I shook my head. "Just checking. You weren't quite yourself when you left."

"Yeah. That was weird, huh? What the hell was that about? I'm thinking I shouldn't do my own mushroom picking anymore."

That sounded like the Paul who had gone with me down into cellar, not the one who had come back up.

"All right, get in the shower. I'll make you breakfast."

"You're the best." He said, kissing me on the cheek. "I'm starving." And he trotted up the stairs.

On the cheek? We went from hot sex to granny kisses? Okay, well, I may have been responsible for his having been possessed by a demon last night, but still...

I made a fresh pot of coffee and started cooking up a veggie and cheese omelet. Soon, Paul was back down. Wet, shiny, new and smell-o-licious. He was wearing one of Tillie's robes and it was ultra short on him. Although, I have to admit, I really appreciated the view of his muscular thighs as well as the barest hint of his well-toned butt-cheeks.

"You smell yummy," I told him. "You look ridiculous, but you smell great."

"Considering how many delectable smells are coming out of this kitchen, I'll take that as a compliment." He set out plates and silverware as if he'd lived with me for years.

I kept watching him, to see if Lucien would pop back up, but he seemed back to normal. Maybe there was some truth to the superstition that things that went bump, only went bump in the night.

* * *

After breakfast, he took a small box out of the pocket of Tillie's robe and handed it to me. "For you."

I opened it up. It was a beautiful pendant, a Tudor rose with a ruby inset. "Where did you get this? It's beautiful."

"We all have our secrets. You like it?"

"Like it? I love it."

He stood up and fastened it around my neck.

"It looks so familiar though. Where have I seen it before?" All of a sudden, I realized. It was Lisette's necklace—the one in the painting. The blood drained from my face.

"I see you remembered where it was from," he laughed, in that same, cold, echoing voice of the night before.

Lucien.

Lucien was back.

I tried to pull the necklace off, but it tightened around my throat, choking me. I was having a hard time breathing.

"What did you do? Spend the night digging up her grave?" I gasped, barely getting the words out.

He laughed.

My body went rigid and spasmed as an entity tried to shove my spirit aside and enter my flesh.

I fought it as hard as I could.

Sweat poured off me, blinding me, as I tried to push the entity out.

But it was too strong. And too determined.

As I vomited my breakfast out on the kitchen floor, my body went into seizures, and then the entity was in.

* * *

When Lisette took over my body, it was like she grabbed my spirit and sat it up on a tree stump, where I could watch what was going on, but she was firmly in charge of the flesh.

She turned to Lucien. "We have so much to get caught up on, my love." Lisette ran her hands over Lucien's new body. "It's not as good as the original, but it'll do." She sniffed and her nose wrinkled up. "What is that rancid smell?"

Lucien laughed. "Your descendant had an accident. I will clean it up."

He grabbed some paper towels and cleaned up the mess. I had to hand it to him—he seemed to have adapted to the modern world quite well. Either he was a quick study, or he had completely assimilated Paul.

"What do you wish do to first, my queen?"

"A hot bath seems in order. And then," Lisette looked around. "What have I missed the most? Mmmm... food. That coffee smells wonderful. And hot baths..." She looked him over. "And then there's you." She held open her arms. "Being with you is what I've missed the most."

He carefully picked her up in his arms and carried her to the master bedroom, where he laid her on the bed and slowly undressed her. "Close your eyes, my love. I will prepare your bath and return anon. Why fulfill only one of your fantasies, when I can give you two?"

She leaned back on the bed and closed her eyes. And mine, as well. All I could see was darkness for a time. And then suddenly, I was in a weird, surrealistic world, where a bear was dancing with a fox and Lisette was flying overhead on a broom.

This was her dream. I was in her dreams. I wondered if I could affect her dreams? Wouldn't that be cool? Maybe I could take control of my body back while she was unconscious?

But all too soon, Lucien was back and Lisette woke up. He carried her to the bathroom. It was gorgeous in there. Not only had he drawn a hot bath, but the tub was full of rose petals. The water was smooth and silky, with a hint of rose oil, and the room was ringed with candles.

He gently lowered Lisette into the tub and slowly washed her hair. "I have so missed these physical things," he said. "The silkiness of your hair, the softness of your skin."

"I am sorry, Lucien. I should never... I thought I would have you in a new body in a matter of days, I never thought it would take centuries. If I had known..."

"Hush, my love. You did what we had agreed on. And now we're together again."

"Yes," she sighed. "We are."

"Hey? Hello?! This is unacceptable. I'm fine with you two getting together for little trysts now and then, but you can NOT be planning a long-term visit. This is MY body." I protested.

"Hush up," Lisette snarled.

"Excuse me?"

"Not you, love. My progeny seems to have an opinion about

this body belonging to her."

"That will fade."

"Thank the Gods. By the next dark moon, these bodies will be ours."

* * *

I had no idea what she was talking about, but none of it sounded any good. What were they planning? And did that mean that Paul and I had until the dark moon to get our bodies back? That was what, in two weeks?

Lisette sighed and reached up, lacing her fingers behind Lucien's neck. "And we'll be together, for eternity."

He bent forward and they kissed.

How could I ever have thought either of them were to be pitied?

I felt so betrayed. And stupid. I bet Tillie was doing an '*I told you so*' dance in her vase. *Damn it.*

* * *

After Lucien bathed Lisette, he dried her off and carried her to the bed. I thought the sex between me and Paul had been hot, but it was nothing, compared to the mind-blowing sex between Lisette and Lucien. I was able watch and share her feelings and sensations. I just wasn't able to do anything that affected my body.

And if I thought I was sexually free, Lisette was a total freak. She went places I would never go. And they kept it up, all night long. I tried to stop her when it got painful, but really, I had pretty nonexistent body control.

"*Hey,*" I nudged her. "*What's going on? When you said we'll be together for eternity, do you mean all four of us? Or just the two of you? We can't keep sharing this body forever, can we? And if you get the bodies, what happens to Paul and me? Where do our spirits go?*"

"Shut up," she hissed.

Lucien looked at her.

"Not you, darling."

She returned to what she was doing and I continued to watch, fascinated. I didn't even know men liked something like that. But Lucien was writhing with ecstasy. I wondered if Paul was trapped inside his body the way I was—a spectator, powerless to stop anything.

I also wondered if we'd get more adept at manipulating our bodies, the longer we were trapped within them, or if we'd lose what tenuous grasp we had and be left floating through the ether, as disembodied spirits.

Could Lisette and Lucien really stay forever? What kind of options I was looking at, realistically?

"Would you please be quiet?" That was Lisette's voice hissing through my head.

Oh, crap. She could hear me. I needed to learn how to shield my thoughts—and pretty damn fast.

CHAPTER FORTY-TWO

WITHIN DAYS, LUCIEN WAS able to access enough of Paul's mind to be able to drive. Which gave me some hair-raising moments, but he and Lisette seemed to be having a blast with it. Fortunately, Lucien's idea of fast and my idea of fast were two different things. I guess when your only experience with forward movement is either your feet or a horse, whipping down the road at 45 m.p.h. is the height of daredevil speed.

I was working on keeping my thoughts quiet, while still keeping my mind open. That way, I could eavesdrop on Lisette's thoughts without my thoughts getting in the way. That was the theory, at least. But no matter how hard I tried to achieve stillness, the best I could do was distract my thoughts for a few minutes.

I really should have studied meditation when I had the chance. Gus was big on meditating. He tried to do at least one hour a day. I guess I just figured he could do the meditating for both of us. Too bad it didn't work that way.

* * *

After a week of eating, sex, TV, more sex, and racing up and down the road, they ran out of food. So they took the SUV down to the Trading Post.

"How much things have changed." Lisette remarked to Lucien. "Look at me. I'm wearing trousers and..." She nudged me with a mental image of her shoes.

"*Blue jeans,*" I corrected. "*And you're wearing gym shoes.*"

"Yes, blue jeans and gym shoes and no one gives me a

second glance. We can stand in the middle of town, holding hands and kissing, and not have to worry about a lynch mob."

"We had to wait a long time to come back, my love," Lucien said. "But it's been worth the wait. It seems we've been gifted with a most opportune time."

"Okay, but these aren't your bodies. You're not back, you're stealing time. And you're stealing flesh. You're nothing more than common criminals. Is that the legacy you want to leave me?"

"Hush up," Lisette thought back at me, annoyed. *"Or I will squash you like a mosquito."*

When Lisette and Lucien got to the Trading Post, J.J. was practicing his guitar.

"That's lovely," Lisette said, flirting with him.

Oh, dear Gods, don't let her get a hankering for J.J.

"I will take whomever I please," she said, her voice a loud whisper in my mind.

"He's just a kid." But I could feel her interest grow, the more protective I got. She really could be a vindictive bitch.

So I immediately and abruptly stopped all thoughts in that direction and tried a different tack. *"He's disgusting and he stinks. But if that's the best you can do with men who aren't under your spell, like Lucien is, well I guess beggars can't be choosers. Have at it."*

J.J. looked up. "Thanks. It's a new song. I just wrote it." He noticed that Lucien/Paul's arm was firmly around Lisette's/my waist. "So you two hooked up, huh? How's that going?"

"Hooked up?"

"Dating each other. Paul and I weren't a couple last time he saw us," my thoughts answered her before I could stop them.

"Oh, yes. We hooked up. Wonderful, isn't it?" Lisette smiled broadly at J.J.

"Are you okay? You're acting a little off." J.J. said. He raised an eyebrow. "Everything okay with you and the ghosts?"

I could feel Lisette panic and poke at me, so I thought about fields of daisies.

"You little bitch, don't screw with me or I'll make you regret it." She hissed in my head.

She smiled at J.J., "Yes, everything's fine. We just came in to pick up..." She cast her eyes around for something and landed on the local newspaper. "This," she said, putting the paper on the counter.

"Fifty cents."

I felt her sharp intake of breath more than heard it. I guess fifty cents was a lot of money to someone who was born four centuries ago. But Lucien was on top of it.

I wish I knew if Paul was more forthcoming with information than I was, or if Lucien had completely absorbed him.

I had a sudden image of a single red rose on Paul's snow-covered grave and the thought of that almost paralyzed me. We had to get our bodies back before we lost them completely.

"Do you know what would be nice?" Lisette said to Lucien, "I would like a rose. A single, perfect, red rose."

Whoa. Did she get that from me?

"Whatever you want my love." Lucien kissed her hand.

"Okay, you two are weirding me out, so knock off the PDAs."

"Public display of affection," I supplied to Lisette before she poked me again.

"If you want flowers, you should go check out the florist on the other side of town," J.J. said. "You can get a dozen roses for fifteen bucks."

I felt Lisette stiffen. The thought of paying for flowers must really chap her hide.

"Hey, if you get just one though, with the baby's breath, it'll look great in that vase you bought."

It was my turn to stiffen. I relaxed and tried to focus on breathing and nothingness. Last thing I wanted was Lisette knowing that Aunt Tillie was captive in the vase. I had a feeling Lisette's revenge could transcend the flesh and, regardless of how bitchy and homicidal she had been, I didn't want to do that to Aunt Tillie.

* * *

When we finally left the Trading Post. I zoned out on the incessant commentary in the SUV about how much things had changed. Instead, I focused on where I had last seen late-blooming roses. In the small cemetery by the cottage. Roses, roses, gardens of roses, different colored roses, wild roses, domestic roses gone wild. *A beautiful, perfect rose on the mantle, displayed in a gorgeous brass vase.* And they were all free.

I know it sounded crazy, but I had a plan. It wasn't much of a plan, but it was the only thing I could think of at the moment.

* * *

While Lucien was reading the paper and getting up to speed on modern day problems, language and viewpoints, Lisette walked down to the cemetery to get her single, perfect rose.

Seeing the cemetery through Lisette's eyes was quite an experience. For her, it had been her home and her prison, for centuries. And she knew everyone who was buried there.

As we walked in, I could see all their spirits. Talking, laughing. Until they saw Lisette and a hush settled in among them.

A young woman came up to Lisette, furious and barely containing it. She looked like my mom, but a lot younger than the last time I saw her. "Lisette, you can not do this. It's anathema."

"Adelaide Katherine MacDougal, I appreciate your feelings, but you have no say in what I do."

"The hell I don't. You release my daughter, immediately."

Holy crap, it was my mom. I guess it's true—when you die, you can pick whatever age you want to be.

"You don't have the strength to stand against me and you lack the stomach to destroy the body I'm in. Please remove yourself from my presence."

Lisette was icy and commanding. There wasn't a single spirit there who didn't cringe and back down in front of her.

* * *

When we got back to the cottage, Lisette went looking for a vase and the one she 'found'—thanks to a nudge from me—was Tillie's.

"Oh my goodness. What's in here?" she said, her nose

crinkling up with disgust. "Is that a mirror? And dirt?"

"I guess. I don't know. I bought it used. I was about to clean it up, polish it and put it on the mantle, when some body-grabbing ghost rudely interrupted my plans."

She felt like she wasn't quite buying my story.

So I pushed her harder, trying to distract her. *"Who's Matthew Gilardi? And why did he kill you?"*

"None of your business," she snarled back at me.

Annoyed, she dumped out the mirror, dirt and bark from the vase and then washed, dried and polished it.

The flower looked lovely on the mantle, displayed in the gleaming vase.

Privately, I prayed that Aunt Tillie had managed to escape. If there was anyone who could be a thorn in Lisette's side, it would be my Aunt Tillie.

CHAPTER FORTY-THREE

THAT NIGHT, WHILE LISETTE was asleep, I asked her again about Matthew Gilardi. This time, I got through her defenses and went straight into her subconscious, because she was suddenly dreaming about him.

* * *

Lisette's baby was in her crib, holding on to Lisette's head with one hand and a blankie in the other. The head vanished and the baby started crying. Lisette walked in the room—whole and alive—and she picked up the baby. Then she sat down in a rocking chair and started nursing her.

I sat down on a bench facing them. "Who's Matthew Gilardi?"

Lisette never looked up at me. She continued looking at the baby's face while she answered. "During the Beltaine festival, when the Horned Lord descended into the men, he descended most successfully into Matthew Gilardi. And Matthew, who never had relations with women if he could help it, impregnated my mother with a child of the Horned One."

Suddenly, we were in a different house, sitting in front of a fireplace, and Lisette looked to be about four years old. She was using a mortar and pestle to grind up some herbs.

The grown-up Lisette stood next to me, watching the child. "Ever since I can remember, Matthew Gilardi has been part of my life. When I was a child, I showed promise in the Cunning Arts, so he took me under his wing. While my mother taught me how to work with herbs and use them for healing, Matthew taught me how to use them for cursing."

The child threw the herbs in the fire and the flames turned blue.

"He taught me how to communicate with spirits and, most importantly, how to master Fate. He taught me how to navigate the realms of the Otherworld. I was his prodigy. He passed his legacy to me."

"But he killed you."

"Things change."

Random images came flashing at me...

Lisette rolling around on a large bed, covered with hides, with a young red-headed boy, who looked about seventeen. Even though the night was cool, a roaring fire and physical exertion kept them warm...

The same boy, now the young King of Scotland, riding off with his troops, Matthew Gilardi at his side...

Lisette, looking at a reflection of her naked body, caressing her burgeoning stomach...

The triumphant return of the boy-king, who had now become a battle-tested man...

* * *

Lisette and I walked through the courtyard of the castle. It was a crisp day, the leaves just starting to turn color.

"I was Prince James's mistress, able to travel the castle at will. It was understood that once he took a queen, my freedoms would be curtailed. But I thought my news would change things. There was a great deal of turmoil and threats of toppling the monarchy. The old rules didn't apply anymore, and I was about to give him an heir. His first-born. And we were in love. Little did I know, I wasn't the only one he had in his heart."

Lisette ran through the courtyard and inside the castle, and I followed. She whispered to me as we climbed the stairs. "I was ridiculously excited that James had returned and I was looking forward to sharing my news with him. I searched high and low and finally found him up in the parapet. But he wasn't alone. Matthew was there with him."

* * *

Lisette ducked into the shadows and listened as Matthew vehemently argued with James.

"She is bewitched, I tell you. I have seen her do things no good Christian woman would even be able to think about."

"That is quite possibly the most ludicrous thing I've ever heard, Matthew." James said, stretching out his long legs.

"My liege, I have spent a lifetime studying this blight on humanity. Please don't dismiss it so lightly. Test her yourself. See if I'm wrong."

"Your idea of testing is a bit overmuch. If she is not a witch, the test will kill her. If she survives your test, she'll be put to death as a witch. It's a ridiculous situation and I won't hold with it."

"My prince, I seek merely to protect you, to open your eyes to the truth."

"Come, come. You know I adore you both. Stop trying to sell Lisette to the wolves. I've given you the title of Witchfinder General, but not so you can use it to control my bedroom."

"If you wish to stay blind, that is your choice. I will honor your wish, no matter how misguided I believe it to be." Matthew said, stiffly.

"Don't pout, Matthew. There is enough of me to go around. There is no need for you to execute your rivals."

Matthew laughed and the two men embraced. An embrace which quickly grew passionate.

* * *

Lisette turned to me. "What was I supposed to do? Matthew and I were rivals for the love of this ambiguously sexed boy. More than just rivals. He was preparing to sacrifice me as a witch."

"Aren't you both witches?" I asked. "Wouldn't he be sacrificing himself as well?"

She shot me a look that let me know—in no uncertain terms—that I was a naive idiot. "Matthew never has only one agenda where two will do. He is sewing seeds so that I am discredited. So I can never reveal the secrets of the new Witchfinder General and be believed. Whether I tell people he's a witch, or whether I tell them he's seducing the Prince. Once

I'm accused as a witch, nothing I say will be believed."

"But he's your father."

"This position gives him the type of power he's always dreamed of. He's got the ear of the king. Anyone who crosses him can be arrested, tried and put to death—all on his word. At the same time, his own actions are hidden, so he stays safe. What small price is the life of his daughter, in the face of all that?"

* * *

As she fell into a deeper, dreamless sleep, I retreated from Lisette's subconscious mind and went off to think. Not that I could go far, but I was able to find a small, quiet corner in Lisette's mind where I could relax.

She'd had quite a life. If she hadn't so rudely taken over my body and—even more rudely—been making plans to permanently evict me from it, I would have wanted to get to know her better. I mean, yeah, somewhere along the line she sold her soul to the Devil, but I almost understood how she got to that point.

While I was brooding, I saw Tillie appear in my mind's eye. "I told you she was trouble."

"That doesn't mean I can't feel sorry for her."

She sniffed. "You're an idiot."

I nodded. "Probably. But are you going to help me or not?"

"Help you? I should kill you. You gave her *two* bodies."

"I'm trying to get them back."

She thought about it and looked around. "Can the evil one hear us?"

I cast an anxious glance over at Lisette, but she was deep in her dream. "I don't think so. She's reliving her death right now."

Tillie paused and listened in. "Oh, that was a loud, bloody mess. Well, that should drown out anything else in her head, as long as we're not too loud."

"Thank the Gods." I sighed, relieved, and told Tillie about my plan. "We don't have a lot of time. If anything goes wrong..." I was going to be completely screwed. But I didn't need to tell her that. She already knew.

She raced off to do her part, leaving me alone with Lisette.

"Gods speed, Tillie." I whispered.

Man, I longed for the days when my only problem was being evicted from my apartment. Facing imminent eviction from my own body gave me a whole different perspective on the past.

CHAPTER FORTY-FOUR

THE NEXT FEW DAYS passed in a blur of sex and food. Every position, every imaginable (and some not-so-imaginable) sex act. And then, Lucien found the wonderful world of the internet and hooked up with a polyamorous group in Trinity Harbor. It made me wonder what exactly Paul did in his spare time.

But still no word from Aunt Tillie. And every day, Lisette grew stronger.

We were running out of time.

* * *

A week before the dark moon, Lucien woke Lisette with breakfast in bed. A tray with coffee, eggs, bacon and hash browns. That must have been Paul's doing. Somehow, I don't think hash browns had been invented when Lisette and Lucien were alive. Next to the coffee was Tillie's brass vase, with a fresh rose.

Lisette sat up and clapped her hands, delighted. "You spoil me."

After breakfast, Lucien drew a milk bath for her. With rose petals. Talk about decadence.

I sighed. The art of romance. I hoped Paul was paying attention. If we ever got our bodies back, I wouldn't mind a little pampering in the bath department. Or in any department. I couldn't remember the last time I had a boyfriend with an ounce of actual romance in his soul.

Lucien washed Lisette's long hair, massaging her scalp. After the bath, he dried and brushed Lisette's hair and then gave her a slow, long, full-body massage with scented oils. I completely lost track of time, luxuriating in the silky feel of the oils as my physical body's kinks and knots got worked out. I may not be able to affect my body, but it was nice to be able to dip in sometimes, and feel what my body was feeling.

I must have fallen asleep, because the next thing I knew, the massage was over.

"Wear something special. I have a surprise for you tonight." Lucien said, kissing the back of Lisette's neck.

He left and Lisette searched through my closet until she found my green, witchy dress. "Perfect."

She put it on and looked at herself in the full-length mirror on the closet door. She looked great. Better than I ever had. Suddenly, I realized that my body, just in general, looked freaking amazing. All the non-stop sex must have melted the pounds off, because my dress had never fit so well before.

* * *

Lucien's big surprise turned out to be a polyamorous party at a swanky house in Trinity Harbor. Right on the shore of Lake Superior. When we walked in, Lisette's outfit turned heads in every room she entered. She was making a bigger splash than I ever did in the same dress.

But when we walked into the dining room, even Lisette got upstaged. Waiters walked around with full trays of drinks, completely naked. There was even a nude cigarette girl sporting a tray of candy cigarettes. And dinner was an enormous sushi feast, tastefully arranged on the naked body of a young woman.

Lisette and Lucien cheerfully jumped into the spirit of things. Lisette was a wild child and her sense of fun and sexual adventure seemed to inspire this houseful of people. Soon, everyone who was in the dining room was naked and smearing each other with chocolate and wine and squishy fruits and anything else that was available and licking it off each other with abandon.

As Lisette strolled through the house, still naked, she noticed that there was a large hot tub out back, the water steaming in the cool night. She looked at Lucien and clapped, delightedly.

"Anyone want to join me?" she winked as she slid open the

glass door and walked out to the hot tub. Lucien was right behind her, sporting a large erection.

Soon, it seemed everyone who wasn't otherwise occupied in the dining room, was in the hot tub with them. Naked, some of them food smeared, looking at the stars. Oddly enough, even though they were all nude, everyone seemed to be on their best non-sexual behavior.

So Lisette stood up, using the cold air to make her nipples stand out even more. She not-so-accidentally brushed them against the cheek of a woman who was staring at her.

"Oh, I'm so sorry," Lisette said, batting her eyes.

"No, anytime, really." The woman barely managed to croak the words out. So Lisette took her at her word and within minutes, the hot tub was full of naked guests who had taken a major turn for the horny.

When the hot tub scene got old, Lisette and Lucien moved back into the house. You couldn't go anywhere without running into naked bodies in the throes of passion. And Lucien and Lisette sampled as many people as possible—guests or employees—in every way they could. Especially Lisette. She had her way with everyone. And she had even more stamina than Lucien.

Somewhere in the middle of the orgasmofest, I became seriously worried that my body couldn't take anymore. How long would it take for an ambulance to arrive in case paramedics needed to restart my heart?

But Lisette ignored me as she continued on her merry way, until she was finally sated. And I was sore as hell. In more ways than one. My body had been abused to its breaking point.

"As soon as I get this body back, the first thing I'm doing is getting it tested. Haven't you people heard of condoms in the Otherworld? STDs? AIDS? Or am I immune to everything while I'm possessed?" I snapped at her.

But Lisette was getting very good at ignoring me. At least, I hoped she was ignoring me. Because if my voice was getting so weak that she couldn't even hear me anymore... well, that thought led down a very dark road.

As Lucien and Lisette dressed and got ready to leave the party, the hosting couple begged them to come back again, party or no party.

Lisette tossed a smug feeling my way. "*I bet you were never this popular before.*"

A-ha. She *could* still hear me. "*I never had to use sex to make friends before,*" I shot back at her.

* * *

As the dark moon approached, I started getting really worried. While I'd had more experiences in the last week than most people have in a lifetime, I really didn't want to be reduced to nothingness, or left to wander the earth for eternity, just so Lisette could get her second go-round at life. And I was pretty sure Paul felt the same way.

Poor Paul. I didn't even know if any of him had survived the transfer. I mean, I was still conscious, but then, I wasn't like most people. I had Lisette's blood in me.

What if there wasn't a Paul anymore?

But then, if that was the case, Lucien wouldn't need the dark moon to make his possession permanent, would he? They would just need to dispatch my spirit. The thought that Paul's spirit was still hanging on, no matter how tenuously, gave me hope.

* * *

Lisette and Lucien spent a good part of the week activating the altar room, gathering herbs and sacrificing chickens to strengthen their magic. I tried to keep my eyes closed as much as possible when they were in the throes of their sacrificial rituals, but Lisette and Lucien positively thrived on the amount of blood they spilled.

Before I knew it, the cottage was humming with power and energy. And the altar room! I was surprised there wasn't a radioactive glow coming from it.

If your body does evil work, while someone else is in control of it, do you still get stuck with the karmic coin?

Finally, the day of the dark moon dawned, and I hadn't heard squat from Tillie.

Was this going to be her revenge? Watching my spirit get

torn from my body? And then what happens to me? Am I utterly destroyed? Do I roam the earth forever? Do I go to the Otherworld?

I shuddered and tried to think of a back-up plan to stop Lisette. Because now, I was officially, out of time.

CHAPTER FORTY-FIVE

WHILE LUCIEN WAS OUT of the house, haggling over a black bull calf, (I shuddered to think why), Lisette was getting the back yard prepped. She gathered large rocks into the shape of a dolmen and set it up as her altar. Then she moved the skull from the hidden cellar temple room to the outdoor altar.

Was she planning to put our spirits into the skull? Were we going to be trapped for eternity in there? Where the hell was Aunt Tillie?!

Lisette planted a large pole in the middle of the yard, with a rope fastened at the top of the pole, so it had free range of motion. She braided the end of the rope into a noose.

A noose?! I shuddered to think what she had planned.

I nudged her, thinking as loudly as I could: "*You really don't want to kill me. We're doing such a great job of cohabitating so far. Why don't we just agree to share?*"

But she ignored me.

Damn it. I was so screwed.

* * *

As Lisette was putting the finishing touches on the ritual space, I suddenly sensed a change in the air.

Gus walked around the cottage and intercepted Lisette as she was about to enter the back door. "Hey, bitch, why you don't answer the door anymore? You get too uppity to be social?" he said, in a fake New Jersey accent.

Aunt Tillie had come through! My heart leapt in joy, but I immediately squashed it. This was going to be my only chance and I couldn't afford to blow things. I could feel Lisette poking around in my mind, trying to dig up memories of who this strange person was.

I focused on a blank chalkboard.

"Hello, remember me? Your best friend?"

What's his name?

I could feel the command from Lisette and before I could stop it, the word '*Gus*' appeared on the chalkboard.

Damn, damn, damn. I ditched the chalkboard set-up and focused on a pointy rock.

"Don't be an idiot, Gus. Of course I remember you."

"What are you doing?"

"What's it look like, silly?"

"If you ask me, it looks like you're setting up a bloody acre."

I could feel Lisette jump in shock. She hadn't expected Gus to know that.

"How's Grundleshanks?"

Grundleshanks?

I projected the image of a puppy to her.

"He ran away."

"Really?" Gus gave Lisette a look. "He must have been faster than he looked."

Before I could stop it, an image of the real Grundleshanks, wearing a tiny race horse saddle, flashed in my mind.

I felt Lisette relax. *That disgusting thing? He's in the temple room, preparing to be sacrificed. We have need of a toad bone.*

"He's a toad. He belongs outside. Not cooped up in some tank. He's around here, somewhere," she said, gesturing at the garden.

"Well, that's a pity. He had potential. So, I came all the way from Jersey just to see you. Think you could offer me a lemonade or something? I'm still on the wagon, y'know."

I focused on a field of daisies. I didn't want to register shock at anything Gus said. He was feeling Lisette out and I didn't want her passing his tests because of my random thoughts.

She shrugged. "Sure, but you can't stay long. I have a date."

* * *

As they walked into the kitchen, Gus threw Lisette into a

chair and handcuffed her hands behind her back. It all happened so fast, there was no time for her to react.

"What are you doing, Gus? This is nuts. Let me go."

"No way in hell. I don't know who you are, but I know you're not Mara."

I felt a choir start singing in my heart. I loved Gus. I could hear him thumping around the kitchen, doing something, but Lisette refused to turn her head and show me. She stared straight ahead, fit to be tied. If she could have popped out of my skin and throttled him, she would have.

"That's ridiculous. Of course I'm Mara. Look at me. Ask me anything. Go ahead."

Don't screw with me, Lisette flashed a warning at me, *or I'll send your spirit into eternal torment.*

"Where in Jersey am I from?"

Hoboken, I thought at her.

"Hoboken."

"Yeah, good guess. I've never been to Jersey in my life." He dropped the phony accent and set a small, brass vessel on the ground in front of Lisette. Then he drew a sigil at her feet. "Mara would know that."

"*I'm going to destroy both of you.*" Lisette hissed, all pretense gone.

Gus took a vial of dark grey powder out of his pocket. "Then it's a good thing I came prepared. I'm getting you out of the body, one way or another. Even if I have to kill it."

"*What?! Wait! No!!!!*" I screamed. Had this been Aunt Tillie's plan all along? Was she finally going to have her revenge?

"*I call upon the dread Queen of Fate and all her minions to free me from your grasp!*" Lisette intoned into the heavens.

Electricity coursed through my body and the handcuffs popped open.

Gus uncorked the vial and threw the powder in my face, just as Lisette was inhaling, before she could get the rest of her incantation out.

The powder seized my lungs and I fought to keep breathing. I couldn't move my hands, my feet, nothing. It was like I was trying to communicate with my limbs through concrete.

Cold...

Cold...

I was so cold...

I could hear my heartbeat slowing down.

Thump...

Thuuump...

Thuuuuump...

The blood in my arteries slowed their movement.

Swiiiiiiissshhhh...

swiiiii... shhh...

swiiiiiii...

Gus drew a circle around me. "*By the Devil and the Dame of Old, I banish you.*"

His words were distant and muffled. Like I was underwater, trying to hear someone yelling at me a block away.

I could feel Lisette seething, furious, looking for any way she could destroy Gus.

But my body was a useless, broken suitcase.

I remembered the cards I pulled. *Death, destruction and sorrow.* Was it only a few months ago? It felt like a lifetime.

I remembered the first time I met Gus. It was at a Halloween party. He was the only one there wearing his normal clothes and yet, he fit right in with all the costumed party-goers.

I always thought I'd spend the rest of my life with him. Even if it was platonically. I just never expected it to be because he was the one who would end my life.

He drew a sigil to my right. "B*y Robin Goodfellow and the Whore of Babylon, I banish you.*"

He drew a sigil to my left. "B*y Lucifer and the Fallen Angels, I banish you.*"

My body thrashed forward and back, in slo-mo, like a human Barbie. I have no idea how. The impulse for movement didn't generate from me.

I focused on breathing. But I was barely able to get any air into my lungs.

How long had it been since my last breath?

Muffled screams and moans of pain squeaked out of my mouth. I didn't think it was from me though. It must be Lisette.

He drew a sigil behind me. *"By the Queen of Fate and the Hags of the Eight Winds, I banish you."*

Lisette squeezed out what air I had in my lungs, in an attempt to use my voice box, to counter what Gus was doing.

I needed to take another breath.

I struggled to remember how to breathe.

Open mouth, inflate lungs...

Something between open and inflate wasn't working...

Gus walked around in front of me and took a second vial of powder out of his pocket. *"Be gone, Witch. Return to hell and leave this girl be."*

And he blew a handful of powder in my face.

My body went into spasms and an unearthly screaming echoed through the room—as if Hell itself was protesting.

It couldn't be coming from me. I didn't know where it was coming from. I just wanted it to stop.

My vision went black and my heart stopped with a thud.

And then Lisette was gone.

I felt a lightness as I rose up. Up, up and out. I looked around. I was still in the kitchen, but I was up by the ceiling, watching Gus as he hovered over my useless body.

I looked around to see if Aunt Tillie or if my mom or dad were going to come for me.

Isn't that how it goes? Family members show up at your death and escort you to a tunnel of light?

But there was no one.

Was this what the afterlife was going to be for me? Trapped in the cottage for eternity? Where was everyone?

I looked down at my broken body. The pendant I was wearing glowed with an ethereal light, like a lit ember between my breasts.

Gus ripped the rose necklace from around my neck, breaking the clasp. He dropped it in the brass vessel and slammed the lid shut.

Then everything went dark.

CHAPTER FORTY-SIX

WHEN I CAME TO, I was on the couch, wearing an oxygen mask and my arm was sore as hell.

I inhaled deeply, drawing the oxygen deep into my lungs.

Wait. I inhaled. Deeply. When had that started? Last thing I remembered, I was dead.

"She's coming round."

Was that Aunt Tillie's voice?

I felt my face. I had an oxygen mask on. I opened my eyes and pushed off the mask.

"What happened?" I croaked.

"Thank the Gods, you're alive." Gus said, kneeling next to me. "I was about to call an ambulance."

"I thought you were going to save me." I said, remembering.

"I did. I did save you. I would have been here sooner, but do you have any idea how long it takes to get zombie powder? Not to mention the antidote? Without a medical license? I had to screw three registered nurses and then talk each one into committing petty theft."

"But... I thought... there isn't any antidote..." I said, struggling to remember.

"No, you're right. If you were in Haiti and you got buried for three days, your brain would have been irreparably cooked. The equivalent of a frontal lobotomy."

"But you saved me? How?"

"Oxygen. Massive quantities of oxygen. And a combo injection of adrenaline to get your heart beating and fludrocortisone to increase your blood pressure."

Then he shoved a piece of black bread, covered in salt, in my mouth.

"Eat it. I've got your body back, but I want to make sure your spirit stays put."

I coughed and choked, but I ate it. Once I was done, he led me to the bathroom, where he had filled a tub with cold, salty water. He made me strip and lie down in it, to shut down the access points on my body. Especially the back of my neck and my forehead.

"Better?" He asked.

"Freezing," I said, shivering. "I could kiss you. The first vial was zombie powder, right? What was that second vial of powder you used?"

"Bone dust and graveyard dirt. All of it courtesy of Momma Lua. We never want to piss that woman off."

* * *

I took a hot shower to warm up, then we went down into the hidden temple room to find Grundleshanks. His tank was on the altar and he was looking thin and forlorn.

"Poor Grundleshanks. He looks hungry."

We took him upstairs and Gus dropped three crickets into his tank.

I was still feeling weak, so I sat on the couch. "You have impeccable timing. How'd you know I needed you right this very minute?"

"It started with Grundleshanks. I kept seeing this totally freaked out little toad in my dreams. I figured if you were freaking out the toad, you were in serious trouble. And then this old lady showed up in my scrying mirror and told me to get my ass out to Devil's Point, Wisconsin a.s.a.p. When I tried to ignore her, she started breaking all of my mirrors. Scrying, magickal, mundane. Even my refrigerator magnet mirror. The bitch. Then, when I wasn't moving fast enough for her, she started haunting my dreams and showing me some scary-ass images."

I smiled. Aunt Tillie. She was nothing if not inventive.

"After that, I went to Mama Lua's and we did a little seer work. We got just enough info to seriously freak me the fuck out.

Even Mama Lua was worried about you and she doesn't worry about anyone."

I looked out the window at the late afternoon sun and suddenly felt like I was going to pass out. *Lucien.* I had forgotten about Lucien.

"Cripes. Are you okay? You're turning blue. Lie down. Breathe. While I take full credit for bringing you back from the dead, I think it's time to get you to a hospital."

"I can't," I croaked. "Lucien will be here any minute." Even with everything that had gone on, I couldn't believe I had almost forgotten about Lucien.

I filled Gus in on Lucien's not-so-final demise, his need for a body, and his possession of Paul.

"You said he was looking for a body so that he could cross over when he dies, instead of being stuck here forever. Problem solved," he joked. "He comes home, we chop off his head."

I glared at Gus, not amused. "Don't even joke about that. I happen to be attached to that particular body."

"We can use the zombie powder, but I don't have any more of the antidote left. If it kills him, it's not a pretty death. And if he manages to survive the first three days, it'll be like someone's given him a frontal lobotomy."

"No!" I said. "It's my fault Lucien was able to co-opt Paul's body. Paul shouldn't have to pay for my mistakes."

"Did you ever think that Paul may not even exist anymore? His brain could just be a pile of mush. He might appreciate us retiring his skin suit."

I couldn't believe Gus was actually being serious. "No. N-O. Do you hear me? Harm one hair on his head and I will beat you senseless. He's been through enough. And if there's any hope we can get him back, we're going to try."

I walked out of there and into the kitchen, where I put on a pot of tea. I was so pissed, I didn't know what else to do. After a few minutes, Gus came looking for me.

"All right, I'm sorry. I don't even know the guy. I'm sure he's Mother Theresa and Captain Kirk, all rolled into one. But we still need to figure out how to boot Lucien from his body and from this realm. From what you told me, he needs to die and cross over. If you know how to do that without harming Paul,

I'm all ears."

I poured us each a cup of Moroccan Mint tea and begged the universe to give me an answer. One that I could live with. Suddenly, an idea popped into my head that was so outrageous, I had a hunch it just might work. Too bad we didn't have any more chickens left in the house.

I had just finished filling Gus in, when I heard Lucien pull up in the SUV.

* * *

Lucien stormed in, furious.

"What's the problem, my love?" I said, faking as much concern as I could, trying my best to imitate Lisette.

"Damnable farmer. He sold the black bull calf out from under me. He gave me two puppies. Purebreds, he said. Guard dogs. He thought it was about money. They are not acceptable."

He handed over two happy, squirming, Doberman puppies. One black-and-tan, one red.

I put them down on the floor and slowly rubbed Lucien's shoulders, kissing his neck the way Lisette did. "Do not worry yourself. You know I never leave things to fate. I have alternate preparations already in place."

I felt him relax under my hands. "That is but one reason I love you so unfailingly. Let me show you the second reason." He turned and I felt him harden against me.

Perfect. I needed to buy enough time for Gus to get everything in place. This should do it. Hopefully, I had Lisette's moves down cold. Because if Lucien tumbled my little secret, things would get very ugly, very quickly.

"We have a few hours before the dark moon rises." I said, reaching down and liberating an important part of him from his clothing. He picked me up and carried me upstairs.

* * *

The thing about Lucien, when it came to sex, I think the man was part horse. He could keep going for hours. And each ejaculation just seemed to make him crave the next even more. It must have been stored up sexual frustration from all those years of being a body-less head.

As we cavorted, I tried to sense any vestige of the man I loved, hidden inside the insatiable beast that had taken over his body. It was fleeting, but it was there. In the precious few seconds when Lucien slipped out of control, usually at the peak of an orgasm, I could feel Paul beneath the surface, screaming for help.

He was still alive, thank the Goddess.

Finally, it was time. I stood up and beckoned to him. "Come, my love, we need that boundless energy of yours for the ritual."

The great thing about being so far away from people— walking outside naked wasn't a problem. So I led Lucien downstairs and outside, to our makeshift ritual space.

* * *

Gus was drugged and tied to the makeshift altar. Next to him, on the ground, I swear it looked like Grundleshanks was bracing himself.

"What's this?" Lucien demanded.

I laughed and stretched, enjoying the cool night air against my hot skin. "I found you a more powerful body. A body worthy of your magnificence. A young witch, who thought he knew more than he did."

"My, you've been busy."

"It was an unexpected gift from the Gods. He thought he could send me back and rescue his little friend. The fool."

I led Lucien to the altar.

"I trust you know what you are doing, my love," he said.

"With the knowledge and abilities locked in this young witch's mind, you'll finally be one of us." I teased Lucien, kissing his neck. "You'll be unstoppable. And once your spirit is in the witch, we can sacrifice this mundane body to gain even more power."

He moaned in pleasure. "My spirit is in your hands, my love."

* * *

I put up a circle and called upon Cromm, one of the old, sacrificial Gods, to attend to this rite. Then I picked up an athamé and cut my palm.

Lucien lay on the ground at my feet. I dripped the blood on his chest in the shape of a pentagram.

"By earth, air, fire and water. By the wind hags of all eight directions. By the guardians of North, South, East and West. I command the spirit of Lucien Odega be mine."

I tried to be so careful not to snag Paul's spirit as well, as I reached into his body and pulled out an entity made of light. It didn't want to let go, but I kept a firm hold on it.

"Lucien Odega, I command you by the Queen of Fate and the Lord of Sacrifice to release this body."

Finally, the entity let go of Paul's body. The light faded from Paul's eyes as he lost consciousness and fell into a deep sleep.

I carried Lucien's spirit over to Gus.

"By my command, Lucien Odega, you whom I have named three times over, thou shalt enter this body and possess it whole." I said, as I hurled Lucien as hard as I could—into Grundleshanks.

As soon as he realized what had happened, Lucien tried to cry out in protest. But the instant he was in his new body, Gus took a blackthorn spike and skewered it through Grundleshanks's heart.

The heavens shook, lightning split the sky and a portal opened above Grundleshanks's head. As Grundleshanks's and Lucien's spirits went through the portal, it sealed up behind them with a loud boom. The ground around us shuddered and went still.

CHAPTER FORTY-SEVEN

AFTER THE RITUAL WAS over, Gus held Grundleshanks's body up to the sky. "Thank you, big guy. Your sacrifice will be honored."

A chill ran through me.

"It's the only way."

I sighed and looked at the poor little toad's body. "If you're doing the toad bone ritual, you're on your own. I've had enough meetings with the Devil lately."

He nodded over at Paul's body, still on the ground. "What'll we do about that one?"

I walked over to him and felt for a pulse. I breathed a sigh of relief. He was still alive. "Let's put him on the couch. When he comes to, maybe he'll just think he's had a bad dream."

* * *

Paul woke up a few hours later, hazy but okay. Gus and I had managed to drag him to the couch and that was probably our saving grace. I think Paul would have completely flipped if he had woken up in the back yard, in the middle of a ritual circle.

As it was, he was disoriented and upset and I really couldn't blame him. His memory about what had happened was spotty and he wasn't happy when I filled him in on the blanks. He didn't even say goodbye, he just walked out, got into his SUV, and didn't come back.

* * *

At dawn, Gus came back from the first step of his preparations for the Toad Bone Ritual and we went down into the hidden temple room. Even without Lucien and Lisette, it was practically glowing with power.

"Damn, what kind of portal to hell did they open down here?" Gus asked. "Every hair on my body is standing on end. I love it."

"Closing this all down is going to be a bitch."

"Good thing I brought my bag of tricks. Let's get started."

So we did. It took a few hours, but we managed to... well, if not completely power it down, then get its power sufficiently under control, so it wasn't an open, pulsating portal to the Otherworld.

Afterwards, we were both exhausted and ready for some sleep. As Gus crawled into bed with me, he couldn't resist a last bout of teasing.

"So, this Lucien guy, he was the disembodied spirit you were creaming yourself over?"

"Shut up. I was not."

"Did he do that Dracula mist thing and get you all hot?"

"You say one more word and I'm going to light your hair on fire."

"Oh, come on. I'm just joking," Gus said.

"Yeah, well, I'm not. I'm tired of everything in my life being held up and mocked for your personal amusement."

"Okay. I'm sorry. Cripes, I drove two thousand miles just to see if you were okay, cut me some slack, okay?" He gave me his best little boy look and snuggled up to me.

"Just keep in mind that you're on thin ice, buddy. So can it with the smart-ass remarks." I snuggled into him and we both fell asleep.

* * *

It wasn't until the next morning, when I was dismantling the backyard ritual space, that I noticed Gus had a U-Haul trailer attached to the Mustang. I was surprised I had missed it the other day.

Gus came out of the cottage, holding two mugs of coffee. He walked over and handed me one.

I took a sip. Strong and sweet, just the way I liked it. I

pointed to the U-Haul. "Do you always bring all your worldly possessions when you visit a friend?"

"Actually, I brought it for you. I figured we could pack up your things and move back to civilization."

"As if that was really an option." I snorted.

"Some things have changed since you've been gone," he said, walking up to the porch and sitting on the oversized swing.

I followed him, curious. "What does that mean?"

"The evil Mrs. Lasio is gone."

"Are you kidding me?" I curled up next to him on the porch swing. "What happened?"

"Lenny caught his hot tamale wrapped around a Greek lamb kebob and he flipped."

"Gus! You didn't!?!"

"I sure as hell did. Did you see him? He was hot. With a capital H. Besides it serves that old prune right. No one disses my girl."

"So that's who your mystery boy toy was? Lenny's Latin dreamboat? You are a skunk."

"And you love me. You want to hear the rest of this? Or do you want to bitch?"

"I'm all ears."

"Well, Lenny told him to pack his crap and move out of his gatehouse, and then he turned around and booted Mrs. Lasio out of the apartment building. So now he's got two apartments up for rent."

"I'm surprised mine wasn't rented the day after I moved."

"That's 'cause no one can afford it. He totally upgraded your place. The minute you left, he had a crew in there, putting in a new bathroom and replacing the skanky carpeting with hardwood floor. And he's jacked up the rent three hundred percent. Now he's going to do the same to Lasio's place. Think he'll let me move in, rent-free? I can be the new building manager."

"After you recycled his boy toy behind his back?!"

"You have a point. Lasio's place too small for me, anyway. The living room is only slightly larger than my penis."

"For someone who lives in a walk-in closet, you're awfully judgmental about size. What were you doing checking out

Lasio's apartment, anyway?"

"Being nosy."

Of course. He wouldn't be Gus if he wasn't nosy.

"But Lenny may let you move back in, now that she's gone," he said.

I thought about it. I really didn't want to leave my cottage. Especially after everything I had gone through with it. It was like a hard-won prize after a long, bloody battle. Most importantly, it finally felt like it was mine. It felt like home.

"I wonder where Mrs. Lasio's going to go?" I said.

"Who cares? She didn't give a crap about you finding a home, did she?"

That was Gus. Loyal to the end. "Are you still bonking the hot tamale?"

"No. That only lasted until he came over and saw my temple room. I've never seen anyone run out screaming so fast. You'd think that church of his would teach him tolerance. Whatever happened to love thy neighbor?"

"Did you miss the Crusades? The Inquisition? Since when has any fundamentalist religion taught religious tolerance?"

"You have a point," he snorted.

* * *

After that horrible night, Aunt Tillie started hanging out with us so much, it was like she had become our preternatural roommate. But she was no longer trying to kill me, which was a big improvement. Gus couldn't see her as clearly as I could— something I lorded over him on a daily basis—but I talked the situation over with him and we came to the decision that, even though she wasn't in the vessel anymore, Aunt Tillie was still trapped here. And it was probably my fault.

Like Aunt Tillie said, messing with magic you know nothing about is not the smartest thing to do. It's hard enough to deal with the consequences when you do know what you're doing.

Looking back on things, I was finally able to see how I had misfired so badly with the fetch. Poor Aunt Tillie. Not only was I inadvertently responsible for her death, I had then trapped her in this dimensional reality and bound her to me, when I put her in the brass vase. Gus and I had some very long talks about what we could do to fix Tillie's situation.

Samhain was right around the corner. And that was pretty much our life as we waited for Samhain to arrive. At Samhain, Gus wanted to turn Lisette over to Gwyn ap Nudd and his Hell Hounds, so we'd be rid of her, once and for all. And hopefully, in the process, we'd find a way to free Tillie, as well.

CHAPTER FORTY-EIGHT

SAMHAIN EVE DAWNED COLD and crisp. The leaves had dropped and the tree branches were bare and stark against the sky. I bundled up in my heavy ritual wear and placed two comfy deck chairs outside, positioning them next to a small table with a bottle of Absinthe, (Gus's first bottle as an amateur brewer), a bottle of water, a bowl of sugar cubes and two glasses.

Tillie shimmered and appeared on one of the chairs. "What are you doing?"

I sighed. "Just behave, would you? No knocking anything over."

"Fine." She smoothed her skirt and looked down at her black Mary-Janes.

"Nice shoes," I said.

"I've always liked these shoes. Comfortable, sensible, good looking. I must say, I'm pleased with the care to detail at Del Angels mortuary. I was afraid they'd bury me in a nice top from my waist up and my skivvies and flip-flops from the waist down. After all, who sees you from the waist down?"

"Who picked out your clothes?"

"That nice boy, J.J.'s, mother. J.J. would never come here. His grandfather—"

"—Is the tree. I know. I've been watering him."

I sat down next to her, to have a serious, girl-to-ghost chat. "Aunt Tillie. While we love having you around, it's time for you to go. You have to cross over. We don't want you to get stuck here forever."

"Why not?"

"Because you need to continue your journey. You can

always come back and visit. I'm just trying to avoid having you trapped here, without choices. Like Lucien was."

Gus walked up, dressed in his ritual garb and carrying Lisette's brass vessel and a jar of ointment. "Look out, Samhain, here we come!"

At the mention of Samhain, Aunt Tillie stiffened and glared at us. "You wouldn't dare."

"It's for your own good, Tillie." Gus said.

Every Samhain, Gwyn ap Nudd rides with the Wild Hunt, gathering lost souls and crossing them over through the veil, to the Otherworld. He also lets his hounds loose on evil souls, to harry and torment them from one end of the earth to the other, before tearing them apart. So it's kind of like getting two birds with one stone.

Gus set the vessel down and handed me the ointment. "Anoint yourself, woman. We've got work to do."

I looked at him. "Are you sure? I mean, what if it doesn't work? We'll be unleashing Lisette, all over again."

"Oh ye of little faith. Have I ever let you down?"

I opened the jar and sniffed at the goo. "Oh my Goddess, that's putrid. What the hell's in here?"

"Aconite, toad sweat, all the poisonous goodies."

Tillie slammed the lid back on the jar and practically threw it at him. "Are you crazy? She can't use that. She shouldn't even have sniffed it." She said, glaring at me.

A look of annoyed confusion crossed Gus's face.

"And you want me to leave you in his bumbling, not-so-capable hands?" Tillie sniffed.

I almost laughed. Gus looked like a puppy who'd just been swatted with a rolled up newspaper.

"It's okay, Gus. I don't think I'm going to need anything to help with my sight. It's been in overdrive for months." I reassured him.

* * *

As midnight approached, Gus and I were both shivering, even in our heaviest robes and cloaks. We could have done the ritual in parkas, but there was just something magical about changing into ritual clothes, it put you into a different head space.

I put up a circle of protection and Gus called upon Gwyn ap Nudd and the Wild Hunt to come for Lisette and Lady Rhiannon for Tillie. There was a crackling in the sky. Far off, I could hear the braying of the Hounds of Hell.

At the stroke of midnight, my sight shifted and I could suddenly see them. Hundreds of white hounds with red ears, streaming through the sky. Braying with a sound like thousands of geese in full voice, flying overhead. Gwyn ap Nudd's pack had been unleashed upon the earth.

"Don't look at the hounds' eyes, Mara!" Gus yelled over the din.

I averted my eyes. Death was said to come to the mortals who looked into the flaming red eyes of the hounds.

Then the Hunt Master himself, Gwyn ap Nudd, galloped out of the portal, riding his Night Mare across the sky. He had the body of a man and the head of a stag. He would ride the hunt to the ends of the earth, as he collected all the lost souls.

Gus opened the brass vessel. As the spirit of Lisette rose up, towering in her fury, two hounds broke off from the pack and harried her, biting at her, herding her into the hunt. She had now become their prey and they would chase her to the ends of the earth. She would either return with them to the Otherworld, where she belonged, or they would rip her to shreds and send her back to the Cauldron of Creation.

Gwyn ap Nudd looked down and I could swear he gave us a salute as he rode by.

As the Hunt continued across the night sky, a female rider separated out from the back of the hunt. Lady Rhiannon, one of the Queens of the Underworld.

The Lady was gentle and beautiful. And she was riding right for Tillie. She stopped in front of us, glowing so brightly and so beautifully, it hurt to look at her.

Aunt Tillie reached up to grab her arm and I felt a sob catch in my throat. Gus put his arms around me. "It's for the best," he yelled in my ear. "You don't want her trapped here forever, do you?"

Aunt Tillie smiled at me and I gave her a teary smile in return. Then she mounted the horse behind the Lady, holding onto her waist.

As Rhiannon whirled her horse around and rode up into the night sky, Aunt Tillie gave us a last wave. Then I watched Rhiannon's horse change from white to grey to black as it jumped over the moon and sailed back through the veil, to the other side.

EPILOGUE

AFTER SAMHAIN, GUS WAS more determined than ever to do the toad bone ritual—he figured that between Grundleshanks's inherent personality and toad-sight, and whatever extra kick the bones had gotten from housing Lucien for a brief nanosecond— he was going to have the toad bone to end all toad bones.

I figured it was just going to be more trouble than it was worth.

But Gus had read, in an old book about East Anglian farmers, that if you can wrest the toad bone away from the Devil, it would give you the ability to charm all animals. Knowing Gus, once he got the bone, he was going to get himself killed trying to charm a grizzly bear. But there was no talking to him once he had his mind made up.

The two Doberman puppies were doing well, although they were no longer so little. We named the black-and-tan one Aramis and the red one Apollo, and they ate everything in sight. They were adorable though. Aramis followed me everywhere, while Apollo was pretty sure Gus had hung the moon.

Me, I'd been debating what to do with my life now that all my ghostly squatters had been evicted and the cottage was finally mine. I started an online witch store, which seemed to be going well. Gus had been carving wands and staffs for me to sell. And we converted part of the cellar for herbal and essential oil storage. Although I had to be careful about what fumes I inhaled, or what I got on my skin. Especially now.

Oh, yeah. All those sexcapades while I wasn't in control? Well, I went to the doctor's office and had a bunch of tests run. No AIDS, no STD's (thank the Goddess!) but the pregnancy test came back positive. No wonder Tillie was so protective of me at Samhain.

The idea of becoming a mom alternately thrilled and terrified me. I had no idea if the baby was Paul's or Lucien's or a complete stranger's. I thought about terminating, but I couldn't. Even now, in the first trimester, this little being inside of me was responding to my thoughts, as if she was aware and could hear me. I don't think it's normal for a fetus to be conscious while still in the womb, but since mine definitely was, I decided to take my chances and hope for the best.

* * *

In the weeks that passed since the incident, Paul had been plagued with nightmares. Every now and then, he'd call me up or come over and I'd try to soothe him as much as I could. But it wasn't often. He was still freaked out about what happened. He said he needed time. And since I was the person who inadvertently brought hell raining down upon his head, I just smiled and nodded and wished him well. I missed him something fierce, but I had no right to force the issue.

Aunt Tillie, on the other hand, had been surprisingly supportive. She often hung out at the cottage with me, just to chat, but the difference was that now, she was definitely a visitor in my home—I wasn't an interloper in hers. She'd been staying on her best ghostly behavior. And she was much sweeter. She seemed to enjoy having the power to cross the veil whenever she pleased.

Gus tried to convince me to move back to Los Angeles with him, but once he found the small cemetery and the stream that ran through the forest, it was pretty clear (to me, at least) that he was going to be here for the long haul. He'd fallen just as much in love with the place as I had. Which was fortunate, because, when he went back to Los Angeles to pack his things, he found out that Lenny had been so pissed at him for 'recycling' his boy toy, he bought Gus's building just so he could evict him.

So Gus moved in with me. He's in Aunt Tillie's old room and I moved into the gorgeous attic room that I remodeled into a bedroom/nursery.

Although we dismantled the bloody acre, we kept the

outdoor temple space that Lisette created, as a place to celebrate the Sabbats and do full moon/dark moon rituals. Unless it was too cold, or pouring down rain, and then we used the indoor temple.

It took a lot of work to clean up the mess Lisette and Lucien left behind with their chicken sacrifices and their black magic, but finally, all the malevolence and negative energy that was so much a part of Lisette's life was gone. Both the hidden room and the back yard were really starting to feel like sacred space, instead of a portal to hell. They filled my heart with joy when I walked into them. And that was a very welcome change.

And now with the baby... Aunt Tillie was so looking forward to being a ghostly great-aunt. She was thrilled at the idea of a great-niece, now that she no longer had to worry about Lisette and Lucien anymore. And Gus was totally psyched about being a MacDaddy. He'd become a font of information on baby-proofing the cottage and prenatal care. You'd think the baby belonged to the two of them, the way they carried on. Even my mom dropped in every now and then, to talk my ear off with parenting advice and nursery-decorating tips.

So how could I possibly leave all of this behind? If home is where the heart is and family is what you make it, I have a feeling I'm going to be here for a long time to come.

-THE END-

To Be Continued In:

SOMEBODY TELL AUNT TILLIE WE'RE IN TROUBLE!

AVAILABLE NOW!

TURN THE PAGE FOR AN

EXCERPT FROM:

SOMEBODY TELL

AUNT TILLIE

WE'RE IN TROUBLE!

Chapter 1

WHEN GUS TOLD ME he was going to do the Toad Bone Ritual, I should have cremated the toad and saved us all a whole lot of misery. But it seemed like a perfectly good idea at the time. After all, Grundleshanks wasn't just any toad. He was something special.

For people who are just tuning in, my name is Mara Stephens and I'm a witch. Not one of those fantasy witches who can wiggle her nose and turn your uncle into a carrot. An actual witch. Which means the Otherworld tends to kick my ass and laugh at me about twice as often as I get to score any wins.

The guy I'm living with currently, is my best friend, Gus. He's a witch too. (And no, warlock is not the *defacto* term for male witch. A warlock is a witch who's betrayed their oaths to their Gods and to their fellow witches. To be warlocked is to be shunned and cast out. Although there is a guy in England who's seeking to reclaim the word as a term for male witches).

Anyway, Gus is... Think Jack Sparrow meets Harry Potter. He's all attitude, fashion, magick and mischief. Although lately, he's been a huge pain in the butt. I blame the toad. Lord Grundleshanks. Or, more precisely, Lord Grundleshanks the Second. Apparently, Lord Grundleshanks the First is living with Gus's childhood friend, Andwyn, out in Utah. Who knew? I only found out when Gus called him, asking about the odds of getting another toad out of the Grundleshanks line.

But our Grundleshanks is currently residing in the spirit world. Or, at least, he was. Until Gus got the bright idea in his head of immortalizing him through the Toad Bone Ritual. *Ha!*

I should have stopped him right there. Or tied him up and

locked him in the attic until he got over it. But I didn't think he could possibly get into as much trouble as he did.

I should have known better. Gus is kind of impulsive and the last time I did an impulsive ritual that sounded like a good idea, I wound up accidentally killing my Aunt Tillie, having to fight off an evil-minded ancestral spirit for control of my body and getting knocked up by a demon who had possessed my boyfriend.

I should have realized that this wasn't going to turn out any better. But like I said, it all started out innocently enough...

* * *

The sucky thing about being pregnant — other than morning sickness — was not being able to take anything but Tylenol for headaches, which didn't really work for me.

I was sprawled out on the couch with a bag of frozen peas over my forehead and eyes, when Gus crashed through the front door with all the energy of a tornado.

"I'm hooooome!" Gus hollered, a blast of arctic wind ushering in his arrival. He was dragging a giant rolling suitcase behind him and looked... different. He had been in Chicago for what seemed like forever, indulging himself in some quality boy toy time. He had yet to crack the gay scene in Devil's Point. Which, to be honest, kind of surprised me. Normally, his gaydar was humming 24-7. The boy was definitely off his game.

Our two Dobies, Aramis and Apollo, eagerly jumped all over his legs, panting and barking in long-legged puppy happiness.

And, just in case I had missed Gus blasting through the door, Tillie shimmered into view on her rocking chair.

"Alert the media," she said sarcastically, as she knitted a pair of baby booties. "Little Lord Fauntleroy has found his way home."

The baby started kicking my kidneys, in some kind of embryonic happy dance. You may think that my soon-to-be child shouldn't be able to hear people talking inside her liquid-filled womb or sense the world around her, and you'd be right.

But thanks to a combination of witchblood and demon seed, my baby who, according to pictures in baby magazines, currently resembled a miniature Creature From the Black Lagoon — was aware, responsive and mobile. Way more developed than any of the books said was possible. Even in her current micro-me size, I could feel magic radiating from her.

"Could you take it down a few notches?" I asked, exasperated.

"Who are you talking to?" Gus responded.

"All of you!"

I dropped the bag of frozen peas on the side table and squinted, shielding my eyes from the sunlight that was bouncing off the snow and rudely shoving its way into the living room.

"Shut the door, would you? You're letting out the heat."

Gus mercifully complied. The baby head-butted my belly, irritated at my lack of enthusiasm.

"Ow! And you can knock that right off." I snapped.

"Knock what off? I didn't touch you." Gus protested.

"Of course, *you* didn't."

"Then, I repeat, *who* are you talking to?!"

"Did your witch senses go on hiatus? Who else is using my organs as makeshift soccer balls? I'm talking to the baby." I said, rubbing my belly in a circular motion, trying to soothe the little monster. "Although, originally, I was talking to all of you."

Gus slapped his hands against his thighs. "What is wrong with you, woman? I have been gone for weeks. Weeks. Nay onto months. Practically years. I wasn't just away for the day. You should be thrilled to see me. Dancing and showering me with offerings. At the very least, have a Scotch and water waiting my arrival. Where's my smiling, happy 'welcome home, I've missed you so much' face?"

"I'm pregnant. Nauseous and stressed *is* my happy face." I said, and felt my eyes filling up with tears.

Damn hormones. I sniffled and reached for a tissue from one of the many boxes I had on the coffee table.

"I should buy stock in Kleenex, I can't even watch TV commercials without breaking down." I sniffled again and blew my nose. "I'm happy you're finally back."

"You certainly have an odd way of showing it."

"What do you expect? You left me alone with Aunt Tillie for too long," I pouted. "I think she's rubbed off on me."

"One can only dream," Aunt Tillie snorted. "You'd be better off."

Gus raised an eyebrow.

"Fine," I said. "I'm a bit cranky today, okay? I'm sorry. Why didn't you text or call to tell me you were on the way?"

"Seriously? You need advance notice to find warmth in your heart? Okay, Wicked Witch of the Tundra. Next time, I'll send flying monkeys to announce my arrival."

I laughed and felt some of the tension in my head release. I had had a tingling feeling all day, like Gus was on his way home, but since I hadn't heard from him, I tried to shake it off as wishful thinking. The constant anticipation had worn on me though, until it triggered a headache.

"If it makes you feel better, the baby's thrilled to see you. She's dancing a jig on my bladder and kicking me in the kidneys."

"You mean *he*," Gus said, grinning. "That's my boy."

"Boy, shmoy. I'm getting a lot of girl energy."

"Obviously, we can't both be right."

"Maybe it's a butch girl," I said.

"Or a femme boy."

I thought about it. "I can live with that."

And I could. Either would be fine, because honestly, the one thing I wouldn't know how to raise was a testosterone-heavy male. They had generally brought me nothing but grief.

"Hold the phone! What if it's twins?" Gus asked, clapping his hands. His eyes beamed. "Wouldn't that be something? One for each of us!"

I groaned. One unexpected baby was going to be work enough. I couldn't imagine raising twins.

Aunt Tillie clucked in disapproval. "Tell the idiot that babies are not toys. They're living beings."

"You tell him," I said.

"Now, who are you talking to?" Gus asked.

"Aunt Tillie. She's sitting right there," I pointed to her rocking chair. "Can't you see her?"

Gus looked a little stunned. "No…"

"Seriously?" I sat up straighter, surprised.

Gus shook his head. "Seriously. That's just… Weird."

"You used to be able to see her though, right? Before you left?"

"Not as solid as you, but well enough."

"Aunt Tillie, how are you blocking Gus?" I asked her, curious and a little concerned.

Aunt Tillie shrugged and continued knitting.

I mean, it was one thing when we were both seeing Aunt Tillie. Gus was like a check and balance for me. But if it was only me... I had to wonder, was I really seeing Aunt Tillie, or was my imagination on overdrive?

When I looked at her again, she was gone. All I saw was an empty chair.

Chapter 2

AFTER GUS DEPOSITED HIS stuff in his room, he came back downstairs. When he found me in the kitchen, he acted like he was going to have a heart attack, grabbing his chest and gasping.

"Knock it off," I said, throwing a green bean at him.

"Barefoot, pregnant and shackled to the appliances. I love it." He whipped his iPhone out of his pocket. "I'm going to commemorate the occasion."

I stuck out my middle finger, just as the tiny camera light flashed.

"I knew if I left you on your own long enough, you'd befriend the kitchen. Have you figured out how to turn the stove on? Or are you just teasing me with promises of nosh?"

"Watch it, buddy." I warned him. "Or you'll be eating your dinner raw."

Gus slid the phone back into his pocket. "Oh, come on. I've been traveling for hours and hours to get back to you. Spoil me a little."

I shook my head and opened the fridge, scanning the shelves for quick-fix carnita meat. "You're lucky I like you."

"I'm lucky you finally learned how to cook. The steady diet of microwave dinners was getting old."

"Is that why you left for so long?" I asked, pulling out the carnitas, a bag of salad and a bottle of dressing. To my dismay, tears started pricking my eyes.

Gus came up behind me and kissed my shoulder. "Isn't that sweet? You missed me. Who would have thought?"

I closed my eyes for a minute and didn't say anything, until I got my equilibrium back.

Gus started setting the table. "I like what you've done with the place. Yule tree, holiday decorations, it's almost like we're real grown-ups."

"Baby on the way," I shrugged. "One of us needed to started acting like an adult."

"Yeowtch. Sheath those claws, bitchy kitty."

"Just putting you on notice. The miniature human will be taking over the spoiled child role for the next eighteen years. You'll have to relinquish your crown."

I dumped the carnitas into a pan and started heating them up. The microwave would have been easier, but I had stopped using it once I found out I was pregnant. I was probably being paranoid, but I didn't want to take any chances.

"Of course, he will," Gus said, soothingly. "I'm not greedy. I can share the role of irresponsible youngster with him."

"With *her*," I said, stirring the pan.

"Just think of all the trouble we can get into together." Gus said as he started working on the salad. "I can take him *or her,* to their first drag queen show. We need to get a baby backpack. Do we have any bleu cheese dressing?"

"Sorry, buddy. It's on the no-no list for preggie ladies. You'll have to deal with French until I go shopping."

"I wonder if they have any baby backpacks on the market with crystal designs? Maybe a little sparkly pentacle? Or a triple spiral?"

I snorted. "You'll have to bedazzle your own witchy backpack. That's definitely a missing niche in the baby items business."

*　　*　　*

After dinner, Gus took care of the cleanup, while I settled down with a book.

"The kitchen is now spotless milady," he said with a flourish, as he flopped down on the couch next to me.

I squeezed over to give him more space.

"I even got rid of the coffee stains on the counter. You really need to clean those as they happen." He popped open the top button of his jeans and took a deep breath. "That's better."

"Between your belly and mine, we're going to need a

sturdier sofa."

Gus narrowed his eyes at me. "I may have put on a few pounds, but I'm not that big."

I snorted. "Have you looked in the mirror, lately?"

"Motherhood has made you mean. Knock it off."

"Sorry," I said, smiling.

"Besides. It's your fault."

"How do you figure?" I asked, making a face at him.

"I blame your pregnancy. I have never been so famished in my entire life. I swear, I've been eating for the three of us."

"I can tell," I laughed.

"Glass houses, honey." Gus stared at my stomach as I stretched and rubbed my lower back. "You didn't have a baby bump when I left, did you?"

I groaned. "You've been gone a long time."

"Surely, not *that* long."

"Last week, I dreamt that instead of giving birth to a baby, a seven-year-old dictator walked out of me, demanding the car keys. The next morning, my pants wouldn't fit."

"You woke up with a belly?" Gus hooted with laughter. "That's impressive."

"I already had a little belly. I just woke up with a bigger one. Check this out." I held up my shirt so he could see the wide elastic band supporting my baby bump.

Gus made a face. "That's spectacularly unattractive. What is it? A slingshot?"

"Pregnancy band."

"I have a better idea. Let's hire an Oompa-Loompa to walk underneath you and support your belly on his head."

I laughed. "I think I'll stick with the pregnancy band."

"Don't be hating on my little orange men. They may be small, but they're mighty."

"You just have a thing for dwarfs."

"Don't judge me. I'm all about equal opportunity," he said, grinning even wider as he lifted my legs on top of his and started massaging my feet. "So, how's our toad doing? Have you been checking on him?"

Gus had made a stone cairn for Grundleshanks outside and enclosed him in it, so he'd be protected from predators while ants and beetles helped him decompose. At least, that was the theory.

"Are you kidding me? I'm pregnant. I can't check on eggs frying without hurling. There's no way I'm going to check on a rotting corpse for you. No matter how much you rub my feet."

Even thinking about it made me nauseous. I shuddered and tried to get the image out of my head. When I opened my eyes, Gus was giving me a pained look and holding out a piece of candied ginger.

"Thanks." I popped it in my mouth. "If it helps, the weather's been a bitch since you've been gone."

"It is winter."

"It's been beyond winter."

"Morgue-cold, by any chance?"

"More like Antarctica, igloo-building, and the Poles flipping. There's cold and then there's Devil's Point cold. Did you see the six foot drifts of snow out there? They're frozen solid. It's gotten too cold to snow anymore. The only thing that's keeping me from turning into an ice sculpture is that this baby has turned my insides into a nice, warm furnace."

Gus frowned. "That's not good. That means Grundleshanks is probably more toadsicle than he is decomposed pile of bones. Maybe I should bring him indoors."

"Oh, no you don't," I said. "How long does it take a toad to decompose anyway?"

Gus looked stumped for a moment, then he stopped rubbing my feet and whipped out his iPhone. "The magic of technology..."

Chapter 3

A FEW MINUTES LATER, Gus was frowning at his phone. "Fifty years. That can't be right."

I hooted with laughter and almost choked on the ginger. Gus's patience was taxed if he had to wait half an hour for his meal at a restaurant. Fifty years might as well be three lifetimes.

I got a sudden mental image of Gus at eighty, camped out at the cairn in a pentacle bedazzled folding chair, with a stopwatch in one hand and a blackthorn cane in the other.

"Didn't your mother ever teach you that it's rude to laugh at frustrated people and internet misinformation?" Gus's frown deepened.

"I'm sure that's not right." I said, patting his arm. "They must be thinking of fossilization, not decomposition."

He made a noncommittal noise and kept scrolling through whatever website he was on. "Weird. Have you ever heard of exploding toads?"

"Spontaneously exploding?"

"Yeah. Boom." He said, gesturing with his hands. "It's a bird, it's a frog, it's a toad bomb. A domestic toadarist. A whole new definition for Toad in the Hole."

Well, that didn't help. I started laughing all over again.

"I'm trying to have a serious conversation," Gus said, grinning. "So, knock it off, Chuckles."

I took a deep breath and tried to think about Grundleshanks and what a special toad he was.

"No," I said, in my most serious tone of voice. "I've never heard of toads spontaneously exploding."

I tried to look over his shoulder at the phone screen, but my eyes were still light-sensitive.

Gus noticed and darkened the screen for me. "Toad liver is a delicacy for crows in Hamburg, Germany."

"I know where Hamburg is."

"Of course you do." Gus said, patting me on the arm.

I rolled my eyes and felt a stab of pain. I really needed to stop doing that, before my eyes got stuck in that position.

"Wouldn't it be a delicacy for crows everywhere?" I asked.

"You would think. But I haven't heard of anything like this happening in the U.S. Maybe German crows have a more advanced palate. *Anyway*. The birds figured out how to get livers out of living toads."

"Wait. Living toads? As in *alive* toads?" I asked, trying to catch up.

"Is your brain ticking along two beats slower than normal?" Gus looked at me, one eyebrow raised. "Generally, yes. That's what living means. I have yet to run into it as a synonym for dead. Alive, living, non-dead. Undead. Hey! The crows created an army of undead toads!"

"That's just... gross."

"Gross and cool. Oh, hold up. You're going to love this," he said, and continued reading. "In retaliation, the toads would swell up to three times their size and explode, spewing their innards up to one meter."

"Ewwww! That's disgusting."

"What's even freakier is the toads were still alive after exploding."

"Are you kidding me?!" I screeched. "That's not even possible. They were alive after getting their livers plucked out?"

"Apparently."

"And then they were still alive after their innards exploded?"

"That's what it says."

"For how long?!" I asked, fascinated in spite of myself.

"All it says is 'a short time'." Gus replied.

"That's just... insane. Freaky. Freakily insane. Attack of the Zombie Toads."

Gus kept reading from the tiny screen. "A thousand toads exploded over three days."

"Holy crap. And then it just stopped? That can't possibly be right. No way can anything still be alive after having their livers plucked out and their innards exploded."

Gus grinned. "Demon Crows vs. Zombie Toads. It's an Otherworldly Smack-Down. There's no other explanation. Crows and toads are both messengers of the underworld. There had to be something supernatural at work. Besides, if birds suddenly developed the ability to pluck their favorite yummies out of living creatures, with surgical precision, why would they stop?"

"Maybe they ran out of toads?" I said, guessing. "Or they got tired of being drenched in toad entrails?"

Gus shook his head. "We're not talking normal toads and crows here. We're talking demonic. Or Daimonic. What if it was Voodoo? Voodoo practitioners can create all sorts of unnatural phenomena."

I shuddered. I had experienced some of that kind of power first-hand recently, thanks to Mama Lua and her zombie powder.

I suddenly got a mental flash of Gus, terrified, ducking, his hands trying to protect his face, as a giant black bird came barreling at him. I shook my head to clear the image out and tried to replace it with a visual of happy Gus, walking through a field of flowers, on a sunny day.

Gus rubbed his hands with glee and raised his eyebrows. "Or... what if toads and crows are just a front? What if the words are code for something else? Like Templars and Crusaders? Hey, maybe we can—"

"—Stop right there," I said. I knew where this was going. "I don't care how bizarre it is, or how Voodoo-ish, or what they actually mean by toads and crows. I am not getting on a plane to Germany to go check it out. You'll just have to let this one be."

Gus shrugged. "If it happened once, there's a good chance it'll happen again. Just in case..." he pointed at me. "Keep one eye on the skies, and one hand over your liver."

I looked down at myself and tried to figure out where exactly my liver was...

Just in case.

Chapter 4

THE NEXT MORNING, I was startled out of a sound sleep by a sub-sonic *boom.* I felt it, more than heard it. Like my body was a drum skin, stretched taut over a kettle drum, and someone had struck a warning thud.

My heart raced. My mind tried to swim through its morning fog. Where had I felt that sensation before?

The house wards.

I jumped out of bed and raced downstairs, the Dobies at my heels. My cottage was known for having a magickally proactive defense system, with a history of having turned at least one would-be arsonist into a rowan tree. There was no telling what the wards would do if they were triggered.

*   *   *

I tore open the front door and was practically knocked over by the wind chill. My eyes teared up from the cold and I tightened my robe around me.

There was a large box on the front porch.

That would explain the wards going off. Someone must have thrown the box on the porch, instead of gently placing it.

I looked around, trying to spot a hapless delivery person sprawled out on a bush, or an additional piece of shrubbery that hadn't been there before, but everything looked normal.

There was a *Sunset Farms* logo on one side of the box. This must be the organic fruit and veggie monthly delivery Gus had ordered for us while he was in Chicago.

I made a face. When I tried to talk him into an all-fruit box, Gus accused me of being a sugar junkie and lectured me about fruit addiction.

I picked it up and carried it into the kitchen, trying not to trip over the Dobie menaces who, for some unknown reason, were feeling compelled to do figure eights around my feet.

After I started a pot of decaf coffee brewing, I fed the Dobes, put winter sweaters, hats and doggy booties on them, and let them out into the run Gus had built for them before he left for Chicago, so they could play. Gus would be laughing his ass off when he saw their wardrobe, but it was ridiculously cold outside.

How did people deal with this kind of cold year after year? I'd only been dealing with it since Samhain, and the novelty had definitely worn off. If I could pick up the cottage and grounds, and move them to Los Angeles, I'd be on the first plane back to sunny California.

I tossed a starter log into the fireplace and lit it. Once the flames were merrily crackling away, I went upstairs to check on Gus and tell him his delivery had arrived. But he wasn't in his room.

I looked around, surprised. I couldn't imagine where he would have gone so early. Gus was a big believer in getting his beauty sleep. I quickly searched the rest of the house, but he was nowhere to be found.

I started feeling anxious. I know he's a grown man, but I'm a worrywart and this was Gus we were talking about after all. If anyone could figure out a way to get into trouble, it would be him. So I went to my bedroom, sat on the carpet in front of my altar, and did a quick check of the web using my sixth sense.

*   *   *

It took me awhile to locate Gus. For me, Gus was usually a gold light on a glimmering green/gold string. Today, his light was partially hidden by a dark cloud. It didn't feel immediately menacing, but that cloud worried me. I'd never seen anything like it before. I tried to poke at it, but my attempts were completely blocked.

The alarm on my clock/radio went off, shooting me back to reality with a nasty screech. I stood up and half ran, half hopped over to the nightstand, my right foot all pins and needles from being under my body.

I slapped at the alarm to turn it off, but — like most electronics — it totally defied me. Every time I turned it off, it would turn itself back on. Finally, I gave up and pulled the plug out of the wall.

Great. Gus was being stalked by something that looked like it was out of the Abyss, my concentration was shot, and according to the alarm, it was time to get ready for my breakfast date with Paul.

I sent up a prayer to the Goddess to watch over Gus, then quickly showered and dressed in my best *hide-the-baby-bump* fashion.

*   *   *

I don't know how I managed it, but I was actually ready to go twenty minutes before I needed to leave. So I stopped in the kitchen, poured myself a cup of decaf and unpacked the box. Of course, the good stuff — oranges, plums, apples — were at the bottom. I had to dig through all the veggies first.

Fennel bulb after fennel bulb. How much fennel can two people eat? And since when did fennel become a vegetable? I always thought it was an herb.

Green peppers.

A head of lettuce.

A bunch of weird-looking green stuff — I checked the invoice, and it was kale.

Small oblong heads of endive.

Human head.

I dropped the head and screamed. From the floor, Gus's face looked up at me.

"*Help me*," it said.

I screamed again.

ABOUT THE AUTHOR

CHRISTIANA MILLER is a novelist, screenwriter and mom who's led an unusual life. In addition to writing for General Hospital: Night Shift and General Hospital, she's had her DNA shot into space (where she's currently cohabiting in a drawer with Stephen Colbert and Stephen Hawking), she's been serenaded by Klingons, and she's been the voices of all the female warriors in Mortal Kombat II and III. If her life was a TV show, it would be a wacky dramedy filled with Dobies and eccentric characters who get themselves into bizarre situations!

The best way to make sure you're notified of future releases, giveaways and sales, is by joining her e-mail list at: http://eepurl.com/LeSnn

To learn more about the author, you can visit her website: http://www.christianamiller.com.

You can also chat with the author on Facebook: https://www.facebook.com/ChristianaMiller.author

You can follow her on Twitter @writechristiana

MORE BOOKS BY

CHRISTIANA MILLER

TOAD WITCH SERIES:
Somebody Tell Aunt Tillie She's Dead
Somebody Tell Aunt Tillie We're In Trouble
A Tale of 3 Witches

SWEET HOME CHICAGO SERIES:
The Thief Who Stole Midnight

NON-FICTION:
Self-Publishing On A Shoestring: Insanely Helpful Links for Indie
Authors

ANTHOLOGIES:
Every Witch Way But Wicked
Love & Other Distractions
Naughty or Nice

To learn about new releases, you can sign up for Christiana Miller's
newsletter by going to http://eepurl.com/LeSnn.

Thank you so much for reading Somebody Tell Aunt Tillie She's Dead. I
hope you enjoyed it!

A THANK YOU

FROM THE AUTHOR

THANK YOU TO ALL my wonderful readers! I couldn't do this without you! If this were a theater, this is where I would come out on stage and applaud all of you. You make this journey worthwhile.

Made in the USA
Middletown, DE
14 August 2015